REMEDY FOR INNOCENCE

REMEDY

for

INNOCENCE

❖

PD WOLFE

Cover design by Peter Selgin
Book formatting by Phillip Gessert

You may contact the author at wolfe22@protonmail.com.

Dedicated to my canine buddies, who add so much to life

TABLE OF
CONTENTS

CHAPTER 1
THE HOOK

IT WAS DURING our junior year of high school that Archie and I most dishonored our teachers, our counselors, our parents (though I had none) in their pious endeavors to mold us into well educated future leaders and good Southern Baptists. Archie was the strategist, of course, the evil genius whose cunning brain earned my reverence, and I merely a drooling disciple. I didn't follow him around like a puppy, but it was something like that. Archie knew things. He was bold. He was smart. He was my General Patton.

Though I didn't realize it at the time, Archie had me figured out. Regardless of whatever hair-brained schemes he concocted, he was always ready with just the right words that would convince me that I would be foolish if I didn't agree to be a part of his exploits. He knew how to hook me. This particular night, it was his word, the word "naked," that hooked me. Naked this. Naked that. It all sounds good. But "naked girl" sounds best of all. "Naked," Archie told me. "She'll be naked."

I was ready for sin, my inclination driven by a toxic distinction I apparently shared with few: my virginity. All my classmates, especially the seniors, crowed about what they did in the back seats of their cars. They bragged about the size of this one's brassiere, the lace and daisies on that one's panties. Even Archie, a mere junior himself, claimed carnal knowledge, though we all knew he was lying. I had no such tales, and genuine lying was unthinkable for a Smith of Smith Station, Mississippi. I was forced to listen to their yarns, embarrassed by my silence, and when my turn came, timidly admit my celibacy. I was tired of it. I wanted authentic firsthand knowledge that could be used to challenge those seniors. So on that Tuesday night in October when Archie offered me a free glimpse of his sister "in the raw," any thought of dishonor or prison, or of being labeled a pervert, was selfishly set aside in favor of the furtherance of my worldly education.

The evening began innocently enough. I had changed clothes—fresh jeans and shirt that Annie, our old black friend and sometimes-housekeeper, had laid out for me—and left my house at the usual time, six-thirty, and per normal routine walked the block and a half to Mary's Cafe. An early-October coolness softened the scorching currents that rose from the sun-baked concrete sidewalk. Summer refuses to recognize its September deadline in Mississippi.

A pungent scent of wild onion mingled with the usual odor of honeysuckle and the soot and sulfur from the recent passage of a southbound freight. There were no vegetables being loaded on the docks across the tracks, no conveyors running, not even a passing vehicle to disturb the calm of evening in Smith Station. I was able to devote full concentration to tromping every crack in the hard surface under my feet, intent upon breaking my mother's back, wherever she might be. Only when the stitched brickwork that was Main Street appeared underneath did I give her a respite and glance up at the cafe before me.

Mary's Cafe. The hub of activity in Smith Station. Located midway of Main Street in the block known as "downtown," Mary's pool hall (as it was referred to by some) was the local rendezvous for lovers, schemers, drunkards, and farmers—and many a student of SSHS. It was as much a part of life in Smith Station as the schools and the churches, and, for some of us, "Mama" Mary was more of a mother than any we'd ever known.

I arrived, and I stopped for a moment to check the day's specials, written longhand on a sheet of spiral notebook paper and taped to the window beside the front door. *"Mary's Cafe. Specials*

Tuesday," the note read, "*Pickeled pigs feet. Fresh. 15 cents a hoof (big hoofs, tho)."*

I hurried inside, hoping she still had some pickled pigs' feet. My friend Archie sat at "our" table, a well-used assembly of greasy pine boards and matching chairs that sat in a corner behind the pinball machine and next to the jukebox, and as the long black spring howled and slammed the screen door behind me, I waved a greeting to him. "Where's Jerry?" I asked as I approached my best friend, inquiring of the third member of our castaway clique.

He gave me the fake smile for which he was well known in our town and rubbed his hands together. "Who knows? I think he drove up to Milldale with his dad."

"But he said he had a date with Teeny Wright. I figured they'd be here."

Archie shook his head. "He couldn't get a date with Teeny."

"Why not?"

"Teeny only dates real studs. Jerry ain't one."

I dragged out a chair and plopped down opposite Archie Jones. His expression, the semi-smile that always reminded me of the smirk on the Mona Lisa's face, remained the same. "Tired," I told him with a shake of my head. "I unloaded six thousand pairs of panties for Mr. Barnes this afternoon. Nearly killed me. There's enough panties in that ten-cent store for every woman in town. And they'll be gone in a week. How do women wear out their panties so fast?"

It was a mistake to ask such a question of the self-proclaimed local expert on all matters related to the female body and its functions. Archie's face lit up in anticipation. Even the acne that covered his cheeks, the worst case anyone in Smith Station had ever seen, reddened. He leaned forward in lecturing position, instantly mirroring the overhead lights atop his sixteen-year-old-but-balding-anyway scalp. "Action," he whispered, drawing close. "Directly proportional to action. Those good-looking babes who are always getting them torn off and always jerking them back on quick... those are the ones whose panties wear out the quickest.

Like Melba." He struck the table lightly with his fist and grinned wolfishly. "I about got all her panties wore out."

"Melba ain't exactly beautiful," I said.

"You should see...!"

"I don't want to hear it, Arch," I growled. "You wouldn't know a pair of panties from a petunia."

Regardless of Archie's status as evil genius, I just couldn't bear the thought that he had actually "done it."

His eyes narrowed now, and I quickly tried to change the subject.

"Uncle Jim's got his woman over at the house tonight again. So I have to stay away from home until after nine. He gets some at least once a week, old as he is. Wonder if it's the same woman every time?"

"Melba's got..."

I was relieved when Archie's words were cut short by the nearby whack of Mama Mary's fly swatter. We both jumped. "Wanna play pool?" I asked before he could gather his wits and continue. "We can eat when Jerry gets here. Pigs' feet tonight. Hot mustard, too. Yummy!"

He left half a bottle of Coke to prevent our table from being stolen, and for good measure I ordered one and placed the bottle opposite his. We chalked our cues, lagged for break, and Archie, of course, opened the game. Pool was his specialty. "Now, about Melba..." he began as he stroked the cue ball.

And so it went for an hour. During that hour, Mary's place filled with the usual crowd. The place began to hum. The farmers, in their dusty overalls, hummed with mutual commiseration, slumped around their tables, occasionally rubbing their worn joints and sunburned necks. The teenagers who were lucky enough to be out on a Tuesday night hummed in anticipation of a quick moment in the back seat before they had to be in for the evening. I got jealous thinking about it. A pair of the local inebriates hummed with every sip from the brown bags they held low as though some member of the police force might spot them and might actually care enough to interrupt their illicit routine. Mama Mary and her able assistant, "Mama's Boy," hummed: There would be a healthy deposit at the Merchants and Farmers Bank in the morning. And after an hour, even I hummed. For the first time this evening, I was winning a game of eight ball.

"Rack!" I shouted at my victory, trying to draw attention, and Archie racked the balls for the first time tonight. I sauntered across to the lunch counter to make sure there were plenty of pigs' feet left, then strolled nonchalantly back to the pool table. Beating Archie at pool was a rarity, and I wanted it to last.

"Speaking of sex," I said as I broke, "Jerry's late. Teeny must be screwing the poor devil's brains out."

"Ha! Jerry ain't never got any from anybody. Especially Teeny. I'm the only one of us three that ever actually did it."

"I don't want to hear your lies, damn it!"

"Anyway, Teeny is too good-looking for Jerry. He thinks he looks like Elvis. But I got news. He looks more like Jerry Lee Lewis than Elvis Presley."

"His hair sure looks like Elvis."

Archie smoothed the few strands of fuzz that curled atop his head. "Hair ain't everything," he said. "Takes more than hair."

"Yeah," I grinned. "Money. New '57 Chevy. Good tan. Blue blood. He's got it all."

"Damn!" my friend said hotly, forgetting the game for a moment. "His mother inherited a pile, and his dad's a gambler! They ain't blue blood!" Archie let out a howl of rage. "I hope his damn Chevy blows up! I hope he gets poor! Then he'd know how it feels. I work all the time, and I ain't got a pot to pee in. It ain't fair!"

The front screen door of Mary's place functioned not merely as a device to deny admission to a portion of the local housefly population, but also as a herald of arrivals and departures. Its strong spring stretched hazardously with each opening, the strain generating a growl that must have caused every cat within two blocks to shiver. The growl was generally followed by a strong whack as the door slammed shut. There had been many growls and whacks as Archie and I dueled over the green felt tonight, and with each we and every other occupant of the place paused long enough to glance up at the door to be sure we didn't miss anything important. Richard Miller and Vince Allen, high school buddies, had come and gone. Carl Hancock, the Chief of Police, visited briefly, along with his best buddy, high school football coach Melville "Meatloaf" Murray. The two stopped at our table long enough to watch us take a couple of shots each. William Brewer came in for a moment and inquired as to the whereabouts of his friend Perry Norman. Whereabouts unknown. Probably out parked somewhere with Miss Saxon Browne.

I felt a terrible surge of jealousy when I heard her name: Saxon Browne. Saxon Browne was my all-time true love, though she didn't know it. I wanted her. Perry Norman had her.

There were a variety of others who dropped in just to check the Tuesday-night action. But after an hour-and-a-half of my one-sided contest with Archie Jones, there came a visitor whose entrance ended the words of every man and boy, and drew the jealous gaze of every woman and girl. The cafe grew quiet and still and Archie and I ceased our play as Mama Mary's noisy door announced the arrival of Linda Murray.

The utterly gorgeous wife of Coach Murray, Linda could have been a model. All of us agreed that she was the ultimate fox, and we all lusted for her, even though we knew that if such an unlikely circumstance ever occurred, her husband would murder the offender. We told each other she was unattainable. Actually, none of us had guts enough to even consider the risk.

She had a pool behind her house, about three blocks from my own, and during the summer when I mowed her lawn every ten days or so in order to make money to blow on movies, pinball, jukeboxes, and pool games, I got to know her. She was my favorite customer. Coach was always gone when I cut the grass; naturally, I became friends with her and her two children. She sometimes lounged around the pool in shorts or a skimpy bathing suit, thus it generally took three hours to cut what anywhere else required thirty minutes.

Now she stood just inside the door, and as male hearts beat more rapidly and female cheeks reddened with resentment, she calmly scrutinized, one by one, every face in the room. She wore a silky nylon dress, glossy vanilla, cut so low in front that the curve of her breasts and the shadowy valley between them were visible. We all had decided long ago that she never wore a brassiere, that she had no need for one. The fullness of her lips, the immensity of her eyes, which seemed always to be only half opened, the mass of blonde hair that flowed beyond her shoulders, all combined to make her head appear too large for her slim body. With her head erect, she always moved with a languid motion that made you uncomfortably aware of her long legs and tiny waist, her tan shoulders and ballooning breasts, though it was nearly impossible to end your stare into her half-moon eyes.

When her survey was done, her eyes once again met mine. There was a minute twitch of her lower lip, a peculiar way she had of grinning. I had admired that seductive smirk many times before. It always made me jumpy. Especially now. She moved delicately between chairs, and I shifted nervously beside the pool table as I realized she intended to speak to me. She stopped before me and smiled. "Hello, Jack," she said.

Though I had gotten to where I felt comfortable talking with Mrs. Murray in the privacy of her home or her backyard, having her approach me in public like this was like revealing to the world our "special" relationship, a cherished "connection" that I never discussed with anyone. I felt the blood rushing to my face. I twisted the cue stick in my already sweaty hands and managed to answer, "Hello, Mrs. Murray."

"Playing pool?"

"Yes, ma'am."

She nodded toward Archie. "I've seen your friend at school, and around town, but I don't think I've met him."

It was only then that I became aware that Archie had slunk

around the table and had positioned himself for optimum viewing of Mrs. Murray's bare parts. "This is Archie Jones," I said, pointing. "Archie, you know Mrs. Murray?"

Archie's head jerked back to a more respectable degree. "Hi, Mrs. Murray," he croaked. "We met before. Maybe you don't remember..."

"Oh, you were the one at the football game!" she said, smiling and touching his arm for an instant. "I remember. You were the one who..."

There was an embarrassing moment as we all remembered Archie being walloped over the head with a bullhorn by a cheerleader who didn't think it was so funny when he told her she had legs like Bob Hope. And that was in front of everyone in the west bleachers, very close to where Mrs. Murray was seated. Mrs. Murray even helped drag the cheerleader off Arch.

Being the lady that she was, Mrs. Murray quickly changed the subject. She turned to me. "How's your Uncle Jim, Jack?"

"Fine, Mrs. Murray," I said. "Especially tonight." Then I thought about what I'd said, and what he was doing about now, and added, "Probably really enjoying his bottle tonight."

She frowned. "I wish he would give up drinking. I worry about him. He's not doing his health any good."

"Yes, ma'am. I'll tell him you asked about him."

She glanced around the café. "Have you seen Melville tonight?"

"Yes, ma'am," I answered, shuffling, "He and Chief Hancock were here earlier. But they left about a half hour ago."

"I was hoping he was here."

"No, ma'am." I shifted my feet again and struggled to make conversation, aware that everyone within hearing range was straining to make out every word. "How are Tommy and Barbara Ann? Do you need your yard mowed one more time this year?"

Her eyes were dreamy, far away. "They're fine. And you can mow it if you like."

I took advantage of the lady's momentary preoccupation,

despite all the eyes on me, to peer downward between her surging breasts into that moist valley where my desires had dwelt many times before. I put on my most innocent face as her bedroom eyes fixed on me again. "Come by. Any day this week or next."

"Yes, ma'am."

"Thanks, Jack. If you see Melville..." She paused. "Oh, never mind."

She turned, lazily, seemingly unaware that every eye was on her, and glided smoothly to and out the door.

"Wow!" Archie breathed in my ear as we stared after her. "Wow!"

"I'd give my left nut," I whispered.

"I'd give both your nuts!"

I let my breath out, aware only now that I had been holding it, and said, "She's the finest thing the world has ever seen. A true goddess. Coach Murray don't deserve that woman. I do. I wish I were married to her. Can you imagine, later tonight, when the kids were in bed..."

Archie loosed a flat whistle from between his lips and shook his head. "She's fine, all right," he said, "but Barbara's finer."

I turned to him in utter disgust. His sister was a beauty, but compared to Mrs. Murray she was a tomboy. "You're crazy," I said.

"Absolutely. Barbara is the best. Mama Meatloaf is number two."

"Arch, they're not even in the same class," I growled. "Comparing Barbara to Linda Murray is like claiming Hoot Gibson looks as good as Marilyn Monroe."

"I can prove it!"

It was a ridiculous statement that didn't deserve an answer.

"I said I can prove it!"

"You can't prove the impossible."

"By god, I will!"

I shook my head in disgust and took my shot, then cursed as I left Archie set up on the eight. Another loss for me. When he failed to squeal with joy I rose to the curious sight of my friend standing motionlessly beside the table, clutching his cue stick as though it were a guidon. There was the usual aura of the devil about him, though his appearance was more Lou Costello than devil. But, looks aside, he would have fit into a pirate movie as well as Errol Flynn. Shrewd. Daring. Resourceful. Clairvoyant, perhaps. He would, for example, unerringly pick the very chair in study hall that would provide the only good view up Teeny Wright's dress. I often wondered if he had a pact with Satan.

"How'd you like to see Barbara naked?" he whispered.

Somehow, I was not overly surprised at the question, though the "Huh?" I answered in reply would have sounded otherwise to anyone listening to us. "Huh?" I said.

"Barbara in the raw. Birthday suit. Boobs and legs and... and... you know. Everything. You'll see why Linda Murray is number two."

"You serious?"

"Serious as a heart attack."

He bent and took the eight without gloating over his victory. After so many victories, maybe he was just tired of gloating. "Yeah, you'd love that, wouldn't you?" he continued with a grin. "Any man would. Any man would give his left nut."

"I suppose so. Sure," I said, though the thought had my toes curling.

"Mama Mary," he called as he straightened himself. The cafe's owner was hunched over her grill behind the counter frying meat for hamburgers. "Mama Mary, what time is it?"

The old lady frowned at Archie, set her spatula aside, wiped her hands on a large white cotton rag that hung from her waist, then reached into the pocket of her apron and pulled from it the medium-sized alarm clock she kept there. It was the only time-piece in her place, and she used its alarm for culinary preparations. "Eight o'clock," she yelled back, "and that's the right time, too, set by the Merchants and Farmers' clock just this afternoon."

"Thank you, ma'am," Archie answered.

"One hour," he whispered to me. "One hour. And I'll prove it to you."

"Why one hour? Why not now?"

He ignored my taunt and we went on with our game.

For most of the next hour, as I was soundly thrashed game after game of pool, I wondered what Archie Jones had in mind. I knew that Barbara would never just stand there and let Archie undress her, much less allow me to do it. She would never do it for us, either. "You pay her, don't you!" I charged.

"Whaaattt?"

"You pay Barbara to undress! How much?"

"Are you nuts?" he said angrily. "No, I wouldn't pay her! That's stupid!" He stalked around the table.

"Then how?"

He refused to answer.

But the slow processes of my frail brain were beginning to put the picture in place. As far as I knew, Barbara was still as virgin as I, and probably only God and Archie's mother had EVER seen her--legitimately--without her clothes. Nor was anyone likely to, certainly not her brother along with one of his gawking friends. So whatever Archie had in mind was predictably devious, indecent, dangerous... and probably illegal. He was, after all, the very guy who'd gotten in trouble for installing an elaborate system of small mirrors in the trees outside the schoolhouse that he used for viewing the girls in the second-floor bathroom. He'd claimed it was part of a chemistry experiment when they caught him out on an oak limb making adjustments to his mirrors. But the principal had seen through that. The more I thought about his offer tonight, the more nervous I became.

"Arch," I said carefully, and after elaborate mental preparation, "what have you in mind at nine, my friend? Are you risking incarceration for the both of us in an attempt to disprove an issue that has been predestined by the gods? Let us not tempt fate. I concede. I will save our lives and our reputations. I concur, though not without reservation, with your assessment. Barbara is number one. Mama Meatloaf is number two." I stretched my arms upward toward the yellow light bulbs that hung bare from the ceiling and begged forgiveness. "Forgive me, Linda!" I whispered.

"You do want to see Barbara's boobs, Jack, don't you?" Archie asked, obviously offended. "She'll be naked, man!"

"Sure I do. But my allergies act up when I get too close to steel bars."

"Don't worry. It's safe." He went back to the game.

"You're sure?"

Archie Mona-Lisa smiled and wiggled an eyebrow; I was hooked.

Though Mama Mary was thoroughly irked at Archie for asking the time every ten minutes or so, and I thought at one point she would jerk him off his feet for an eyeball to eyeball discussion of his lousy manners, the moment finally arrived. "Ten minutes 'til nine," Mama Mary answered from behind her counter as she studied her pocket clock. She rolled her lazy eyes at him, wisps of gray hair falling before them. "Got a hot date, hot shot?" she drawled. "Cinderella gotta get in before midnight?"

"Nope." Archie carried his cue stick back to the wall rack as he made the mistake of sounding a bit brash. "Just got an appointment, that's all."

Mama Mary raised an eyebrow and barked, "WHAT DID YOU SAY, Archie Jones?"

"I said no, MA'AM."

"That's better."

"Yes, MA'AM."

She looked in my direction. "Still want them pigs' feet, Jack?"

Pigs' feet no longer seemed so appealing. I answered, "Lost my appetite, Mama Mary. I'll just pay you for the Cokes and the games."

"Oh." She was obviously disappointed with the paltriness of my purchase. "Well, I might have some of them hoofs left over for tomorrow night," she said. And after Archie and I had settled up, she waved us out the door. "You be good, Cherokee Jack Junior," she called, making use of my late father's nickname with a "junior" added on.

"Yes, MA'AM," I answered.

And we marched out her door and into the night.

CHAPTER 2
"IN THE RAW"

A S WE LEFT Mary's Cafe, heat still billowed from the hot sidewalk that led toward Archie's house. I fell in step beside him. "Gotta hurry," he mumbled. "Almost nine o'clock."

"Why nine?" I asked. "You can tell me now."

I thought of Peter Lorre, of "Casablanca" fame, as Archie turned to answer. Instead of "Rick, I hope you are more impressed with me now," Archie said, "BATH TIME, Jack. Barbara takes her bath every night at nine o'clock. Straight up."

My suspicions had been accurate. Peeping Toms! I felt that sinking, weak feeling in the pit of my stomach that all novice criminals must feel just prior to their first caper. I said, "I hope for your sake we get cells in different counties, Arch. Cause if we get caught..."

As we scaled the Main Street railroad overpass the lonely howl of a distant freight train reached us. Its solitary light was but a faraway dot, a tiny beam that straddled the shiny rails in twin streaks of imminent brilliance. It would pass in a moment, gushing smoke and puffing steam, and coating in the process the streets and buildings of downtown Smith Station with a layer of fine black ash and soot. The town would reek of sulfur as a hundred cars clattered and squealed past, each with its own distinctive accent, until the final red caboose and its red and green lights faded to quiet again.

As its forlorn wail reached us now, I shivered instinctively and reluctantly yielded my thoughts to an unrelenting "memory," a familiar sensation of panic that caused me to step a bit quicker, to urge Archie along, faster, to distance myself from the bridge and the tracks before the hated engine arrived with its load of creaking cars.

I shuddered involuntarily and turned my eyes to the sidewalk before me... and hurried Archie along. Only when I heard the caboose would I be at ease again.

We arrived. The dark passage between the Jones' house and its encircling line of shrubbery loomed ominously as I leaped after Archie from the sidewalk to the damp grass of the yard. "Quiet," Archie advised, his head weaving expertly side to side as he peered about searching for possible witnesses. All was still and peaceful. The house was dark as well, the only light coming from a window somewhere in the rear. Without evident emotion he whispered, "Muddy," as we tiptoed our way. "Always muddy through here. Water line leaking."

"You sure this is okay, Arch?" I asked, knowing better.

"Shut up, fool. Be quiet."

"We'll ruin our loafers. And our jeans."

"They'll wash. Just keep quiet, will you? You'll wake up Mom and Dad. Walk silent. On your toes. Like an Indian."

"Heck," I said, "it's so muddy in here you couldn't hear a team of mules square-dancing."

Archie exhaled almost noiselessly as he stopped to point, as we rounded the corner, to the old brick building, dimly lit by a small luminous window, which had been a kitchen serving the house in the years before a more modern one was installed inside. The near wall of the building was no more than six feet from the main house. The entire structure was steeply roofed with copper that in the light of day had paled to green. A large oak tree enveloped much of its upper portions in limbs and leaves. "Up there," Archie whispered.

Staring upward, I observed a reprieve. "The roof's too steep!"

"Stop whimpering. It's okay. We got limbs to hold to."

I followed him around the ancient kitchen to where a wooden crate and several additional pieces of lumber had been stacked against the rear wall. Even in the dimness, I could see that the worn makeshift ladder had been used quite often. With a bound Archie leaped from the boards to an oak limb, then pulled himself to the roof. "Come on," he whispered anxiously as he peeked through leaves to where I stood below. "Jump up here. Hurry!"

"This is illegal, Archie," I said from the ground. "It's called 'criminal snooping.' The penalty is thirty years. It ain't what I'd call exactly 'honorable,' either."

"You chicken-shit," he growled. "Get your butt up here. We'll miss the show."

"Think how many shows we'll miss while we're picking cotton over at Parchman."

"I'm gonna tell everybody in school what a chicken bastard you are!"

He would, too. Cursing him under my breath, I repeated Archie's maneuver, and in a moment we were creeping along, one on either side of the crown of the roof, toward the edge nearest the main house. We held to the tree limbs, and if not for them would have slid off the slick metal roof toward an unpleasant casualty ten dark feet below. After we briefly struggled with limbs and leaves, at the furthermost end of the roof there appeared before us an open, screened window.

"The upstairs bathroom," Archie giggled, jerking a thumb. "Ring-side seat."

"We're so close. Are you sure she won't see us?"

"Naw. She never has. We're practically invisible, up on this roof, behind these limbs."

"At times like this I wish I was colored."

"Quit worrying. That bathroom is like a cave. I did some tests a long time ago. Can't hear nothing. Can't see out at night, neither."

I thought about the ladder. "You do this often, Arch?"

"Quiet, fool. You're talking too much."

We had just made it. The freight train had roared through town, and the Merchants and Farmers Bank clock had just begun its nine-o'clock serenade when a light flashed on in the bathroom and Barbara Jones entered. My first impression, as always when I saw her, was that her deep red lips and red fingernails, of matching shade, were somehow suspended, independent, standing out from the rest of her body. Perhaps, I had surmised, that was due to the amount and color of her lipstick, and to the contrasting paleness of her skin. "Show time!" Archie grinned, bumping me with his elbow. I grinned back at him, for the bathroom light illuminated us rather well. In fact, damned well. We were not entirely invisible! If I could see Archie, and Archie could see me...

"She can see us if she looks out here!" I whispered with a sense of dread.

"Shut up!" Archie hissed.

"But, good god..."

"Look!"

Barbara Jones was already strewing clothes all over the bathroom floor. Her shoes. Her dress. Her stockings. A slip. Stripped to bra and panties, she leaned across the edge of the tub, directly opposite the now-smoldering eyes of Archie and myself, and began to run her water. She stood erect, reached behind her back, and gently eased her bra from her breasts. "Oh..." I said. "Oh..."

"Shut up!"

"My god!" I gawked, "What a pair of..."

Archie's elbow hit me in the ribs and distracted me momentarily. Strangely, I felt no pain. I whispered in awe, "LOOK AT THAT, Arch!"

She was a bit plump, though that was of slight concern, and had the thick black hair and pale white skin that, with the exception of Archie, was common to her line. Her breasts were large enough that their weight caused them to droop. But since they were the first real pair of breasts I'd ever seen, they were absolutely astounding. They made me feel dizzy as they swayed and swirled and bounced with her every movement. This was a lot better than Uncle Jim's girlie magazines!

After a moment she stood back to await the filling of her bath, and I was surprised to see in her face the same smirk that lit

Archie's face when he beat me at a game of pool. Another Jones' quirk. A leer that said, "I'm the best! Just ask me!"

There must have been a mirror over the tub, for Barbara's doe-eyes mocked it. She admired herself in it, her gaze almost directly into the open window and very near where I hung on a limb, afraid to move for fear she would notice me. Satisfied with her self-examination, she took hold of her panties with a thumb on each side and wiggled them away, exposing another mass of curly dark hair. The mound of curls reminded me of the fuzz on Archie's head, except there was much more of it. My mouth fell open. This was a first for me. Barbara's breasts swayed and bounced before my eyes like the headlights of a lurching automobile, a hypnotic, dazzling spectacle. Now I knew how the bullfrogs in Davis Lake felt when we blinded them with a flashlight. Dizzy. Captivated. Paralyzed by spectacle. My eyes leaped from breast to breast to pelvis and back, unable to concentrate on one for fear of missing the other.

After a minute of intense examination of Barbara's goodies, however, I was struck by an unpleasant stab of pain. It was passion. And it was in my belly.

I had always experienced less violent spasms of this nature whenever, for example, a beautiful woman would walk past me on the sidewalk. Or I'd catch sight of Teeny Wright's naked knees when she was scaling the long staircase at school. But now, as Barbara's pale body bounced about before my eyes, what began as a tingle in my center grew rapidly to a searing gash. Someone, it felt, had been drawing a zigzagging line across my belly with the fine tip of a very sharp knife, and had decided at last to leisurely shove the blade hilt-deep.

I held to the limb, bent to ease the cramping, and tried to keep an eye on the activities inside. Unfortunately, as I kneeled to relieve my knotted stomach muscles, Archie's head blocked my view. He had early-on positioned himself nearer the action than me, but with my height advantage that had been no problem, for I had been able to peer over his head and shoulders. But now, with my body kinked behind his, I was unable to continue my inspection of Barbara's finer parts. I struggled to look over or around him, but each time I shifted position, Archie shifted his. In a moment we were pushing at each other, each wrestling for a better angle. I shoved him; he shoved me back. I cursed him. He cursed me back. "Move!" I whispered angrily.

"You move!"

"You see this all the time!"

"And don't never get tired of it."

"I can't see!"

"Tough. You can..."

His words trailed and I felt him stiffen, his gaze fixed on the scene before us. I shifted slightly and peeked around his shoulder, a premonition of doom flooding over me, hoping I wouldn't see what I was afraid I would.

She had covered her breasts with her arms and hands, had bent nearly double to hide the rest of her body, and the look on her face was one of complete terror. She was staring right at us. Her lips had curled, her mouth was half open, her eyes were popping, and I knew she was about to scream like no woman had ever screamed before.

I didn't wait to confirm my observation, but as Archie and I scattered limbs and leaves and rocked the entire neighborhood with the sound of our feet slapping and slipping on that copper roof, Barbara let loose the most formidable sound that has ever been uttered. It began as a low-pitched warble that might have been a passing fire engine, then increased to a crescendo that echoed a recording I'd heard of the sirens that shook Londoners awake during the air raids of World War Two. If our predicament hadn't already "lent wings to our feet," the sound of Barbara's wailing did so. Neither Archie nor I bothered with his ladder; we instead dove feet-first from the far end of the kitchen. Thanks to the muddy earth and to Mrs. Jones penchant for flower gardening, neither of us suffered broken legs.

We ran with a speed that if observed by him would have

prompted Coach Murray to add our names to the team roster. Fortunately, there were no low-hanging clotheslines to decapitate us as we blindly tore through the neighbors' backyards. I ran recklessly, close on the heels of Archie, who amazed me with his acceleration. When we hit the sidewalk we turned back toward town, still at full gait. We ran as if Barbara were right on our heels. In mere seconds we covered two blocks, and in mere seconds more, threw ourselves upon the long low lawn that bordered the ICRR depot, rolling on the ground until we were hidden from view of anyone on Main Street by a small hill east of the tracks. We lay for a long while puffing and wheezing and thinking our own thoughts about the debacle.

"Reckon they called the police?" Archie asked finally, after his breathing slowed. "I ain't heard no sirens."

"I don't know," I answered. "I just hope Barbara didn't recognize me. I'm too young to spend the rest of my life in prison."

Archie cringed a bit. "The rest of your life?" he said, as though it were news. "They wouldn't give us life, just for doing that, would they? Hell, after all for god's sake, she's my sister!"

"Yeah," I said. "They'd let you go. I'd be the one to get the chair."

Archie was silent for a minute, then spoke with sudden confidence, and even giggled as though he'd discovered some hidden joke. "Barbara didn't recognize us," he said. "I ran those tests."

"You and your damned tests."

"And they didn't need to call the police. The police probably heard Barbara from downtown."

I nodded agreement. "I've never heard anything like that. Hollywood would hire her for their horror movies if they could hear her scream one time."

"You didn't even have to hear it. You could feel it."

"It was Hiroshima, only louder."

We were silent for a moment, each of us, I guess, contemplating a long stretch at the county penal farm. Then I said, "We need an alibi, Arch. We're gonna have to be ready when they question us."

He looked at me as if I were crazy. But he began to wring his hands, and he moaned slightly under his breath, a fact that made me perversely happy. Archie wasn't as tough as he made out. "Alibi? You think they'll question us?"

"I don't know. Probably. We gotta be ready. So... Where were we when the crime was committed?"

Archie thought for a minute. "The Grande Theatre?"

"The ticket lady will know better."

"Oh, god! And Mama Mary knows what time we left her place, too. Cause I kept asking her what time it was."

I snapped my fingers. "I know!" I said. "My house! We were at my house, playing with Willie. Dogs can't talk, and Uncle Jim is no doubt thoroughly inebriated by now. It's perfect. You just go on home, like nothing's happened, act surprised by all the cops hanging around twirling their rope neckties, and I'll sneak over to my house, making sure nobody sees me, and act like I've been there all along."

Archie raised himself to an elbow. "You're making me nervous, Jack. There ain't gonna be no cops at my house."

"Just be ready anyway."

He dropped back to the grass and began to wring his hands more violently. "I'm under the gun! How can I face them?"

"You've got to convince them you don't know anything about it, Arch. You can do it. I know you can. You're the most accomplished hypocrite I've ever known."

His chest swelled suddenly at the compliment. "You're right," he breathed confidently, "I can do it."

"I better get on home." I pushed myself from the lawn.

Archie dragged himself upright and, peering into the darkness, sighed, "I gotta give the acting job of my career." He turned and stuck out his hand. I took it and shook it. "If they get me, Jack," he said earnestly, "I want you to know I ain't gonna turn you in."

"Thanks, Arch. It was your damned idea anyway, you bastard. See you tomorrow."

The moment I used that word I regretted it. I didn't even know why it had slipped out. It was a word I didn't even like to think about. That, and "illegitimate."

"Tomorrow," Archie continued, "I hope when I see you tomorrow it ain't from that adjoining cell."

I turned to go. "Me, too."

"Jack?"

"Yep."

He grinned as I turned back to him. "Them's great tits, ain't they? It's that Jones' blood. Mrs. Murray ain't got tits like that. I proved that, didn't I?"

"They're wonderful, Arch," I said. "Your sister is a Monet with nipples." I thought about it for a minute, then said, "You know, it's not really a sin, what we did tonight, Arch. It might be illegal, but it's no sin. God Himself truly understands. For us to lust for Barbara is merely to succumb to our appreciation for His good taste." I hesitated for a moment, then continued, "We just better hope the judge is a Christian gentleman."

Archie gave me a hollow smile.

I crept into the shadow of the trees that grew beside the depot and alongside the railroad tracks, and paused for a moment to watch my pal plodding back to the sidewalk. As he walked slowly in the direction of his house, the normally conspicuous spring in his step was missing. He was worried. And that worried me. I feared my reputation was in his hands. What would Uncle Jim, not to mention the rest of the townspeople, think of me?

But I could hardly blame Archie. All I could do was cross my fingers and hope for the best. I sneaked along the railroad tracks, keeping to the shadows, and made my way home to Cherokee Rose.

CHAPTER 3
UNCLE JIM

C HEROKEE ROSE. I loved the sound of it. A rambling wild flower, "Cherokee Rose" was the name chosen by my Great-great-great-great grandmother when the house became headquarters for Smith Plantation over a century ago. Afterwards it was birthplace and home to generations of our line of Smiths. During the War, as the South was raped, Cherokee Rose suffered desecration along with it. The Yankees camped on its grounds, plundered its cellars, swilled stolen wine as they watched from its balconies the looting and pillaging and burning of all else that was Smith Plantation. The begging of my maternal ancestors saved the house from the torch, but not before the foreign "army" stole the furnishings and the silver, "confiscated" the livestock and cotton, and shipped the plantation bell north. Stripped bare, Cherokee Rose survived. But things would never be the same. The Yankees left a legacy of hatred that would survive along with our house. Barbarians, Jim called them. A horde of barbarians.

For me and for my uncle, Cherokee Rose was refuge. Its magnificent profile stood out across the tracks, almost hidden in the darkness as I approached. White columns. Porticoes. A temple roof caressed by the branches of mossy water oaks. Forgotten beds for flowers. An exquisite aberration, it was, a noble stage prop that outshone its setting. Not that it was perfect. Time and neglect had taken their toll. Ivy hid much of the outside walls. The eaves had rotted, and occasionally water-soaked bits of wooden cornice crumbled and fell to the old gardens and brick courtyard below. Someday, Uncle Jim claimed, Cherokee Rose would be restored to its former grandeur. Out of loyalty, I believed him. In the meantime, he and I lived in a few rooms downstairs and let the vines and mold have their way with the rest.

I had reached the south end of the docks, carefully picking my way and keeping my eyes peeled for any sign of life, when a splash of light from a vehicle turning onto Depot Street from East Main momentarily bathed the docks, and probably my scrambling form. I dropped from the platform into the recess between it and the iron rails and held my breath, hoping I hadn't been spotted by a carload of vigilantes intent upon restitution. After a few seconds of waiting, during which there was no indication that the vehicle had continued along the street, I experienced the same feeling of panic that had gripped me while atop the roof of the Jones' old kitchen. I couldn't afford to be caught slinking toward home scant minutes after a vicious "Peeping Tom" had scared the daylights out of Miss Barbara Jones.

Cautiously, I lifted my head above the platform floor, just far enough to make out a Plymouth Fury pulled alongside the dock at the far end. Its headlights were burning. I had the impulse to break and run. Could I make it to Cherokee Rose without being seen? No, the odds were against me. I settled back into my sanctuary; best to wait in the shadows and see what developed. Unless, I thought with a chill, the entire town had been alerted, and every last citizen was now out searching for the reprehensible curs who spied on a young girl as she bathed.

A new cream-colored Plymouth Fury, I noted with another careful glance, fully a hundred yards from me, pulled into the shadows, much too far away for me to see the driver. But I recognized the car now. Coach Murray. Coach Melville "Meatloaf" Murray. Husband to the same Mrs. Murray who had been out looking for him earlier tonight. And lo! Here he was, parked in the darkness beside the farmers' dock. What strange conduct for Coach Murray!

At a click as the passenger door opened, the vehicle's dome light gleamed anemically. A passenger shifted to exit the vehicle.

This was my chance. Both passenger and driver were probably temporarily blinded by the dome lamp. I scurried to the safety of the darkness across the tracks, bent as low as possible while still able to run, sprinting until I was among the trees of the front yard of Cherokee Rose. Once behind the base of a thick oak, I turned to be sure there was no one around to see, peered once more in the direction of the Fury, then darted across the wide veranda to our front door. I jumped when I felt movement at my knees, then let my breath go when I realized it was only Willie, out to greet me. He was ready for his supper, and he stayed on my heels as I pushed my way inside.

The first time Archie told me my Uncle Jim reminded him of Fred Astaire, I was indignant. At the time I wasn't sure why his words upset me. But later, after thinking about it, I came to what I considered a rational assessment of my anger: Jim was superior not only to Fred Astaire, but to every other human being on the planet. To compare him to mere mortals was only to diminish his stature.

Lean and handsome, dapper and polished, my Uncle James Longstreet Smith, even at age fifty-six, turned the ladies' heads. His movements were as graceful as those of a ballet star. He spoke eloquently, particularly after a few drinks, in elevated prose that sent even those of the local teaching profession scurrying for their Webster's. He proudly claimed lineage from General E. Kirby Smith of the Confederate States of America, the very last commander to surrender to the hated Yankees. He often walked the streets of Smith Station with his head held high, always clutching the walking cane that had been passed down through generations of Smiths, and which was reverently dubbed "Rattler" since its shank was a silver casting of a striking rattlesnake. He would sometimes twirl the Rattler with the grace of a high school majorette. He was the envy of every cripple in town.

Resting in our "living room," Cherokee Rose's huge parlor that still flaunted corroded chandeliers and peeling plaster embellishments, he was sprawled in his favorite cushioned chair as I walked inside. An ash-laden Camel dangled from one hand, thrown across an arm of the chair. A brown bag containing the customary pint of his favorite cheap liquor, Early Times, was nestled to his chest with the other. His gray hair and graying mustache were tousled, his skin pale, his nose thin. The gauntness of his features, his hollow cheeks, sleek as a piece of fine china, were illuminated by a sprinkling of freckles. When he heard me approach he opened his eyes and smiled, thin lids and arched eyebrows exposing the serene blue eyes that, happily for me, we shared through common heritage. He was a bit sober, for he was able to look me in the eyes. "Where you been, boy?" he asked in the rich Mississippi brogue that I imitated quite naturally.

"You oughta know," I said. "In exile. Exiled from my own living quarters while you have been here indulging yourself in conduct inappropriate for a Smith."

He grunted. "You wouldn't have thought it was so 'inappropriate' if you were the one that just got through wrestling with a wild woman."

"Wild, huh?"

"Wild and wonderful."

"You look like you've been wrestling with an ox. It must have been that same one tonight that you had last time. Big fat gal? Bout two-twenty?"

He chuckled and replied, "You obviously don't know her. Young gal. Relatively. Built. Wonderful body. Full breasts. Damn good in bed, too. A ravishing angel."

"I don't want to hear it," I said. "I'm stuck with Archie Jones while you lie around copulating with some horny young woman. It ain't fair."

"Hell, I figured you were out catting yourself. What about that Browne girl you're always talking about? The young goddess?"

"She's still going steady. With the main meathead."

He grumbled. I caught a glimpse of his straight white teeth, "You're a Smith, boy. Take her away from him."

I glanced at a chandelier, then back to him. Making love must sober you up, I observed. Jim didn't act like he'd had more than a drink or two. "What have I got to offer Saxon Browne," I said, "that compares with a jacket with a football letter? I could show her my stamp collection, I guess. That'd really turn her on."

He gave me a pained expression. "You're too hard on yourself. Women want more than high school jackets."

"I'm not rich, either."

"Money's not everything."

I sighed. He mimicked me, and said, "What did you and Archie do tonight?"

"We played pool and listened to the jukebox. Elvis has a new song out."

"Elvis!" he scoffed.

"Great song. You should listen to Elvis, Uncle Jim. You'd like him."

He shook his head while he drained the last of the bourbon from his bottle. "Never!" he said then. "I prefer real music, my boy. Sinatra. Crosby. Hell, boy, even the Andrews Sisters are the harmonistic superiors of that long-haired hillbilly from Tupelo. Damn, even Willie Wing's howls are more enjoyable! That dog is more an artist! Rock-and-roll devours your mind, boy. If you continue to endure that tripe, you will surely wind up a pauper begging beignets in the back alleys of the French Quarter."

"Sounds like fun!"

"See? The process has begun."

"I think you're just getting old," I teased. "Fifty-six! Grizzled. Senile. Out of touch. Probably impotent, too."

After shifting in his chair and tossing the empty bottle at me in jest, he answered, "You impertinent young rogue! Senile, perhaps. Impotent, never! However, if such a state were necessary to respect art and to admire excellence, than I would welcome it with great satisfaction. I have, however, obviously failed to meet my obligation. I have failed in my efforts to instill in my nephew an appreciation for the accomplishments of true artists. Bach. Da Vinci. Robert E. Lee. Betty Grable. Ingrid Bergman."

"Especially the latter, right?"

"Correct, my boy."

He produced another bottle partially filled with liquor from beneath his cushion and held it up. "The liquid shepherd of salvation," he preached as he opened it and turned it upright, draining what remained. He dropped the empty to the floor and continued, "which regal flavor and stimulating properties have eased my troubled thoughts for the concluding moments of this evening." He eyed the bottle where it lay on the floor, sadly shook his head, and turned his attention back to me. "Didn't make out tonight, eh?"

"Your only nephew will always be a virgin, Uncle Jim," I sighed. "If I ever get any, I'm gonna have to pay for it."

"You're just a kid," he scoffed, pulling at the Camel and spewing a stream of smoke over our heads. "Your time's coming. Don't rush it."

"I think I'm the only virgin left in high school. Everybody's done it but me."

"Talk. Nothing but talk. Don't you believe them."

"Pretty convincing talk. Archie can describe every flower on Melba's panties. Richard Miller has claw marks on his back that he shows us in the boys' bathroom. Jimmy Parker comes to school with a fascinating odor to his fingers. He claims it's you-know-what. Perry Norman claims he..." I paused as the sudden vision of Saxon Browne and Perry Norman straddling a seat in Perry's car brought another surge of jealousy.

"I'd get you a whore," Jim said thoughtfully as he regarded the floor, "but it wouldn't be right. There's no honor in buying a woman." He thought about what he'd said. "Of course, at my age, it's acceptable. But your first time ought to be special, with the love and tenderness of your youth. It'll mean a lot more. You'll remember it the rest of your life, and it'll be a good memory. One you'll cherish. You don't want to start out with a whore."

"Heck, no," I said. "How much are they, anyway?"

"Just bide your time. It will happen when it's supposed to. And you'll be glad you waited."

"I ain't got much choice. I'm broke."

Jim scowled at me. "Use proper English, Jack Junior," he said. "There's no such word as 'ain't.' And you're smarter than these farm hands around here. Understand?"

"Yes, sir. I know better. How do you feel? Have you eaten anything?"

He shook his head against the cushioned back of the chair and let his eyelids slide shut again. "Nope. Not hungry. But I feel okay. Just tired. Need a drink."

He'd been my father and mother, cook and teacher. I loved Jim by instinct, but if I had not had instinct, I would have loved him through homage, and later, perhaps, because I recognized the indelibility of blood. Even though I was eventually forced to admit to myself that he was not flawless, such admission did not diminish my respect and affection for him. I accepted his faults as the inevitable influence of man upon god. I said, "Wonder if it's about time for you to go north..."

"No!" he blurted with a jerk as my words registered on him. He raised himself a few inches from the chair. His blue eyes flashed. "I'm not ready to go!"

"You're close. You've been on it for a while now."

I expected a dirty look, and I got it.

But he knew as well as I that the time was nigh when he would have to be taken to the Sanatorium, a mile north of Smith Station on Highway 51, for a week or two of forced recuperation from his bout with alcohol. It was a regular thing and, I told myself, necessary for his health. He had his own reasons for going, I suspected, for once he made up his mind, he went peacefully.

"I need another bottle, Jack," he said after a minute. "Another pint. Tell the Boy to put it on my bill."

I wrinkled my nose at him. "That'll be three, maybe four, today, Uncle Jim. Don't you think you ought to slow down?"

He smiled. "Hell, boy, I'm about to sober up. Can't you tell? I can't do without my whiskey. Mr. Times and I are like love and marriage. Can't have one without the other."

"You need a divorce."

"You won't run back up to Mary's and get me another bottle?"

"Sure." I sighed and frowned at him again. If I didn't go for him, he would stagger up there himself. "Maybe a half-pint, though?" I said hopefully.

"Get me a pint and," he sighed heavily, "and I'll do what you want. I'll let you carry me up to that fucking Blake's place tomorrow or the next day. Or maybe the day after."

"It's a deal." I said. "I'll be back in a few."

I took a couple of minutes to empty a small mountain of food into Willie's bowl. The dog was just a leg-shy mongrel, but he was huge, he loved me, and I loved him more. Jim had insisted on naming him "William Wing Smith" after Confederate General W. W. Loring, who lost an arm in the Mexican War. Willie had lost a front leg in similarly dramatic fashion: doing battle with a freight train.

I stopped at his chair long enough to ask Jim if he needed anything else from Mary's place. "No," he said, "Just a pint." He grinned hugely as I breezed from the room and out the front door.

With not an inconsiderable amount of apprehension I retraced my steps of earlier this evening at a deliberate pace, glancing toward the loading docks to make sure Coach Murray was gone. There was no sign of the Fury, or of anyone else. Neither was Main Street lined with patrol cars filled with big men demanding information that would lead to the arrest of a sneaking, ruthless "Peeping Tom." I breathed a bit more easily.

Many of Mama Mary's regular customers had departed for the evening, but as I threw her front door open I saw that at least one new one had arrived. She was not really a customer, though at times, in violation of the small "White Only" sign that hung near Mary's front entrance, she had a meal or drank a soft drink from a stool at Mary's lunch counter. Josephine was special, so special that the white patrons of Smith Station did not mind the intrusion of this particular sixteen-year-old colored girl into Mary's all-white establishment.

Her father was white, an Italian named Rossetti who failed to observe the same strict rules of separation of the races that was a part of the upbringing of all native Mississippians. The transient spent a few nights with Josephine's mother, then disappeared. After her mother died giving birth to her, Josephine was raised by her grandfather, "Mama's Boy," the old colored man who was Mary's most trusted helper with the restaurant.

Her skin was naturally a lighter shade than that of her maternal ancestry. I had heard her called a mulatto and a quadroon, and even a "high-yeller" by the less tactful of my friends. Names didn't matter. She was "colored" despite her white father. But she wore her curly dark hair shoulder-length, had learned to use makeup, and dressed better than most of the white girls in town. And unlike most other colored women in this part of the country, she had adjusted her diet to avoid the obesity that was the misfortune of many others. She was clever, spirited, a dramatic oddity. In a small Mississippi town where colored women were generally poorly clothed, portly, uneducated, where most worked as cooks, waitresses, laundresses, and farm hands, Josephine's wit and stunning looks were both intriguing and sanctifying. Had it not been for the unwritten code that positively discouraged such, many of my high school buddies, me included, would have crossed the line and asked her for a date.

Mary and Josephine were my friends, the natural conclusion of their oft presence and my daily patronage of Mary's Cafe. As I entered, the two were engaged in a lively conversation, one on either side of the lunch counter. Mama's Boy smiled at them from his station beside the rear door, a proud grandfather perched upon the stool that accommodated his posterior during those periods each evening when he was the "runner," the traditional title for "he who runs to get the liquor from the illegal stash out back." He knew what I wanted, and as soon as our eyes met and we had exchanged the familiar knowing glance, and I'd held up the "pint" finger, he jumped from his stool and disappeared through the back door, leaving me a few seconds to leer at the curves of Josephine's finer parts. She had leaned forward, arched over the counter, one foot lifted so that the tip of her shoe curled around her other leg. Her skirt was drawn almost to one knee. She wore high heels. I felt the dagger in my middle for the third time tonight.

"Hi, Josephine. Hello again, Mama Mary," I said, placing my elbows beside Josephine's on the counter. I forced myself to look away from her thick curls and gold earrings, only inches away, long enough to smile at Mama Mary. Josephine smelled good, too. "A pleasant evening to you both."

Mary nodded and Josephine giggled. "You're so poetic, C. J. Junior," she said. "You could write poems."

"With the proper inspiration," I said, one eyebrow jumping, "I could write hundreds of them."

"Oh, you wolf!"

"Just like his old man," Mary said.

I said, "Thank God for that! An appreciation for beauty was one of his better traits. Or so I've been told."

Mary said, "He was just a little eager. That's all."

"A wolf in sheep's clothing," Josephine mused. "And I always thought you were a nice boy, Jack."

"Wolves need love, too. Don't they?"

They both shook their heads in disapproval.

"So, what's going on?" I said lamely.

Mary pulled deeply on a crumpled cigarette as she responded, "Josephine has a new boyfriend. She was telling me all about him, except for who he is."

"Darn!" I said.

Josephine's eyes had a dreamy quality to them as she looked at Mary and told us, "I can't tell you who he is. But what a night! It's been like no other night that ever was. There were shooting stars in the sky a little while ago."

Mama Mary and I looked at each other.

"And the moon looked down," Josephine continued, "and it spoke to me. The moon said, 'Josephine, you're the luckiest girl in the whole world. You've found your knight in shining armor.' And what a knight!"

My mouth fell open. "Talk about poetry! We ought to record this conversation. We could sell it!"

Josephine's voice was a sing-song of happiness. "I just may lift my arms and fly away," she crooned. "I feel like an angel. An angel who's just earned her wings."

Mary shook her head in wonder. "I forgot what love did to a person," she complained. "I'm damned glad I'm too old for it."

I said, "Not me. I'm jealous."

"I've never met a man like him," Josephine chimed on. "I've been dating boys before him. Nothing but boys."

"I'm gonna be sick," I said in disgust. "Tell me who he is. I'll neuter him."

"You'd be surprised!"

"So would he. Someone we know?"

Josephine only smiled.

Mama Mary gave the counter a swipe with her rag. "Don't let him break your heart, girl," she said earnestly. "Men ain't worth it. And you look like you're running a temperature over him."

"About a hundred and four," I said.

Mary and I laughed again as we turned away. The Boy appeared with the brown bag I had ordered, and I told them all "good night" and left the cafe. As I warily walked toward home I wondered about Josephine. Most of the colored males who lived in and around Smith Station worked as farm hands or laborers; it was hard for me to imagine any of them creating such a reaction in Josephine. Still, I was white, and white people probably find it hard to imagine life and love among colored people. Too, ours was a small community, and most of the local girls, of whatever race, ended up married to local boys. Josephine, despite her remarkable talents and looks, would probably do the same. Probably just a local farm hand, I decided.

After I delivered Jim's pint and he had begun to nurse the bottle's tapered neck, I undressed in my room and fell wearily into the big tester bed that had once been my father's. Before I went to sleep, I could not help but briefly speculate on Archie's success or failure. I hoped that his natural inclination toward fabrication was especially unwavering and effective tonight. And I wished that I'd asked him to call me after the confrontation at his house, for now I would have to wait until tomorrow to determine what happened.

The ordeal had drained me, and despite my anxiety, in a moment I was fast asleep. That did not last, for it was to be another night of the cursed nightmare. Sometime after midnight, awakened by the clatter of steel wheels on steel rails, I bolted upright, confused at first. Then I forced a laugh at the absurdity of my mental ramblings, my impossible "memories." Warm milk. A bath in warm milk. Preposterous! Still, my sheets were soaked with perspiration, as though there were something ominous about floating about in a tub filled with warm milk. The snores coming from the direction of Jim's bedroom were comforting; he'd made it to bed all right. He was there to save me if I became swamped in pabulum.

And so, once again, I concealed my fear with ridicule. It was my way out. The nightmare came so frequently nowadays that the distinction between dream and reality had become uncertain. The ethereal had become blurred with the corporeal.

I wondered if I were going crazy.

CHAPTER 4
NIGHTMARE

IN A TUB filled to overflow with steamy water, I relaxed and soaped myself from head to foot. The sun had not yet brightened my quarters, and in the darkness of the warm bathroom this morning there was finally solitude and solace. Dawn, I hoped, would lift my spirits. Eyes closed, body tranquilized by the moderating lather, I felt the spirit of my mother, the vague memories—kitchen smells and clattering dishes—of my grandmother, and her offspring. I wondered then if my father had been as honorable as Jim made him out to be.

As was customary of my lazy deliberations during such apathetic moments, I mourned the loss of my parents. But for mere seconds only. I considered myself lucky! I had never been bothered with a father or a mother, nor even a grandfather or grandmother. Only Uncle Jim, who was more brother than parent. Following the death long ago of my grandmother, Jim saw to it that all my needs were attended to. He walked me to school, and was there to meet me when I came home. He tutored me. He lectured to me. The two of us spent hours together, more often than not in our library, where he made my education a study of the ancient works that abounded therein. "They won't teach you this in school," he would say with a finger poised alongside a salient proverb, "but a Southern Gentleman needs to know." He refused to discipline me. "Your conscience will be burden enough." He was friend and counselor. Never parent. Now that I was older, he had given me free rein. Nowadays he drank more and preached less. I learned to drive his station wagon. I kept late hours. I spent nights with Archie, and invited my friends over whenever I wanted. Uncle Jim was there if I needed him, occupied with his own interests and his bottle if not.

I learned that there is an extravagant and wonderful freedom that comes with lack of parental authority. I savored my uninhibited education, the advantages of my freedom. I was a better person because of it. Unabridged. Uncensored. Untainted by the guidance of parents. Complete as I could make myself. As liberated as I wanted to be.

After I dressed, I slid noiselessly down the hallway to Jim's room. He lay covered only in a light sheet, for even October nights in Mississippi can be brutally warm. His body was stretched diagonally across the bed, one leg hanging partially from the mattress. His snores were loud and strong, and with each there came a warm and sour breath that stank of digested alcohol, a putrefied odor rank enough to bring on nausea. I backed away and shook him at arm's length without effect. I shook him until his eyes popped open and he jerked, startled, and half rose from the bed. He settled back into the mattress and peered at me in surprise. "What's the matter?" he said thickly. "Something wrong? What's happened?"

"Are you awake?"

His face wrinkled. "Well, if I wasn't before, I sure as hell am now. God! My head! Get me a cigarette. Over on the bureau. And some aspirin."

His head sank back into the down-stuffed pillow and his eyes closed. I retrieved a pack of Camels and stuck one between his lips, at which his eyes opened and he drew strongly as I offered a tip of flame from his lighter. Now our breathing space was contaminated with searing smoke as repulsive at this early hour as the fog of regurgitated booze. After a moment I brought a glass of water and two aspirin, which he noisily swallowed. He pushed his eyes wide open for an instant, then settled back lazily into his pillow. "What time is it?" he asked as he blew smoke blindly across the room.

"Nearly seven."

"Damn!" He peered at me from his pillow. "What's the matter?"

"The dream, Uncle Jim," I said. "I had it again last night. I want you to listen to it."

He shook his head, stared for a moment at the canopy of his bed, looked away, and said, "I told you, Jack. It's nothing. It'll fade away in time."

"But it's not, Uncle Jim. And I think there's more to it than just dreaming. It's so real."

The smoke drifting overhead seemed to capture his attention. "You know it's not real."

"When it starts, I'm all wet. Warm. Like in a steam bath. Only it's not a bath. It's like being in a bathtub filled with hot milk. I can even taste it. I crave it. It IS milk. The funny thing is, it's such a comfortable place to be that I don't want to ever leave. I could lie in the hot milk and taste it forever."

His eyes rolled. He wasn't really interested in hearing about my dream again.

I went on, "You're going to laugh at this, but at this point the dream turns sexual. I get a hard on. I'm making love to a woman in the bathtub, in the hot milk, rocking back and forth, with her petting me and kissing my cheeks and neck. I can hear her heart beat. She starts singing to me. I can feel the words in her chest, hoarse, like she has a cold. It's an old song that I've heard before. Maybe an old slave song, like Annie used to sing when she was ironing. She's making me feel terrific with her naked breasts and her skin rubbing all over me, in the hot milk, and all the time she's singing. Weird, huh?"

"Weird," he agreed, fumbling with another Camel as he lit it from the stub of the old one. "A bona fide wet dream."

"I want to keep on forever, because I know we're safe in our bathtub, and I'm loving every minute of it. But she's restless. She keeps looking at the door, like she's expecting somebody. She looks at her wristwatch. It must be nighttime, because the drapes over the windows are almost dark, and there's no other light in the room. The door is locked. We're safe, like we've always been. We must do this every night, huh? Nobody can hurt us in here. It's a sanctuary for us."

I felt myself begin to shudder. "But tonight is different. In a little while, I can feel her start to tremble, and the milk in the bathtub has ripples all over the surface. They're such big ripples that we start to come apart. There's a roar, too, like a freight train coming through the house. I can hear the whistle, and I can hear the wheels clacking on the rails. She starts breathing fast, and I can tell she's really afraid. I think she's afraid of the train, and I try to comfort her. But that's not it. She pushes me away, and accidentally pushes me under. I'm drowning. She saves me. She drags me back up, out of the milk. I go under again. She pulls me back up, and pushes me away again. I'm suffocating, and I cling to her as hard as I can. We pull and push at each other. Then, in a while, I float in the milk by myself. I'm really afraid now."

Jim rolled to his side and placed his chin on a palm. "I need a drink, boy," he mumbled. "Any liquor left? I always need a drink before I can diagnose a dream."

"No, sir," I said. "Then, all of a sudden, there's a loud noise, and the door opens, and she grabs for me so we can make love some more, I guess. But it's too late. I see a man, a man I thought I knew once, but that I've never seen before, standing in the doorway, weaving from side to side like he's drunk. But I don't think he's drunk. Maybe he's sick. Later on, I smell his breath, and it's sour, alcohol sour, so maybe he is drunk. The light behind him is so bright I can't see his face. He's standing beside our tub. He's yelling and cursing like he's mad as hell. By this time, the naked woman is standing by the tub, too, screaming at him, and there's milk running everywhere. There's so much milk gushing out of the tub that I'm afraid I'll get washed away. It's the train causing all the ripples, and I hate it.

"The lady smiles at the man, but he pushes her. She falls on the floor, and raises herself up enough to look into the tub. I see her eyes. They're smiling at me. Eyes can do that, can't they? She reaches for me, but the man grabs her hair. He drags her away. All the time, while she's being dragged toward the door, she's looking at me, and crying. Loud cries, like she's being tortured. Wild, wild cries. They scare me, but I start laughing at her. That's the weirdest thing. I can't stop laughing all the time she's crying.

"Then the man stops. The woman's head bounces off the floor, and he comes back for me. I think he's about to kill me, because he raises his hands. But he pulls me from the tub, and he holds me very still, right in front of his face. I don't know him. I've never seen him before. He stares at me for a long time, while I shake and tremble and wait. His eyelids droop, and his eyes are red. He looks at me, and shakes me, and then he does the strangest thing. He smiles at me, and he throws me back into the bathtub. Then he grabs the lady's hair again, and pulls her on through the door. He closes the door, and locks me in."

"That all?" Jim asked impassively. "No mutilation? No hatchets and rip saws?"

"That's not quite all of it. I hear the caboose. Then the door opens again, and the man – I'm not sure it's the same one—sticks his head in. He looks at me, and he says, 'Murdering little bastard!' And then he locks the door again. There are voices on the other side, and some yelling, and I lie in the tub and wait and listen. Then I have the most terrible feeling I let all this happen. If it weren't for me being such a chicken bastard, I would have stood up for her. Instead, I didn't do a thing. So I always wake up feeling guilty as hell, like I failed her."

"You think this has something to do with your mother, Jack?"

I really wasn't prepared to answer. I hated that question.

"What do you think, Uncle Jim?"

He frowned and lay back on his pillow, where he took another drag from his Camel and stared into his canopy once again. "I guess it's time," he said finally.

"Time?"

"Time for you and me to take a trip north."

"Doctor Blake?"

"Sure. I'll get you a room next to mine."

"Be serious," I said, hoping he wasn't. "The dream means something, though, don't you think?"

"Floating around in a tub of milk?" He turned to me and chuckled. "Sure. We used to bathe you in milk all the time. Your mother insisted on whole milk, too. Ninety-five degrees." He snorted and smiled. "Come on, Jack! How can that be real?"

"Well, maybe that part's not true."

"And a baby making love to a grown woman. How many babies have you known that could manage that?"

"Maybe not that, either."

He studied the silk starburst that hung above his head. "I'll talk to Doctor Blake and see what he says. Maybe he'll want to talk to you." He paused, then continued with a rye grin directed upward to his canopy. "In fact, I'm sure Blake will want to see you."

For a second or two I didn't know what to say. The idea of telling someone, even a doctor, that I often dreamed of taking a bath with a naked woman in warm milk was about as appealing as explaining why I felt the urge to masturbate three times a day. I might do it. But it was going to take a lot of convincing.

"Let me think about it," I said.

"It really strikes me as a good idea!" Jim said eagerly, warming to his great plan. "I should have probably suggested it before now."

"Let's wait until the next time it happens. It ain't really as bad as all that."

"Don't say 'ain't.'"

"I'm off to school." I leaped from the bed.

"Before you go," Jim called before I made the door, "I think I'm going to need a drink right away. Your fault, too. Woke me up too damned early. Will you go by Mama Mary's? Get me two fifths. Then you won't have to go again so soon."

I shook my head. "Two fifths is too much."

"Yeah, well, it's going to be a two-fifth day."

I didn't relish him getting that drunk, for now and then when he crossed some fine line Jim's personality suffered a distinct shift. He was still "Uncle Jim" during his binges, but no one would know it by his language; his mastery of the oath escalated exponentially to include curses that were regarded by many of the townspeople as genius. His ability to scald an offensive person, animal, automobile, or even a tree, with obscenities staggering to those within earshot, was admired by all of them. Worse, his skills were held in such esteem that his fabrications were repeated, and strangers to our town were often stricken in awe at the profoundness of the curses that flowed freely from the mouths of common men. It was a trait of his of which I was not proud. It was downright dishonorable. "You promise to go north?" I said warily. He nodded.

I visited with Mama Mary briefly, discussed the weather with a couple of customers, and ate an order of toast after the Boy retrieved the whiskey. Then I delivered both bottles to Uncle Jim, fed Willie, made a bologna and mustard sandwich for my lunch, and walked on to school. By the time I walked out the door, Jim had downed half a fifth.

CHAPTER 5
ARCHIE'S REVENGE

O NE OF THE many advantages of living in a small town is
that practically everything of any importance is within
walking distance. Mary's Cafe, the most pivotal of the sprinkling
of downtown structures, was within a block and a half of Cherokee Rose. Mr. Barnes' Five-and-Ten-Cent Store, where I worked
most afternoons after school, was two blocks from home,
squeezed between Danny's Drug Store and the Merchants and
Farmers Bank. The Grande Theatre was across the street from the
cafe, two doors east of Jake Ainsworth's Barber Shop. Somewhere
farther down my internal list of key structures was Smith Station
High School, across the tracks only a block beyond the Main
Street railroad overpass, an easy ten-minute stroll from home.

My walk to school took me past the grassy field where the
football team was hard at practice. They had endured such each
morning this week. Coach Murray's team had won five straight
games so far this season, and was expected to win the remainder as
well. Early morning practice sessions were the norm for the cham-
pions. The coach was standing on the far side of the field when
I recognized him, face to face with one of his recruits, apparently giving him an earful. Typical, I thought. Coach Murray was
a tough trainer, but his methods paid off. His teams won confer-
ence championships so regularly that the failure to do so cast a
pall upon the entire town.

I followed the sidewalk in the long oval path that encircled
the playing field, and that would, at its end, bring me within spitting distance of the coach. As I neared him, he was ending the

heated abuse of his understudy. Seeing him reminded me of his car, parked at the docks last night. He glanced toward me and grinned, and I waved to him. He then patted his player on the behind and sent him scurrying back into the huddle.

The coach was muscular, broad, six-feet-four, two-twenty, and had the reputation of a brawler. Only a few weeks before, he and his wife Linda had been having a Saturday-night beer at Ginny's Drive Inn, twenty miles north at Milldale, when an off-duty Milldale policeman by the name of Al Mohoney dropped by to show off his latest girlfriend. Al was a strutter, too, and before long he and the coach had words, then a session outside in the parking lot. The ambulance attendants carted Mohoney off to the hospital as Coach Murray swaggered his way back inside to brag a bit; his embarrassed wife waited outside in the car. Though the remainder of the Milldale Police force must have been chagrined at the rough treatment given one of their own, retribution had not been administered, at least, not to my knowledge. Perhaps they feared receiving the same treatment given Mohoney.

Coach Murray was also known for his hunting ability, if you could call it that. According to the tales of those who accompanied him to the woods, he loved killing wildlife, and would shoot anything that moved. Hunting season didn't have to be open for him to kill, either. Once, when seven white-tails had gotten themselves trapped inside the chain-link fence at the garment plant, the coach took it upon himself to destroy them all, the last one, a doe, by strangulation after she had broken a leg in the fencing. The carnage was not well accepted by the townspeople, but no one came forward to tell him so.

He'd asked me several times to try out for the team, practically assuring me each time that I would be allowed to play. Football, however, was not for me. The coach accepted my rejections with tolerance, suggesting that anytime I changed my mind, just let him know. I couldn't figure why he was so friendly to me when he showed no respect for others who had no interest in sports. I thought for a while he might be queer, but discarded that notion when it became clear he was an aggressive womanizer. Eventually I learned to accept his fraternity, glad in the end that he treated me with more tolerance than most of the other kids in school.

I reached the corner of our large red brick schoolhouse at an opportune moment; a block away, Archie pranced along the sidewalk toward me. His feet danced along in a happy jig, and my heart was lifted. The world-champion liar had done it again.

"Hi, Arch," I called when he had reached my side. We walked together toward the wide steps that led upward to the second floor of the school building. "You don't have to tell me. They bought the story, didn't they?"

"Of course," he answered matter-of-factly. "Even Chief Hancock was there. I fooled him, too." He paused at the flagpole, stretched and yawned, turned to wave at the other students who were filing toward morning classes, then sighed deeply and yawned again.

"So," I said irritably, "what happened? Hurry up. School bell's about to ring."

He covered his mouth and belched politely. "It was a great piece of acting," he said. "You shoulda been there."

"I wasn't. What happened?"

"My best performance. Of all time."

I whispered, "Get on with it!"

"Well..." He burped again. "Carl was talking to mom and dad. Barbara had calmed down. She was only shaking a little."

We were nearing the top step. I urged him on with, "Hurry up, Arch! Class is about to start."

"I acted real surprised when I went in. I saw old Carl and asked him what he was doing in my house. Like I didn't quite like him being there. He shouldn't surprise people like that, you know."

"Sure, big man. I know he was concerned about your little complaint."

"You want to hear this?"

I nodded and held my tongue.

"Then mom hugged Barbara—she had clothes on—and told

me a Peeping Tom had been spying on her poor little daughter. Ha! Get that! Poor little daughter? Best tits in the whole state!"

"I know, Arch," I said. "Then what?"

"Carl said Barbara's screaming probably scared them so bad they wouldn't come back. He said he'd do some checking around, though."

"Barbara didn't recognize us?"

"I told you. That bathroom is like a cave. Can't see nothing..."

"Then what?"

"I suggested to Carl that he might want to check on Charlie Mitchell, next door. Charlie's been acting kinda spooky lately, anyway. I wouldn't put it past him to do a little peeping."

We stopped on the wide terrace alongside the second floor entrance. I pulled Archie to one side. "You set the law on poor Charlie?" I whispered. "When you know he didn't do a thing? God, I can't believe you'd do that, Archie! Poor Charlie!"

He looked at me like I was crazy. "Better Charlie than Archie and Jack, huh? That'll throw them off track!"

"But Charlie's not but ten years old. It'll scare him to death! Did they go talk to him yet?"

"I don't know. Anyway, I told Barbara how sorry I was, and that I'd beat the hell out of the trashy bastard what spied on her poor naked body, if I ever caught him. She hugged me and thanked me. Then I went upstairs and went to bed."

I shook my head in admiration and disgust. "I never met anyone like you, Arch," I said. "You ought to go on to Ole Miss. You'd fit right in with all those crooked lying lawyers."

Relieved that I wasn't in danger of being arrested, I breezed through my morning classes. English. Algebra. Recess. American History. I joked with my classmates, and even the teachers. I diagrammed a sentence without help, solved a complex polynomial, quoted a few lines from the Declaration of Independence so authoritatively that Mrs. Hardy smiled with joy. I passed Saxon Browne traipsing down the stairs after English class, and her eyes met mine. I could have sworn she winked, and an instant vision of my lips nuzzling her ears, buried in that profusion of long, musky brown hair, brought the dagger back for a moment. Life was good!

After a quick sandwich and Coke during lunch break, Archie and I performed what had become the routine at this time of day: We sought out our friend and benefactor via '57 Chevy, Jerry Bass. The Senior always parked his Chevy half a block from the schoolhouse in order to smoke Lucky Strikes without the threat that the school principal would catch him. We spied him there as always, alone, his lean figure propped against a shiny fender, huge clouds of smoke bellowing from his lips. I imagined already that I smelled the acrid fumes and the charred cardboard scent of his nicotine-scorched fingers.

"Trying to look tough," Archie whispered as we trudged in his direction, "with that greasy black hair. First thing he'll do is jerk out his damn comb and slide it through his sideburns. Then he'll flex his muscles and start in on me. Or you. And we'll take it, like always, so we can ride in his damn car."

"Ignore him, Arch," I said. "He does look a lot like Elvis, especially since somebody told him so and he started spending most of his time preening in front of a mirror."

"Well, I ain't taking his shit."

"We're gonna miss you, pal."

"Reckon he really dated Teeny?"

I shrugged. "I don't know. I'm surprised he had the nerve to ask her out. You know how bashful he is. He stutters when he tries to talk to more than one person. Except for you and me. He's a Jekyll-Hyder. He's nice to everybody else, and just the opposite to you and me. I think it's cause he's at ease with us. I'll bet he even stutters when he's grooming and cooing sweet nothings to himself in front of his mirror."

"What you're saying is, he hates anybody who's friendly to him. Right?"

"He hates only his close friends. Us."

"Weird."

"Enigmatic."

"For sure. Enigmatic. The guy's strange. I wouldn't be surprised if he's a cousin to Boris Karloff. He probably collects throats."

"Hound dog!" I shouted as we left the sidewalk and neared our friend. "Hound Dog" was the nickname Jerry preferred once he discovered he was an Elvis look-alike.

"Howdy, boys," he answered, lolling against the fender.

"How's it hanging?"

"Left side. Bout thirteen inches," he drawled.

"You wish!" Archie snickered. "Yours don't hang. All it does is droop."

"Damn, Archie!" Jerry countered, as though he had just noticed him. He placed a hand gingerly atop Archie's head and patted. "My god, boy! I believe you've worn a few more hairs off your scalp. Had your head up the principal's ass again, eh?"

"Drop dead, Jerry Lee."

"You're just jealous, son. I could pass for Elvis the Pelvis, and you could be mistaken for that beast what was jump-started by a lightning bolt."

Archie grimaced. "Elvis would commit suicide if he ever heard that you claimed to look like him."

"Your acne looks worse, too, Stub. Looks like maggot bait."

"How was the date with Teeny last night, Jerry?" I asked. "You must have finally got some, you were out so late with her."

"Well, you know me. I ain't like some people." He sneered at Archie. "I ain't gonna lie." Pulling a comb from his pocket he slicked his glistening hair and sideburns while maintaining a grip on the Lucky with two fingers. Archie bumped me with an elbow. "I came awful close," Jerry continued, eyeing us to catch our reaction. "Not quite all the way. I believe next time, though, that little miss Teeny is gonna let me have some. You boys will be the first to know about it, too."

Archie glanced at me, spat on the ground and said, "You might want to tell Teeny, too, Jerry. Otherwise she might not notice."

"Listen, you runt!" Jerry snarled. He was highly sensitive about the proportions of what we all considered our principal organ. "I'll compare mine with yours anytime."

Archie took a deep breath and stared nonchalantly into the limbs of an oak tree.

"We went out to the gravel pit, boys," Jerry continued proudly. "When you date a woman as hot as Teeny, you don't waste time at a pool hall with the kids. That kind of woman is READY, if you know what I mean."

"You really went to the pit?"

"Stayed two hours out there! The pit!"

Located just off a paved road about three miles west of Smith Station, the gravel pit was the late-night parking spot of choice. In its dark and sparsely-vegetated crater was ample space for harboring a half-dozen vehicles, each in relative obscurity. The tales of what went on there were legend. If Jerry had been there with Teeny, he had accomplished more than we ever expected.

"And you didn't get any?" Archie said pointedly.

"Hell, I told you, I came close. Next time."

"Well," Archie said with a wave of his hand, "you'll be surprised how much fun it is. When you finally do it. I remember years ago, when Melba and me first..."

Jerry stiffened like a cat readying for an attack. "Melba and you nothing, runt!" he said. "You and Melba ain't never done it!"

"We have, too!"

"Just shut up!"

"Amen," I said. "We're tired of those stupid tales of yours, Arch."

"They're not tales!"

Jerry chuckled gleefully and turned to beat a staccato rhythm on the hood of his car. The peculiar Jones' smirk flitted across Archie's face, and I thought of his sister immediately. I naturally thought also of her breasts.

"Not to change the subject, Jerry," Archie hissed, "but guess what I heard? About Teeny."

Jerry scoffed, "Nothing I don't already know, runt. How would you know anything anyway?"

"It's just a rumor. But from a pretty good source. A usually-reliable source, I would say."

"A rumor? About my girl?"

Jerry was REAL interested now.

Archie shook his head. "She ain't your girl, Jerry."

"The hell she ain't."

"Well..." Archie's wheels turned for a minute. I watched as one eyebrow cocked. A slight grin passed across his face. His posture shifted ever so slightly. That Peter Lorrie slyness was unmistakable as he said, "I know you two are pretty close, Jerry, so I thought you needed to know. More than anyone else, I guess. Especially if she's your girl."

"She's my girl, all right."

My best friend shrugged. "That's too bad. I was kind of afraid of that."

"What?" Jerry demanded. "What have you heard, runt? Tell me!"

Archie leaned to pat Jerry's arm and said with the utmost sincerity, "I'm your friend, Jerry. You know that. So don't blame me for telling you this. But friends are friends, right? That's why we're put on this earth. To look out for each other."

What a crock! I thought. And Jerry was falling for it!

"Sure, Archie," the Senior said softly. "What is it, pal? What did you find out?"

"Well..." Archie looked about to be sure no one was within earshot. "Well, I heard Teeny was dating Richard Miller on the sly. You know. Ole Muledick himself. Nothing steady. Nobody knows about it. I just heard that when Muledick calls, Teeny drops everything so she can run out and meet him."

The effect on Jerry was one of immediate disbelief. He leaped backward against his Chevy. "Muledick?" he yelped. "Teeny ain't never dated Muledick!"

I grinned inwardly – Arch had done it again – as I turned him with a hand to his shoulder. "Not Muledick, Archie!" I cried in his face. "Why, that bastard'll ruin her!"

"Better believe it. I tell you." Archie pulled from my grip, shook his head sadly, and studied his loafers. "I don't even go the bathroom the same time he goes in there. It's too embarrassing."

"Poor Teeny!"

"Maybe."

Archie's face could have been that of a doctor informing a dying patient of the lack of hope. He said gently, "But most women just love them big ones. Maybe Muledick ain't hurt her. She's so... teeny, though. I remember him telling about that girl in his pickup truck at the drive-in that time. That girl just couldn't get enough of his monster. She wouldn't let him quit."

I just had to add, "But he may seriously wound Teeny with that thing!"

"She may just howl with pleasure."

"She's a size larger now, for sure."

Out of the corner of my eye I had been watching Jerry. He was nearing a state of shock. The words limped from his mouth: "You're lying, Archie."

Archie shrugged. "Well, that's what everybody says, Jerry. I'm sorry."

"Not Richard." Jerry's shoulders sagged, like a flower wilting before our eyes. "Anybody but Muledick." With a pitiful, almost fearful expression he looked at Archie and said, "You ARE lying, Archie. Aren't you?"

"I didn't really want to tell you, Jerry, old pal. You're my friend. I wouldn't have, except for that. You really ought to know. You'd do the same for me. Me and you's buddies."

"Yeah," Jerry said hoarsely.

"But it's just a rumor, Hound Dog. Might not be anything to it."

Jerry shook his head. "No," he said, "she drops everything and runs to meet him. I know she does. No woman can resist THAT..."

"If I were you, Jerry," I said, "I wouldn't follow that act for nothing. Teeny won't be able to feel anything smaller than a baseball bat for three or four days after that brute gets through with her. She's probably worn out at seventeen years of age. She's a woman now. And ruined for any other man for the rest of her life."

"Especially Jerry," Archie moaned, patting Jerry's shoulder again. "You know he ain't got much anyway, and compared to Muledick, well, maybe he can order one of them enlarger things and add enough so that he won't feel like an absolute fool when Teeny gives in and he finally jerks it out of his jeans. Huh, Jack?"

"Sure," I answered, "Uncle Jim's magazines advertise them all the time. They're guaranteed, too. I'll bring you one of the ads, Jerry."

"Thanks, Jack," Jerry said. He groaned at the pavement. "I still can't believe it. I feel sick. I think I'm gonna throw up."

"Don't take it so hard," I said. "There's other women. Just get there ahead of Richard."

"Don't really hurt them anyway," Archie said nonchalantly, throwing up his hands, "to get stretched a little. Long as it's just a little. Those things are elastic, like a sock, long as you don't overdo it. After a while, they're all stretched to hell anyway. I know. From Melba."

"Hence the quaint expression," I added, "big ol' gooduns and good ol' biguns. We ought to ask Teeny to take measurements."

"Boys, I think I'm gonna take a drive." Jerry pulled the driver's side door of his Chevy open and slid onto the seat. "I'll see you tonight at Mary's place. Same time as usual."

"You gonna skip class?" I asked.

"Uh-huh."

Archie and I watched as Jerry backed away from the curb and turned his car toward town. "Poor Jerry," I said.

"The bastard deserved the truth."

"The truth? The truth?" I asked with a scowl. "There ain't no truth to that! Teeny never has dated Richard."

"That's not the way I hear it."

"But if that was so, everybody in school would know it."

"Not necessarily."

I shook my head. "You're the greatest liar I've ever known, Archie. You even lie to me."

"I hardly ever lie."

"Like last night. You know little Charlie Mitchell's not a Peeping Tom. That was a lie."

"Oh yeah? Suppose I told you Charlie's seen the same thing you saw last night?"

I drew back in astonishment. "My god!" I cried, "has the whole town been back there on that roof?"

Archie didn't answer, and I didn't know what else to say. The school bell rang, and I followed him back inside, eager for my last school period of the day. Study hall. The only "class" where students of different grades occupied the same room at the same time. My favorite time of the day. Saxon Browne had the same study hall as I.

She walked in after I had taken a seat at a table near the one where she always sat. She came very near me, and surprised me again by eyeing me as she passed. She sat down and eyed me again!

Something happens between eyes, I thought as we played the game, as if eyes themselves have a face all their own. Eyes smile. Eyes frown. Eyes suggest. Just like faces. Or so I imagined. I imagined Saxon's eyes asked me for a dance, for a touch, for a smile in return. My own told her SAXON, DARLING, I'M YOURS! I had to brace myself each time she shook her long brown hair or grinned across the table at someone. I couldn't keep my mind on my books. Her long legs were clearly outlined under her skirt, under the table, the curve of her fair thighs plainly visible. The dagger visited my belly button. My stomach wrenched into knots each time her throat swelled when she swallowed, or her eyes blinked while she read from her textbook. She caught me staring, again and again, and she stared back. Her naughty eyes delivered the same veiled message each time: WHAT ARE YOU GOING

TO DO ABOUT THIS, BIG BOY? YOU HAVE TO MAKE THE MOVE. HAVE YOU GOT GUTS ENOUGH TO ASK FOR A DATE?

I had trouble believing it was happening. The muscles in my stomach felt like piano wire. Unaware of how tense I had become, I almost fell on the floor when the last bell rang and I tried to stand on a leg that had gone to sleep. She was gone by the time I recovered and looked around to see if she had observed my moment of disgrace. Probably gone to meet Perry, I thought.

I wondered if Perry could read her eyes the way I could.

CHAPTER 6
THE PLAN

W E PLANNED TO meet at the cafe at six-thirty. But first there was the matter of work. When I entered his office at the Five-And-Ten, Mr. Barnes glanced up from a long paper tape curled from the impact of a thousand numbers, and ceased tapping keys and pumping the adding machine's operating lever. The usual saturated stub of cigar hung from his lips, spirals of smoke adding to the cloud that had settled around him.

"More panties today Mr. Barnes?" I asked. "Or maybe I get brassieres today, huh?"

"Jack." The old gentleman pushed his eyeglasses forward on his nose and peered at me with a twinkle in his eyes. "I wouldn't think a boy your age would get tired of playing with panties."

"Empty panties aren't much fun, Mr. Barnes."

He was a seventy-year-old with a buoyant sense of humor; his laugh was a medley of grunts and giggles. "I believe I remember that to be the case, too, Jack," he griggled. "Well, we're not ready to put out that shipment of fabric. Or the sanitary pads. I guess you'll just have to make do fondling that batch of brassieres all afternoon."

"Maybe I'll learn something."

"Maybe you'll find one that's got something in it."

So in my after-school capacity as Chief Flunky at Barnes' Five-And-Ten-Cent Store, I unpacked and shelved brassieres and other goods from three o'clock until five, with only a break or two helping at the cash registers up front. Mr. Barnes was the type of boss to give employees their head. Only a couple of times did he wander, in the shuffling gait that always reminded me of someone pushing a loaded wheelbarrow, from his office. Perry Como was his favorite singer, and he hummed Perry's latest as he padded about with his arms hanging before him.

Two hours passed quickly, and at five o'clock I took off, pausing for a moment across the street at the windows of Murphy's Dry Goods to ascertain that Archie had already been released for the afternoon. He was nowhere to be seen. Melba, the plump young girl with whom he claimed intimacy, and who also worked for Mr. Murphy, waved to me from far back in the store. I waved back, then jogged for home.

The disagreeable odor of Jim's whiskey at our front door was a sharp reminder that it was nearing time for his confinement. A quick peek into his room confirmed that he was out of this world. Recumbent beneath a tangled sheet, he slept, his heavy snores rocking the venerable walls of Cherokee Rose and lending its sanctuary a familiar surge of desecration. Never me, I thought. Never will I drink alcohol.

I could not wake him to ask if he had eaten, even though I shook him, so I left him where he lay. He would probably crawl from bed sometime during the night and remain awake smoking his Camels and resting in his stuffed chair until daybreak. He might walk to Mary's for breakfast, but more likely for another bottle.

After washing our dishes and superficially sweeping the floor, I bundled the week's soiled clothing and placed it outside the back door for pickup tomorrow by the old colored woman, Annie, who had been taking care of our laundry as long as I could remember. Jim remained comatose. I took a last look around, then began my robotic walk toward the cafe, stomping cracks and backbones along the way.

Jerry's blue-and-white Chevy was posted in its usual parking space in front of the cafe, like a thoroughbred, reined and head bowed, awaiting the return of its rider. A beautiful automobile, it had proven its mechanical merit on the improvised strip just outside of town. The car was Jerry's pride, and he always parked it so that anyone who wanted could merely glance out the front window of the cafe and admire its sleek form, savor and covet the potential extension of mind and pelvis it offered.

They were seated at our table. My mouth watered as I beheld the juicy pig's foot upon which Jerry gnawed hungrily. Archie sat impassively, almost contemptuously, watching, a brown Orange Crush bottle before him. The jukebox boomed, balls ricocheted and cracked upon the pool tables, pinball machines chimed, and a number of customers lined the lunch counter, seated upon the procession of ancient stools that sprouted like grotesque weeds from the cafe's fertile floor. Mama Mary was busily frying hamburgers while sucking on a wad of chewing tobacco that would shortly join its soggy comrades in the Crisco can near her feet. She was a smoker as well, and generally alternated cigarettes with liquid tobacco, although at all times she was capable of carrying on a conversation on any subject germane to Smith Station or any of its citizens.

I yelled for her to bring another platter of pigs' feet, please ma'am, and an Orange Crush, then took my place at our table. "Shit, Jack," Jerry said as I sat. I wondered for a moment why I had never noticed that nearly all his sentences began with a four-letter word. "You're about too late. She's almost out of pigs' feet."

"I guess the Boy will have to run out back and pickle-up another batch," I said. "He has a big cage with lots of stray cats he's collected. He only uses the hind legs for pigs' feet, though."

"Cats' feet!" Archie howled.

"Hell, you claim to have eaten worse, runt," Jerry chortled. "Even though you're lying."

"Women love it," Archie said, "if you French kiss it."

"Great Scott!" I coughed, "Wait until after I eat my pigs' feet!"

Jerry leaned back, slid a stub between his greasy lips, and blew a cloud of smoke into the steadily-worsening atmosphere around us. Archie regarded him with a face twisted with sincerity and passion and said without warning, "By the way, Jerry, I got confirmation now."

"Yeah? Confirmation of what?"

"Teeny. She usually goes to the pit with Muledick on Thursday nights. That's her mom's bridge night, and she can always get out. My usually-reliable source claims the sounds of her screams of pleasure reverberate for miles around the pit. Most of the other couples out there can't get nothing done for all the groans and moans coming from Richard's pickup. It's a real problem. A real distraction. Something really needs to be done about that guy's dong."

Jerry puffed on his cigarette and appeared calm as he studied Archie. "You're lying, runt," he said evenly. "You might as well admit you're lying."

An angelic smile covered Archie's face. Somehow, I thought, that was the most damaging response he could have made.

"You're lying, Archie," Jerry repeated.

"What are we going to do this weekend?" I said. "The fair's been going on all week up at Milldale, and we haven't even gone once. Maybe we ought to go up there one night, maybe tomorrow night."

"I'm too broke," Archie said, as his eyes dropped before Jerry's blistering glare. "Besides, it'll be the same old stupid rides. Same old cotton candy. Same old games. Screw it."

"Well," I said, "so much for that. What I'd rather do anyway is to invite a bunch of women over to my house for an evening of pleasure. An orgy. I believe I could handle thirty or forty women in one night. I'm getting desperate, too. If I don't nail one or two soon, I'm gonna explode in a gooey fireball of protoplasmic disillusionment."

"No danger in you exploding," Jerry chuckled. "Bet you relieve the pressure all the time."

"Ain't the same," I said. "Just don't satisfy like a woman would."

"How do you know?" Archie asked. "I'm the only one..."

"Shut up!" Jerry and I shouted simultaneously.

"I'm telling you, we do it!" Archie raged. "All the time. She gets up against the shelves, where we store the shoes..."

"At which point you get a heel in the ass," Jerry snickered. He snickered, but he did it without a hint of a smile.

"...and she pulls up her dress, and..."

"And you just walk right over and stick it in, eh? Just like that? Right, runt?"

"Exactly!" Archie pounded the table with his fist.

"Hell, Archie." Jerry smiled now. "You couldn't get that little weenie up that fast. And what about Mr. Murphy? You sell him tickets so he can watch?"

"We don't do it until he's gone."

"You're lying, runt." Jerry looked at me. "He's lying. Right, Jack?"

"Absolutely," I said. "He's the world's greatest liar. He better be. We'd have to kill him if he actually did it."

"She begs me. She loves it," Archie ranted.

"She begs? She loves it!" Jerry bent to pretend nausea, then snickered again. "God help us, she loves it!" he said wearily. "We really do need to ask Melba about him, Jack."

"I got some before you did, Jerry. That's what makes you so mad."

The front legs of Jerry's chair hit the floor with a bang as he reached across the table, grabbed Archie's collar, and pulled him close. "You little squirt," he growled, "If you don't shut up, I'll take you outside and feed you a knuckle sandwich. You got that, squirt?"

Chins quivering above Lucky butts and pig bones, the two stared into each other's eyes. Archie wavered, and in a moment Jerry released him, satisfied that there would be no further mention this evening of Archie's sexual exploits.

"Let's lighten up, guys," I said. "I've been sitting here thinking. Maybe only eight or ten women per night could keep me satisfied. I'd be willing to try, anyhow."

Archie was still hot, and since he couldn't very well risk a beating at Jerry's hands, he turned his rage on me. "You wouldn't know what to do with them if you could get them, Jack," he said. "I'd have to come show you."

"Sure you would," I said. "Thought we got that settled. You want to start it all over again?"

"I'll bet you wouldn't even know what position to use, would you?"

I was caught off-guard by the question. In desperation I frantically recalled the black-and-white photographs in Uncle Jim's girlie magazines. No help there. I had a good idea of how it should be done, but in none of the books in Cherokee Rose's library were there explicit details to prove my assumptions. All I had in the way of hard facts were my discussions with the guys in the john. So I procrastinated, reasoning suspended in a reproductive hinterland. Finally, I decided to rely upon the basics garnered in those secret discussions at school. "I'd get on top!" I said. "That's how men do it!" And if that were not the precisely correct answer, I added, "Usually."

"Usually?" Archie's eyebrow arched. He seemed so sophisticated that I prepared myself for a stinging contradiction. But instead he said, "Yeah, most of the time, I do it that way." He saw the warning look in Jerry's eyes and said hastily, "That's right, eh, Jerry?"

Jerry was now busily lighting another Lucky Strike, too concerned with the arc set off by the flint of his Zippo to get involved in a conversation about sexual procedures.

"That's one way," Archie continued smartly. "But you can do it rear ways. Sideways, too."

"Sideways? Rear ways?" I said, looking again to Jerry for help. Now our Senior friend seemed thoroughly absorbed with a pool game being played twenty feet away. I said, with all the confidence I could muster, "And the woman can get on top, too. They REALLY like it on top!"

"Oh, my god!" Archie's mouth dropped open in obvious shock

and I saw my lie falling apart. "Jack! You don't know any better than that?"

Counting on his support, I punched Jerry. "Right, Jerry?" I said.

Jerry pointed at the pool table. "Good game," he said. "We ought to play a little pool."

I turned back to Archie. "You don't know what the hell you're talking about, Arch!"

Archie assumed lecturing position – tabled elbows – and with a sigh obviously meant to communicate patience said, "Jack, you can't let the woman get on top. You don't know why?"

"No, and you don't either."

"Think about it. If the woman was on top, her vital fluids could run out. A woman can die when her vital fluids run out like that. You gotta be careful."

Suddenly Jerry decided that the game could get along without his surveillance. He turned his attention back to us. "Yeah, Jack," he said, even more patiently than Archie, "there's a lot more to it than just sticking it in. You gotta read up on it. You gotta know what you're doing, son."

"I don't believe it."

"Why?"

"Well... Well, their vital fluids don't gush out on the ground while they're walking around. You're both nuts."

"That's what Kotex is for!"

"Uh-uh. Kotex is for when they have their period, once a month."

"It only happens when they're stretched open," Archie insisted. "They can walk and run, just like men, as long as they keep their muscles tight. You ask one. You'll see I'm right."

"Damn!" Was there wisdom in Archie's logic?

"We'll teach him all about it, won't we, Jerry?" Archie said as he bumped Jerry's arm. "He's young. He'll learn."

They were wrong. Weren't they? "You are both nuts" I said.

Mama Mary brought my feet and drink, and I silently gnawed

while I contemplated this new concept of the most important part of the sexual riddle. So much to learn. Archie to teach me. I gagged at the thought.

Jerry suddenly burst out with a laugh. Archie and I looked at each other. "What's so funny?" I asked

Jerry continued guffawing. "I was just thinking about that study hall," he managed through his snorts of mirth. "Mrs. Walters, and Archie, and him getting kicked out of school."

Suddenly I was laughing just as hard as I recalled that day. But Archie's face was screwed into a growl of rage. "Fuck you," he growled.

"Who saw it first?" I asked. "Did you see it first, Jerry? Damn, I wish I could have seen it."

"Bobby Pitts saw it first," Jerry said while trying to control his glee. "I'm surprised it wasn't Archie saw it first. Bobby came over to our table and told us about it, and we all jumped up and got in line. Archie got in line after a minute. That line was clear back out to the stairs. All boys, all wanting help with their homework. I think she was getting suspicious by then. Kept reaching up and pushing at the part of her dress that covered her boobs."

"Get to the good part," I said.

"Well, Mrs. Walters ain't a bad looking woman, you know, and that day she had on a brown dress that was low in front, but I think something was wrong with it, too, cause of the way it flopped out up top. You could see all the way to her navel. Anyway, when I finally got there, standing behind her while she was showing me how to get square roots, I could see them boobs. Beautiful boobs! It musta been an old brassiere she had on, cause them big babies was just laid out there, just begging to be smooched."

I groaned. "God! And I missed it."

"Them big boobs was beautiful," Jerry continued with a sigh. He looked from Archie to me. "I bet Mrs. Walters ain't getting enough at home, boys. I bet she shows them things off on purpose, hoping one of the guys will ask her for some."

"Okay, okay," I urged Jerry on while trying to control my laughter. "Tell us about Archie now. We've heard it, but it gets better every time you tell it."

"Well, like I said, she was getting suspicious, what with every boy in study hall in line at her desk. Then Archie finally made it." He had a huge grin on his face. "That shriek of hers coulda been heard all over the building. More than a shriek. It was like a wolf howling. Somebody even called the cops."

"I heard it, and I was downstairs in the office," I said. I was almost in tears from laughing. "I thought somebody was being murdered."

Archie hadn't said anything up to now. But now he mumbled, "Well, I couldn't see them boobs very good. The top of her dress was flopped over..."

"So you just reached down and pulled it open..." Jerry and I were laughing so hard we were about to fall out of our chairs.

"Well, I got a better look than anybody else," Archie boasted. "And three days suspension, too!"

Poor Archie. For once he couldn't think of any retaliation befitting the moment.

"And I didn't get a look at them," I moaned.

Archie glanced at the two of us and snickered discreetly. He wasn't about to let us have a laugh at his expense. "Yeah, boys, but I've been thinking. I know how we can see some up close," he said. "Lots better than just Mrs. Walter's boobs."

I gave him a wide-eyed look of warning, sure that he was about to invite the remainder of the county's residents to an evening's entertainment outside his sister's bathroom window. But Archie had something else in mind. "Not only can we see tits, we can see everything else, too," he said. "Maybe even see two people hard at it."

"I don't want no part of it," I said immediately.

Jerry's left eyebrow arched with interest. "Hmmm...," he said. "Let's hear him out, Jack. How we gonna do that, runt?"

"Simple," Archie said. "We go where the action is! We drive

out to the gravel pit, ease about in the darkness until we find a car where there's a totally dynamic screwing taking place, and we observe. And take notes."

"You're nuts," I said.

"Hmmm...," Jerry said. "Hmmm...."

"We'll take along a camera, too," Archie continued. "We may want a picture or two to study later."

"How the hell are you gonna get a picture to take in the dark?"

"Flash bulb. Or flashlight."

"Hell. You'll get us shot!"

Arch grinned. "Yeah. I was just kidding about the camera. We might catch Muledick out there, though, with Teeny howling at the moon. Then you'd know for sure about that rumor."

"Uh-uh. Not for me," I said. "We'll end up breaking rocks for thirty years."

"But it ain't no crime," Archie continued after a frown in my direction, warming to his idea. "It's really research. The resolution of scientific curiosity. I've thought about it. It's a perfectly justifiable undertaking. An investigation of human anatomy and the interaction of the male and female parts. Newton would have done the same thing, if he'd thought about it. And it'll be a lot more fun than watching apples fall out of trees."

"My god! You have thought a lot about it!" I yelped.

Jerry regarded Archie with new respect. "Damn! Let's do it!" he said.

"Now, wait, guys," I said, pushing away from them.

"Chance of a lifetime," Archie rattled on. "You two can see how it's done, and maybe I can pick up a few pointers, too."

There was a light in Jerry's eyes I'd never seen before. "Let's go tonight!" he breathed fiercely. "Car's right out front." He half rose from his chair, and Archie reached for the table to shove himself erect.

"Wait! Wait!" I yelled. I leaned across the table and pushed them back into their seats. They bared their teeth at me, but they sat. "We need a plan first, don't we? We can't just rush out there without a plan! We'll get killed! We need dark clothes so we won't be seen. We need to walk the pit beforehand, so we'll have a layout of the land. Body armor. We need that. And we need a bunch of guns to carry along with us. Maybe a machine gun or two. Hand grenades."

"Hell, we've all been to the pit. In the daytime," Jerry said in disgust at my caution. "We know every inch of it. And I can carry my twenty-two revolver along. It's in the car."

"We ain't wearing dark clothes, though," I said. "One of those studs will surely pick you off with a well-aimed slug."

"You worry too much."

"Well, we can be ready tomorrow night," Archie said. "And, anyway, that's when Teeny and Richard will be there." He glanced at Jerry. "If that rumor is true, that is."

Jerry slowly nodded his head, a dull gleam in his eyes. "Yeah," he said. "Yeah. Tomorrow would be better..."

"This reminds me of my first time with Melba," Archie said. "You two will..."

"Shut up!" Jerry and I screeched.

Unnoticed by the three of us, Mama Mary had begun making her table rounds, a chore she performed only when business was slow and the Boy was occupied with other drudgery. At other times, when the cafe was crowded and noisy and the Boy had his hands full, she took orders by a "screech and scream" process that might consist of a screeched "What'll it be, Hal?" followed by a screamed, "Hamburger. Fries. Lots of catsup. Ma'am." Most of us regulars had become acclimated by constant exposure to her circus behavior, but newcomers were always surprised by the bazaar atmosphere.

She had shuffled up behind Jerry tonight in her ambling gait that always gave the appearance of one leg being shorter than the other, which, I had decided, she used purposefully to secure sympathy and thereby larger orders of pigs' feet, and tapped him on the shoulder. He jumped. "Didn't scare you, Jerry, did I?" she croaked happily as she sidled beside our table. Mary rolled her own cigarettes, stale yellow things that were bent, bulged, and matched her teeth in color and texture. One jutted from her lips now, tiny flakes of ash drifting from it onto our table with each syllable. "You got a guilty conscience, boy?" she continued.

"No, ma'am," Jerry answered quickly.

"How was them pigs' feet?"

"Great!" we all said in unison.

"How about some more?"

"No, ma'am," Archie said. Jerry and I shook our heads. Mama Mary silently retrieved dishes and wiped our table with a damp rag, spreading crumbs onto our laps, the floor, and even into adjacent chairs. Then she ambled to another table, trailing yellow smoke and ashes behind, to begin anew her pigs' feet sales pitch.

"Suppose we get caught tomorrow night?" I whispered.

"Hell, we been slipping around this town at night for sixteen, seventeen years," Jerry said. "We know the ropes. Nobody will see us."

"It's awful quiet out there at the pit. Except when you-know-who is out there. People in cars can probably hear every branch crack under our feet."

"So, we won't step on branches."

"Of course, if we do get caught, it won't be so bad. If we survive all that lead those mad studs will be throwing at us, we can form our own chain gang at Parchman. That'll be fun. We can come up with a catchy name for it, too, like Archie's Peekers. Or Jerry's Rock Crushers. Something really sophisticated. It'll be fun."

"Or Jack's Chicken Shits," Archie said pointedly.

I stared at the ceiling, tacky from layers of the greasy mist that boiled from a never-ending chain of frying burgers, at the naked light bulbs and cotton cords that hung at odd intervals, and briefly wondered why Mary chose yellow bulbs. Maybe her cigarettes and teeth were yellow because of the glare from the yellow bulbs. Maybe we all had yellow teeth. But what did that matter anyway? We probably would not survive the kamikaze attack on the gravel pit, so, so what if we had yellow teeth?

"We better carry a flashlight," Archie said.

I hadn't realized it before, but our heads had become clustered together at the center of our table while we were in the process of communicating. And we were speaking in hushed tones appropriate to a group of hardened criminals plotting a bank robbery.

"We don't need no damn flashlight, Archie," I whispered. "Someone is sure to see that."

"I'll only use it in an emergency."

Jerry cocked his head and stared for a moment at Archie. Then he said, "We better hope the moon ain't out. If the moon is out, and it hits the top of Archie's head, hell, we might as well build a bonfire." His body rocked as he held his stomach and silently laughed.

Neither Archie nor I cracked a smile. "What about our reputations?" I said. "I've got a sterling reputation in this town. People look up to me, like unto God. They expect more of me than mere Peeping Tommery. Besides, Uncle Jim will kill me. I'll despoil the Smith name. Hell, if we get caught, they'll change the town name from Smith Station to Britt Station, after the Britts, and I'll have to move to Milldale to escape the wrath of the community. That is, if they don't toss me in prison. A man's honor is his bond. Or something like that, Jim says. We're risking my stature and esteem among the townsfolk with this prank. Count me out."

"My ass," Archie growled. "You got an active imagination, Jack." He settled back in his chair and appeared to concentrate. "But we'd sure have to leave town. Only Milldale wouldn't be far enough. Probably have to move to Alabama."

"Alabama!"

"Hell," Jerry said, "you mean Alaska!"

"Death," I said. "Imprisonment. The scorn of the world's great societies. Our futures down the crapper. Is it worth all that for a quick shot of tit, et al?"

They looked at each other, then at me. "Hell, yes!" they cried in unison.

Jerry grinned. "We'll go out there about midnight tomorrow

night. They ought to be screwing like a bunch of mad dogs by then."

Archie shook his head contemptuously. "Hell, fool," he said, "they'd be through and gone if we waited until midnight."

"Some of them studs really know how to do it," Jerry argued. "They go for hours and hours."

"It only takes a minute. Remember, I've been there. I know. We need to be in the pit about nine o'clock. Thursday is a school night. Everybody'll have to get in early."

Jerry was forced to agree. "Yeah," he said sullenly. "You may be right for once, runt. And we don't want to miss anything. We'll meet up here at six-thirty, play a few rounds of eight ball, then execute The Plan."

"Right." Archie looked at me. "Right, Jack?"

"I'm too young to die," I said.

"Too chicken to live."

"Always figured him for a lily-livered ass-hole," Jerry added.

I said, "My buddies."

"Ex buddies."

There was dead silence then. They stared at me accusingly. The pressure was on. I squirmed, but said, finally, "Okay, but you two have got to promise to throw yourselves in front of me if there's any gunplay. To lie to Uncle Jim if he hears anything. To swear in court you forced me to go along. To tell them you drugged me. Deal?"

"Deal," Archie said.

"You'll take care of Willie? If you survive and I don't?"

Archie nodded and said solemnly, "Tomorrow night will be a night to remember."

The die were cast. We settled into speculation regarding our expedition, and tried to think of anything and everything that could go wrong. The prospect of being caught in the act of spying on people who were engaged in what must be considered a most personal affair, was repugnant, but even I, after examining "The

Plan" from the perspective of Archie's "resolution of scientific curiosities," gradually became enthusiastic.

"The Plan" was not all that Archie had in mind, however. He envisioned this as the first of a series of excursions into the pit. We would learn, he contended, new techniques for the persuasion of the unwilling female. Compile a list of girls who would. By use of a stopwatch, time the various participants for inclusion in a database by which we could judge our own performances. And last but not least, perform an objective analysis of Richard Miller's performance based upon the length and decibel level of Teeny Wright's screams of pleasure. "We can publish this," he said gleefully. "A scientific study of The Act. We'll be famous."

"We'll be dead," I said.

As we sat in a haze of smoke beneath the yellow bulbs and schemed to remedy our carnal ignorance by unorthodox means, I observed yet another digression from the norm. Jerry bumped my arm and nodded as a couple entered through Mary's front door. Archie did not notice for a moment, so engrossed in describing our now noble conspiracy was he, that he no longer had our attention.

Perry Norman had arrived. And with him was a beautiful girl. But the girl was not Saxon Browne.

"Wonder where Saxon is tonight?" I said to Jerry. "She and Perry are supposed to be steadies. Who's that?"

"Poor Perry probably needed a little strange," Jerry said softly. "And that ain't bad."

"Hell, Perry ain't never done it with Saxon," I said angrily. "Saxon's a virgin! She's a lady!"

"You nuts? Perry tells everybody how he takes her out to the gravel pit all the time."

Archie had now craned his neck around toward the counter where Perry and his new friend, a voluptuous blonde whose hair hung damp and stringy, now sat and awaited Mama Mary and her order pad. "Looks like Perry and that gorgeous blonde have been out to the pit," he said. "Look how sweaty they are. Perry sure musta needed a little strange."

"Damn it, Archie, Perry ain't never screwed Saxon," I said, making sure my words were low enough that Perry couldn't over-hear.

"He does all the time," Archie snickered. "I got it from a usu-ally-reliable source."

"Well, this time your source is wrong."

"You really got the hots for Saxon, don't you?"

"Any man in his right mind has the hots for Saxon," I declared. "She's a goddess. Mississippi's version of Claudette Colbert. A future Miss America. She's just not quite fully developed yet, that's all."

"You mean she ain't got no tits."

"They'll come. Next year, when she's eighteen, she'll make Bar-bara Jones and Linda Murray look like anemic boys."

"Well," Archie's eyebrow raised as he glanced at Jerry, "well, since you love her so much, you ought to ask Saxon for a date. Now's your chance. Perry's been unfaithful to the girl. And I'll make sure she knows about it, too."

A queasy premonition of failure and disaster always accom-panied thoughts of my asking Saxon for a date. Perry Norman had been deterrent enough, and now, with what appeared to be an opening... "She's a year older than me," I babbled. "And she's too good-looking. I got a full schedule, what with feeding Willie and buying booze for Jim. And that's probably Perry's sister he's with tonight, anyway. Hell, maybe it's Saxon's cousin, fresh in from New Orleans or something, just doing Saxon a favor. Saxon's probably sick. That's it!"

"Perry ain't got no sister," Jerry charged. "And Saxon ain't sick. You're just chicken." He turned to Archie. "Boy's chicken-shit, Arch."

"I knew it," Archie agreed, nodding. "Biggest chicken-shit in the entire county."

"We ought not even associate with the coward."

"Let's leave him here, the gutless, mangy dog."

"Perry will kill me!" I whimpered.

"You wouldn't have a chance anyway," Jerry shrugged. "Saxon Browne would never go out with you."

"He's a loser, all right," Archie added. "Anyway, after years of making love to Perry Norman, Captain and star quarterback of the Little Dixie Champion football team, what the hell would she want with Junior here?"

"Now wait a minute," I said. "I ain't THAT ugly."

Jerry slicked his Elvis haircut with his comb. "Pretty ugly. Ain't got a chance with Saxon, anyway."

"The hell I don't."

"One way to find out."

"All right," I said without thinking, "I'll prove it. I'll ask her..."

The rashness of my commitment settled like a cloud of nerve gas upon the troops. So I added, "I ain't saying when I'll ask her, though."

They grinned at each other with satisfaction. They're looking forward to the carnage, I thought. My buddies! The two of them had worked me the way Archie and I had worked Jerry earlier. Archie! The man with the pact with the devil!

CHAPTER 7
SANATORIUM

WHEN THE MERCHANTS and Farmers Bank clock chimed ten, my two friends and I parted company outside Mary's Cafe. Jerry offered to drop Archie at his house, since it was on his way, and I stood for a moment staring after the Chevy as Jerry left scraps of his rear tires on the bricks of Main Street. Then I turned the corner and started for Cherokee Rose. Halfway there, Squeaky Bishop, one of Jim's best drinking buddies, met me on the sidewalk. The two of them had apparently been having a round together. Squeaky was not a favorite of mine, since I considered him a bad influence, and, despite the greeting and an obvious inclination on his part to chat for a while, I barely spoke as we passed. A brief minute later I waited with Willie outside the front door of Cherokee Rose until the hacking coughs of my uncle subsided.

The atmosphere around his chair was tainted by the familiar fumes of charred tobacco and simmering alcohol, along with the foul odor of vomit. Thoroughly soused, he was nevertheless cognizant and able to communicate.

"Hello," I said as I circled his chair. "Didn't expect you to be up. Figured you for a zombie for another six or eight hours at least."

An empty he raised in a silent toast, after which he succumbed to another ragged cough.

"Saw Squeaky leaving. Have you eaten? Are you hungry?"

His eyes blinked foolishly as he focused on both us Jacks and said, "Thirsty. Need 'nother fiftha whiskey. Mister Times. You gonna gimme some more whiskey, boy? That sot Squeaky drank parta mine."

"Nope," I said. "You've had enough already. I'm amazed you can still talk. You and Bacchus would have made a great team."

He grinned crookedly, head weaving, and raised his empty again. "Us Smith's good at one thing, sure, boy. Hell, yo dad, Cherokee Jack, was better'n me. My lil brudder could drink that whiskey. Bettern even me."

"You both deserve medals."

His face wrinkled in sorrow. "I miss my lil brudder. You know, Jack?" His eyes lifted and he tried again to focus on my face. "I was just twenty years old when that lil kid was born. I loved him more'n anything on God's green earth. I practically raised him. Wif yo grandma's help, of course. He was a hoss. And he was prime when he died. He didn't deserve to die like that. Not like a dog who'd been given strychnine."

Seldom was Uncle Jim mournful during his drunkenness. Tonight, however, he appeared on the verge of desolation.

"Don't get melancholy, now, Uncle Jim," I said. "Cherokee Jack died of ptomaine poisoning or food poisoning or something. It was just an accident, I guess." I sat on the sofa opposite him. "How about something to eat? It'll make you feel better."

"Feel fine. Ain't hungry." He hung his head in misery. "Wish Cherokee Jack was drunk that day," he said. "Maybe he wouldn't been hungry. Maybe be still live and kicking today. And still drinking his whiskey."

"There's some moral here, I'm sure."

"Damn poison. Germs."

"Home cooking. Mary and mom and the café. I know! The moral is, if you get married, avoid your wife's cooking. You sure you're not hungry?"

I helped him light a cigarette after he tried and failed. As he dragged at the fiery weed, I said, "Reckon Mom poisoned Dad, Uncle Jim? I've been hearing that ever since I can remember. I don't even know who told me about it first."

"No. Hell, no! Blake. Blake said ptomaine. Jack ate at Mary's. Maggie ain't no blame."

"Reckon Mama Mary poisoned him?"

"It was ptomaine. Nobody poisoned my brudder."

"Then why did Maggie take off without saying anything to anybody?"

He shrugged his shoulders and drained a drop or two from his bottle. His hands were shaking. I said, "People say it was another man. That Maggie killed old Cherokee Jack to be free of him, then took off with her lover."

Jim's face took on a scowl. For a minute I feared he would throw his empty at me. "Talk like that just starts damn rumors," he growled. "Us Smiths been in Missippi for a hundard fifty years, and we ain't had no scandal." He grinned at the floor, then looked up at me and said evenly, almost soberly, "Think you and me can perpetuate the renowned Smith line without fucking up the record?"

"You and me? You planning on having a few late bloomers?"

"You then," he grunted. "Reckon you can have us some rug rats without some kinda gossip?"

"If I can ever figure out how. Did you ever hear from Maggie? They say she went to California. Hollywood. Or that she's being held prisoner in the jailhouse. Even that she was murdered. What do you think? "

He sighed heavily and stuck his tongue as far inside his empty bottle as it would go, then said unevenly, "Bout time to go north."

"You never heard from her after that day?"

He shook his head side to side in long, exaggerated movements. The way he did when he was lying. Jim was, above all, an honorable person, and he hated lies and liars. His ability to lie was hence defective. "She wouldn't call me anyway," he lied.

I dropped to my knees on the floor beside him so that we could be face to face, so that I could exploit his drunkenness and his weakness for truth. I'd take advantage of him while he was soused. Eyeball to eyeball. Nose to nose. Then our eyes met, and at close range I recoiled as I recognized in his ashen pupils a mirror of my dream. I knew it was only some kind of mental phenomenon, but in the depths of his eyes I thought I saw the vacant, bewildered stare of a naked, screaming woman. I backed away, unnerved by the delusion. Slowly Jim's lids slid shut as he fell victim to another coughing seizure. He turned away, and I returned to the sofa and waited, ill at ease at the physical manifestation of an illusion that had haunted me off and on forever.

"Need a drink," he said after a moment as he straightened himself. "Go to Mary's, Jack."

"You need to go see Dr. Blake, Uncle Jim," I said. "Right now. It's time. No, it's past time."

"Think so?"

"Think so."

Another long sigh of despair and frustration was heaved into space. He glanced over at me, a reluctant frown on his face. "In the morning," he sighed. "I'll go in the morning."

"Okay."

"But you have to go to Mary's. Deal?"

"Half pint?"

"Fifth."

"Pint, then. Okay?"

He nodded. He was through. He lay his head back and closed his eyes. Ten minutes later, after my trip to Mary's, Jim was waiting, and he thanked me for the pint, which he promptly began to drain. I told him good night and dropped into my bed. I lay still for a while, fighting the insane urge to call Saxon Browne and ask her for a date. I even got up, dashed down the hallway, and jerked the receiver from its cubbyhole in the wall. But when I heard the switchboard operator, Gertrude, say "Number, please," I chickened out. I told her I'd accidentally knocked the receiver off the cradle. Then I went back to bed.

Sleep did not come easily. I tossed and turned and thought of all the people in Smith Station who probably still thought my mother poisoned my dad and took off with another man. What if it were true? Who could he have been? The townspeople would have noticed if one of their own had disappeared the same night Maggie left, so that meant it had to be someone who did not live in Davis County. What did that prove?

What bothered me most, though, was the possibility (the fact?) that people were talking behind my back. When they saw me downtown walking down the sidewalk, or having a Coke at Mary's place, were they asking themselves, "Wonder if Cherokee Jack was his father? Or is he the son of her lover? A bastard? Or just, technically, "illegitimate?" I even wondered if Archie and Jerry talked about me.

God, it hurt! I fell asleep after a while, despite Willie's barking and Jim's violent coughing.

A thin sheet of bright autumn sun slicing through the half-opened window drapery woke me with its warmth. Was winter ever going to arrive? I wondered. It was only seven o'clock, and already the bed sheets were suffocatingly warm.

I would be late for school, an inevitability since I was taking Jim to the Sanatorium. It didn't bother me to be late. The school principal would raise Cain, but afterwards he'd let me go on to class. I'd tell him I was ill again, and that he was a lucky fellow I even managed to get out of bed to show up today. He'd be grateful. He'd probably thank me for the effort. Yeah.

After a hasty bath, a hastier clothing, and a hurried bowl of food for Willie, I shook Jim awake. A cigarette helped dispel his grogginess, and, grunting, he maneuvered himself from the bed with only a boost from me.

"How do you feel?" I asked.

"I ache."

"Where?"

"Brain."

His brain always ached after a long drunk and just before his trip north. An alcoholic, he told me, was always swearing to himself that he would abstain. Next time. Next time, after he'd fallen off the wagon again, he would have another guilty conscience.

He'd let himself down again. So he had an ache in the head. The brain's pangs of conscience, Jim claimed.

There was no need to help him dress; he'd slept in his clothes. He refused a hairbrush and claimed he didn't need to go to the bathroom. After he had brushed his teeth, and as the hallway clock chimed eight o'clock, we packed a suitcase, then I took his arm and guided him outside to our only means of transportation, a well-worn 1949 Plymouth station wagon that wallowed pitifully beside Cherokee Rose in a drift of damp oak leaves. Along the way to the vehicle I held my breath to avoid strangling on the foul odor of Jim's unclean body. Drunks, I had decided in one of my more enlightened moments, smelled like cadavers. I decided then that "cadaver" was a pretty good definition for a drunk.

"Need a drink, Jack," he complained irritably as he leaned on me, stumbling across the verandah. "Don't think I can make it without a drink."

"My god!" I said. "They've had to build two new distilleries up in Tennessee just to keep up with the demand here in Smith Station! They'll probably hire a hit man to knock me off when they learn I've taken you to the Sanatorium!"

"Don't be cruel," he said testily. "I'm an old man. Your elder. Your only living relative. You should respect my wishes."

"As you are well aware, Uncle Jim, it ain't a lack of respect. You're killing yourself, and I don't like that. Don't you listen to Dr. Blake when he lectures you?"

Jim scoffed. "I've known Blake for forty years," he said. "I wouldn't trust him to diagnosis old Willie Wing's worms, much less treat them."

"That makes a lot of sense. He doesn't scare you with his hints of doom?"

"I don't give a rat's ass, boy. We've all got to go sometime. May as well go happy. Speaking of happiness. Your dream. I'll set you up to discuss it with Blake. Maybe do it the same day I get out, and save a trip."

I felt myself tense, and I said, "No real hurry about it. I wish I hadn't mentioned that damned dream again."

"It's the best thing."

"Hope Doctor Blake has an open mind. Otherwise he really will reserve a room for me afterwards, near yours, so we can convalesce together."

"Good. You'll love it there. Now, stop at Mary's so I can enjoy one last pre-incarcerative sample of the distiller's art." He pushed me away with a hand as I helped him into the car. "I forgot the Rattler," he cautioned. "Can't leave without the Rattler."

I went back for his suitcase and the pedigreed cane, then seated myself behind the steering wheel on the cracked leather seats of our repulsive but reliable old station wagon. The six-cylinder engine cranked as soon as I touched the starter. Standardshift, dirty windows, black wall tires, the frustrating tendency to buck... A source of pride for me it was not. But Jim loved it, just as he adored all his withering possessions. I hugged the back roads when I drove the thing.

After the stop at Mary's, Jim leaned back and let out a contented sigh with the first sip of liquor. I shook my head at him. "You love that stuff, don't you?"

"Not really." He stared through his open window as we passed a herd of milk cows munching grass from a hillside beside the highway. His liquor bottle was already half empty. "Actually, I hate it. I hate what it does to people. This, dear nephew, though you may fail to recognize it as such, is truly my redeeming worth to society. I drink to save mankind. I will drink all whiskey, if possible, and thereby prevent the ruination of many another."

"A true humanitarian."

"A philanthropic boozer."

"I tried a beer once. Harold Barker stole some from his dad's refrigerator. I hated it."

"Good. It's evil. It'll make you impotent. You won't be able to rouse the little dandy when the time finally arrives."

"By the way," I said, "Mrs. Murray asked about you the other night. I forgot to mention it."

He turned with a quizzical expression and said, "I make a reference to sex, and you mention Mrs. Murray. Is there a hidden message here?"

"Hmm...."

"She is indeed an extraordinary creature."

"A regular forest nymph. She said she was worried that you were drinking too much. Though why she would worry about your drinking is beyond me."

"How nice."

"I told her you were drunk all the time, that she better come over right away to save you."

He chuckled and tossed his empty bottle from the car. "I suspect," he said then, "that you have attempted to use your poor uncle as a mere instrument in a scheme to gratify your potent teenage lust."

"Any way that works."

"Uh-uh," he said. "I'm not sure I want it to work."

"Hmm...," I said, glancing over to him. "Have you a yen for Mrs. Murray yourself, Uncle Jim? I couldn't blame you."

"She's a beautiful woman, in spirit as well as in form."

"A fitting mistress for a Smith. Maybe Jim Smith?"

He chuckled again. The intensifying effect of the additional alcohol had become evident in his more methodical speech. He said, "Have you heard of a 'Meatloaf' Murray, a barbaric simpleton who teaches our youngsters to pummel one another?"

"Yes," I said, "I have. And it seems that you told me once, in a similar instance, 'You're a Smith. Take her away from him.'"

"He beats her from time to time," Jim said with no emotion in his voice. "He beats her worse if she even acts interested in another man."

"No!"

"Yes. Nothing that shows, of course. He couldn't have people know he beat up a hundred-pound woman."

Suddenly I had a visual image of Mrs. Murray in her bathing suit, lounging around her pool. She'd had bruises a time or two, but not enough to make me suspect foul play. Did he abuse her breasts, her private parts? The thought was sickening. "Why would he do that?" I asked. "How could Coach Murray hurt such a lovely woman?"

"She's a threat to his manhood, Jack."

"Which means what?"

"That Murray is an insecure, ill-bred simian who beats his woman for his own gratification. He can't handle the threat of another man. He reminds her of that all the time, by giving her a little punch, a little pinch. Maybe a kick every now and then."

I'd never heard any such rumor. "How do you know, Uncle Jim? Does everybody in town but me know?"

We were nearing the entrance to the Sanatorium. I slowed the Plymouth. Jim attempted to light a cigarette, but failed on two attempts and finally threw it from the window. "Need to quit anyway," he said vaguely.

I persisted. "I've never heard any rumors about Coach Murray beating Linda. How did you hear about it?"

"Have my ways, boy. Have my ways."

I parked in a vacant space near the entrance to Blake Sanatorium, killed the motor, then turned to my uncle. "I'll miss you, Uncle Jim," I said. "Call me if you need anything."

"I won't need anything." He slid slowly across the seat and lurched to his feet, the Rattler dragging behind. "Blake will take good care of me."

"I know." I circled the wagon with his bag in one hand and grabbed his arm with the other. "I wouldn't leave you if I weren't sure of that."

Doctor Blake had built his "Sanatorium" some fifteen years back, and it had since become very successful in the treatment of the alcoholics, the mentally-ill, and the degenerates-in-general of Davis and surrounding counties. The series of squat red brick buildings had been constructed on land owned by the old Smith

Plantation, donated to The Blake Foundation by Jim. Jim was quite proud of his part in the center's success; his benevolence was rewarded with at least one substantial dividend: He was granted treatment for any of his illnesses at no cost. And that included whatever therapy was required to periodically remedy a bout with the booze. He had required rehabilitation so often lately that I wondered if Doctor Blake thought Jim's gift such a great bargain after all.

Jim was acquainted with every doctor and nurse, and many of the patients, and was always greeted by them with such elation that it seemed to me he was embarking on a therapeutic sabbatical instead of serious therapy, Personally, I loathed Blake Sanatorium. The place had an air about it that sent me gagging to the bathroom. The smell of it: Alcohol, ether, every smelly drug known to man. A fragrance in the air too clean, too sterile for the living. A smell you could taste. The look of the place: Every room, every corridor abnormally bright. Light reflecting off the walls, the floors, the furniture. A peculiar light that made you yearn for sunshine. A light that made all things harsh. A harshness you could touch, if you wanted.

But whispers and sobs were the Sanatorium's most loathsome peculiarities. I had never been to Jim's room; they always took him from the receiving area. But I had been in the corridors and seen other rooms. Most were lonely with a single presence. From some, though, spewed the sounds of faith and of hopelessness, one as persistent as the other. Love, and the agony it inflicted. False reassurance and the suspicion it created. The sounds at times of families and their mourning for unalterable loss. And God. God this, God that, God everything. God and His repulsive obsession with funerals. God and his disregard for life.

I always thought of my parents when I entered Blake Sanatorium. That was what it was for me. The odor and the feel and the specter of the end of life. The enveloping cloak of death.

I held my breath when I had Jim inside, determined to forestall for as long as possible the coating of my tongue and throat, the seduction of my passion for life, by the repugnant cloud that oozed from the sick bodies and sick brains trapped within the Sanatorium's red brick walls. How had Jim tolerated it all these years? I wondered.

The plump old receptionist with purple hair greeted us beyond her sliding-glass panel and immediately picked up her telephone. She knew what we were here for. In only a moment an orderly appeared, smiling broadly in welcome. "Howdy, Mr. Jim, Mr. Jack," the colored gentleman in white uniform said. I couldn't remember his name, though he and I were old buddies. He took the bag from me, and patted Jim's shoulder. "Time for you to come see us again, Mr. Jim? We missed you."

If not for the redness in his eyes, his unsteadiness, and the meticulous enunciation of each word, I would not have suspected Jim was drinking, much less literally smashed. "George, you old scalawag," he said cheerfully, "it's good to see you. Is our checkerboard ready for another series?"

"Yassir," George answered. "Won't take me a minute to get it down. Yassir, we'll have a time! Soon's I handle them other chores, I'll be right there."

Jim stopped to wave to me. "See you when I'm emancipated, Jack," he called. "Hold down the fort."

"I will, Uncle Jim."

"And remember. If anybody asks about me, it's my heart. Remember that? Bad heart."

"Yes, sir," I said. "Bad heart."

The only people who would fall for that line were people new to Smith Station. Jim was only fooling himself.

The drive back was uneventful. After parking the wagon in its assigned space beside Cherokee Rose, I jogged to the schoolhouse and made my apologies to the principal for being late. After a short lecture on the virtues of punctuality, he allowed me to go on to my regular class. The day thereafter was routine, with the exception that I ate lunch with Mama Mary. Jerry skipped school for some reason, and Archie had to do an errand for his mother during the lunch break. We had no time together to discuss The Plan.

After school, and after two hours with Mr. Barnes and a truck-load of feminine fundamentals, I trudged homeward, alarm growing within me with every step. Tonight was the night. Tonight, my two buddies and I would visit the gravel pit to spy on some unsuspecting philanderer. As if to add to my sense of foreboding, dark clouds loomed upon the western horizon, threatening rain later in the evening. I hoped a storm was brewing. Maybe a shower would put a halt to our foolish expedition.

They were waiting at six-thirty, soft drinks before them, their elbows on our table, smug grins across their faces. The look of them angered me. I felt like an unwilling collaborator being led to the guillotine by two irresponsible accomplices. But I wondered, too, if it were only my own cold feet that made me angry, and not at them, but at myself.

A Lucky hung fuming from Jerry's lips. He had been making smoke circles, and several hung in disarray over his head. Archie slurped catsup and French fries while eyeing the rounded rump of Margerie Dalton, who sat beside her boyfriend on one of the counter stools. My friends looked oddly rustic, for The Plan called for each of us to wear dark clothing. Indeed, the three of us were dressed like field hands. Old jeans. Dark work shirts. Black socks. Drab, worn-out shoes. I pulled out my chair and plopped wearily into it. Jerry pulled the cigarette from his lips, exhaled, and said, "Howdy."

"Howdy," I replied.

"Ready for some action, son?"

I sat straight and glanced around us. "Don't say that so loud, Jerry. You want to have to move to Alabama?"

"Oh, are you worried about that? Well, heck, I won't tell anybody else, then."

"What?" I said quickly. "You told somebody else?"

"Don't have an organism, boy. I was kidding."

"Relax," Archie said, pulling his eyes from Margerie's backside. "Nothing's gonna go wrong."

I slumped back into the chair. "I recall those were Custer's last words," I said. "Sure looks like rain."

"Nothing in the forecast."

"Tell it to those thunderheads out there."

"Rain's about as likely tonight as you getting a date with Saxon Browne. You asked her yet?"

"Nope."

Jerry giggled. "Can't blame you. Rejection is high on my list of undesirable experiences, too."

"Well, keep on with Teeny, and you'll accumulate your quota of rejections. Especially after you bare certain extremities."

But I was the one to squirm. Jerry was right. Saxon would get a good laugh if I called her and asked for a date. Are you nuts? she would ask. Or just stupid? Then she would tell everybody in town. They would smile and whisper secretly as I passed. There goes Jack Smith, they would say. Called Saxon Browne for a date. She put him in his place, though. Damn fool will never have the nerve to call HER again. Never had a chance with that beautiful young thing anyhow. Boy ain't got good sense. Wacko.

Then Perry Norman would find out, and I would have to spend the rest of my life on the road.

Due to the thinness of the crowd, Mama Mary was serving via personal visit to each table, screech and scream unnecessary tonight. Liquid tobacco was her choice this evening, and she paused between armloads of the specials of the day—pickled boiled eggs, biscuits, and fried strips of fat-back pork—to center her Crisco can, strategically located near the grill, with a stream of brown extract. The periodic spurts from her mouth were well aimed, we had all noted before, for we calculated her accuracy at over ninety percent. The occasional inaccurate squirts were cleaned from the floor or grill or customer or whatever with a long white cotton rag that trailed from her waist. She also used the rag to wipe tables, a practice we chose to ignore. Her gray hair was bushy and wild tonight, as though she had just washed and brushed it straight, only to have it mussed as she strolled through a hurricane. Her thin, dark mustache was tinted with a few strands of white. She'd had a glass of milk.

"Hello, Mama Mary," I said as she paused beside our table.

"What'll it be, Jack Junior?" She held her pad and pencil ready. "Special's pickled eggs and fat back."

"Ain't too hungry, Mama Mary," I said. "No appetite."

"Hamburger? Fries? How about a Coke?"

"I'll have a Coke."

"Lost your appetite, canary?" Jerry asked when Mary was gone.

"Tweet, tweet, ass hole."

"I had a brainstorm," Archie said, leaning forward to indicate a huddle was called for. "I got us something that'll make us practically invisible in the dark."

"Ha," I said, "I've heard that 'invisible' bit before."

Archie's face reddened. "This is different," he answered. "War paint. I got us war paint to rub on our faces."

"We ain't fighting no war, runt," Jerry said, grinning at me. "But it is a good idea. We better grease the top of his head with it, Jack. If the moon's out, well... No sense in giving our position away before we even get started."

Archie's face reddened even more. "Bite my ass, Jerry."

"I'd sooner eat a cow paddy."

Archie eyed the jukebox, then collected all the nickels Jerry and I had on us. Coins were dropped and buttons punched in tandem. The conversations of the dozen customers were soon immersed in the thumping bass of rock-and-roll. "Like to have me a 'Little Darlin' tonight," Jerry said as the song played.

"Call Teeny," I said. "Maybe she's recovered from her last date with Richard."

Jerry scowled and squinted in my direction.

"Think about this," I said. "Suppose it was you out there at the pit tonight, Jerry, in your Chevy with your girlfriend, just getting it on, and some guy stuck his head in the window and looked at your dong and said, 'Don't mind me, buddy, I just want to watch.' What would you do, Jerry?"

Jerry snorted. "Hell, I'd blow the bastard's head off!"

"I rest my case!"

"We got everything?" Archie asked. "Gun. Flashlight. We're wearing dark clothes. Camera?" He grinned.

"Bandages? Bullet-proof vests? Good lawyers?" I added.

"The yellow-belly will be okay," Jerry said to Archie, "once he sees them sweaty bodies tearing at each other. Them moans and groans and screams will cure him."

Archie gave us a knowing smile. "I'm going to write an essay about tonight," he said, "giving names, dates, sizes, and productivity. I may not let you read it, Jack."

"I'm crushed."

"I'll use my findings for blackmail, too. I'll own this town. Let's play pool until time to go."

Both of Mary's pool tables were taken. However, a brief argument between the two cronies at one table ended their play. The dispute began when one participant claimed his opponent had relocated the cue ball while he was out back taking a leak. There were un-Christian words. Then, as suddenly as it began, the quarrel ended when the larger player threatened to shove a beer bottle up the other's hindquarters. The two walked away, arms around each other's necks, swearing eternal friendship.

"Let's go," I said as the two chums exited the cafe.

A three-player game of eight-ball can be a boring affair, since one member of the trio is always idle. Not so tonight. We were anything but bored. The minutes flew. We had to know the time after every game. Mama Mary glared each time we asked. Eventually Jerry and Archie, to my satisfaction, began to show signs of uneasiness. Nervousness was obvious in their trembling hands and in the absence of banter. "We better skip it," I warned them gleefully. "The pokey is a nasty place to spend Christmas."

"I know what we need," Jerry said after a while. He leaned his cue stick against the wall and walked to where Mama's Boy manned his station. I knew what was coming, but I didn't stop him, for, despite my disinclination to strong drink, this was an urgent occasion. Was there really salvation in a bottle?

In a moment Jerry returned, laden with three brown bags. "Schlitz," he said as he distributed the beer. "Ice-cold Schlitz."

"I'm not much of a drinker," I said.

"Drink it. It'll make a man out of you."

"Jim said it would make your dick shrivel."

I drank anyway, gagged on the first swallow, and nearly sprayed my pals with foam. The second mouthful was better. The third went down smoothly. In no time I began to imagine that I enjoyed the taste. More importantly, drop by drop, bravery trickled into my veins. "Not bad," I said when Schlitz can number one was empty. "We should have another or two or three."

"Your turn to buy a round," Jerry said.

Archie had chugalugged his beer as if he were born with a can in his hand. "I'll get the round after that," he promised.

Game by game, beer by beer, we waited for Mama Mary to proclaim that nine o'clock had arrived. She no longer griped each time we asked her to check her clock. Instead, she watched with a glow of satisfaction. She winked at the Boy once. He grinned back at her. Three evolving customers for her booming beer business, I thought. The good old free enterprise system.

"It's time, gentlemen," Jerry said after a final visit with Mary's pocket clock. He raised a fist into the air. "Let's crash the pit!"

"Maybe we ought to have one more round," I said.

"One more, and we'll have to carry you out of here!"

"I believe I'd like that."

We probably appeared almost sober to the casual eyes of the customers as we trooped through the cafe's melodic screen door onto the sidewalk outside. The Chevy awaited us in its usual space like the good steed it was, eyes gleaming in the dark, gaping, snorting, its muscular frame coiled and eager to charge into the night's calmness and to sacrifice its passengers to Armageddon. Archie took the rear seat, while I climbed in front, the 'suicide' seat, won regularly from Archie in arm-wrestling matches. The glass-packs rumbled softly until we passed Cherokee Rose and turned onto the paved road that led west past the pit and onward toward Louisiana. Then Jerry accelerated. We were on our way.

CHAPTER 8
DISASTER

THE CLOUDS AND their promise of a liberating rain had dissipated, and in their place a half-moon brightened the horizon. With the Chevy's windows open a cool breeze circulated in the car, and I shivered, dreading what was coming. Suddenly Jerry begin singing a loud, boisterous rendition of "Dixie." Archie and I sang along with him. The exercise helped merely to suspend my trepidation—until we neared the small gravel road that led to the pit. The approach of that dark, forbidding path ended our chorus, and we spoke then in whispers.

"Dark up there," Archie whispered as Jerry drove slowly past. "Spooky. The little bit of moon makes it worse, with all the hazy shadows."

"Better for us," Jerry said. "We can't be seen. Bet them studs are up there tearing them things up right now, too."

"Wish I had another beer," I said.

Archie agreed. "Damn it, we shoulda brought more."

After peering into the blackness beside the road I said, "It's so dark we can't find the old logging trail," and with an embellished moan, "Darn! Might as well turn back and wait for a night with a full moon."

Jerry growled, "Hell, I'll find it." And in a moment, perhaps a hundred yards from and opposite the pit entrance, he steered the car off the paved road onto an overgrown trail left by loggers years before. After the car was hidden from view he doused the lights. We sat for a moment in silence. When my pals spoke, they reminded me of the sound of an old war movie.

"I got the gun," Jerry said.

"I got the flashlight," Archie said.

"I got the shits," I said.

Jerry jiggled his keys for a second. "I'm gonna leave the keys in the ignition. Just in case we have to make a quick getaway. I don't want to have to dig for keys while I'm having a gun battle with a jealous stud." He snickered and opened his door. Archie and I followed suit.

After thrashing about in the vines and tall grass, we stood on the old trail. Archie pulled a tin from his pocket and began smearing dark cream onto his cheeks. "War paint," he explained. "Want some, Jack?"

"Yeah," I said.

"Want some, Jerry?"

"Naw. Sissy."

Archie held the tin out to me. "Put some on my bald spots, Jack, will you, right on top? Make sure no white shows."

"Good idea," I said. "Let's don't take any chances."

I waxed the top of Archie's head, hiding the shiny areas as directed. After a moment Archie and I were hidden behind a screen of dark brown. We might have earned a spot beside Al Jolson while he performed his pantomimes. "You're invisible, Archie," I said admiringly. "This was a good idea."

"Yeah," Jerry chuckled, "now them mad studs can't see you when you're running away."

"And," Archie said, "I'm glad Jerry don't want any, Jack. The mad studs won't see us. Jerry's ugly white face will draw all the gunfire."

"Great!" I said. "A decoy!"

"Now wait a minute," Jerry waffled. He stood with his hands on his hips for a moment, then said, "Gimme some of that war paint."

Archie and I waited as Jerry dabbed brown cream on his face. The three of us then turned to walk back toward the paved road and the gravel pit, as imperceptible to the eyes of mad studs as the trees and bushes that surrounded it. The flashlight was lashed to Archie's belt loop. Jerry's pistol hung from his belt. On the road, the warmth of the asphalt underfoot was soothing after the chill of the ride. An owl hooted nearby. Crickets and tree frogs chirped. The half moon peeked over the treetops.

The gravel pit was a small mountain of clay gravel that had been cleared of vegetation years before. Then, and occasionally now, gravel was scooped from its center for use on county roads, thereby creating what resembled a miniature volcano. The crater, entered via a small road leading abruptly upward from the paved highway, was perhaps a hundred yards across, and, because of its height above the surrounding countryside, could not be seen from the paved road. Scrub vegetation—noxious plants, vines, briars, native flowers, and small trees—had grown wild along the slopes and their meandering gullies, and within the confining walls of the crater, resulting in the creation of several "oases" in the bowl that conveniently sheltered parked cars from the view of others who also made use of the pit's unique configuration.

A sharp, tangy odor filled our nostrils as we began our ascent. "Bitter weeds," I whispered, and wondered why I had. Gravel crunched loudly beneath our feet. We walked shoulder to shoulder, each step synchronized as though that were part of The Plan.

"Quiet up there," Archie whispered. "I don't think there's anybody in there."

"You expect them to hang out a sign, runt?" Jerry chuckled. "Or maybe have a welcoming committee?"

"Can't really see." Archie flashed his light into the gravel at our feet.

"Damn it! Archie," I said. "Don't turn that damn light on! Somebody may see it!"

"Roads too steep," he countered nonchalantly. "They can't see over the rim."

"Besides," Jerry added, "them studs are too busy with them little juicy tenders to worry about a little light."

"Wonder if Muledick and Teeny are up there?" I said. "It's Thursday night. Their night."

"I'm counting on it!" Jerry snarled.

The way he growled, "I'm counting on it!" brought shivers. My god! I thought suddenly. Jerry's planning on killing Muledick! Maybe Teeny, too! That's what this is all about! That's why Jerry is so eager!

"Why don't you let me carry the gun, Jerry?" I said.

"Why?"

"I'm a good shot."

"I'm better. And I don't mind using it."

This had to be stopped. I had to think fast. I grabbed their arms and pulled them to a halt. "What if somebody else pulls in here?" I said, nodding down the hill. "We're out in the middle of the road! They'll drive right up on us!" I looked up and down the highway. "We better haul ass!"

Jerry snickered, "If they do, I'll just put a few holes in their windshield. They'll turn around and go right back out."

"Good thinking," I said.

I followed them to the rim, all the while worrying over some way to prevent Jerry from murdering Richard Miller and Teeny Wright. We were breathing hard when we reached the edge, and not entirely from the uphill trek. Jerry scanned the interior of the crater, where the oases of vegetation threw dim moon shadows on the desert-like gravel floor. An obscure background of treetops rose above and behind.

"I don't see nothing," Archie said.

I said, "Of all the nights to pick, we choose the one when nobody's horny. Let's go home!"

"Not yet!" Jerry said, grabbing my shirt.

"Spooky," Archie whispered, staring hard into the crater. "Real spooky."

I said, "Wonder if they can see us up here, bathed in all this moonlight and outlined against the sky like we are?"

"They ain't worried about us."

"I think I see one!" Archie pointed to a clump of small trees directly opposite our position on the road. "Let's ease around..."

All hell broke loose.

While we were straining our eyes to try and detect the car Archie claimed he saw, the headlights of the car suddenly blazed. The sudden brightness blinded us. We were those bullfrogs in Lake Davis, dazzled by a hypnotizing beam of light in the darkness. We instantly grabbed at each other as though the other might be our salvation.

The lights dimmed as the starter did its work. The engine roared, and the headlights brightened. There was a lurch as the car was put in gear. Then came the sound of gravel spinning from its rear tires, the roar of its engine. The bright beam from its headlights swept across us once, twice, three times as the driver stepped on the gas and the automobile swerved. It began a violent charge toward us.

"Haul ass!" Jerry shrieked. There was a touch of glee in his shout, as though he were actually enjoying his "great adventure." And there was no need for his warning; Archie and I were already doing the Highland Fling.

My last perception of the oncoming car, glimpsed in terror as I dove for the ditch alongside the road, was one that would reside in my memory forever. The automobile pitched from side to side as the driver struggled to control it. From its rear spewed a swell of dust and gravel brightly tinted in red by the vehicle's taillights. The rumbling roar of the charging motor, the scream of abused tires, the patter of rocks falling back to the barren landscape after being hurled high into the air, were sights and sounds never to be forgotten.

Jerry jumped the ditch on one side of the road and disappeared among the sounds of his body tearing through branches and briars. Archie leaped from the road on the other side; I followed, the sound of his body crashing through the underbrush guiding my own flight. My feet slipped and churned in loose gravel, limbs and vines and thorns scraped across my clothing, my face and arms.

The darkness confused and disoriented me, yet the only choice was to continue to plunge sightlessly through the jungle-like terrain. I fell repeatedly in the loose gravel, bruising my hands and face. My fingers throbbed from clawing at loose rock. Finally I sprawled within sight of the road, stunned by a small tree that rose in the darkness in line with my sprinting head.

Fortune was with me. As the roar of flying gravel and the scream of the automobile's engine came to an abrupt end, I found myself prone in a gully, hidden from view by one of the serpentine ruts formed in the slope by countless rains. For an instant there came the sound, farther back, of Archie's efforts to push on through the jungle. That ended, however, when he realized that the automobile had stopped on the road opposite our positions. Only by becoming still as death could we hope to escape detection.

At the sound of a car door being slammed I flinched. Someone was out on the road. Richard? Perry? One of my other high school classmates? Had they already recognized me? God! I hoped not. How humiliating!

Moving carefully to avoid making a noise, I raised my body enough to allow myself a view over the sandy lip of the gully. I was chilled by what I saw. Not twenty feet away a man towered beside a Plymouth Fury. 1957 model. Cream color. Headlights still blazing. Oh, my God! I thought as I quickly ducked again. Coach Murray!

I couldn't help myself. I peeked again. The big man stood motionlessly beside his car, easily visible in the scattered light of the Fury's headlamps. Skintight shirt. Hunting vest. Jeans. Huge brass belt buckle. Cowboy boots. Arrogant stance. My heart sank.

He spoke. I was surprised at how easily I heard him say, muttering under his breath, "Goddamned Peeping Toms."

A feminine voice whispered from inside the Fury, "Let's go. Please."

The coach walked to the open window on the passenger side

and looked down. He shook his head and said softly, "Suppose the bastards saw us? You feel like leaving Smith Station for good?"

"They didn't see us. They just got here."

"You don't know that. They could have been coming out when we saw them. If they were down there..."

The ominous tone to his voice made me shiver. I hugged the ditch and began a prayer.

"Damn!" the coach shouted.

The girl said nothing.

"Wish I had a flashlight," Coach Murray continued. "I'd go out there and find them three little perverts. And strangle them, right where they lay."

"That would just make things worse," the girl answered. "Let's go. I'm scared."

"No. Not until I put the fear of God in them."

I cringed when I saw the coach's gun. With what appeared to be deliberate aim, he raised his arm straight out and pointed it directly at me. As he pulled back the hammer of the large pistol, I ducked. Three terrific, unhurried explosions shook the countryside. Rocks and bits of branches showered my body. Leaves floated from branches overhead. There was a moment's pause, then he fired three more times, the explosions shaking the earth once more as he emptied the pistol in Jerry's direction.

He spoke again, more loudly, and with a note of joviality to his voice. I could hear every word without raising my head. "Bet they won't try that again," he said. He snorted. "Bet the cock suckers have to empty their pants after that. Hand me that box of bullets out of the glove box."

"Suppose you hit one?" the girl asked with what I took to be anger in her voice. "You might have killed one of those boys!"

The coach chuckled, then bellowed in Jerry's direction as he began to reload his weapon, "I'll kill you goddamned Peeping Toms if I find out who you are. I promise you! I'll cut off your balls and stuff 'em down your throat!"

"I'm scared, Melville," the girl said from the car. "Let's go. Please."

I raised myself enough to get a look at Melville Murray and the pistol in his hand. "Bastards had dark makeup," he said. "You recognize any of them?"

"No."

"Funny clothes, too." He kicked gravel from the road and peered out into the dark vegetation. "Bet they're halfway back to Smith Station by now." The coach kicked more gravel as he rounded the Fury and reopened his door. "You stay down. Keep your ass down and out of sight!"

He had spoken too late. The girl's hair and one hand were dropping below the window ledge when the dome light popped on. I couldn't see who she was, but one thing was certain: Coach Murray's girlfriend was not white. Coach Murray was cheating on his wife with a colored girl!

The Plymouth's engine roared again. Gravel popped as it slowly rolled down the gravel path. When it turned toward Smith Station on the paved road and accelerated, I jumped to my feet and began brushing leaves, briars, and dust from my clothes. Behind me, Archie was likewise dusting himself. "Great godamighty!" he said loudly enough for me to hear.

"Come on!" I yelled. "Let's get the hell out of here, Arch! If there's anyone else in the pit, they may decide to leave now. I wouldn't blame them, after all the artillery. And Coach might even double back."

"I hurt my foot." Archie winced as he broke free of the vines and briars and stood beside me. "Might have broke it."

"Hope it heals fast," I said, "cause I'm hauling ass."

The foot wasn't hurt nearly as badly as Archie had figured, for he kept up with me, stride for stride, until we had torn aside the jungle and reached the pit road. Jerry was standing there, waiting. There was disbelief in his voice. "Holy Jehovah!" he said. "Coach Murray! I thought we were dead!"

"Yeah," I said. "Of all the people to deal a round of coitus interruptus tonight, we would have to pick him."

"One of those bullets almost hit me," Archie complained. "He coulda killed me!"

"I started to shoot back at him," Jerry bragged, "but I didn't want to shoot coach. He was an easy target, though. Good thing for him I didn't."

"Yeah, yeah."

"But," he continued, "we're standing here talking. We should make like whores and blow."

"Let's make like whores," Archie agreed, "before somebody else swoops down out of that pit with their guns blazing."

The three of us galloped, Archie a moderately limping gallop, for the Chevy, not even pausing long enough to congratulate each other on our escape. The moon still lolled on the horizon, crickets and owls had resumed their symphony, and the dark sky was animated by a few churning clouds and the flickers of a million stars. It hardly seemed possible that moments before this serenity had been violated by gunshots.

In less than a minute we were roaring back along the road toward Smith Station. No other vehicles appeared, and it looked as though we had survived our encounter with a mad stud. After our initial fright had eased, we laughed nervously about it, then, as is the nature of morons, became cocky and began to mock the now-hilarious ordeal. We congratulated each other for bravery under fire. My two buddies even jokingly suggested another trip to the pit tomorrow night. I knew they were only trying to get a rise from me, and I refused to let them.

Halfway home, Jerry raised another hair-raising issue: "What if Meatloaf figured we'd be driving back to town on this highway? He could be up here waiting for us!"

Archie and I hadn't thought of that, and after Jerry's ominous prediction we road scared. Jerry slowed from his normal ninety miles-per-hour to less than thirty at each crossroad and turnout, as though we might slip past unnoticed at the slower pace. "We'll have a hard time out-running that Fury," Archie said as we all peered anxiously into one of the many dark farm roads that criss-crossed the highway.

"For the rest of our lives," Jerry added.

However, no Plymouth Fury appeared out of the night, and we arrived back on Main Street worn out by the strain of the ordeal. Jerry whistled softly and said with evident relief, "Thought we were gonna have to move to Louisiana for a while. But we made it. Let's go have a beer to celebrate."

"Have you looked in the mirror, Jerry?" I asked, shaking my head. "If we go in the cafe with this war paint on, people might be somewhat suspicious."

"Damn!" he said, swiveling his rear-view mirror and stroking his hair. "We better go wash up before anybody sees us. It's a dead giveaway. And I wouldn't want to be seen anywhere like this, nearly as repulsive as Archie." He laughed. "I sure am glad we're all spending the night at your house tonight, Jack."

"Nobody there to bother us," I said. "Uncle Jim's in the tank."

This, too, had become part of The Plan, once Jim was safely tucked away in his room at Blake's. With their parents unaware of his absence, Archie and Jerry had the freedom to stay out as late as they wanted without the worry they would ever know.

After Jerry had parked the Chevy behind the wagon, we trooped together inside, our first thoughts to visit the bathroom and remove the war paint. I leaned against the lavatory and scrubbed with a soapy rag. "We're scratched up," I said as I examined my face and arms in the mirror. "If Coach sees us tomorrow, he might guess where we got all these wounds."

"We'll lay low," Jerry said. He scrubbed his pretty face vigorously. Archie waited patiently. "We'll avoid the football field and the ladies' lounge. Those are his hang outs."

"And Mama Mary's," Archie added. "We'll have to give up pool for a day or two."

Jerry and I rubbed our faces with all the energy old Annie used on her scrub board when she washed clothes. My skin felt raw after a while, and I was making little progress for all my efforts. My face looked like a bruised pumpkin. "This war paint won't come off," I said. "It wipes off on the rag, but it smears. It's stained my face."

"Mine, too," Jerry said, turning to Archie. "How do you get this war paint off, runt?"

"Just rub. It'll come off," Archie said. "Eventually."

But it would not. The more we scrubbed, the deeper our cheeks were stained. Archie began trying to remove the waxy concoction from his face and the top of his head, with the same result. "Damn!" he said. "It really WON'T come off!"

I said, "If Coach sees us like this, there won't be any question about who interrupted his diddling. He won't miss next time, either. What is this stuff, Archie?"

"War paint, fool!"

Jerry and I looked at each other. There was something in Archie's voice... "Runt, you better come clean," Jerry growled, "or Jack and I will beat it out of you. What is this stuff?"

"Why, it's..." The boy paused and stepped back. "I couldn't find no real war paint..."

"And?"

"And since I work in the shoe department..."

"Shoe polish!" Jerry screamed with sudden comprehension. "Brown shoe polish! We'll never get it off!"

Archie gulped and backed away to the bathroom door. "Sure we will," he said. He pulled the tin from his pocket and examined it closely as though directions for removal would be printed right there on the side of the can. "Just rub hard...," he said under his breath.

"You hold the bastard down, Jerry," I yelled, "and I'll castrate him!"

"And I'll shove 'em down his damn throat!" Jerry shouted as he lunged for Archie's throat with both hands. Archie dodged and dashed out the door. Jerry's hands dropped to his sides in despair.

"We gotta get something to cut this stuff," I said. "There's only one thing we have that might do it."

"Sulphuric acid? Or sandpaper?"

"Turpentine. Uncle Jim mixes turpentine with something else to oil up the Rattler. He hates it when that cane's not slicked up. I'll get it."

I found it in his closet. With a dry towel and a few capfuls of the pungent liquid, Jerry and I succeeded in removing the waxy residue from our faces. It took a while to coax Archie from his seat on the dock across the tracks, but finally we were able to wipe his face and balding head clean. He took the turpentine to his cheeks. "Told you it would come off easy," he said after a minute.

Jerry moaned in exasperation, "Just be glad we let you live, runt. One more trick like that..."

"People can smell us before they even see us, now," I said, sniffing the air. "Hope it wears off by morning."

"I'm dog-tired," Archie moaned, his eyelids drooping. "Gun battles wear you out. Let's hit the hay."

Jim's absence meant that Archie and Jerry could sleep in his big bed, thereby eliminating the necessity that the three of us sleep together. I didn't want to sleep with either of them anyway, but particularly Jerry. Jerry could be dangerous. Once, when he and Archie had been bunking together in Jim's bed, Jerry had had a wet dream. Archie screamed bloody murder. Jerry's caresses woke him, and, he swore, were reason enough that he would never sleep with him again. Jerry denied it all; but I figured not even Archie could make up a tale like that.

I pulled fresh sheets from a bureau drawer where they were stored after each of Annie's scrubbings, and with my buddies' help replaced the smelly bed covering that still lay tangled on Jim's mattress. Afterwards we reclined and sat together beneath the canopy of the old tester, content to relax for a moment before turning in. "We can never tell anybody about tonight," I said. "If Coach found out it was us... Well, you heard what he said."

Jerry replied, "He was just mad. He'd never actually do anything like kill us."

"Remember Al Mohoney, up at Milldale?" I said. "Ask old Al. He'll tell you all about Coach Murray. Al's head wobbles when he walks now. You can't understand what he's saying unless he holds his head with both hands."

"You know," Jerry mused, "I can't understand why Meatloaf was out there with another woman when he has the sexiest woman in the state waiting at home."

"Pussy makes a man crazy," Archie said.

They had not mentioned the most astounding revelation of the evening. Had they seen the colored girl? I wondered... I said, "Could you two see who the woman was?"

"I could hear her say something. Barely," Jerry said. "She was scared. I heard that much. Funny accent."

"I could hear her sometimes, too," Archie said. "Coach's hollering and shooting though... Could you see who she was, Jack?"

I shook my head. "No. She was crouched down in the seat."

"Maybe it was his wife!" Archie said with sudden inspiration. "That's it! They do it in the pit, just for kicks!"

"Lord! Archie," Jerry gasped. "They're gonna sneak off from their two kids, drive to the pit, take their clothes off, do it in the car, and rush back home? When they could've just done it in their bed?"

"Maybe."

"Uh-uh. Meatloaf has a special little honey he don't tell nobody about. He goes out there where his wife can't catch him."

I wasn't going to tell them what I'd seen. What might they do? Archie had already mentioned blackmail. He would do anything for money. He would probably blab the whole story eventually anyway, and though that would be bad enough, having a colored girl involved would make it ten times worse. Suppose Mrs. Murray found out? And her children? Talk about embarrassment! They would have to move to Alaska with us.

"We gotta heal fast," I said. "You both look like Brer' Rabbit would've if he hadn't been a rabbit. And that turpentine blistered your cheeks. Coach will surely be suspicious if he sees us."

"But think about that," Jerry said. "If Meatloaf finds out it was us, there's not much he can do about it. One word from us, and he's liable to lose his wife and his job. He'd be afraid to say much to us."

"Coach Murray's got a temper like a spring bear," I said. "He would take that thirty-thirty of his and use us for target practice."

"Better than being choked on balls," Archie said. "Quicker, anyway."

"And suppose we did tell about tonight," I said. "Then we'd have to explain how we knew. Archie, you can be spokesman. You can tell everybody it was your idea to sneak around the gravel pit in the middle of the night."

"Not me!"

"Then we gotta keep quiet. Otherwise, we will have a rampaging mob after us."

Jerry sighed. "You're right."

"Might be good to have a cover story for these scratches," I said. "We go out to Lake Davis a lot, night fishing. Suppose we say our flashlight quit, and we had to walk back to the car in the dark. Through that briar-patch jungle on the west end."

"That'll do it," Jerry agreed. "Good idea."

Archie was almost asleep. He mumbled, "Did we catch any fish?"

"Yeah, runt. A twelve-foot shark."

CHAPTER 9
THE PRICE OF BLAB

I DREAMED AGAIN, not of tragedy, but of that which is most important in life.

Saxon Browne loomed over me, a stimulating fantasy, her provocative brown eyes staring into mine, the long brown curls of her hair gently lapping at my neck. Her daring lips, pink and glossy without the embellishment of lipstick, nipped at my throat. Her dainty tongue lingered on my ear, moisture-laden and maddening. I smelled fresh country air and parched new hay and the special scent that was her own. I willed her hands to the elastic band at my waist, tingled as the tips of her fingers roused chill bumps from my belly and took my breath. Her nails pricked my tender skin with the finesse of a feather. I stiffened in expectation...

And Archie shook me. "Jack," he shouted. "Wake up. Time to rise and shine."

"Damn, Archie," I said angrily before I opened my eyes and sat up. Jerry had come in, too, and the two of them sat on my bed. "I was dreaming about Saxon Browne! It was just getting to the good part, too. You ruined it."

"Well, EXCUSE ME."

I glared at him while I thought: Here I am, upset because I couldn't finish a wet dream. What's wrong with me? My sex life, if you could call it that, consists of fantasy, of manual stimulation, of dreams of what could be instead of what is. My fictitious sex life resides within the confines of imagination and surrogate fingers.

Were we all three of us having sex by proxy? Disgusting! When were we going to have the REAL THING?

I sighed, "How'd you make out during the night, Arch? Jerry have his way with you?"

"I put two pillows between us," Archie answered. "I wouldn't let him cross the line." He turned to Jerry. "Much as he wanted to."

Jerry's lips curled. "Runt," he said, "if I was gonna be queer—which I ain't – you'd be the last person I'd choose. I was just dreaming about Teeny that other time. Didn't have nothing to do with you."

"It was MY nuts you had hold of."

Jerry bristled.

The two tip-toed around each other as we prepared for school, doing our best to camouflage scratches and traces of war paint. "Remember to avoid the coach today," I warned as the three of us piled into Jerry's rod. "Today's Friday. It's critical. By Monday, maybe our scratches will be healed. Until then, we look like victims of the Plague. And remember to stay upwind. Turpentine wears off in three or four days, though."

Archie was especially marred. Spread randomly along the acne veneer of his face, rows of punctured skin covered his cheeks. They resembled a travel map of dotted highways scribbled among small mountains of red whelps and smudged valleys. Jerry was scarred here and there, too, and there were stubborn smudges of brown near his sideburns, but overall he was in better condition than Archie. Probably, I thought, he had run with his hands covering his face to protect it. The both of them smelled like the Rattler. Or was it me? My own face and arms were scraped and cut, and I had a small bruise on my forehead where I had conked the tree. Separately, our injuries might pass for routine ignorance. Side by side, it would be apparent that the three of us had faced the same demons. "We shouldn't be seen together at school today," I warned anew as we headed for class. "We need to stay as far apart as possible."

"You're making too much of this," Jerry said. "Meatloaf ain't that smart."

"Do you want to risk it? Remember what he said. And if he catches one of us, we're all caught."

"Yeah," Archie said, "Any of us would spill the beans once he started the nut-cuttin.'"

"Archie, you have a foul mouth. See you later." I trotted away, intent on getting to class and hiding my face in a book. Coach Murray taught a couple of history classes as part of his keep at SSHS, but each of us had completed work at his elementary level of training. The textbooks that Coach used in his sessions had big print and lots of pictures. But we had to watch out during class changes and, as Jerry had mentioned, shun the ladies' lounge and the football field.

Morning passed naturally enough, with a few glimpses of the loftier portions of female limbs to make the educational experience more tolerable. Questions regarding my face I disarmed with fleeting references to a fishing trip cut short after an encounter with a new, dangerous species, "cat" fish. I bumped into Archie between English and Algebra classes and was about to beat a hasty retreat when he grabbed my arm and indicated with his eyes the long wooden staircase that linked first and second floors. "Guy that designed them stairs ought to get a medal," he breathed. I followed his line of sight upward to where students were forced to turn and reverse course on their trek up or down. Margerie Dalton leaned against the railing conversing with one of her friends. Her skirt had billowed, and her knees and thighs were visible.

"Damn!" I said. "Damn!"

"Makes the juices flow, don't it?"

"I can't watch." I said. "I'll embarrass myself, right here in the hallway."

But Archie and I nevertheless tarried until Margerie disappeared. "I don't have any energy left," I said then. "I'm drained. If Coach showed up now, I couldn't even run."

Archie agreed. "I'd die happy, though."

Noon break arrived, and I ate a solitary meal. Then I wandered blindly about in bored seclusion. Being apart from my two best friends, I found, was an oppressive ordeal. I thought of walking to Mary's Café for a quick game of pinball, then decided I'd better save my money. Jim was not at home, Willie was probably making his rounds, so Cherokee Rose was not too appealing, either. There was nothing to do but await the bell that would signal the resumption of classes. Boring! I thought. Soon I became so annoyed with doing nothing that I succumbed to the temptations of habit and turned up the sidewalk toward the parking space where Jerry usually parked his Chevy. To my surprise I saw that Archie was there, leaning against the Chevy's fender, having apparently yielded to similar enticement. Jerry was nowhere around.

"Ain't like Jerry not to be here smoking his weeds," Archie said as I approached. "Wonder where he is?"

"Coach is probably cutting on him right now," I joked as I took a position on the fender beside Archie. "Just kidding," I added as Archie's eyes widened. I felt a strange elation that he was showing signs of good sense. "He's probably just off somewhere trying to convince Teeny of the merits of the petite penis," I said. "And of the vaginal damage invariably inflicted by a non-petite one."

Having observed in the past Archie's transcendental knowledge of events that should otherwise have been clandestine, I decided I might have reason to be as nervous as he appeared to be. "Reckon he's okay?" I asked.

He shrugged and peered along the street in either direction. Minutes passed. With no sign of him, I became jumpy. "Maybe he had to spend the lunch hour in the principal's office," I said. "Maybe he got in trouble."

"Not Jerry," Archie replied. "You know how shy he is around other people. He never gets in trouble at school."

The noon hour ended and Archie and I were compelled to return to classes. Our restive eyes met occasionally as we sat before our desks, immobile and apprehensive. At study hall we scarcely glanced at Teeny Wright's ankles or Margerie Dalton's bulges, or even at Saxon Browne's curls. Instead we made visits periodically to the water fountain, where from the second floor window we had a view of Jerry's Chevy. "Nothing," I reported after a sixth trip to quench a very real thirst. "No sign of him."

"Meatloaf killed him," Archie whispered with a fatal resonance in his voice. "And we're next."

"Things like that just don't happen here, Archie," I said. "This is Smith Station. Mississippi. This ain't like it is in Boston, or New York, where murderers and rapists run wild in the streets. Get a grip!"

"Things like this don't happen except where Meatloaf's concerned," he answered. "I think Meatloaf has killed Jerry."

We walked together to Jerry's Chevy at the sound of the final bell, each of us occasionally touching the other as if to ascertain that a friend and messiah was only a step away. Our classmates rapidly disappeared, either on foot or in automobiles, and soon we were left alone beside our friend's car. "Don't make sense," I said for the twentieth time.

"Let's go to the cafe and see if he's there," Archie suggested. "If he's not, we'll wait on him. There'll be lots of people there, too. Safe."

"We gotta work."

"This is an emergency. We can be late."

We set out for the railroad overpass, heedful of every sound or movement on the streets, and had traversed only half that distance when Coach Murray's Fury rounded the corner ahead of us. "Uh-oh," I said as we stopped to grip each other's arms. "Run like hell!"

"No!" Archie said under his breath, "We'll really look suspicious if we run. Act natural. He won't try anything out here in the open."

So we strolled as if bored with the world. The Plymouth neared us and slowed, then turned into a parking space ahead. "Oh, no," Archie whispered, "Jerry's in there with him!"

I could see Jerry then, huddled on the passenger side seat. I stopped in my tracks and uttered the most sensible words that came to mind: "Who cares now if we look suspicious? Hell, let's haul ass!"

"What about Jerry?"

"It's every man for himself."

"We can't just leave him!"

"Maybe you can't, Tonto. Leave him to the wolves, I say. Let's haul."

But our reluctant though deliberate stroll had brought us near enough the coach's Fury that we made eye contact, and when the big man stuck his arm out the open window and motioned Archie and me closer, we stood spellbound, not knowing what to do next. "We can't run now," Archie whispered.

"Why not?"

"We just can't."

The coach didn't take his eyes from us as we ambled nearer; at ten feet, he smiled at us. It wasn't a friendly sort of smile, more a cat-that-caught-the-mouse one, and as he waited for us to draw close I observed that he was flexing the muscles in the huge arm that covered much of the Fury's door panel. He could kill any of us with a single blow, I thought. A single squeeze of his hands. Maybe even with a thump from a forefinger. "Greetings, you little Peeping Tom fuckers," he said by way of welcome. His western hat was pushed back, framing his great round face like a misplaced halo. "You two been fishing, too, ain't you? Get in."

"Coach!" I cried, raising a hand in greeting. "How's it hanging, man?"

He looked at me as if he thought I was crazy. "I said, get in." He pushed the vehicle's door open, leaned forward, and pulled his seat with him. "In back. Now."

"We gotta go to work, coach," Archie squealed. "Jerry, too. Come on, Jerry."

"Either you get in, or I put you in," he growled. "And it ain't gonna be pleasant if I do it."

Archie and I crawled inside, past the coach and his immense body that reeked of the flat gray stench of the locker rooms. Jerry watched as we struggled through the restricted opening. His face was very red. Was that the imprint of a hand across his cheek?

The coach cranked the Fury without another word and backed from the parking space. I wondered what people would think, if anyone saw us. The students were gone, however, and none of the teachers were outside the school building. And Coach Murray didn't intend on being noticed. Taking a route that skirted the downtown streets, he guided the car west on the paved road that led to Louisiana.

He's taking us to the pit! I realized with horror. He's going to take us there and kill us! "How's the team nowadays, coach?" I said gaily. "Little Dixie champs again this year?"

No answer.

"Milldale Central has a helluva team this year. They'll probably be our toughest opponent."

"Shut up," the coach said, keeping his eyes on the road.

Where did he keep the pistol? Under the seat? Could I get to it before he did? Did I have the guts to shoot him? And if I did? Coach Murray had the neck and shoulders of a bull, the biceps of a water buffalo. Six slugs from a thirty-eight would probably slow him down. But would that stop him?

Archie, Jerry, and I exchanged secret, terrified glances as we neared the familiar and totally unappealing gravel road that led up to the pit. As rocks flew from the road beneath the car's rear tires, I was reminded of a similar scene only last night, an evening that seemed a hundred years past. Why, I wondered, had I listened to those two half-wits?

The coach brought the Fury to a skidding halt nowhere near any of the small oases. As dust settled about us, he turned in his seat. I strained to push away, forcing my body into the rear seat, as far from his as possible. "Now," he said, turning to eye Archie and me, "I've got the story from Jerry, here. I know it was you three out here last night. He's told me what he saw. Now, you two tell me. And it had better be the same story."

"We didn't see nothing, coach," I lied.

He twisted in his seat. "Don't give me that, Jack. Talk!"

"We really didn't, coach," Archie said. "We heard you, and we heard a girl. We figured it was Mrs. Murray. That was all. With you shooting that gun that way, we didn't even raise our heads."

"You didn't see the lady?"

"No, sir."

"You were coming in when I saw you? Not going out?"

"Yes, sir."

"How about you, Jack?" He twisted again in his seat in order to better see me, and as he examined my face he shook his head in disappointment. "I'm really ashamed of you, Jack," he said. "More than these other two. I thought better of you. What the hell did you think you were doing? Now, what did you see?"

I knew what he was driving at, though Archie and Jerry did not. I also knew that things would be a lot worse if he knew that I knew. A white "pillar of the community" parked out at the gravel pit with a colored woman? Ruination! "Same thing, coach," I lied. "I could make out your car. I could barely hear you and that lady, whoever she was. We really thought it was your wife."

Coach Murray pursed his lips and stared, his fingers drumming the seat beside Jerry's head. "Why the hell would I be out here with my wife?"

"Lots of people do that," Archie chimed in. "All the time."

Now the coach looked at Archie as though he thought HE was crazy. It's not going to be that bad, I thought after a few seconds of silence. Just a little tongue lashing, and it'll be over. And from here on, we'll all be good little boys.

Coach Murray stared out the front windshield for what seemed a long while, steadily drumming the seat with his fingers. His neck, I noted as I examined it at close range, was a big as my waist. His hat size was probably measured in feet, not inches. Wonder, I wondered, if every other thing about him is big....

"You boys have put me in a bad predicament," he muttered to the windshield. "I dislike killing." He turned to give each of us in turn a toothy grin, then said, "No, I take that back, boys. I enjoy killing. It's just that if I kill all three of you at once, somebody might get suspicious."

Archie, Jerry, and I exchanged glances. "We won't say anything, coach," Archie said hoarsely. "Will we, guys?"

"No!" Jerry and I said simultaneously.

The coach gazed indifferently out his window. "I could go ahead and kill them now." He seemed to be talking to himself. "The killing would be fun. But I don't want to if they're telling me the truth. Hell, a man gets tired of killing. Wonder if I can trust these boys?"

"You can trust us, coach," Archie said quickly.

"But death. It's such a permanent solution to this problem."

"We won't say nothing!"

He sighed and turned back to us, his introspective moment having had the desired effect: we were shaking like leaves on a windy day. "There's no need to kill you?" he asked as though he were surprised at the idea. "You boys won't mention a word to anybody?"

"No, sir!"

"No, sir!"

"No, sir!"

"Cause if you do..." He shook his head. "If you do, I'll come after you. One at a time. You won't know when, either. Maybe a bullet through your back that'll explode your heart like a balloon full of water. Maybe a knife. Maybe I'll bring you back out here, and cut your dicks off first, before I kill you. I don't know, though, really, right now, this is such a great opportunity for me." He paused and sighed and looked almost bored for a moment. Then he said, "But you say there's no need for me to kill you? You can keep your mouths shut?"

"Yes, sir!"

"Yes, sir!"

"Yes, sir!"

"Well, if I heard the slightest rumor..."

"We won't say a thing, coach," I said. I meant it.

"I might ought to just kill you anyway," he muttered, turning away with a sorrowful expression. "I don't know. I just have to think on it. It'd be such fun!"

"Please coach," Archie begged. "Don't kill us. We'll never say nothing. We all three promise we won't."

The coach sighed dejectedly. "Well," he said without turning back to us, "I've been in a good mood all day today. I guess it's a lucky day for you three." He reached for the ignition key.

Not another word was spoken on the return trip. We were afraid, I suppose, that if we spoke, and the wrong words came out, Coach Murray might change his mind. We piled out of the Fury when it stopped alongside Jerry's Chevy and watched silently as the coach drove away after leaving us a final bit of advice: "Watch your backs, boys."

"I'm going to Sunday School and church Sunday," I said when he was out of sight. "The Baptist Ladies can have me. I may even become a priest. How do you say 'Hail Mary' in Southern?"

"Holy fucking shit!" Jerry chirped.

"I'm going straight home after work," Archie said, "and hug my mom. Maybe even Barbara, too. And I ain't leaving home for a month. What an afternoon!"

"Same here," Jerry said. "Except I'm going now. I ain't setting a foot out until Monday morning. And I ain't walking no dark alleys for a while. Wow! Let me tell you how it happened!"

Jerry shivered as he spoke the words. Archie and I listened breathlessly.

"I was hanging out behind the gymnasium. Figured that was safe, since Meatloaf thinks basketball is for sissies. But he was right there! All of a sudden, he just showed up. He asked me about the scratches, and I started to tell him our cover story. Then he slapped me! Hard! He said I was lying!" Jerry's face flushed and he hung his head. "I told him the truth after that."

"That bastard!"

"We would have done the same thing, Jerry. What happened then?"

"He made me get in his car. We drove back roads until time for school to let out. You know the rest."

I said, "I sure wish Uncle Jim was home. Wonder if I can get a room at the Sanatorium close to his?"

"Glad I ain't going home to no empty house," Archie said. "You can come home with me and spend the night, Jack."

"Thanks, Arch."

We swore ourselves to secrecy. Jerry dropped us at our respective places of employment and drove away toward his home. Archie reported to Mr. Murphy, and I reported to Mr. Barnes, who was in his office, running up figures on his machine and humming the usual Perry Como song. "Got a few scratches, there, Jack," he said when he looked up. "Been in the woods? Or did some eager female get hold of you?"

"Fishing. Light quit. Walked out in the dark. Briars."

"Better take two flashlights next time."

"Yes, sir. Sorry I'm late."

He gave me cash-register duty for the final thirty minutes of the day, but my mind was not on making change, and when five o'clock arrived I could scarcely remember to what useful purpose I had been employed. I told him "good evening" when he allowed me to leave, and left the five-and-ten by the rear door. As I rounded the corner in front, I caught a glimpse of Archie's rear as he chugged along the sidewalk toward home. He hadn't been kidding. He intended to go home and stay home. I didn't blame him. The specter of an enraged football coach lurking around every corner was reason enough to seek the safety of parents and the quiet of one's own bedroom. Ah, the safety of my wonderful home, Cherokee Rose!

CHAPTER 10
FORT CHEROKEE ROSE

T HE SAFETY OF home. There is no safety at my home! I thought with a shudder. Cherokee Rose is as easy to get into as an apple orchard! Should I spend the night with Arch? Or stay all night at the cafe, playing pool and pinball? Eight or ten beers would certainly change my attitude. I could drink a little bravery and then trot along to my elegant hovel as tranquil as a milk cow. I might not even feel the bullets when they struck my back. The café. The café...

Downtown Smith Station always became subdued, though a more powerful word might have been more apt, after the store closings at five o'clock. By six o'clock the streets were usually deserted except for the vehicles parked near the cafe or movie house. Later there would be the occasional squeal of tires as teenagers searched for restless others. The vagabonds and shysters, who during the day profited by their prey upon the naive of Mary's patrons, would congregate in small groups in alleyways where they would squander their hard-chiseled loot in games of chance. Chief Hancock would drive by every now and then, patrolling the quiet streets, making sure all was well in his little community. The town tonight was, as every other night, a melancholy relic of hours before, silently awaiting eight AM and a return to bustling normalcy. That, I thought as I entered the café, is exactly the way I want it tonight. Quiet. Deserted. And safe.

Few customers were huddled about the tables or perched upon the stools in Mary's place. The supper crowd was not yet hungry, and the time was early, the sky too bright, for leisurely philandering and covert boozing. The jukebox was a low-pitched boom, a palpitation more felt than heard. A pinball player shook his machine as he confronted the irresistible force of gravity upon the shiny steel marbles. I took a stool at the very end of the lunch counter, graciously surrendering "our" table to whomever first spotted it, and awaited the attention of Mary or her Boy.

There was to be a delay in service, I soon found, for Mary had embarked upon one of her periodic housefly-killing sprees. Someone had left a door ajar earlier in the day, and there were an inordinate number of the villainous insects buzzing about. Mary hated them. As I sat down, the battle had been opened.

Mary shook her long-handled swatter with the dexterity of Babe Ruth, muttering things that sounded like "guddamn flies," and "gotcha little bastid" while she smeared tiny guts and broken wings across tables and counter alike. Her performance was something to behold, and the sight of her in combat, slinging her swatter and cursing with every slap, was enough to eliminate the squeamish from the ranks of frequent diners. I cringed as I watched and looked away and remembered another time... Jerry... Jerry, as he had been about to make a shot on the eight ball...

His neck had "chilled," as he later described it, from the rapid breeze near his left ear as Mary walloped a luckless fly that had made the mistake of finding Jerry's just-like-Elvis hair tonic irresistible. Jerry leaped back in surprise as the unfortunate fly ricocheted across the room and struck a corner in a double bank that imparted just the right amount of English to create a long, graceful arc that sunk the fly's carcass in a side pocket. Jerry was astonished. All the pool crowd was. And Mary graciously claimed she hadn't even been aiming for that particular pocket.

Perhaps the fly-swatting incident most memorable to us, however, occurred when Archie's cousin, Josiah Quincy Adams, of Boston, Massachusetts, was in Smith Station for a visit. Josey, as we called him, had made fun of our "accent" and our manners, while constantly stressing the significance of Massachusetts's cultural climate and the artistic, political, and scientific gifts made by the people of his great state to the fortunate remainder of the country. He also bragged about how "our side" won the War. We were therefore exceedingly pleased when he suffered at the hands of our own Southern Warrior, Mama Mary.

As it happened, Josey, Archie, Jerry, and I were having a round of burgers and fries one afternoon when Josey launched into a vivid description of the fine cuisine that was served in the fancy club on Boston Bay where he and his parents often dined. Above us, a thin sheet of sunlight that had sneaked through the window blinds illuminated the anxious fluttering of a lone fly that had apparently escaped an earlier tirade by Mama Mary. We three veterans took note of the crazed insect, and of Mary's instant mutation from cook to killer, and prepared ourselves as the fly staked claim to a portion of Josey's burger. Josey had turned to a tale of his ancestors' part in the Revolution when the ear-piercing crack of Mary's long-distance swatter ended his soliloquy. We watched eagerly as Josey gazed in wonder between hands poised to accentuate the significance of Massachusetts's role in American history, to a scene appalling to eyes virgin to the sight of strewn entrails and inanimate eyeballs. Hands yet poised over the remains, Josiah burped so loudly that the gurgle could be heard above the now-resumed screeches-and-screams. We waited. We hoped he would be sick, there and then. We wondered, too, as Josey reeled slightly in his chair, if we would be so lucky as to witness the imposition of a permanent affliction on the Yankee. We all sighed with disappointment, though, as he slowly rose and left the cafe, never again to roam amongst the fertile growth that rooted in its slithery concrete floor. Our laughter afterwards could have been heard in Milldale.

The slaughter of houseflies tonight ended with a triumphant declaration of total victory by Mary: "Happy days is here again, folks!" Immediately thereafter her customers regained their self-possession, and the buzz of joyful conversation, so rudely discouraged by Mary's offensive, was resumed following a myriad of sighs. In a moment, after explaining the scratches on my face, I had a soft drink in hand. I drank it leisurely in order to extend my stay while I watched Mary fuss about her grill preparing greasy sandwiches and French fries by the score. Apparently she was expecting an army for supper.

I screamed an order for another soft drink and for a bowl of the special, beef and vegetable soup with plenty of salt and pepper, wondering if I could stretch my meal into two hours and that much nearer Coach Murray's bedtime. The cafe was half filled with customers now, the screen door squawking almost continuously as hungry new ones arrived or sated ones departed. I had brief conversations with several of my high school friends, and wondered what my two best buddies were doing at the moment. Though I missed them, I felt a surge of satisfaction at merely being a part of the unwinding process that was accomplished here in the café each afternoon by variant numbers of the local populace. Though Mary probably did not realize it, her place provided a ration of psychological rehabilitation along with every bite.

As was the normal order of things, I glanced at the front door each time it announced an arrival, hoping, as was the normal order of things, that a voluptuous blonde would come slinking inside whispering my name and begging for sex. That seldom occurred, of course, nor did it tonight. Instead I got Squeaky Bishop, who was, in my book, not only Jim's drinking companion, but the other extreme. He entered after Mary had served my soup and soft drink, into which I buried my nose and cheeks in the hope that Squeaky would not recognize me and would instead bother someone else. It was not to be, however.

"Hello, Jack!" he shouted, slapping my shoulder as he pushed onto the stool beside me. "Mind if I join you?"

Of course, I was delighted to have his companionship, and told him so. "How you been, Squeaky?" I asked after he was settled.

"Great!"

"You sound almost sober. You must be broke."

"Naw. Got a poker game later. Need to stay sharp."

He was sixty years old, with the face of Theodore Roosevelt minus the glasses, except that his nose, pounded flat by some pugilist of the past, resembled in size and mottling one of Mama Mary's buttermilk pancakes. He used hair oil that glued the thin gray strands to his scalp and left his forehead glossy. And he always wore blue jeans and knit shirts that could in no stretch of imagination contain his blue-ribbon watermelon belly which, incidentally, or perhaps by design, helped conceal the handle of the thirty-eight revolver that was ever on his person.

As he rambled on cheerfully beside me, I was reminded of yet another reason for my lack of fondness for Squeaky Bishop: He had the breath of a dung-pile. Worse, because his breathing was labored by the onset of Emphysema, he shared his wheezes and the horrific odor with everyone within range of his gusts. There was no way, I thought, I could sit here and hold my food down. Much as I dreaded that walk home, a bullet between the shoulder blades seemed merciful relief from Squeaky Bishop.

With a nasal twang caused from holding my breath I said, "Gotta go, Squeaky. Late for an appointment."

"Wait! You ain't finished," he complained, a hand on my shoulder. "Besides, I wanted somebody to sit and eat with and talk to. Mary!"

A comforting waft of lye soap and scorched cotton accompanied Mary as she stopped before us. Squeaky quickly ordered his food—"something strained good, Mary"—while preventing my departure by gripping my forearm. "Lost my damn teeth," he said under his foul breath after Mary was gone. "On the way to the coast to gamble. Didn't miss 'em 'til we went to a fancy restaurant." He grinned at me and pushed me back onto the stool. "Had to order soup, Jack. Soup! And the rest of the boys was eating shrimp and flounder and raw oysters. After a few beers, I ordered some anyway. Had a hell of a time getting it all down. Except for the oysters."

"Too bad," I said. The rubbery slap of Squeaky's unshackled lips upon one another was fascinating to behold, the sort of revolting fascination that Medusa no doubt used to turn her victims to marble. He pulled a cigarette from his free pocket and lit up, and I watched, spellbound by his baggy mouth. "Why do you go all the way to the coast to gamble, Squeaky?" I asked, just to observe the action. "Mr. Bass always has a game, just around the corner."

"Hell, boy," he said, "that'd be like having one woman. You get awful damn tired of just one woman. Same thing with poker games."

"But you're playing at Mr. Bass' place tonight, right?"

"Yeah. Me, Bass, George Montelbano, and Meatloaf Murray."

"Coach Murray?" I asked, suddenly very interested. "Coach is coming up here?"

"He'll be late. He's got another little engagement to take care of beforehand." Squeaky gave me a knowing look. "If you know what I mean."

"Well, I've got to be going," I said. "Gotta feed Willie. Got a thousand things to do."

"Hell, boy, stay a while! Boy your age, you ought to be thinking about love anyway. You can do them other things another day."

"Soon as I get caught up with the chores, Squeaky, I plan on falling in love."

"Love," Squeaky said, gripping my arm with renewed vigor, a mellow touch and a sigh in his voice, "love is like an ice cream, Jack. Good and sweet and enjoyable at first. Then." He paused and turned his eyes to the yellow light bulbs above our heads. "Then it starts to melt. Just drips away. First thing you know, it's all gone, melted to shit."

"Damn, Squeaky, I didn't know you were so poetic."

"But you know what, Jack?"

"No. What?"

He pulled me closer despite my attempts otherwise, intent upon whispering advice of great portent. "What you have to do then is to go get you a fresh cone, boy. And try something different. Strawberry! Banana! There's all flavors out there besides vanilla, son!"

"You're quite a philosopher, Squeaky," I said. "I've got to go!"

"Oh, all right," he sighed. He smashed his cigarette out in what was left of my soup. The odor of scorched tomatoes and sizzling tobacco mingled with the barnyard stench of his heavy gasps. When he covered his mouth to belch, my stomach rolled and I jerked from his grip.

"See you later," I said as I headed for Mary's cash register.

"See you, Jack," he called. "I'll come by when Jim gets out."

That reminded me. Squeaky was a bad influence. I paid Mary for supper and walked back to where he sat. "Squeaky," I said as he waited expectantly. "When I get Jim out... I... We need to help him stay off the booze for a while. It's bad for him. He's getting old. I'd appreciate it if you wouldn't..." Hell, I thought. Get on with it! "Don't bring him anything to drink, Squeaky," I said. "Tell him no. And if you're drinking, please stay away. Okay? You know what I mean."

Squeaky twisted on his stool. "Jim can decide that for himself, can't he?" he said with a pout. "He knows when he's had enough. I wouldn't do anything to hurt him anyhow. You know how much I think of him."

"I need your help, Squeaky. You're one of his best friends. If you care about him, you'll help him slow down. Doctor Blake says he's damaging his health."

Squeaky's face softened a bit, and his garish lips puckered in a manner peculiar to the toothless mouth. "I sure wouldn't want anything to happen to Jim," he murmured. "Maybe you're right. I'll see what I can do."

"Thanks. Hope you find your teeth."

"Probably under a cushion on that old sofa," he said. "I'll find 'em."

Though Smith Station had streetlights, there were dark alleyways along either side of the street that led to Cherokee Rose. As I dashed past each of them I kept my eyes peeled. Coach was supposed to be taking care of "another little engagement," the nature of which I could easily guess, but, nevertheless, I was not about to let my guard down. As illogical as it might seem to the normal mind, the coach might be planning a little sport killing later this evening.

There was no lighting inside or out of the house to make the old antebellum seem more charitable than the dark mental image I had formed when I left the cafe. The scene was right out of a horror movie. A cool breeze from the northwest had chilled the air, signaling the overdue arrival of fall, the brisk gusts rousing the live oaks. Their branches groaned with the unexpected strain, the ominous chorus of alien vibrations adding tension to the already intimidating clap of a loose shutter whipping in the wind. Hedges planted along the sidewalk in front writhed and heaved like so many hoodlums flexing their muscles in preparation for mischief. The nearest street light, a half block away, only added to the macabre image by casting flickers of vague movement about the grounds. There was no sign of Willie. As I surveyed the bleak scene, I considered reversing my steps and making the short walk to Archie's house and the comfort of his bed. But I was a man, wasn't I? I was a Smith! I walked to the front door, listened for any unusual sounds for a moment, and went inside.

The light from several lamps helped dispel my fear, and I felt ashamed for being frightened of my own house. Cherokee Rose was my sanctuary, my country, my world. In her I could always find peace.

But she was no Fort Knox.

Room by room, window by window, door by door, lock by lock, I secured her. Where there was no way to make her secure, I arranged a barricade of furniture through which Coach Murray would have to struggle, and in the process create enough noise to wake me if I were asleep. Chairs tilted under the knobs of all the outside doors made them safe. The only balcony accessible from below, and that only by scaling a rotten rose trellis, was secured by similarly blocking doors and windows. A padlock denied access to the unused coal bin in the basement. Lastly, I drew every drape and blind on every door and window and turned out all lights.

I would have freedom of movement within my fortified dwelling without being seen from outside. There was just enough light inside now that I could barely see to get about.

"Willie?" I called from the back door as I prepared to bolt the last unfettered entrance. "Willie, where are you boy?" I gave a sigh of relief as the old cripple hobbled from his favorite station near the base of one of the live oaks and wagged his tail in greeting. "William Wing," I told him, "I love you a lot. Especially tonight."

I fed him an unusually generous portion of food and stroked his fur, a ploy I hoped would encourage him to stay home. "You stay here in the backyard tonight, Willie," I explained. "Bite anybody who sneaks around back here. I'll guard the front door. Okay?"

Willie ignored me and kept eating. I poured him even more food. If he were extra full, perhaps he would be content to wallow all night in the leaves.

After bolting the back door and once again satisfying myself by inspection that my domicile was fortified, I pulled from its hiding place in Jim's closet his old thirty-eight caliber revolver. Though the gun was rusty and worn from its years of being lugged about in back pockets, it was loaded and capable of firing. Jim and I practiced with it on the occasions that we were in the woods or at the lake together. I stuck it in my waistband and immediately felt much safer. Coach Murray was in for a surprise if he fooled around with me!

The grandfather clock that towered against a wall in the hallway chimed. Only seven-thirty! I noted with surprise. It seemed much later. I took time to crank the pendulum and chime weights back into their dark recesses, and wondered if the faded face and warped hands of the old timepiece were lying to me. Probably not. The clock had always been fairly accurate, though its precision was suspect after a cog slipped somewhere inside. Occasionally now, on the hour, a few extra bongs shook its wooden frame as though the clock were caught up in happy clamor. Jim and I joked about it, chastised it sometimes with a few well-chosen but friendly words. It was just a piece of furniture, albeit a living one, and a treasured part of our lives. Old grandfather LIVED with us, all the more a member of our decaying family because of his imperfections.

My favorite part of Cherokee Rose was the library. Located off the parlor, our "living room," the library had doubled in earlier times as a "smoking room." A long walnut mantel of near shoulder-height, appointed with hollows to receive long-lost glass ashtrays, ran the length of one wall. Faint scents of charred tobacco yet remained, a memento of ponderous councils conducted by early Smiths. Except for one large window, the remainder of the room was bookshelves and volume after volume of books. This was where I had spent much of my youth, inspired by Jim to confront the mesmerizing influence of the observations and imaginations of great writers. I was seized by their work with a zeal, a passion, that surprised us both. The room had become a sanctuary within a shrine, and I paused now for a moment at the door to take pleasure from it. The overstuffed and lumpy cushioned chair where I had slouched and read for hours on end beckoned from its station near the fireplace. Another old friend. I dropped into it, patted the thirty-eight for reassurance, and closed my eyes.

I fell asleep. The tension of the day and the lack of sleep the night before must have overcome my fear. In a moment I was dreaming once more, not of mellow milk or killer coaches or of sex, but a bizarre nightmare that centered on Saxon Browne:

Saxon latched the door to my room and turned to face me with the smirk of Barbara Jones. She wore an ankle-length thin red kimono that buttoned from neck to hem. It billowed slightly as she approached my bed.

"Ready?" she asked as she sat and reclined alongside my naked body. "Ready to look some more?"

"Yes," I answered, "I'm ready."

"*Where? Do you know where?*"

"*Yes,*" *I said, pointing.* "*I'm sure it's in there, Saxon. There's no place else it could be.*"

She plucked a few buttons and my mouth watered. I stared. "*Check here,*" *she said as she pulled my hand to her bare shoulder.* "*Is it there?*"

"*No,*" *I answered.*

More buttons fell at her touch. Her breasts were bare. "*My breasts,*" *she said with a scorn in her voice that didn't matter.* "*Want to check my breasts?*"

I cupped one breast in my palm and shook my head.

"*You have to find it, Jack,*" *she said.* "*You have to look everywhere.*"

"*Yes,*" *I said.*

"*Hurry.*"

All the buttons were open now. "*It's close,*" *I said. I placed my hand between her thighs and tried to force them apart.* "*Very close. I think it's in there.*" *I pointed to the spot.*

"*I should have known,*" *she said.* "*Men! If you had to lose your mind, Jack, I wish to hell you'd lost it someplace else.*"

"*It's my Smith blood.*"

"*And suppose Perry finds out? His mind is in there, too, you know.*"

"*No,*" *I said,* "*his mind is someplace else. Maybe in a football.*"

The door to my room flew open and there, angry and vengeful, swatter held high in fly-killing stance, stood Mama Mary. "*You're just like your daddy, Jack!*" *she shouted as Saxon aloofly departed through the door behind her. "I'll have to treat you the same, too!"*

"My mind!" I shouted. "It's getting away!"

"Your mind has been where it ought not be! When I find it, I'll teach it and you a lesson you won't forget!"

With a flurry of whacks she went for my fanny...

I was sure I had heard something. The whacks from Mama Mary's weapon faded, and in their place I heard a tap-tap-tap coming from somewhere near the front of the house. Coach Murray! I thought as I jumped to my feet. Melville Murray, knocking on my door! Willie, where are you? The phone! The phone! Call the police! Jack, you fool, pull your gun!

The tapping came again. I jerked the pistol from my waist and ran for the hallway and the telephone. Gertrude! I yanked the phone from its cubbyhole.

At "number please" I yelled and begged as if Gertrude were Chief Hancock himself. Then, between supplications, I realized that my name was being called. A woman's voice.

A woman. At my front door?

There was no threat at all. I felt like a complete fool. I stood for a moment listening as Gertrude frantically yelled my name, dreading the need for telling her the truth. I would never live this one down. "Gertrude," I said finally into the mouthpiece, "I had one hell of a nightmare."

"Jack! You scared me to death!"

"Don't tell anybody."

"Are you okay?"

"Yes, ma'am. That nightmare was so real, I thought I was being beat up."

There was silence for a moment, then Gertrude said, "Think I'll go have a drink."

"Yes, ma'am. Sorry."

A woman? I thought as I hung up. What woman would come by here at night and knock on my door?

I tiptoed to the front of the house and eased the drapes aside. Slim woman. Shoulder-length blonde hair. Heck of a body. Long tan legs hanging from white short shorts. Hugging herself to keep warm. Whispering my name. Mrs. Murray! Linda Murray!

CHAPTER 11
CHARGE!

P RACTICALLY DANCING WITH chill, she darted inside as soon as I opened the front door. I hung my head out and craned from the doorway, half expecting her husband to appear out of the darkness. There was no sign of him. I closed the door and bolted it securely as Mrs. Murray apologized for the intrusion. "I'm sorry to impose on you like this, Jack," she said from behind me. I turned to face her, suddenly apprehensive. Another good reason, I thought, for Coach Murray to shove portions of my anatomy down my throat.

"It's no intrusion, Mrs. Murray," I said, trying to keep the shiver from my voice. "I had dozed off. I didn't hear you until I woke up. Sorry it took so long for me to let you in."

"I didn't expect you to be asleep." She glanced at my clothes and I knew she was wondering if I had gone to bed in them. I looked like a beggar. But she... She looked like she'd just stepped from her shower and dressed for a tennis match. "In fact, because there were no lights on," she continued, "I nearly didn't stop. I wouldn't have, if I'd been in my car."

"You're walking?"

"I walk a lot."

"Really?" I said. "I never see you out."

"I usually walk south of here, along the old lake road."

Me and Mrs. Murray, alone, here, in the dark... But why? "

I didn't forget the lawn," I said hastily. "One day next week."

"That's not why I'm here."

"Do you know what time it is?"

"I'd tell you." She held her arm out. "But there's not enough light in here to see my watch. It must be about nine o'clock."

"Oh," I said. "I slept over an hour."

"Feel better?"

"Yes, ma'am."

"I know Jim's not here."

"No, ma'am. He's back at the Sanatorium. His heart again."

"His heart?" she chuckled. "He's such a dear. Honorable to a fault. Contemptuous of the truth. When will he admit to himself that everybody in town knows about his drinking?"

I shrugged. "He has his pride, I guess."

"I should leave, shouldn't I?"

"No," I said quickly while I eyed what I could see of her legs, "I haven't even asked you to sit down. Sit down. Please. Stay awhile. I'll turn on a light."

She turned slightly and took a step down the hallway. "I do need to talk to you," she said, pointing to where my hands were hanging beside me. "But is that a gun? I do wish you'd put that gun away."

Jim's pistol dangled, forgotten, at the end of my arm. I held it out and looked at it stupidly. "Sure," I said.

"Are you planning on murdering someone tonight?"

I placed the pistol on a side table, gingerly, as though it were a piece of garbage. "I was just straightening things up," I said. "I was just putting it away. Uncle Jim must have left it out."

"You clean house in the dark? While you're sleeping? How novel!"

In the darkness I could hardly make out her bare tan legs and arms, but her shorts practically glowed. The bulges that swelled her knit blouse brought to mind the rumor about her not needing a brassiere. Once and for all, I told myself, I should make a conclusive determination of the truth so I could share the confirmation with the rest of the world. How? How? I followed her down the hall. Peering through the open door at Jim's bedroom she smiled and said, "Him and his tester bed." After a short pause she continued, "He told me he had a tester bed."

"We have seven of them," I said as I worried over just how long Coach Murray would play poker tonight. "Two down here we use, five upstairs without mattresses. I'll turn on a light. You're cold. I'll get one of my jackets."

"A blanket would do. And don't bother with the light. My eyes are getting used to the dark." She turned toward the parlor. "I'm sure no one saw me stop here," she added, pausing for a moment at one end of the sofa. "So don't worry. Your reputation is secure."

"Oh, that doesn't matter. Nobody would think anything anyway. I'll be right back."

From an armoire in Jim's room I pulled a light cotton blanket, then hurried with it to the parlor and awkwardly draped it around her from behind. I watched as she arranged her body on one end of the sofa, pulled her feet beneath her, and drew the quilt about her. I took a seat at the opposite end.

"How is school?" she asked.

"Fine. I'll be glad when Christmas break comes, though."

"Typical," she said. "I was that way, too. Always wanting summer to hurry. Now, I wish I were that young again."

"How are Tommy and Barbara Ann? Where are they, anyway? Are they okay?"

"Of course," she said. "They're spending the night with my next-door neighbors. The Shepards. You know them. They have a boy and girl nearly the same ages."

"Yes, ma'am," I said.

"You're really fond of my children, aren't you?"

"I guess being around them when I was cutting your lawn this summer... We had some good times."

"We all did. The four of us. Tommy and Barbara Ann love you like a brother. We all think the world of you."

And I was thinking while she spoke of such trivialities: I'm alone in Cherokee Rose with the most gorgeous piece of female flesh in the entire state. Talk about lucky! Just she and me. Might

I impose myself upon her? Is it possible I can convince her to stay over for a few hours, just for a little hanky-panky and a healthy dose of sex? After all, the kids are away, and Coach is busy with some stupid card game, and Mrs. Murray is home with me... ✧

Good God! I thought then. Are you nuts? Coach Murray's wife?

But I could feel a tingle inside like nothing I'd ever felt before, not the usual dagger, but something that I couldn't control that had taken charge of my mind as well as my body. I could think of nothing but her thighs, her breasts, her shoulders and arms, and how they might feel if I could but stroke them. My body was as taut as a fiddle string, and would no doubt whine if stroked. Archie was right. Pussy makes a man crazy.

Her two perfect calves stretched to the floor before her as she pulled the blanket from her knees and adjusted her position. She stretched and pillowed her hands behind her head and stared absently at the oil painting of my grandfather that dangled over the mantle above the fireplace. I heard a soft sigh as she began, without looking my way: "I had a personal reason for coming over here tonight, Jack."

The plot thickens. Now, I fantasized, she'll tell me she finds me irresistibly attractive. She's been following me for days, whispering my name and admiring the bounce in my back pockets. She can't sleep for thinking of my aphrodisiac face and erogenous body. My husband, she'll assert, is a mere pansy compared to you, Jack. I'll leave him if you say the word. And right now, what would make me happier than anything else in the world would be for you to allow me to remove all your clothes so I can cover your entire body with soft kisses. Right now. This minute. Can't wait.

What other reason could there be for her visit? "I can't imagine why you came by," I said. "I've been sitting here wondering..."

"Melville is playing poker tonight," she said. "It's almost providential that I could get out tonight without him knowing. I certainly wouldn't want him to know that I'd come to see you. Don't ever tell him!"

And the plot thickened even more. The darkness and my erotic imagination and whatever had control of me got the better of me; I spoke with blind instinct rather than good sense. "It's only nine o'clock," I said. "We've got all night. They'll probably play poker all night."

"This won't take all night," she said as she turned to stare at me, an eyebrow raised. "Jack, I don't want you to get the wrong idea..."

"God, you're good-looking, Mrs. Murray," something inside me blurted out. "You're beautiful! You're the most beautiful woman I've ever seen!"

For a few seconds she gaped, then straightened in the sofa and pulled her blanket closer around her. She said, "Well, of course, Jack, I appreciate that, but don't mistake..."

"You're a gorgeous woman! No man could help but love you!"

"Now... That's nice, Jack." Her hair billowed slightly as she shook her head. "But aren't you getting carried away just a little bit?"

I would have sworn that little twitch of her lower lip was the same I'd seen a thousand times before when she was grinning inside. A smile in the darkness. It means "okay." Under these circumstances it meant: "CHARGE!—FULL SPEED AHEAD."

"Let us love for awhile," I said, "you and me, for a year or so."

"What?"

"F. Scott Fitzgerald."

"Well." She settled back into the sofa and inspected me from a corner of her eye. "I believe I understand your remark, Jack. And I believe we have a slight communication problem."

"Ma'am?"

"For God's sake, quit calling me 'ma'am!'"

"Yes, ma... Mrs. Murray."

"If you're going to try to put the make on me, you can at least call me Linda."

Wow! Who could have misunderstood that one? I leaned forward to touch her arm and to stroke it very tenderly, very carefully with the tips of my fingers. "Making you, Mrs... Linda," I said, "is the hallowed consummation of my wildest dreams. You have beautiful arms. Beautiful skin. Wonderful full lips. Delicate little ears. Bite size. I love your ears especially. But I also love your long blonde hair. And your eyes are like no woman's since Cleopatra. And everything else..." I glanced at her blouse. "...is wonderful, too."

"My god," she said, aghast. "What a line! You must read a lot."

"No, it's just that I've always loved you, Mrs. Murray. I'd slay a dragon for you."

"Linda," she said slowly. "Call me Linda." And then, thoughtfully, "Nobody's killed a dragon for me in a long, long time."

"I will. I'll find one tomorrow."

Her nose wrinkled. "You've always seemed like such a quiet, innocent boy. But damned if there isn't a lot of Jim in you."

"I'm not innocent. I'm a real cad. I'm just like Jim. I hustle women all the time."

"Really?" She frowned. "I'm disappointed in you then."

"No, not really," I said quickly. "I lied. I hardly ever hustle women."

She straightened. "Well, anyway, that's certainly not why I came over here tonight. To be hustled. I want you to know that."

"I don't care. I lose control when I'm around you."

"My god!"

Should I pounce?

I was chicken.

"It IS beginning to sound like a good idea," Linda Murray continued, slowly from her end of the sofa. I heard the giggle in her voice. "Melville's out for the night... And you've made me so hot... I'm practically throbbing now, and it's been so long...."

"Wow!" I said, wondering what I should do now. She gave me directions.

"Put your head right here." She patted between her breasts to show me where, then held her arms out and shifted her legs to accommodate my body. I fell between her legs and between her breasts, in awe of the instant warmth. "Just relax," she cautioned after a minute. "Not so rough. Let me just hold you for a while. I'm not sure I can do this. Give me time."

She pulled one of my hands around her, behind her back; the other she held loosely, her fingers intertwined with mine, at her hips. It was not an entirely comfortable arrangement for either of us, and she adjusted her body, putting her arms around my shoulders. In a moment both my arms were around her and my face was burrowing between her breasts. The rumor was confirmed: no bra. "Easy," she whispered as we held each other. "Just be still."

The scent of her filled my nose; my cheeks blistered from contact with her bronzed skin. Eyes closed, I explored her back and shoulders and ranged downward to the swell below, marveling at the sensation. I opened my eyes and adored her wonderful dim curves. Was this really happening? Heaven on earth! I could hardly wait to tell the guys; it was too good to keep to myself. A thirty-six-year-old woman and me! The finest woman in the county! "I love you," I mumbled into her bosom.

"Don't you think I'm a bit old for you?" she whispered. "And what about my husband? He may be upset when he finds out you love me."

"I don't care," I said, wondering if she would let me pull that knit blouse off so I could REALLY get the feel and taste of things. I was afraid to ask. "I'd die for you. But there's no need to tell your husband so I have to prove it."

"Believe me, he's the last person on earth I'd want to know," she said.

Which reminded me of what Jim had told me. The beatings. The bruises. No wonder she wouldn't want the slightest suspicion raised. Coach would kill her!

"I'll never tell a soul about tonight, Linda," I said. "I promise. And I really do love you. I have for a long time."

"Jack." She kissed my forehead while her fingertips slid along my shoulder blades. "I know you love me," she said. "Teenage boys naturally love women. Nearly all women. And I love you, though not quite the way you want. But like I said, that's not the reason I came over tonight."

I raised my head from her chest for a moment to feign interest in the real reason she came over tonight. That proved to be a great excuse to allow it to fall back again, this time with a breast strategically located much nearer my mouth. Could I reach it with my tongue without being too obvious? Would she like me to bite it? Maybe she just liked them licked. Maybe she would knock hell out of me. It was worth it. My confidence grew by leaps and bounds. I opened my mouth and readied a sneak attack.

"No," she said as I plotted, "I wanted to ask you about a rumor I heard. I was told by a friend that you and your two pals saw Melville out at the gravel pit with another woman."

There is nothing, I learned then, that is quite so confusing as the sudden turn of emotions that accompanies the transformation of one's mental state from that of overwhelming sexual desire to one of panic. Breasts and all the other good things I had planned to explore were forgotten in an instant. Surely, I thought, there is some mistake. I pulled my face from steam and bosom and slowly straightened to face her. "You heard WHAT?"

She could have been asking if I'd played any pool lately. "Did you and your friends see Melville with another woman, Jack? Just tell me the truth."

Like my uncle, I had an aversion to lying, especially when there was a good chance of being caught. And like him, I avoided lying by use of deviousness and by phony innocence. With all the disdain I could muster I said, "Who in the world would say a dumb thing like that? Rumors. I just don't understand people who sit around gossiping all the time."

"Then you didn't?"

I couldn't help but squirm, and she couldn't help but notice. "You don't think your husband would be out with another woman anyplace I could see him, do you?" I said. "How the devil could I ever do that?"

"You were out at the gravel pit. You and Archie and one other boy. Jerry, I think. I'd like to hear how that came about, too."

"The gravel pit? Me?"

"Jack," she said patiently, cupping my chin in her hands so she could hold me and stare directly into my eyes, "you can tell me about it. This wouldn't be the first time that Melville has done something like this. It used to hurt, but it doesn't matter that much anymore."

"If it doesn't matter," I said from the opposite end of the sofa, to where I had now retreated, "why do you want to know about it this time? Why don't you just ignore it?"

She shrugged. "You're probably right. Maybe it only matters because it's just another excuse to leave Melville. I wasn't going to so soon, but with everybody in town whispering about his affairs... I don't think I can take that. I have some pride. I won't have people whispering about me or my children behind my back."

"It's only a rumor," I said dully.

"Jack, you're lying," she said hotly. "You and your two friends were at the gravel pit. You saw him with a woman there. He even shot at you."

"No..."

"Why were you three boys at the gravel pit at night? Without girls." She looked at me inquiringly. "Are the three of you...."

"No, ma'am!" I cried. "We're straight!"

"I'm curious, then. Why?"

"I didn't want to go," I squealed. "They forced me. It was all their idea."

"Yeah. I bet."

"They just wanted to look around. You know. Just to see how they were... You know..."

"Teenage voyeurs." She clasped her hands and giggled. "How interesting."

"We didn't get a chance to see anything."

"Instead of lovers, your little spying expedition netted a mad bull and his little heifer. Did you see who the heifer was?"

"No."

"No idea?"

"No."

"Probably that same floozy from Milldale," she said, contempt in her voice. "Well, it doesn't really matter who. It did happen, and you've just confirmed it."

And now what? I thought. What happens to Jack, Jerry, and Archie? The possibilities were endless: Death. Dismemberment. Torture. Exile. If Mrs. Murray had heard about us, Coach Murray could be next. Then: End Of Life As We Know It.

"Will you tell Melville you know?" I asked.

"No. At least not right away. I have to think about it. Make plans. But he's sure to hear about it sooner or later, Jack. This is too juicy for a town as small as Smith Station. Everybody in town will know tomorrow."

"You think so?"

"Of course."

I put my head between my knees and moaned, "I may be leaving for Alabama right away."

"Smart move."

Who? I wondered. WHO? I straightened with a growl. "How did you hear about it, Mrs. Murray? Linda."

She shook her head. "You three have gotten yourselves into a pickle."

I nodded.

"One of you didn't take Melville seriously when he told you to keep quiet. That, I regret to mention, was a huge mistake."

"You know everything!" I cried. "Which one was it? Archie? Or Jerry?"

"What would you do to him if I told you?"

"I don't know." Murder was high on the list of probabilities. "I can't understand why either of them would do it. They both have too much to lose."

"Big man," she scoffed. "Big man had to brag and make himself look big."

"Archie!" I cried.

"Archie," she repeated. "The boy in the cafe the other night."

I repeated the name slowly. "Archie."

"He has a girl friend named Melba. He bragged about it to her. He told her that you three went out there just to check up on Melville, and that you caught him in the act. Dodged bullets. Outsmarted him. Made him look like a fool. Made you sound like some kind of avenging angels. Even backed him down when he confronted you. Melba has told half the people in town."

"My god!"

"The little bitch. I almost wish she'd kept her mouth shut."

"But Archie didn't even see Melba until three o'clock today!" I said. "She must have sent telegrams!"

"Little fool!"

Despite its jolting impact, the intimate nature of my conversation with Linda Murray was having a humanizing effect on our relationship. The more we talked, the more I realized she was no goddess. She was not unattainable. There was no pedestal. She was just a beautiful and sexy woman who could be charming or, probably, as bitchy as the average unhappy housewife. The insight had the effect of bringing my image of her down to earth. As she cursed her husband and the others involved, I felt a strange sense of loss. The infatuation with which I had always regarded her became a casualty of our familiarity. Though I now felt more her equal, already I grieved for the comfort of her illusory perfection. I said nervously, "Do you think your husband has heard yet?"

Her answer was small comfort, "The funny thing about rumors, Jack, is that the people who are the subject of them are the last to hear."

"So there's no need to worry tonight."

"And he'll be late with his precious poker game."

That seductive twitch of her lips appeared. Her "okay" grin.

With thought of what was to be, my concern for tomorrow was as fleeting as my mourning of her mortality.

"Come," she said as she pulled the blanket from her body and leisurely rose from the sofa. She tugged at the hem of her knit blouse and with one fluid motion exposed the wonderful breasts that I had long revered. Her bright white short shorts were next.

I sat for a moment and stared. Was this really happening? Gorgeous Linda Murray, standing here before me, naked, horny, and ready for a good time? I was entranced. More than that. Despite all my big talk, I was scared to death.

"Jack?" she asked hesitantly, "Jack, don't you want..."

The moment had arrived. Either I jumped up and did what I had wanted to do for as long as I could remember, or else I bolted for the front door.

She made up my mind when she held out her hand. I took it and followed her to my bedroom. I didn't even wonder how she knew where it was. In another moment I was wondering why I had ever thought there was anything "angelic" about Linda Murray.

Older women, I quickly found, do not worry about their vital fluids draining from their bottoms. She gave me no time to mention it anyhow, for when our bond was first made, she was dominant, and while in her dominant position there were no more tender words from her, but rather a wild exhilaration and reckless abandon that allowed me the pleasure to marvel at the way she used her body to please herself. I was in awe.

Later there was laughter, and whispers. They were close, and soft, for once we embraced our bodies were never far apart. After a while I belonged there, my body kneaded and shaped to symmetry, a pattern meant for hers. Our unison was a common rhythm that we discovered together and that we greedily seized for our own. No other two people on earth could have it the same; I just knew it.

She left my bed sometime before sunrise, and after a tender kiss good-bye and a few moments spent scanning the streets outside, she walked away into the night.

I lay awake for a while afterward and mused that my life would never again be the same. And I had discovered what I wanted to do with the rest of it.

CHAPTER 12
LET'S MURDER ARCHIE!

ELECTRIFIED, INSPIRED, AND satisfied, I soaked in the tepid water of my early-morning bath and observed with contented man-of-the-world satisfaction that there was nothing more stimulating than making love to a woman. And what a woman! She must be an expert! Visions of Linda Murray's firm body, tantalizing reminders of what was and what would be, kept flashing before my eyes, rekindling my rapture. The intensity of the experience was overwhelming! I floated—dazed, drained, numbed to the world of reality.

The physical pleasure, I decided after thorough consideration, had been no more gratifying than the sense of fulfillment that came with the warmth of her kiss, the touch of her hand. A mystical state love was, from which physical euphoria spontaneously exploded. Passion. Affection. Devotion for and to the moment. Best of all, the toe-curling certainty that my sentiments were shared. We loved each other! She said so! Together, enfolded in that warm, moist cocoon of emotion that excluded all else, no one else mattered, and no unpleasant thought could possess the mind. We were lovers!

The experience was not, however, without its moments of uneasiness. For a few vaguely disturbing seconds during my hours in bed with Linda Murray I floated with her in my dream tub of warm milk, and in the darkness I imagined her eyes were no longer provocative half-moons, but listless scraps, relics of anger and conflict. Her husband was the culprit, I decided. His cruelty to her had roused that vision.

After her departure there were unsettling, completely unexpected flashes of guilt. I dozed for a few moments after she was gone, and when I awoke the guilt settled on me like a chill. I had become an adulterer. The very sound of the word... ADULTERER... committed that zenith of conflicting states... HONORABLE... to the dust heap of unheeded moral law. It had not been an honorable act. I felt shame. I would do it again, but I was shamed nonetheless.

I silently mourned my sin as the still small voice smothered my blissfulness. Then came the light of day, the real world that drives away the gremlins who bring turmoil to darkness; my concern with ethics was replaced by a very real concern for my life. I could readily understand Coach Murray's anger if... not, IF... WHEN he found out that Archie had let the cat out of the bag. But Great Scott! If he learned his wife was gone all night, and if he found out where she had been... It would be the end of me!

Archie! I thought maliciously. Today was Saturday, one of our all-day workdays. Jerry would meet the two of us at morning break for cokes and ice cream. We would kill Archie, Jerry and I, right there on the tiled floor of Danny's Drug Store!

Unaware that I knew the truth about his absence, Willie was waiting for his morning snack, wagging his tail and pretending he'd been outside guarding the house all night. "Bad dog, Willie," I scolded him. "Some pretty bitch pranced by here last night, didn't she? And you just had to check her out. You were out catting when I needed you most. You're a disgrace to the guard dog profession." Then I remembered my own illicit activities and continued, "But you're a true Smith. You're forgiven."

A thirty-eight revolver had never been one of those accouterments that I normally included as part of my daily dress. However, I was now determined to be prepared for anything. I retrieved the pistol from the table where I had placed it in such contemptuous fashion last night. With Jim away, and Willie inclined more to flirtation than to security, this steel-gray revolver was my only protection.

Squeaky Bishop, I recalled, always carried his pistol in a pocket of his jeans. But when I tried a similar arrangement this morning, the butt of my revolver protruded well above my waist line. Squeaky's pistol, I decided, despite the protection of his belly, must have a shorter barrel.

It was too heavy to slide into a sock, and, besides, the legs of my jeans were too tight. A long-sleeve shirt would hide my waist if I wore the tails out, but it wouldn't hide my pockets. Anyway, the gun felt so awkward stuck in a pocket or under my belt I was afraid it would tumble out at the slightest movement. There was, however, a solution.

There was a time when I was a sophomore in high school that great interest was given by all the boys my age to jockey straps. Coach Murray unwittingly instigated this fascination with protective undergarments by deciding one day that all his football players must wear them, along with other protection, when they were on the field. The notion then became widespread among the rest of us, for some reason, that if you were well endowed in the pelvic regions, jock straps were necessary to protect your most valuable asset. Naturally, every male kid in school, myself included, was soon wearing one, some even stuffing their elastic shields with toilet tissue to substantiate the need for protection. We would strut around the school grounds during break, often using one hand and a swaggering motion as we walked to yank the mighty contents of our jock straps back into place.

Then came the rashes and the suffering. After a few days of squirming uncomfortably in our classroom chairs, we found the contraptions unworthy of the pain. One by one, they were shoved out of sight to the backs of drawers of every bureau in town. We all went back to our normal line of underwear: none at all.

I pulled one of my old discarded jock straps from its cache, jerked free of my jeans, and pulled them both on. My waist had expanded since sophomoric days. With the cold thirty-eight shoved in beside my pride and joy, the elastic waistband dug into my backside. But the scheme was functional. After adjusting the position of the pistol within the jock strap so that its contour suited that of my belly and pelvis, I fastened my jeans and admired myself in a mirror. Not bad, I thought. Macho! An enhancement of that prize which all the world would crave if they could but get a look. But I worried that I could shoot off my finer parts while trying to extract the weapon, in which case I'd then turn it on myself and my troubles would be over. Or, since I would likely have to drop my jeans in order to get to the gun, I might be so embarrassed that I would still decide to use it on myself.

There was no sign of Coach Murray or his car, but I glanced this way and that as I trod stiff-legged upon the sidewalk's cracks toward town. A truckload of bright orange pumpkins was being packed into a rail car across the tracks at the docks, destined, no doubt, to decorate many a home for Halloween. The Grande Theatre's residuum of ticket stubs and stale yellow popcorn crunched under my feet as I passed, then a pungent odor of hair oil and talcum preceded my approach to the door of Jake Ainsworth's Barber Shop. Across Main Street someone had already fed Mary's jukebox its dowry of nickels; its primitive throb affirmed the presence of life in downtown Smith Station. That meant more this morning than most others.

Although the five-and-ten didn't open until eight o'clock, Mr. Barnes always left the rear door unlocked for his employees. He was seated at his desk when I arrived, puffing as usual on a stub of tobacco while humming Como. He would never suspect, I thought, that I am a Peeping Tom, and one who befouls married women. Or that nowadays I carried a thirty-eight strapped around my crotch. I waved to him as a normal person might, and he returned my salute with his usual cheerful greeting. "Shipment pulling in anytime now, Jack," he yelled in his gruff but subdued voice. "You help unload the truck."

For the next two hours, with various interruptions, some to adjust my jock strap, I hauled boxes of goods from a delivery truck into the storeroom, never once wondering if they contained new insight into the sculpturing of ladies' underclothes. A vision of a naked Linda Murray kept blinding me to everything else that went on around me, and several times Mr. Barnes had to repeat things before I heard. When could I see her again? It would be risky. It could be fatal. But, God! I wanted her. Again. And again. It was, I thought as I began to re-rationalize all my rationalizations, okay to be an adulterer with Linda Murray. She was, after all, leaving her husband.

I wanted to share the details of my conquest with someone, and relished the thought of the look of surprise and envy and disbelief on the faces of Archie and Jerry when I told them. But I couldn't. I had learned better. I had learned that even your closest friends can't be trusted, that they can deceive you, perhaps they easier and better than anyone.

With the arrival of ten o'clock I saluted Mr. Barnes once more and gained his nodding approval to take a break. Out the back door and around the corner was Danny's Drug Store, where Archie should be waiting. I took a long breath before entering, then walked inside and spotted my "pal" seated at one of the glass-topped black iron tables near the windows that faced the sidewalk outside. From a straw immersed in a tall glass of malted milk, he sucked as though he had not a care in the world. Jerry, too, was there, leaning against the marbled bar where Danny prepared his savory concoctions, awaiting the druggist's preparation of his order. I took note that the scratches on their faces, like mine, were healing nicely. And I failed to detect the odor of turpentine from either of them. Not that either was of great import now that Coach was aware of our identity.

I paused and could not help but enjoy the smell and feel of the place. Danny ran a tranquil drug store, a pleasant place to visit. Many of Smith Station's mothers, fearing the corruption of their children's morals, would not allow them inside Mary's Cafe. But Danny's Drug Store was different. Because of its reputable proprietor, always spotless in his white uniform, its clean black-and-white tile floors, and the trade attended it by the more upstanding of our citizenry, its drug store/soda fountain atmosphere was considered a safe environment for proper young people. The place was therefore generally spurned by those of us who craved the excitement of the seamier side of life, that which abounded at Mary's Café. But a Saturday-morning malted milk swigged in an atmosphere free of cigarette smog and a mist of bacon grease was welcome relief from the pool hall.

I made my way to Archie's table as Jerry received his ice cream and began heading in the same direction. Danny, too, had an eye on Archie, for the young man had just dribbled milk onto the shiny glass table. Archie took note of Danny's grimace and frantically began sopping his mess with a napkin. Jerry spoke to me, and I returned his greeting as we took our seats. Archie's mouth took over before we could get another word out. "Too bad about your dad, Jerry," he blurted without taking his eyes from the depths of his glass. "That was a lot of money to lose."

Jerry grunted and frowned at him. "Shit. You heard, huh?"

"Heard?" Archie asked. "Hell, yeah! Everybody's talking about it."

"What happened?" I asked, forgetting for a moment my mission of death.

"Jerry's dad...," Archie began before being interrupted by a scowl from Jerry that meant "shut up."

"My dad lost a lot of money at poker last night," Jerry said. "Damn Meatloaf. I hope somebody kills him before long."

"Coach Murray won?" I said. "How late was he out?"

Jerry scowled at me now. "What the hell difference does that make? Late enough. Probably daylight. My old man didn't get in until after mom served breakfast."

"All right!" I grinned.

"Three thousand we lost, give or take a few coins," Jerry sighed. "I think the bastard cheated. Nobody can win from my dad like that. He's the best poker player around."

"Jerry's dad was dealt an ace-high flush when the pot got so big," Archie informed me. "Meatloaf stayed with a pair, even with Mr. Bass betting high. That was stupid. Wasn't no way he shoulda drew out against an ace-high flush. Not when he had to draw three cards."

"Full house," Jerry groaned. "The bastard filled up on a three-card draw. Ain't no doubt he cheated."

Archie leaned across the table. "The good part, though," he said, "aces and eights. Dead man's hand. Meatloaf ain't gonna live to enjoy all that loot."

"Speaking of Coach Murray," I said, remembering the mission, "have either of you had any run-ins with him?"

"Naw," Jerry said, a questioning look on his face. "We're okay."

I watched Archie. He gave no hint that he had spilled the beans. He was, I observed once again, the most gifted fraud I had ever known. I said, "Well, it's doubtful that the three of us will be alive tomorrow."

Archie scoffed, "You ain't still scared, are you? I bet you didn't sleep a wink last night, did you?"

"Not a lot," I admitted, grinning inwardly.

"Probably had all the doors and windows locked, too."

"Yep."

"Chicken-shit!" Archie bellowed. Then, softly, head bent forward, "I ain't worried about Meatloaf anymore. All that talk of his was just bluff."

"Is that why you told Melba all about it, Archie?" I said. "You were so sure it was bluff you told her? And now she's told everybody in town? We're good as dead, you bastard!"

Jerry's mouth fell open. He looked at me in disbelief, then at Archie, who had paused in mid-slurp. Archie's face took on an expression that instantly reminded me of one of Mount Rushmore's sculptures. Rigid. Expressionless. As if he had just died and no one had bothered to pull his eyelids closed. A dribble of milk drooled from his lips as he swallowed. "No," he said weakly. His eyes darted from Jerry to me and back. "No. Melba wouldn't say nothing. I mean, I didn't..."

"God Almighty!" Jerry hissed as he rocked noisily backward in his chair to the cold stare of Danny. "You didn't, did you, runt?"

With my lips close to Archie's ear and reaching for it, I whispered, "I want to cut your throat, Archie. If it weren't for getting blood all over Danny's clean floor, I would."

Jerry growled as he placed his fists atop the table, "I'll de-nut you for sure this time."

"We better wait," I said. "Danny will throw us out."

Turning his attention from Archie to instead search the tables around ours, then to glance up and down the street outside, Jerry said, "We've got to get out of town. Now! Let's blow for Biloxi!"

"Melba wouldn't tell," Archie repeated dully.

"Hell, she's practically set up a gravel-pit information booth!" I said. "I wouldn't be surprised if they announce it over that Nashville rock station we're always listening to. She's a one-woman public address system. Tell her to shut up!"

"I can't believe she'd do it."

"Coach hasn't heard yet, though. If he had, we would have heard from him already. Maybe nobody wants to tell him."

Jerry perked up. "Yeah! Who the hell would have the nerve? I sure wouldn't want to be the one. He might just blow up and kill whoever told him, just for general principles!"

"Sure," Archie agreed. He had the gall to smile at us. "Nobody's gonna say nothing to Meatloaf. He ain't got no friends, anyway." Archie hung his head. "But mom. Somebody will tell her, for sure. When she finds out I'm a Peeping Tom..." He looked up at us and mumbled, "Alaska don't sound so bad any more."

I was so tempted myself. Jim. I knew what Jim would say when he found out. "Our reputations!" he would shout, "My God! You've sullied the Smith name!"

"I'm going back to work," I said, rising. "I don't feel good, exposed in this front window this way. It's an easy shot from down the street."

"I don't feel like eating ice cream, either," Jerry groaned.

They pushed away from the table leaving their uneaten deserts for Danny. Archie fidgeted, clasping and re-clasping his hands. I was glad he was frightened. "Let's meet at Mama Mary's for lunch," he said, "so we can decide what to do."

I said, "Damn, Archie! You've practically sealed our fate, and you want us to meet you for lunch? I'd rather have sandwiches and Arsenic with Adolph Hitler and Eva Braun."

"Aw, come on," he begged. "I don't want to have lunch by myself. We gotta plan. How about it, Jerry?"

"I may not be able to control myself next time I see you, runt," Jerry warned through clenched teeth. "I might kill you before Meatloaf gets the chance."

"I'll talk to Melba. I'll tell you both what I find out at lunch. Maybe it wasn't her. Hey!" He looked at me with an accusing squint. "Who told you, anyhow?"

I wasn't prepared for the question. "Anonymous telephone call," I answered, squirming.

They looked at each other, and I could tell they didn't believe me. I didn't care. "All right," I said, "the café at lunch. Lunch with a rat."

Jerry agreed as we walked out.

No one at the five-and-ten acted as if they had heard the latest town rumor. Not that I expected one of them to point and shout PEEPING TOM! in my face. They seemed their normal selves, and I silently performed my duties and thought of Linda Murray's breasts. I wished I could talk to her, but I certainly wasn't going to call her house. Maybe she would call me. She knew where I worked. Maybe she could get out tonight....

I was living on the edge, I thought, panicky for an instant. The next few days could be grim. Death. A good beating. The humiliation of exposure. Perhaps taking leave of Smith Station for good. As for the latter, I wondered if I could bring myself to run. This was home. This was Smith country. And there was Jim, the most tragic casualty of all. I was guilty of criminal snooping, so he was guilty as well. His honorable name, his emblem of respect, would be tarnished with scandal. The notion that I had to face him with my story was sickening at best. Alaska really was sounding better all the time.

In something of a dazed awareness of the rest of the world, I walked at noon to Mary's Cafe. Archie and Jerry were waiting. Archie wore his Mona Lisa rather than his Mount Rushmore and spoke as soon as I was seated. I wanted to hit him. "Melba didn't say nothing to nobody, Jack," he said immediately, shaking his head. "Somebody else told on us."

"Well, who else did you tell, Archie?"

"Maybe it was you, Jack. Maybe you told somebody."

I gave him my best look of scorn. "I didn't."

Jerry eyed me suspiciously and said, "It was one of you two. And I ain't sure I believe that 'anonymous telephone call' bit, either, Jack."

Archie's eyes took on a triumphant look. "Who told you, Jack. Who was it?"

I avoided lying by saying, "You know it was Melba."

"Who was it that called you?"

"How about a 'usually reliable' source?"

"You blabbed to somebody."

"I haven't mentioned it to anyone, Archie," I said. "You're just blowing your usual smoke." I looked at Jerry. "Like he always does. I hope big mouth here catches the first round of slugs. Let's order some food and eat."

By the time we finished our meal, and despite the animosity felt all around, Archie had convinced Jerry and me to meet him at the cafe after work in order to further assess our plight, and maybe shoot a little pool. Our lives couldn't end just because of Meatloaf, he argued, and the coach wouldn't try anything in the café, would he? So why not relax a little? I agreed that it sounded better than waiting around at home to be murdered. And despite my weariness, it was Saturday night. I almost slipped and offered to let them spend the night with me at Cherokee Rose. But what if Linda Murray dropped by? Regardless, neither of the two was likely to want to sleep in a death trap. I would shoot a few games with them, I decided, then head home early, fortify myself inside, and hope that Linda could slip over later.

As the three of us left the cafe, a light rain began to fall, one of those infrequent, fleeting, and curious October rituals, for though there were puffy clouds miles away, overhead the sun shone brightly. Huge raindrops glittered in the rays of the great Helios, prompting Jerry to stare heavenward and say, "Devil's beating his wife. Devil's beating his wife again." An omen, I thought immediately. A harbinger of doom.

Mr. Barnes noted with what apathetic disposition I approached the afternoon's chores, and in a good-natured way tried to cheer me up. "I need to light a fire under your ass this afternoon, boy," he said. "You act like a dog that's just been kicked. What's the matter?"

"Tired, Mr. Barnes," I answered from my position astride a push broom. "Didn't get much sleep last night."

"Another of those all-night fishing trips, I suppose?"

At afternoon break I had a Coke and struggled to keep my eyes open. When five o'clock finally arrived, I dragged myself through the rear door and considered bypassing the cafe and going straight home. Was the coach waiting there? I wondered. I didn't want to find out. I told myself it was the lure of the café's refreshing vice that guided me to it. Actually, I was scared to death.

I stumbled inside, again the last of our trio to arrive. "You look like shit," Archie said in greeting. "I believe you've aged thirty years since last Thursday night."

"Meatloaf's scared the boy so bad he won't go to the bathroom by himself," Jerry snickered. "Always said the boy was chicken-shit."

"Thanks, Arch. Thanks, Jerry." I pulled a chair from under our table and fell into it.

"Let's have a beer," Archie said. Again, he had his Mona Lisa smirk. I doubled my fists and snarled at him.

"And shoot some pool," he continued without notice. "Ah, beer and pool. The essence of life."

"Don't forget pussy," Jerry added. "And Chevrolets. And Luckies."

"Sounds good to me," I said. "Maybe a beer will make me as brave as you two. Or as stupid. Hell, I'll take stupid right now."

After beers and French fries and fried onion rings, we seized a vacant table and began another round of eight ball. "If I weren't afraid for my existence, I'd be bored," I told them. "The essence of life does not consist of bending over a pile of ivory balls while balancing a can of beer on the edge of a pool table. Nor even of Lucky Strikes and Chevys. Now pussy, I'm not so sure about."

"When you grow up, you'll appreciate the finer things," Archie said.

"Son of a bitch," Jerry muttered from his chair leaned against the wall. Archie and I looked up to note the entrance of Richard Miller and Teeny Wright. "It's not Thursday night, is it?" I said gleefully. "This is not their night, is it?"

Archie grinned and turned to peer at Jerry. "Hee-hee," he chuckled under his breath. "I was right. Teeny and Muledick. My usually-reliable source was reliable." He turned to stare at the newly-arrived couple. "Teeny don't look no worse for the wear, does she?"

Richard glanced our way, and to our dismay waved and started in our direction. "Hope there ain't no fight," Archie whispered to me.

"Teeny" was a tiny blonde, compact and pretty, who wore a smile most of the time. She was very popular with both male and female students, and seemed an odd companion to Richard, who was tall and gangly and wore glasses that magnified the size of his eyes. Because of the goggling effect, his face always reminded me of a starving bullfrog. However, he was a friendly character who moved blandly within school social circles, seldom bragging of his Special Gift. He's not beautiful, I thought. But he had what the girls wanted, and size was what counted. Archie said so. Jerry agreed. They must have been right, I observed, because that was all the talent Richard possessed, and he had Teeny. I greeted them as they approached. "Hello, Richard, Teeny."

"Hello, guys," Richard said amiably. Teeny spoke to us and waved to Jerry, who returned the gesture and remained in his chair. "Playing a little pool?" she said.

"Yep."

Teeny's tiny bulges made her a fascinating girl to watch. But her tiny giggles may have been the real reason for her nickname. She was a cheerleader, of course, whose tinny squeals had inspired many a Davis County gridiron warrior. I'd heard rats make similar sounds when they were frightened. Or maybe birds. South American birds. "Who's winning?" she cheeped. "Jerry?"

Archie stuck his chest out and elbowed me aside. "I am," he said. "I always do."

"Poor Jerry," she chirped.

Archie tapped his cue stick into the palm of one hand. His chest swelled. His nostrils flared. "I'll teach him how to play, Teeny, if you want me to," he said graciously. "Don't worry. With my help, he'll learn."

"Are you that good?"

"Sure I am. Just ask. Jack?" Archie crooked a finger and motioned for me to come nearer. "Tell her, Jack."

I did. "Sure, Teeny," I said. "He's so good we genuflect and beg to stroke his big stick after every shot. We're gonna set him up a game with Willie Mosconi. And after he's dead, which won't be long, I suspect, we plan to have his head shrunk down to half-size so we can use it for bowling. "

Archie growled. Teeny Parakeet snickered. "Where are you boys going after you finish your pool game?" she asked. "Maybe a little sight-seeing trip, huh, Archie?" She looked at him. "Maybe out to the gravel pit, huh?"

Archie sputtered as though he had experienced a seizure.

Teeny continued, "What is your mama gonna think when she hears?"

Richard and Teeny sniggered and held on to each other all the way to the lunch counter, glancing over their shoulders as they went. "Damn!" Archie hissed.

I turned to resume the game, then noticed that Jerry had risen from his chair and was staring intently toward the café's front door. Chief Hancock. And where Chief Hancock lurked, Coach Murray was generally found as well. I grabbed my crotch protectively and circled the table. "Some of them hot-hot hot tamales, Mary," the Chief called after he was seated. We listened intently. "Lots of them hot peppers on the side, too. You know how I like 'em."

Hot-hot hot tamales. One of Mary's specialties. I had tried them, but they burned worse coming out than they did going down.

As we continued our game while nervously watching the front door for any sign of the coach, it was soon apparent that Coach Murray had made other plans this evening. I could guess what they were, too. In a while we relaxed and returned to the useless chatter that was the norm. Soon after, the Chief left and Richard and Teeny rose to leave as well. They had reached the door, ignoring the wrathful gaze of Jerry Bass, when Richard, all smiles, turned and walked back in our direction.

"Imagine if Coach Murray hears that rumor!" he said before reaching us. "He'll probably get so mad he'll cut your nuts off!"

Archie and I eyed each other

"So don't repeat it," I suggested to him. "Just keep it to yourself, Richard."

"Won't do any good. It's all over town already. Heck, it was Mr. Peabody at the court house that told me."

"Damn! He knows everybody in town!"

"Yep." Richard turned to go, then thought of something that made his face break into a wide grin. He sidled back, close to us, and looked around before speaking. "Did you guys get to see Sabrina?" he said confidentially. "At the fair?"

Archie and I glanced at each other. "No," I said. "We didn't even go. Somebody said it was the same old rides and things."

"It was. Except for Sabrina. Of the Sultan's harem. Man! What a body! What talent! I have never seen anything like that, guys!"

"What did she do?" we asked eagerly.

"Man!" Richard looked around again before whispering, "She could squirt a Ping-Pong ball all the way across the tent! It was wild!"

"Great gobs!" Archie nearly shouted. "From her...?"

"Yeah. Right out of there, like a rocket!"

"How?" I asked.

"Muscles. Air? I don't know. But she was great! I caught one of the balls, too. Got it at home. Don't smell no more, though."

"Wow!"

"Too bad you boys missed it. Maybe she'll be back next year. You guys gotta see her!" Richard waved as he left. "Stay outta the pit at night!" he chuckled as he went through the door.

We informed Jerry that Richard was headed for the pit with Teeny for a little recreation, then told him about Sabrina and her remarkable talent. Jerry grieved for a while over the loss of "his" girlfriend, but, like Archie and me, his words soon suggested that he was more preoccupied with certain innovations that were a part of the Davis County Fair than with blonde cheerleaders. Soon we circled our pool table talking only of Sabrina of the Sultan's harem and her amazing ability to launch a Ping-Pong ball without a racket.

"How does she do it?" Archie fretted. "Are they regular Ping-Pong balls? Does she have any of her clothes on? How many does she stick in there at once? Does she have to reload? I gotta see this for myself."

"We'll have to wait until next year," Jerry moaned. "Fair's over."

"No, it's not," Archie said.

"For all practical purposes, the fair is over, Arch," I said. "This is Saturday. It's Colored night."

"I'll bet Sabrina still puts on her act tonight, though."

"Archie," Jerry said patiently, "like Jack said. It's Colored night. White people can't go to the fair on their night."

"I know that. But I bet they wouldn't mind if three white boys came by, just for a little while. Just to say hello to Sabrina."

"Well, this is one white boy that ain't going to the fair on Saturday night," I said. "I'm highly devoted to all this white skin, and I don't want it mutilated by a cheering mob of big black men wielding switchblades and straight razors."

"Wonder how she does it? Air? Big muscles? Bet she has a hell of a set of muscles down there! We could see them ALL, too."

"How would you like that to be your last view of female anatomy?" I asked. "It's too risky. Haven't your crazy ideas got us in enough trouble already anyway?"

"Billy Pryor and Andy Sullivan went down on Saturday night one time," Jerry said, "and nobody bothered them."

"No!" I said. "Count me out."

Archie took his cue from Jerry. There was a wild glint in his eyes. "Let's do it, Jerry," he said. "Let's go!"

Faced with making a choice, Jerry wavered. "I don't know, Arch."

"This is the last night. The girls are always the wildest on the last night. Sabrina will be popping them balls out like a machine gun."

"I don't know..."

"Wonder if she can aim the thing? Wonder if we could catch us one of them Ping-Pong balls!"

"That WOULD be something," Jerry said. He hesitated a moment and looked over at me where I cowered against a wall. "Let's do it, Jack," he said eagerly. "Let's go up there and see Sabrina!"

"Not me! I gotta go home. Willie awaits me."

"Would you go if you knew it was okay?" Archie asked. "If someone who really knows said it was okay?"

"There ain't nobody I know who could guarantee that."

"Boy!" Archie shouted as the old colored man trudged toward the small kitchen with an armload of dishes. "Boy, come over here for just a minute, will you?"

Mama's Boy continued toward the kitchen, but when he emerged in a moment he came directly to our table. His gait was unhurried and shuffling, his thin black face friendly and innocent. The Boy confronted life at a leisurely plod that included frequent pauses for procrastination. He was Mary's most reliable and trusted employee. If required to do so, Mary would have shared her fortune less begrudgingly with him than with any other person in town.

"Boy, we want to go to the fair tonight," Archie said, leaning on his stick. "But, you know." He glanced at Jerry and me for encouragement. "It's not our night tonight. Do you think anybody would say anything if we went? We wouldn't stay long, just long enough to see one show. What do you think?"

"Well...," The Boy straightened himself and looked down his nose at Archie as he considered the question. He hooked his thumbs into his pockets. "Well, Mr. Archie, it is Saturday night," he drawled, "and that's our night, you know. You white folks just let us have one night."

"But we won't be but a minute, and we'll be gone."

"It ain't that nobody would get mad," the Boy continued, "it's what's right. We don't go to the fair on other nights. We just get Saturday night. And still, there's some white folks come then anyhow. Do you think that's right?"

"Some white folks go on Saturday nights?"

"Ever now and then."

"So nobody would say anything to us, then? Nobody would start a fight with us?"

"Colored folks ain't like white folks, Mr. Archie," the Boy continued. "Long's you let us be, we ain't gone cause no trouble. Colored folks got 'nough misery without gone out and looking for more."

"Thanks, Boy," Archie said as he patted the Boy on the back. The Boy turned and shuffled away, but glanced over his shoulder as he ambled away. His lips were drawn, if not in anger, something near to it. Resentment, I thought. His frown made me feel sorry that we'd bothered him.

"There," Archie said triumphantly after Mama's Boy was out of earshot, "the expert has spoken. We can go to the fair and check out the Ping-Pong balls."

"That's one man's opinion, Archie," I argued. "You can never tell what will happen."

"You're just chicken-shit, Jack." Archie sank the eight ball to win another game, then nonchalantly tossed his stick atop the table. "Let's do it. Let's go see Sabrina. How about it, Jerry?"

"Sounds like fun." Jerry placed his stick in the wall rack. "I like the element of risk. I'll carry my twenty-two, just in case. It's in the Chevy."

My own weapon had gnawed a raw spot on my pelvic bone. And I could feel a rash developing around the elastic edges of the jock strap. "There'll be five thousand people there!" I clamored. "You're gonna defend us with six bullets?"

"Come on, chicken," Archie taunted, "We won't even need a gun. Nothing's gonna happen."

I thought of Cherokee Rose, of its darkness, and glanced to the stool recently vacated by Chief Hancock. Coach Murray was somewhere out there, maybe waiting behind that hedgerow along the sidewalk. Wouldn't I be safer with my friends? The thought of walking home alone made me shiver. I would rather face all those irate colored people at the fair than one Coach Murray.

Jerry and Archie paid for their games and pulled on their jackets. I likewise anted up.

We climbed into the Chevy and turned north toward Milldale. Overhead the sky had turned dark, and a chill wind blew out of the northwest, bringing to mind a line from Poe: "It was night in the lonesome October, Of my most immemorial year." I wondered if Poe had died the same year he wrote those lines.

I am a lot like Uncle Jim, I thought, just like Linda said. Not a back-sliding alcoholic, though. No, a back-sliding nit-wit. I was even neglecting my pal, Willie, tonight. The chill wind shook the car, and I shivered. I'd make it up to Willie. If I survived.

CHAPTER 13
SABRINA OF THE SULTAN'S HAREM

T HE MILLDALE FAIRGROUND was a long, very gently slop-
ing field of some thirty acres that was grassy in the spring
and early summer, worn and dusty or soggy by fall and winter.
Not only was the facility used for the annual carnival, but also for
a variety of sporting events that included baseball, softball, volley-
ball, and football, and sometimes the hosting of statewide sporting and cultural events. The grounds were tonight, as a
consequence of several days with little rain, barren and dusty.

Cars lined the fence surrounding the festivities this evening,
an assortment of vehicles typical of tonight's con-
stituency—Fords without headlights, Chevrolets without
bumpers or fenders, Plymouths with cardboard windows. They
were packed into a parking lot near the main entrance gate. Jerry
parked the Chevy in a space at its rear, and we sat for a moment
gathering courage and evaluating our odds of survival.

"Nothing but colored people," Jerry said as we watched a group
of children chattering happily as they raced for the gate. "Not a
white person in sight."

"What'd you expect?" I said. "No other white people are dumb
enough to be here tonight."

"We'll probably know a lot of them," Archie insisted. "We
probably have some friends here. Nobody will mess with us."

"We need to write those words down and leave them here in
the car, Archie," I said, "so the newspaper can include them in your
obituary."

Jerry pushed the pistol into his waist belt and pulled his shirt over its butt. "Just in case," he said. "Let's go, men."

"Sabrina, baby, here we come!" Archie giggled.

The white ticket seller at the gate eyed us with surprise from within the hollow of his booth. He shifted to peer at the sea of dark faces beyond the gate as though checking to be certain, then turned to us with a shake of his head. His eyebrows raised in warning. "Saturday night, boys," he said, one finger poised upon the quarter Jerry had placed before him. "Don't you know it's Colored night?"

"Yes, sir," Archie said from around Jerry's shoulder. "We won't be but a minute. Can you direct us to Sabrina?"

"Oh," the man said with a knowing grunt. "Sabrina. So that's it. You three came to see Sabrina."

"Yes, sir."

"You know what you're doing, then?"

"Yes, sir."

"Well," he said, his head tilted toward us, "If I were you, I wouldn't tarry too long. Wouldn't stay too late. Go see the girls, then leave. One of these bucks gets too much liquor in him, and you might wish you'd stayed home."

"We can handle ourselves," Jerry countered.

"Maybe we ought to listen to the man," I called from my position in the rear.

The ticket seller leaned from his booth and pointed. "The sideshow with Sabrina is on the far side. You'll recognize it. If I were you, I'd walk near the fence and stay out of the midway until you're close to her tent. Then just cut through."

The ticket sellers' advice was worthwhile, for there were few people standing or walking beside the fence. Our way was clear. We stumbled in the semi-darkness, Jerry and Archie joking as we hurried along. The sky was bright overhead, raucous music blared from tents and whirling contraptions, and there was the smell of pronto pups and cotton candy. We braced against the chill in the wind. My spirits began to rise as the few colored faces of which we had momentary inspection seemed unconcerned with our presence.

Her tent was large, held tautly in place by ropes tethered to iron spikes. We spotted it across the midway as we approached from our position alongside the fence. Colorful paintings of veiled women wearing transparent gowns of red and yellow adorned the sides and front of the canvas. A flag of red stood out stiffly in the breeze from a short pole at the peaked crown of the structure. Above an entrance blocked within by a broad flap were the welcoming words, "See the Women of the Eastern World! Watch as They Perform Amazing Feats! Only 25 Cents Admission!"

"There it is!" Archie whispered. "Sabrina, here we come!"

A virtual rolling sea of dark heads jammed the midway between the tent and us. "Just act normal," Jerry advised as he headed into the stream of humanity. I adjusted my crotch one more time, then followed Archie into the crush of movement. We were jostled and even given some hard looks as we wiggled our way across the midway, but no one seemed inclined to question our presence.

A tall, mustached white man guarded the entrance to Sabrina's tent, from within which came a flow of soft oriental music. "You won't believe your eyes!" he bellowed. "Tickets are limited. The show's about to start! Step right up. Get your tickets right here!" A short line was queued before him.

"Direct from the Orient to the plains of Milldale, Mississippi," I said in awe. "The Sultan and his harem."

"Let's get on up there," Archie urged, and we fell in. In a moment Jerry and I had our tickets, and after swearing that Archie, too, was eighteen years old, we watched as he received his.

"Runt!" Jerry giggled. Archie smiled happily at the dig.

Inside was a bursting, boisterous, jovial crowd of colored males aged fifteen or less to ninety or more, all swaying with curiosity and anticipation before the heavy hemp rope that separated us from the chest-high stage floor. We squeezed our bodies among them, amidst scorching foul breaths issuing from mouths recently clamped about onion-laden fare, and gradually worked ourselves toward the front center of the mob. "Easy," I warned. "Don't make anybody mad."

"But I can't see from back here," Archie whispered. Then, as courteously as one could expect, he requested passage from each of the audience who blocked his way. To my surprise, they seemed willing to accommodate his bold inquiries. Jerry and I followed, and were rewarded with good vantage points with which to view activities once they began. "You are a fool, Archie," I whispered to him once we were stationary. "I predict you will go completely bald, but in no natural manner."

An oriental drum rolled, and the ticket-taker-now-Master-of-Ceremonies appeared. "Gentlemen," he called, "from the Sahara Desert...," and with a handsome flourish of hands he stepped away from the parting drapes behind... "Sabrina and her entourage!"

Eagerly we all pushed forward as the curtains parted. An awed silence fell over us as a fat white woman dressed in a transparent gown and covered with sparkling costume jewelry emerged. Gown, veil, and jewelry failed to hide her dark panties and brassiere, which in turn failed to disguise the rolls of fat that wrinkled and winked with every gyration she made to the accompaniment of an oriental tune. Her thick makeup had melted from the exposure endured during earlier performances, her eyes were black orifices from which an occasional glint of reflected light suggested life at the bottom of the pits. The crowd fell back as eagerly as it had leaned forward.

"Damn!" Jerry cried. "I seen better looking women in coffins!"

"Sabrina?" I said. "Oriental? She looks American. Redneck American." Then I added defensively, "She's gotta be a Yankee, though. No Mississippi girl ever looked that bad."

"Sabrina must come on next," Archie said hopefully.

I thought it an act of kindness that the fat girl ended her performance without removing her clothes. Immediately another fat woman slithered from the gap in the curtains and began a similar dance. A very slight improvement, she removed her gown to display bull's-eye patches on her breasts and a triangular patch of black cloth between her thighs. The crowd grew restless then, and there were mutterings of "She a haint," and "Bring on that Ping-Pong gull." Archie joined in a couple of times, yelling, "We-want-Sabrina! Bring-on-Sabrina!" Jerry and I tried to shut him up, but he paid us no attention. "Bring on them Ping-Pongs!" he yelled.

"Maybe Sabrina got sick," Jerry ventured. "Maybe she tried to shoot a ball too far and broke something."

The crowd was inspired to sigh as the second lady bounced heavily from the stage. After a spattering of applause, all of them grew quiet. Some of them have seen this before, I observed.

Oriental music of a more provocative nature ushered bare toes and a slim ankle from the drapes, and soon a long, smooth, bare leg followed. The deliciously tan leg wiggled and twisted to the music. "Sabrina!" Archie hissed.

"Sabrina! Queen of the Sultan's harem!" the MC suddenly bellowed from his perch beside the stage. "Crown jewel of Persia!"

She slipped seductively from the curtains, eyelashes fluttering above a transparent veil, hips fluidly rotating. The slant of her eyes, whether a product of genetics or of mascara, conveyed what I considered the first evidence that these were truly "Far-Eastern" girls. Arms held high, hands clasped over her head, Sabrina began to thrust her hips and breasts at the audience. First her breasts, then her hips, then her breasts again, all in time to the tinny beat of strange music. Her gown parted as she moved to reveal the now-familiar bull's-eyes and triangular patch that covered her small breasts and hypnotic pelvis. Though Sabrina had obviously not missed too many meals, compared to the previous dancers her body was emaciated.

"Wow," Jerry whispered, "she's something else."

"I'm in lust," Archie groaned.

"She's positively lewd," I cried. "I love her!"

The crowd cheered wildly as Sabrina began to remove the trifling bit of gaudy cloth she wore. First the gown, then a bull's-eye at a time, and finally the patch lay at her feet on the wooden stage, all discarded to the mesmerizing rhythm of oriental strings. Bare except for a garish belt that encircled her waist, Sabrina then sat gracefully in the center of the rough wooden stage upon a beach towel delivered there by the MC, who also placed a bowl containing a number of Ping-Pong balls near one knee. A hush fell upon the entranced observers. "Look at that thing!" Archie whispered excitedly, pointing. He didn't have to prompt us. Jerry and I couldn't keep our eyes off it.

The music faded as Sabrina smiled into the crowd, looking from one man to another, enjoying the lust and desire and insane cravings that were evident on fifty or sixty faces. With her dark hair and skin, she reminded me of a Lebanese girl who attended our school. I wondered for an instant if the schoolgirl would look that good with her clothes off.

At the sound of another oriental drum roll Sabrina raised and spread her knees, ankles entwined, and leaned backward to rest on one palm. With an eye on the crowd, she ran her tongue along the inside of her free hand, then, fingers glistening, used it to pluck a Ping-Pong ball from the bowl. She fondled it with her lips, kissed it, licked it until it was wet, all while eyeing the eager faces before her, winning groans from collective throats, and then, daintily, with two fingers and her thumb, placed the moist white ball amidst the thick, dark hair of her pelvis. In an instant, it was gone.

"Wow!" Jerry said. "Just slurped it right up!"

"Get ready!" Archie gibbered wildly.

As the drum roll swelled, Sabrina again surveyed her audience, finally squinting and nodding slightly at a fan who stood far in the rear. She seemed to draw air into her plump belly, which extended even farther as she stretched, until it appeared taut and hard. Both palms now propped her lengthening body as she inhaled and concentrated on her objective. The drum roll intensified. A tense hush came over us all. Not another sound was heard. Her eyelids fluttered. Her round belly shuddered and went flat. There was a resounding hollow "thwop!" The missile was launched!

"She CAN aim the thing!" I cried in amazement.

The Ping-Pong ball exploded from the talented lady's woolly innards and sailed in a long, patient arc to our rear. There were sounds of a frantic scuffle as patrons fought for the projectile. Meanwhile Sabrina cocked her weapon for another barrage, and in a moment another missile was being eagerly pursued by souvenir hunters. "That's the damnedest thing I ever saw," Jerry said admiringly. "How does she do it?"

"She musta practiced for years," Archie said. "Since she was a little princess."

Sabrina proved to be a crowd pleaser. With each drum roll her fans became more enthusiastic, cries of "Over here!" and "Gimme one" filling the gaps between firings. And she was an excellent markswoman. With each shout she did her best to comply with a shot in that direction, her eyes following the course of each ball, after which she would giggle with happiness at whoever's good fortune. Then she would reload and fire again. As she worked, the tent became even more uncomfortably warm, and uncomfortably smelly. Beads of perspiration ran along Sabrina's pulsing stomach and from the hot foreheads of each of her devotees. We wouldn't tolerate this steam oven under any other circumstance, I thought. But nobody's doing any complaining right now!

We watched, enraptured, as shots were fired at a dizzying pace. The bowl of balls was being emptied. "I gotta have me one of them balls!" Archie whispered as he frantically waved in a vain attempt to catch Sabrina's eye.

"I'll get you one," I said.

"How?"

"I'm taller and a helluva lot better-looking than you are," I said. "She'll see me. You watch."

So I stuck my hand high in the air and motioned wildly. Only two or three balls remained in the bowl now. I shouted her name as my arms flapped, and, in a miracle of timing, caught her eye.

Immediately I held a forefinger over Archie's head and gestured furiously at his balding crown. "Right here, Sabrina!" I shouted. "Put one right here!"

She got the message. She grinned at Archie as she loaded the last projectile into her simmering cannon and took deliberate aim. "Get ready, Arch," I said. "Here it comes!"

Drool ran from Archie's lips and open mouth as he thought either of his prospective trophy or of the spot from which it was about to be hurled. Sabrina spread her knees for the coup de grace. She grinned at Archie. Her belly bulged, her pelvis protruded. Hair rose on end.

THWOP!

The final Ping-Pong ball hummed through the air, hurled in a short flat trajectory toward Archie's waiting fingertips. Jerry on one side, I on the other, watched as the ball zipped between Archie's clutching hands. Right into that wide-open mouth! I hoped.

But it struck him center temple. Then it whizzed away up and over and into a breathless crowd who cheered in appreciation of the finest shot of its kind that any had ever witnessed. Jerry and I rocked with laughter. Archie's expression was once again one of Mount Rushmore's presidents.

"Wild!" Jerry screamed.

"Too much!" I shouted.

As Archie stared, crestfallen, at the stage before him, Sabrina pushed upright from her beach towel, and with a wave, a smile, and a flaunting twitch of her rear, danced behind the waiting curtains. The crowd continued to howl and applaud for minutes after her disappearance, but Sabrina's act was over. We drifted with our comrades toward the exit and into the thronging midway, where we hesitated.

"Hit in the head with a Ping-Pong ball fired from you-know-where!" Jerry chortled. "Archie, you're gonna be famous when I tell everybody."

I added, "He was staring at the lady's thing so hard, I don't think he ever saw the ball."

"Right between the eyes!" Jerry chuckled.

"You better not say anything, Jerry," Archie warned. "I'll tell everybody about you-know-what."

"Damn!" I said as my stomach growled. "I'm so hungry I could eat a horse." The crowd, I observed, was paying no attention to the three white boys who had crashed their party. "Wonder if we could safely buy a pronto pup before we go? I ain't had a pronto pup since last year."

Warily scanning the midway, Jerry succumbed: "Reckon it's okay,"

Archie pointed across the way. "There's a food booth," he said. "I'm hungry, too. I don't think we'll even be noticed."

We struggled once again through the mob of fairgoers toward our destination, an open booth from which exuded the maddening odors of hot wieners and scorched corn meal. "Great!" I said, eyeing another booth when I had a mouthful of greasy dough and fat red wiener. "They have sauerkraut and sausage sandwiches over there at that next booth. Let's try one of them. Fried pork skins, too! Then I want something sweet."

So we had another sandwich and pigskins, followed by fried chicken legs that had a taste like charred rubber. "Damn!" Jerry grumbled as he spit chicken, "tastes like a damn inner tube. Well-done inner tube at that."

Archie wiped greasy hands on his jeans and looked around. "Time for desert," he said. "Peanut brittle." He pointed. "And maybe some cotton candy and popcorn."

"We're gonna be broke when we leave here," I said happily. "We'll have to put in some overtime next week."

We had now become cautiously seasoned to the unaccustomed environment of Saturday-night-at-the-fair, scarcely heeding the fact that except for the men who manned the rides and the various food and game booths, we were the only white people on the fairgrounds. When Jerry suggested that we try the whirling airplane ride, Archie and I agreed with little more than passing uneasiness. "Good god, I'm full!" Archie said as we were swept toward the airplanes by the disorderly crowd. "I wish I hadn't eaten that innertube chicken."

"I had my quota of grease for two months. Wish I hadn't ate that last cotton candy," I said, holding my stomach and crotch. I was sure to have a raw pelvis tomorrow.

"I ain't never gonna eat again," Jerry groaned as we bought our tickets and took our places in line. "I'll be ready to go after this."

"Me, too," Archie and I agreed.

Overhead, two small metal boxes hammered into the shape of tiny airplanes whirred at the ends of long, rotating steel beams. Frightened and delighted dark faces peered from the open windows of the crafts, their excited screams fading and rejoining with each revolution, their clutching hands pawing for equilibrium. People are fools, I thought as I watched from my position in line, for subjecting themselves to such punishment. And here am I.

Soon the ticket line shortened and Jerry and Archie were seated together in one of the tiny craft. As luck would have it, I had to wait until the next flight. In a way it was worth it, for the sight of my two friends twisting and turning, screaming at the top of their lungs, and waving to me when they weren't, was a spectacle to be placed into a permanent part of memory. Times like these were the fireside tales of tomorrow.

After their landing, they staggered on solid ground from their plane, laughing together and warning me of the horrors about to befall me. I brushed them aside with a boast of my superiority and slid across the metal seat of my craft as directed by the attendant. After scooting in alongside me, a small colored boy and I were securely fastened by a steel chain across our waists. "Hi, kid," I greeted him. "How's it hanging?"

He looked puzzled for a moment, then answered, "Hi."

"Ready to fly?" I asked.

"I reckon so. What's your name?"

"Jack."

"I'm Deron."

Our airplane smelled of a metallic blend of grimy fingers and vile sweat, the consequence, I imagined, of terror, dribbling pronto pups, and an eternal absence of cleaning. Round bars welded above our heads were there for the obvious purpose of bracing ourselves; I vowed not to even so much as touch the filthy things. Must be a billion germs to the square inch, I thought. No telling what I'd catch.

The exterior of the plane had been gaily-painted reds and yellows at one time, though smudges and bare spots now obscured the original bright coating and attested to the years of human horror and excitement to which it had been subjected. As our craft was placed in orbit, I sat cross-armed and enjoyed the sight of the milling throngs below, while my companion gripped his brace and panted. "Don't worry, Deron," I shouted to my new friend, "we won't fall."

But the sudden wild gyrations and gut-wrenching rotations made me wonder. I cursed at the need, but grabbed the round brace for support. My copilot and I were being forced from one side to the other, all the while being flipped and rolled and twirled, upside down one moment, on our sides the next. Faces below became a blur. The bright lights of the rides and booths, the Ferris wheel and the sideshows, spun around us at a dizzying pace, a kaleidoscope of smeared color and streaking arcs. Great fun, I thought for a few seconds. Almost nauseating. Nauseating? Yes. SICKENING.

Sickening! A knife of pain stabbed my stomach. My stomach began to draw itself into a large knot. Oh, no, I'm gonna be sick! I thought. All that greasy food! No! Not me!

But there was no stability for my eyes to fix upon, no permanence in this free-falling world that my grappling hands could seize upon to settle my roiling guts. Visions of greasy pig skins and slimy mustard-covered dough and deep-fried inner-tube... I needed a moment to focus, to calm...

"Stop the plane!" I shouted at the top of my lungs from my metal window. "Stop the goddamn plane!"

"Let me off!" I yelled with what was left of my strength. Now I was too weak to fight it. Get it out and feel better, I thought. My head hung foolishly from the window, the turbulent air whipping my dangling tongue against a spot worn bare by a thousand other tongues, and no doubt covered with a billion germs. I hardly cared.

There were two choices: My pistol-packing crotch, or the crowd below. An awful mess in my lap? Uh-uh. It would end up all over the inside of the plane and us. Would it evaporate before landing on the heads of all those squirming people below? Now was no time for physics. You all better move, I thought, staring down at the blurred images. Better dodge...

So, as demeaning the act and the admission, I made the dishonorable choice of emptying myself of pronto pups and peanut brittle into the unsuspecting swarm below. We whizzed along. They stared heavenward. Theirs were happy faces, pointing and laughing, enjoying their night out, unaware that they were about to be pelted with soggy bits of my last meal. I will be killed tonight, I thought. But if I survive, and after I've healed, I'll never do it again.

After the eruption, which must have settled in a wide arc around the speeding aircraft, I pulled my head back inside and wiped my mouth with a sleeve of my shirt. The contraption was slowing, beginning its descent. I had momentarily forgotten about my copilot, and now turned to offer apology and explanation. His eyes were wide in awe. "You fool white boy," he said pointedly.

"I couldn't help it, Deron," I said. "I didn't mean to."

"You puked all over ever-body."

"Yep. I had no control. I feel a lot better now. It was an accident. I can assure you, I'll never ride one of these things again."

"I'm gonna tell my mama."

"Now, wait, Deron," I croaked. "You don't want to do that." I had an instant mental image of Deron's mother shouting at me and pointing as I skulked away: There he is! That's the sorry white fool that puked on you all. Get him!

No way! I had to get away from here without being discovered! "Deron," I said, "give me five minutes head start. Okay?"

He lazily shook his head.

"They'll kill me!"

He nodded. "Theys ought to kill you, white boy."

"I'll give you a dollar." I dug frantically into my jeans pocket for my last dollar. We were almost to the ground. "Here. Five minutes. That's all I ask."

Deron reached for the bill and pulled it from my hand. "How long's five minutes?"

"Count to five hundred."

"I can only count to ten."

"Well, count to ten fifty times."

He was perplexed for a moment, then slowly nodded. "Where you live, Jack?" he asked.

"You think I'm gonna tell you? I wish I hadn't even told you my name. Forget we ever met, Deron."

Our airplane came to rest, and the metal door creaked as the attendant opened it. He looked at me in disgust, and was about to say something, but once the chain had been removed, Deron jumped out and I followed, immediately heading toward where I had left Archie and Jerry. They were nowhere to be seen. After a few anxious moments of scanning the crowded midway for a friendly white face and not finding one, I decided that my buddies must have gone on to the car. Probably left when they first saw what was happening overhead. Bastards. Some buddies.

The time required to say ten fifty-times was being rapidly expended as I searched fruitlessly for my cowardly pals. I finally put my head down and without making eye contact with anyone began what I hoped was a well-disguised sneak toward the safety of the fence line, not far away, but on the other side of a crowd probably fifty yards in breadth. As I crept along, striving to avoid bumping or shoving anyone, I heard mutterings nearby. "Das de one dat puked," I heard. And, "...oughta whip de bassid's ass," and even, "We get a rope, we hang the white mudder-fucker." Worst of all, one strong voice said loudly, "I'll cut de bassids balls off wit my switchblade!"

What was the likelihood that one would lose his virginity and his life on the same day? I wondered. Small, no doubt. Except among a few species of spiders. But my chances for survival were improving the quicker I covered territory. I hustled rapidly through the pressing herd of people, some of whom stood their ground in an apparent show of challenge. When that happened, I avoided a test of strength by the cowardly act of tip-toeing around. At this point, Smith pride was something to avoid think-ing about.

The midway was half traversed, and with each step I was gain-ing confidence, when without warning a strong hand gripped my arm. My arm halted, but my high-powered stride caused the rest of my body to whirl about. I was suddenly nose-to-nose with a man no taller than me, but twice as wide. He wasn't fat, either. "Where you going, white boy?" he asked, his dark face against mine. Do all of them call us 'white boy?' I wondered. "You in a hurry?"

"Yeah," I said, trying to pull back and away, "Gotta go. Gotta catch up with my buddies. They're right over there. Big Guys. Football players. Waiting on me."

He wore black pants and a black T-shirt. His hair was trimmed closely to his scalp, accentuating two surprisingly bright scars that ran from his forehead back as far as I could see. Knife wounds, I thought. That ain't good. But there was worse. On his shirt. Evi-dence of puke.

The supposed superiority of the white race was supposed to intimidate and strike fear into the heart of any colored man. Just a contemptuous look was supposed to do it. A gesture of author-ity always ensured it. I looked him over, head to foot, haughtiness in my every facial muscle. I glared arrogantly at his wide, flattened nose, his bulging lips. I showed disdain at his barrel chest and his large arms laden with muscle. He had beautiful, snowy-white teeth. Splendid teeth. They were grinning at me. "Gonna jus puke on everybody and leave?" he said. "Not even gonna say you sorry?"

He smelled of beer, and I was reminded of the words of the gatekeeper: "One of these bucks gets too much liquor in him, and you might wish you'd stayed home." Lord, I thought, I wish I'd stayed home.

"I didn't mean to puke on all you guys," I said. "Nobody would vomit on someone on purpose, would they? How about letting go of my arm?"

He swayed slightly, and stuck his free hand into a front pocket. He was not drunk, but he was feeling his liquor. "I don know," he said as he fumbled in his pocket. I looked about me and saw with escalating concern that every face in the crowd had beautiful, snowy-white, grinning teeth. "You puked on us," he continued, "and I gonna teach you a little lesson."

I watched in disbelief as his hand emerged from his pocket holding a large switchblade knife. A gasp from the jam of onlookers, who had quietly observed us until now, coincided with their rapid retreat to a distance several feet away. He and I were now surrounded by a packed throng of avid fight buffs who began a steady undertone of conversation. Probably making odds, I thought. And I can guess what they are: a hundred to one. "There's no need for that knife," I said, groping behind for an opening. "I'm leaving. Give me thirty seconds, and I'll never set foot in Milldale again. I'm giving up county fairs."

"Well, I gonna jus cut one of yo ears off fore you go, white boy," he said. "Get down on de ground. On yo knees."

Did he think I was crazy? "I don't think so," I said. I retreated as far as I could, almost until my back touched a solid wall of people.

Would only six bullets be enough to stop him? Could I get to my weapon? Could I unzip and drop my drawers in time? Would they laugh so hard when they saw it they'd slap me on the back and tell me I was a silly fool, then let me go?

Next time, I thought, I'll wear a better holster than a jock strap.

A wild run for it was my only chance. I readied for a leap away. But I had scarcely moved when my antagonist charged. I had time to brace myself, but when his shoulders hit me in the middle I doubled and rolled first into a forest of legs, then onto the dusty plains of the Milldale Fairgrounds. There was no escaping him. He was too strong. I was pinned to the ground.

I smelled dust. I tasted dust. Dust ground to fine talcum by a million plodding feet. From my position on my back, through a fine fog of dust suspended in the hazy light, I watched in horror as my straddling adversary pressed the button that released his blade. At the audible "click," he said, "Which ear you wanta keep, huh?" He grinned with his pretty teeth. "Lef or rat?"

"How about both?" I whined.

I had managed to get a hold on one of his wrists, and as he brought the knife down I grabbed the other. He was strong. Stronger than me, by a lot. I was about to lose an ear. Colored muscle: One. White superiority: Zip.

Behind me, over my head, I caught sight of the curious faces of those who watched, spellbound by the knife and my ear. Toothy grins abounded. But some faces were filled with horror. The good guys, I thought. They'll stop this. "Get this black bastard off me!" I shouted.

Immediately, I knew I had erred. Now all the faces had toothy grins. I shut my eyes and held him away with all the strength I possessed, then opened them wide at the shrill young voice of protest. Over my face, Deron's small hands pushed at the head of my opponent. "Don hurt him!" Deron cried. Tears streamed down his cheeks.

"Tell him, Deron," I panted. "Old pal."

"Don hurt him," Deron sobbed again, striking my adversary

upon his head as the two of us strained at each other. "He didn't mean to."

But Deron disappeared to the sounds of his mother's admonitions. I heard him struggling with her as he was dragged away. All over now, I thought. Good-bye, Deron. Good-bye, ear.

I tried to improve my position by turning to one side, but he was too powerful. My arms weakened, and the blade dropped nearer. Maybe, I thought as the end drew near, maybe Jerry and Archie will come and save me. Or maybe the guy was only kidding, and once he knows he can do it, he won't. Nobody really ever cuts off another person's ear.

The keen edge of the knife above my cheek, the beginning of a sawing motion that would make for a quick end to my ear, were persuasive clues that this nightmare would not end until my little flapper lay wrinkled and alone and gathering dust under all those feet.

But suddenly, the awed silence of the crowd was jolted by a feminine voice that shouted a command: "STOP IT, LEROY!"

Leroy stiffened. His arms relaxed a bit. And I had hope.

There was no doubt that Leroy recognized the voice behind the order. He turned his head to peer over his shoulder, and then, apparently confirming his suspicion, relaxed his arms even more. Leroy's girlfriend! I thought. God bless her!

"I'm scared you'll hurt him!" she continued, "Get up! Get up, Leroy!"

Leroy, of course, had heard this voice before. And, in the back of my mind, I knew I had, too. Recently. On a Thursday night. It was the way she said, "I'm scared... I'm scared you'll hurt him..." The last time I'd heard her say that, it had been, "I'm scared, Melville..."

Why I hadn't figured it out before now was a question that would later perplex me.

Leroy eased his body backward to sit more solidly on my stomach, but he kept the knife blade above my head. He turned to face Josephine Rossetti.

"I'm scared you'll hurt him, Leroy!" Josephine yelled again. "Get your ass off him! He's a friend of mine. And I mean, now!"

"Aw, Josephine," he whined. "Just an ear..."

"NOW! Don't you know they'll put you in jail?"

Framed against a dusty sky streaky and radiant from the bright lights all around, she stood over us, hands on her hips, a scowl on her face. Leroy glanced at me, then back to her, as though he hadn't made up his mind to obey. "Damn," he sighed as he folded his blade and looked down at me. "Yo one lucky white boy."

I pushed myself upright as he removed his rear from my chest, and began to beat the dust from my clothes. The eyes of the spectators were still on me, so I kept my own trained in the dirt.

When I finally got the courage to raise my head, I saw that Leroy had an arm around Josephine's waist. "I was not gonna cut his ear off," he was saying. "I just wanted to scare the bassid. He puked on me!"

"You don't cut somebody's ear off just because they have an accident," Josephine barked. "Anyway, you'll get into a lot of trouble if you hurt a white boy. Don't you know that?"

Leroy answered with a sullen, "No, I won't. I don care."

"You're a fool, Leroy. A drunken fool."

"But baby..."

"You go somewhere and sleep it off."

"Okay, baby. Okay." As he stumbled away, bristling, Leroy shot me a look that James Cagney would have died for.

The interest of the fight fans having returned to rides and sideshows, now that a good ear-cutting had been thwarted, they slowly disbursed. I looked around quickly for Deron, but he, too, had apparently been whisked away by his mother. Well, I thought. I'll remember Deron. One day I'll do him a favor, too. And now I'm getting the hell out of here. After I thank Josephine.

I wasn't particular anxious to face her. It's not a manly thing, to be saved from a beating by a girl. I felt like a first-class sissy. What must she think of me? A fool for being here on "their" night? A weakling for being so helpless? Josephine had seen me at my worst. I could sure forget about crossing the line now, though the knowledge that she was having an affair with a man of my own race made the thought that much more intriguing.

The dust was dry enough that it disappeared from my clothes under the beating I gave them. I straightened my hair and, despite the instinctual desire to run like mad, wobbled toward where Josephine stood without expression, regarding me through the marching columns. She wore a white turtleneck sweater and red skirt, glossy white shoes, and gold jewelry more flattering to her than it would have been to a movie star. Arms hanging loosely at her sides, she reminded me of a queen mingling with her subjects. Her dark hair had been washed and curled, and it tumbled down upon her neck and shoulders in fluffy ringlets. She looked clean and fresh, and that made me yearn likewise to rid myself of my dust and dirt. I probably smelled like vomit, too. "Thanks, Josephine," I said when I was near her. "If you hadn't come along, I'd be minus an ear."

"I don't know why I stopped him," she said icily. "I should have asked him to cut both your ears off."

"Damn!" I said. "What did I do?"

"Why are you here? This is not your night. You have no right to be here."

"I know," I said, hanging my head. "I'm sorry."

"Why did you?" she demanded.

"Well, " I stammered, "it was a spur-of-the-moment thing. We didn't want to miss the fair. We talked to your grandfather."

She cocked her head in disbelief. "Grandfather said it was okay?"

"Not exactly."

Looking down her nose at me, she replied, "I thought so." I felt like a school kid being admonished by a teacher. "You are as big a fool as Leroy, Jack. But not fool enough to come up here alone. What other fools came with you?"

"Archie and Jerry." I looked around, halfway expecting to find them nearby. "I guess they cut for the car. Look, I'm sorry for the trouble I've caused you. I really appreciate the help, though."

She stamped her foot, causing a small cloud of dust to drift between us, but said nothing. Arms folded across her chest she stared expectantly at me. It took me a moment to understand why she was behaving so strangely. Then it dawned on me. She had heard Melba's tale!

"You should have let him cut my ear off," I said.

"Is that rumor about you and those other two true?"

"What rumor?"

"You know what rumor, damn it! You and the gravel pit. Thursday night!"

"The pit?"

"You son of a bitch!"

We backed away from each other, she in hostility, me in surprise. Why was she so upset?

Of course! Josephine probably thought we'd seen her with Coach Murray that night! But hadn't Coach Murray told her about our little ride, and our oaths to the contrary? Didn't he tell her that we hadn't mentioned a colored girl?

"Damn you, tell me the truth!" she cried.

I hesitated for only a moment. I was the only one who had seen her. Jerry and Archie had been too far back in the woods to be able to make out her hand and arm. Her secret was safe with me. And there was no harm in telling her so. Was there? "I won't ever tell anybody about that night, Josephine," I said. "Nobody will ever know."

"Damn you! Half the town ALREADY knows!"

"I never told anybody, Josephine."

Josephine hadn't been mad before. Now, I discovered, she was MAD. As her face hardened and her fists clenched, I decided I preferred facing Leroy to her. "You son of a bitch!" she barked. "Where are those other two sneaky bastards?"

"In the car. The parking lot."

She had become an avenging devil. "You go out there and tell them to wait! I want to tell them, just like I'm telling you. You better not mention my name to ANYBODY!"

"I'm not, I'm not," I began.

"Just shut up!"

"But Josephine..."

"You shut up, or I'll scream bloody murder!" she yelled. "And then they won't stop with just your ears!"

People were already staring at me with what could hardly be described as sympathy and understanding. I thought about all those rows of toothy mouths that had a little while ago been anticipating the severing of my body parts. I never wanted to see a scene like that again. Rather than risk saying a word and ending my chances for survival, I merely nodded to Josephine. "Tell them to wait for me!" she shouted as she wheeled and disappeared into the mob of people.

I returned the gatekeeper's wave and a moment later found Jerry and Archie seated in the Chevy. Their eyes, darting and staring round and anxiously over the dashboard of the car, reminded me of the sand crabs Uncle Jim and I had watched on the beach at Biloxi once. "He's alive!" Archie yelled as I walked up. "He escaped!"

"It's a miracle!" Jerry said. "What took you so long?"

I certainly didn't want to admit the truth. So I said, "I went back to visit Sabrina. Got a quickie. You guys should have hung around."

"Naw..."

Archie giggled, "We figured they had strung you up after you vomited all over everybody." He snickered under his breath. "But you got away okay? Definitely a miracle."

"Yep."

I pushed Archie aside and sat on the front seat as he hung his head and faked gagging. "You stink like... What is it Jerry?" he said gleefully. "Day-old goat turd? Or is that curdled pronto pup?"

"More like Willie after he's had a night out," Jerry snorted. He reached for the ignition key.

"Wait, Jerry. We've got to stay here a minute," I said.

Jerry paused. He and Archie looked at each other. "Are you out of your mind?" Archie asked. "Why? Did you get into trouble? They after you? Or you gotta puke some more?" More snickering.

"No. A lady wants to talk to you two."

"A lady?" They looked at each other again. "What lady?"

"You'll see. Just wait."

Jerry let his hand drop from the ignition key, pulled his pistol from his waist, and dropped it on the seat beside him. I hung my elbow from the window and watched for any sign of Josephine. I planned to stop her before she let the world know. "Why did you two run off and leave me?" I asked.

"Hell, man," Jerry said, "they knew it was you. They were gonna beat you up."

"So you two were just going to let them? You had your gun, didn't you?"

"A twenty-two ain't too effective against five thousand people."

I turned to face them. "So you and Archie just left me? Do you think I would have run off and left you two?"

"Hell, yes!" they cried in unison.

"Well, that's all I wanted to know," I said. "And you're right. I would've left you."

"We've been sitting here talking," Archie said, "and we figured that what happened back there tonight would probably lead to prestige and glory for you. For sure, if they'd killed you, you would have been famous. But even though you got away, there's some glory to be culled."

"How you figure that?"

Archie managed to get into lecturing position, even in the center of the front seat of the Chevy. His fat red cheeks glowed. "The sheer numbers, Jack," he crowed. "How many people did you puke on? A hundred? A thousand? Whatever it is, it has to be a world record! We'll send it to Guiness, and..."

"Fuck you," I said.

"You'll be famous as Archie!" Jerry cackled. "Only man in the world who got shot between the eyes with a pussy-to-puss missile. Only man in the world to single-handedly puke on three thousand other people. At once. And I know them both!"

"Here she comes," I said, pointing to where Josephine Rossetti was walking briskly across the parking lot toward us. She was not alone. Leroy strutted along beside her.

"Josephine?" Archie said. "I thought you said a 'lady'. Who's that with her?"

"Her bodyguard," I said as I jumped out of the Chevy. "Better keep your weapon handy."

Before I reached her, Josephine angrily shook her finger at me. "Just go on back to the car, Jack," she yelled. "I'm not saying this but once, and I'll tell all three of you together."

"But Josephine," I shouted, "I need to talk to you! Alone!"

Leroy snarled when he saw me. "You heard her!" he bellowed as he took several steps toward me. I angled away. As Josephine continued toward the Chevy he yelled, "She say it was okay to cut yo damn ear off now!"

"But Josephine!" I yelled again, "they don't know!"

Leroy charged, and I burned shoe leather maneuvering away from him. He rushed again, and I retreated still further. Then, apparently satisfied with the distance between his "girlfriend" and me, he trotted quickly to her side and resumed his march. "I've got to talk to you, Josephine!" I shouted from a hundred feet away.

Whether she did not hear, or thought I was lying, or was so upset that she wouldn't listen, she ignored me. By the time I had tip-toed back to a position near the car, on my guard lest Leroy charge again, Josephine was threatening Archie and Jerry with all manner of hell if they disclosed to anyone a secret of which they weren't even aware. "Don't you tell another soul about that night at the gravel pit!" she screamed. "If you do, Leroy here will make you wish you hadn't! Right, Leroy?"

Leroy nodded dumbly.

"If anybody asks you who you saw, you better not mention any names! You hear me?"

Archie and Jerry nodded dumbly.

"Bastards! No good bastards!"

On his toes, fists held chest-high, dancing left one second, right the next, Leroy hopscotched a warrior's minuet conducted to the rhythm of Josephine's words. But the look on his face was one of bewilderment. He was ready to defend the woman of his dreams, though he wasn't sure when or why he should begin. Archie and Jerry shifted their gaze from Josephine to Leroy, back and forth, wide-eyed, precisely like those eye-swiveling sand crabs. I could have laughed out loud, except that everybody would have known I'd finally lost it. So I leaned against a fender and maintained a watchful eye on Leroy.

Into the open window of the Chevy Josephine emptied her lovely mouth of its entire vocabulary of nasty words, while Jerry and Archie sat dumbfounded and listened. She straightened after a minute, then shook her fist in Archie's face. "You little faggot," she shrieked. "You're the most low-class of all. You and your big mouth!"

Archie cringed. Jerry, too. Me, too. Even Leroy cringed. None of us had ever seen Josephine behave like this. She was, I observed, Donna Reed's face and body, with King Kong trapped inside. I definitely preferred Leroy in a fight to the death. After a few more hisses at Archie, she spun around and stalked away. That caught Leroy, who was still dancing his minuet, by surprise. He dashed after her, then turned and dashed back to the Chevy. "Yo better not tell nobody," he said fiercely. He raced away for good.

The three of us watched silently for a moment as the two brawlers stalked away. I opened a door and crawled into the back seat of the Chevy. I had never been so tired in my entire life. "Let's go home," I said as I sprawled across the back seat, "before we get in more trouble."

"Good God!" Archie said. "I never knew Josephine could be such a bitch!"

"What the fuck was it all about?" Jerry asked as he cranked the Chevy and pulled to the road. "The girl is nuts!"

I listened from the rear seat cushion in a state of apathy, barely comprehending words, and caring little for what they said. "Don't you get it?" Archie was saying. "She was with Meatloaf that night at the pit! That was why Meatloaf wanted to know so bad if we saw who she was. He was at the pit with a COLORED girl, Jerry! An underage girl! Josephine! My god!"

"Hot damn!" Jerry shouted as his hands beat a rhythm on the steering wheel.

"An UNDERAGE COLORED girl," Archie continued. "If this gets out, Coach Murray will be the one moving to Alaska!"

"He won't be such a hard-ass after this, by god!"

"Hell, they might lynch him! Or at the least, run his ass out of town."

"We've got him now." Jerry beat the steering wheel with both hands. "He can't do anything to us! If we let this out, he'll be finished!"

Archie said slyly, "Let's use our heads. I got an idea."

"Yeah?"

"Yeah. Don't breathe a word of this to anybody, Jerry. Remember all that money he won from your dad? Well, there may be a way..."

When they woke me in the driveway of Cherokee Rose, I wanted to ask Archie if I could spend the night with him. But I had my pride. I went inside after they pulled away, unloaded my jock strap, checked the doors and windows, fed Willie a heaping mound of food, fell into my bed, and slept until dawn.

CHAPTER 14
MY TRUE LOVE

WILLIE RECEIVED AN extra helping for breakfast next morning. "Good boy," I told him as I sat in the backyard and scratched his ears. "Sorry I was so late feeding you last night. I'll go by Mr. Kosser's store and get you a soup bone to make up for it. Okay?"

Of course, that was fine with Willie. He and I lounged in the warm morning sun for nearly an hour, he with his thoughts of squirrels and bitches, me with mine of doom and humiliation. A few of the trees that were scattered across the grounds of Cherokee Rose had begun to sprinkle the yard with leaves, dotting the grassy lawn that had sprouted little since my last trimming. Winter is on its way, I thought absently. Another year, another universal milestone, another scene in life's relentless march toward death.

Thankfully, the damage done to my face and arms during the wild rush through the briars and saplings that grew along the slopes of the gravel pit was rapidly healing. The bruising had begun to fade, though the many thin lacerations and scrapes were still faintly evident. But I was pleased with my more or less rapid recovery. Even the formidable odor of our turpentine cleaning efforts had been reduced to a point of vagueness.

Josephine had saddled me with despondency. Those angry words of hers had peeled away the artificial layers of self-defense—the self-serving vindication and denials—that I had used to disregard my own corruption. Her words—those cursed blades of contempt!—had exposed me. Now I was repugnant and cheap in my own eyes. A low-life Peeping Tom. A liar. An adulterer. I even puked on people. I prayed Uncle Jim never learned of my sins.

Sprawled there in the warm grass, trying hard to justify behavior that was unforgivable, I found myself hungering once again for the comfort I'd found in the arms of Linda Murray. There, in that dark bedroom, after our breathing had slowed, I had found something for which I had been unconsciously searching: A peacefulness, a contentment I had never known and, I suspected, only two people who love each other could know. A warm, wet, delirious hideaway where fears and cares are suspended in time. An exclusive province secure from alcoholics and bullies. A snug domain where concern for the future did not exist. Josephine's opinion of me would be of little consequence if I were in bed with Linda this morning. Neither would the pending entry of my name into the "Gastronomical Curiosities" section of the Guinness Book of World Records. The physical act of making love was insulation from the real world, a private respite from mere existence. But, I was dismally aware, the spell was cast only from the moment you slipped beneath the covers until the moment you were forced to leave them.

The telephone rang, and I ran back inside to answer. My friend Archie returned my hello and asked what I had planned for the day. I had planned a brief trip to Paris for dinner and drinks this evening, I told him, but decided to cancel so that I could hang around and play a round of eight ball with my buddy. No, Archie said, he'd just called to tell me he had "things I gotta do around here. Come on over if you want to. It's safer over here."

"Barbara around?" I asked without thought to honor. "Does she bathe in the mornings, too?"

He said no, Barbara was visiting a girlfriend. So I declined the invitation. "Call me back if she comes in early," I told him. "Maybe I'll spend the night."

"Sure thing. I got some things to talk over with you anyway. Some plans."

"Like what? A plan to get Jerry's dad's money back?"

"I don't want to talk about it over the phone. Remember, this phone has ears. It can wait. By the way, I'm sorry about running off like that last night. It was Jerry's idea."

"Forget it," I said.

"Josephine was hell. What a bitch!"

"Yep."

"That was something, wasn't it?"

"Yep."

"Sabrina, I mean. Woman sure has a mean curve ball."

He'd already talked to Jerry, who also had some very important yard work planned. Yeah, sure, I thought as I hung up, any excuse to stay home where you're safe. I may be chicken, but I'm not by myself.

So I was faced with a lonesome Sunday. Maybe...

If Coach Murray's car was not in their driveway, maybe...

No, I shivered. I ain't brave enough to even call her, much less visit her at home. There was that invitation to cut the lawn, though...

Maybe later in the week.

Breakfast, then. Fried eggs and crisp salt pork, grits, and eight or ten of Mama Mary's huge brown biscuits, all coated with a thick layer of fresh country butter. Maybe a pancake or two drowned in a big puddle of black sorghum molasses. And some French toast. Doggone! I thought. I must be hungry! And what if Coach Murray happens by the cafe? I'd just shoot him, I decided, and finish my breakfast.

I saddled up in jock strap, pistol, and pants, pulled on a warm shirt, socks, and shoes, locked the front door behind me, and shouted for Willie. "Come on, old buddy," I told him when he rounded the corner of the house in his trademark three-legged gallop, "you can tarry outside the door and covet what you smell on my plate inside the cafe. If there's any left over, which I doubt, I'll bring it out for you. Ain't I good to you, boy?"

Willie, of course, once again agreed, and we strolled together toward the cafe. The breeze of yesterday had died down, the clouds had disappeared, and already the sun had warmed the sidewalks of Smith Station to a temperature approaching an invigorating comfortableness. Must be nearly sixty-five degrees already, I thought happily, and it'll get to seventy-five or eighty by mid-afternoon. Maybe I'll spend the afternoon lounging along the shore of Davis Lake. Maybe some of the girls will be water-skiing in short shorts or skimpy bathing suits. Willie would like an afternoon at the lake, too. Maybe there'll be a squirrel to make the afternoon interesting for him, or a bitch to make him crazy.

The cafe was nearly empty. Only one reprobate, a rascal no doubt miserable at his loss in a poker game of last evening, sat in a far corner loudly gulping his coffee. For, despite the wicked appeal of Mama Mary's gay music and the maddening aroma of her seasoned fried sausage, most of the people of Smith Station were sufficiently pious that Sunday mornings were generally reserved for family, Sunday School, and church. Only those of us of selfish and immoral persuasion ignored the Call of the Baptist Ladies and engaged in less demanding and more enjoyable entertainment on these reverent occasions. I, like my uncle, was aware of my eccentricity via my colorful ancestry, and of the accepted indulgence by the citizens of Smith Station of our heathen mania. The same irreligious behavior in those of lesser name was often viewed in an entirely different vein.

Willie took a seat outside, and Mama Mary waved me to a stool and took my order with an unusually serene and cheerful tranquility. Her mellow euphoria was reflected in the soft sound of the jukebox. Instead of Elvis pounding the walls with rock, Johnny Mathis and Pat Boone hummed tender love songs. "Nice," I said as I watched her cook and thought irresistibly of last Friday night. "Some mornings are made for love songs."

She wiped her lips with her all-purpose rag, smearing and then removing the powdery evidence of a taste-test from her prim mustache. "Suppose so," she drawled in her gravel voice, wisps of gray hair flying. "If I was sixteen again, I'd know damn well so."

Her spatula clicked and scraped about the hot grill in a metal-lic ceremony I knew by heart. "Shoot!" she said once. Her wrin-kled yellow cigarette drooped with ash as she turned to me and placed her elbows on the counter opposite me. She said, "You're looking more like your dad every day, Jack." A bare smile lit her face. "Hope you ain't the cut-up he was."

Aha! I thought. An opportunity to learn a little history. "What did he do that was so bad, Mama Mary?"

She thought for a minute. "Nothing I want to mention, Jack. He was just wild."

"Wild? That don't tell me much. I want something nice and juicy."

She grinned wickedly. "Uh-uh. Wouldn't do to tell."

"I wish he hadn't died so young. Tell me about that, Mama Mary."

She tapped her cheek with the butt of her smoke and glanced about the cafe. "It was a shame," she said, pushing away from the counter. "A real shame."

"He got sick right here in the café, didn't he?" I asked before she could get away. "Uncle Jim told me that. He died at home, though."

Without turning to me she said, "I really don't want to talk about it."

"He ate something that didn't agree with him."

"Toe-main," she mumbled. "Died. At home."

"They never did find out what he ate that caused the ptomaine, did they?"

Mama Mary's cheeks had reddened as she wheeled about. Her mellow euphoria had disappeared. "No, they didn't, Jack. Didn't Jim explain that to you?"

"Yes, ma'am. Some."

"Whatever it was spoiled he ate, Jack," she said frostily, "he didn't eat it here. I can tell you that. He had them hot tamales, with lots of peppers the way I fix 'em. He always liked them hot tamales, the hotter the better. But that ain't what killed him.

Twenty other folks had them tamales that day, and none of them got sick. You ask Doctor Blake. He tended your dad. He'll tell you. Ask him."

"I didn't mean..." I began. But Mary had stalked away.

A frigid silence ensued as she opened her freezer and removed several packages of frozen meat and vegetables. I squirmed, angry with myself that I had been so insensitive. "Sorry, Mama Mary," I said as she walked past. "I didn't mean anything."

A sigh indicated she had forgiven me as she paused to lean again on the counter opposite me. "I believe you. But didn't Jim tell you about it?"

"Sure. But he doesn't like to talk about it much, either."

"Good. It's better left alone."

Mary pulled the bent butt of her cigarette from between her lips so that she could speak more plainly. She must have wondered if I still had doubts about her innocence, for she continued, "Doctor Blake said Cherokee Jack could have ate something bad the day before."

"I know, Mama Mary. I'm sorry if you got the wrong idea."

"Your mama had some of them same tamales, but not so hot. She didn't get sick."

"Did she go home, too, when they helped my father get back to Cherokee Rose?"

"I think so."

"She didn't make it to the funeral."

Mary shook her head. "Nobody saw her after that day. Nobody knows what happened to her."

Which made me wonder again just how my mother got away without anybody noticing. "Were any of their cars missing next day?" I asked.

Mary shook her head "no," then, "How would I know? I never heard if there was."

"Then she must have met somebody else," I said, "and they left town together."

Mary tossed her head and almost lost her stub of roll-your-own. She grabbed it before it flew across the grill, then fumbled clumsily before clamping the stub between her teeth. She grunted, "There wasn't anybody else, Jack. Your mother was a good person. It's the men that are usually the skunks." She pulled at the remnant of butt, then held the dead scrap upright between two fingers. Tiny smears of white paper clung to her wrinkled upper and lower lips where the disintegrating wrapper had resisted her efforts.

I nodded. "I know you're right, Mama Mary."

A triumphant glow lit her face as she backed away and smashed the distorted fragment of cigarette on the concrete floor. "Ready for them eggs?"

As additional customers arrived, I ate breakfast in the muted clamor of a clicking spatula, cracking eggs, and conversation subdued by the Sabbath. I couldn't help but wonder where my mother might be. The Caribbean? Hollywood? Graveyard? Or murdered, quartered, and flung into an old cistern? Maybe Jim did it. Maybe he murdered her when he figured she poisoned his brother. I didn't really believe that. I felt I would never know exactly what happened. People were just too closed-mouthed, probably for good reason.

"Toe-main poisoning," I thought. Our "Encyclopedia Britannia" indicated the illness was caused not by "ptomaine," but by "botulism microorganisms." They could have lived in a can of spoiled beans. What an unromantic way for my father to die.

This was Willie's lucky day. My conversation with Mary, premonitions of disaster and scandal, and possibly the subtle fear that Coach Murray might suddenly appear, all combined to repress my appetite. A breakfast fit for Lassie was Willie's reward for guarding the door.

How best to tuck a thirty-eight into swim trunks? That was the question of the moment after Willie and I were home preparing for our trip to the lake. The prospect of being labeled "Muledick Smith" was not an unpleasant thought, though it soon became obvious after the gun was in that critical position that swim trunks had not the support of jeans. The barrel, the whole thing, jock strap and all, would tumble into view alongside other valuables at any immoderate stride. Experiments at various positions and angles failed to satisfy the need for both protection and confidentiality, and I finally decided to leave the pistol in the station wagon and trust that I could reach it quickly if I needed it. Surely the coach wouldn't visit Lake Davis today. But what about Linda and the kids? The prospect was stimulating.

Old Grandfather clock was striking eleven when Willie and I left the driveway of Cherokee Rose and headed south toward Lake Davis. Willie road the suicide seat with his head hung from his window, barking at every movement along the streets and highway of our route. I made no effort to curb his rowdy behavior; this was to be a day strictly for our relaxation and enjoyment. How better to cheer an old dog than to put the wind in his face and consent to his howls of pleasure?

There was one stop I wanted to make before going on to the lake, one I had put off for some time, and Sunday was the right day for it. When we neared the arched wrought-iron gate that led into the Smith Station Cemetery, I slowed and turned into the gravel road that wound its way up and down the shallow slopes of the graveyard. Our family plot occupied a prominent position near the center of the grounds, its vaults and stones rising above the enclosing iron fence. Several generations of my ancestors resided here, and there was room for more. The Smiths planned for the future.

While Willie bounded from stone to stone engaged in a frenzied whirlwind of awkward territorial marking that would have horrified the Baptist Ladies, I approached the gravestone that marked the spot where my father's remains were lain to rest. Cherokee Jack's stone was identified not by his alias, but by the name given him at birth: Jefferson Jackson Smith. Beneath were the dates of his life: 1919—1942. The rest of the large headstone contained the usual hopeful rhetoric, a verse from the scriptures, and a worn "Gone-But-Not-Forgotten." Tiny angels haloed the perimeter. I stood before the marker and suffered the usual depression that comes with the regret and the silent wishes for what might have been. I was alone. Alone now, alone, it seemed, despite my uncle, for all my life. The bright morning sun was no cheer. I was alone. After a few minutes reflection, I spoke to my father:

"Who are you? Are you really my father?'

There was nothing to indicate that my words had stirred him to response. No sudden breeze. No cloud to hide the sun. The ground didn't shake.

"Don't you know I needed you?" I said. "For homework. For advice. To tell me how best to find and screw girls. Just to be there?"

I waited for a reply and got none.

"You went and died on me. You'll never be able to tell me the truth about my mother. I'll never forgive you for that, dad."

Graveyards are most always quiet. They can be located near a highway or a steel yard or an apartment complex, but they always have a special stillness about them that commands at least some respect, even from the least devout among us. The psychological chill that comes with entrapment within a cemetery's iron boundaries gripped me now, and with a shiver that was fear and remorse, but not true repentance, I continued, "Sorry, dad. If you are dad. I know this was not the way you intended things." I turned to go to the wagon. "Have a good day," I called over my shoulder. "See you next trip."

Lake Davis was a man-made lake of approximately one-hundred-fifty acres, an algae-laden, stump-filled, drab pool of green water trapped by tree-covered hills on three sides, and a dirt levee on the other. A gravel road traversed about one half its perimeter, its course intersected often by gravel turnouts to the waterline. The remaining shoreline was frequented only by those willing to hoof it, a complication that increased its appeal to the younger crowd. Generally, they could walk a hundred yards, more or less, along a tree-studded trail that began at the end of the access road, and find sanctuary from parents, adults, and peers.

I visited here often; the spot I usually chose for lounging and napping in the sun was frequently selected by others as well. "Bare Butt Cove," as some youthful bard had christened it, was something of a teenagers' watering hole. Several hundred yards from road's end, pines, oaks, dogwoods, magnolias, sweet gums, sycamores, and a variety of similar species of trees shielded the small hollow from anyone traversing the walking trail. Yet it was quite visible from the lake, and the hooked-arm channel that permitted access to the main body of water was a favorite of those of us who spent much of each summer fishing, skiing, and swimming its murky depths. After sunset, because of its unique advantages, Bare Butt Cove was often exploited in the name of love. Archie's ideas regarding the endurance of the average pair of panties were possibly inspired by his perceptive observations in this hollow, for a torn pair drooping from a tree branch was not an unusual sight.

After shoving my pistol under the front seat of the station wagon, I grabbed my towel and called Willie. Together we followed the worn path through the woods until we reached the less obvious trail that meandered farther and ended finally on a slight ridge overlooking BBC. As most of Smith's Station's residents were either still in Sunday School or church, or were otherwise observing the holy day, the hollow was deserted when Willie and I reached it, and I was able to select an advantageous knoll near the center to place my towel, remove my jeans and T-shirt, and stretch contentedly in the cool air and warm sunlight. Across the lake at the boat landing, another sacrilegious soul was launching his boat, and soon the buzz of an outboard motor added to the numbing influence of sunshine. A breeze whispered among the pine needles overhead. Nearby, a squirrel barked. Birds chirped noisily. My watchdog lay at my feet. The most delicious sense of relaxation I'd felt in a week dazed me, mind and body, and, as per plan, Willie and I were soon engrossed in that most pleasant of adventures, dozing and dreaming.

Trials and tribulations were forgotten. Reminiscences of wet kisses and damp skin were summoned. In a wandering coma I dreamed good dreams. I pined for Linda, and supposed she loved me, that she would leave her husband and come to live with me. We would stay awake together for hours every night, our bed trembling from the onslaught of our passion. I would eventually take Tommy and Barbara Ann for my own. Uncle Jim would approve. Coach would approve. Then both would conveniently disappear.

An hour passed. Two. The rattle of the solitary outboard motor was replaced by the churning of several. On more than one occasion, laughter and Willie's reliable barking marked the approach of newcomers to Bare Butt Cove. I was not so disturbed that I was completely revived, but each time I raised my body just enough to assure the harmlessness of the new arrivals, waved half-heartedly if I knew them, then returned to the drowsy rapture of sunlight and fantasy. This was ecstasy. And since home meant only loneliness and fear, I would, I decided, stay here in BBC all afternoon. And I might have done just that, contentedly snoozing and dreaming the day away, if Saxon Browne had not awakened me.

The persistent efforts as I lay dozing to recollect every detail of the night with Linda Murray must have addled my brain and stimulated the creation of dozens of curious mental images, each of which had two themes in common: nudity and sex. The fantasy being played inside my head at the moment Saxon bent to nudge my shoulder was centered between the comfortable thighs of Sabrina of the Sultan's Harem, and the difficulty she was experiencing with an encumbered Ping-Pong ball. Of course, I was always one to help a lady when she had trouble with her Ping-Pong balls, and had stooped to examine the difficulty when Saxon first spoke. Through a haze I imagined Sabrina's voice, and with sure finesse attempted to tweak the ball from its lodging. My fingers surrounded it, and gently squeezed. Sabrina sighed. Saxon bumped my shoulder and spoke more firmly. "Jack! Wake up!"

I tugged gently at the ball and whispered my undying gratitude to Sabrina for allowing me to help with her problem. Sabrina groaned and responded by squeezing my free hand.

"Jack!"

Sunlight blinded me as I tried to open my eyes. For a moment I stared disbelievingly as a face moved to block it out. Saxon Browne's long hair tickled my cheeks. Her beautiful white teeth shone in a smile. Her hand was on mine. My other hand, I realized with a jolt of horror, was in my swim trunks. And that was no Ping-Pong ball I had grabbed.

Saxon Browne was a lady. If I had not known before, I recognized this now as she turned aloofly to examine pine trees and squirrels' nests, allowing me time to discreetly withdraw the scandalous hand from my trunks. I quickly pushed myself to my knees as she seated herself carefully upon a corner of my towel and pulled her darling legs beneath her. Willie stretched beside her and watched her movements. So I sat, too shocked to speak, and stared, the dagger piercing my belly with familiar fierceness.

She wore a dark blue bathing suit of the kind meant to cleverly cover all the right places, yet be cunning enough to expose tempting fringes of protrusions, as well as to divulge the body's delicate impressions to even a barely imaginative observer. I examined her every bulge, every crevice, intently, covetously, until the moment she turned to speak.

"We were skiing," she said demurely. "I saw you lying here, and decided to stop and say hello."

"I'm glad," I said.

With a jolt I recognized an internal uneasiness. I even sounded nervous! And where were the words I wanted to say to the woman to whom I had mutely given my eternal love when she was ten and I was nine? "I'M GLAD?" Lousy! Not only lousy, but now, nothing better came to mind. I was a blank. A speechless blockhead.

A simpleton. We sat in awkward silence while I desperately struggled for verse.

"Daddy will be back to pick me up in just a minute," she said finally. She turned to gaze at the boats circling the lake, their tethered escorts in close pursuit. "I just wanted to say hello."

Her skin was naturally pale, and the sun had begun to color it. She would have a light sunburn. I wondered if her skin would have a warm taste from the sunburn. Her lips were a wonderful pink without the need for sun or makeup. I wanted to see her tongue, too. Did it match her lips? I wanted to lick her teeth. Were they as slick and clean as they looked? Maybe bite her neck and nibble her ears...

"Let's start over," I said. "I'm awake now. Hello."

"Been here long?" she asked as she turned back to me. "You're getting burned."

Eyeing her legs, which were somewhat reddened from exposure, I responded, "So are you. Your beautiful knees will ache tonight."

"Oh?" She snickered delicately. "You think my knees are beautiful?"

"God, yes! I really like you, Saxon," I blurted with sudden audacity. "Every since I was in the fourth grade."

"Really?"

"Yeah."

"Well, I don't remember you in fourth grade."

My face must have become a crimson beacon of embarrassment. I turned away and coughed. I wished, as I turned back to her after that uneasy moment, that she would ask a question with an easy answer. But she only watched with seeming indifference as I struggled. I finally managed, "I could never forget you."

"I was kidding." She grinned. "I remember you well in fourth grade."

Suddenly, everything was okay. "You were just playing with me, weren't you?" I giggled. The moment the words were out I pictured myself with a straw hat and a weed between my teeth, making yuk-yuk-yuk noises.

"Maybe I wanted to see you squirm."

I giggled stupidly. Yuk-yuk-yuk.

"Did you really sneak up on those people out at the gravel pit? What did you expect to see?"

Damn Melba and her big mouth! Was there anyone left in the county except Coach who hadn't heard? "I have no idea how my name was associated with such a crude and disgusting affair as that," I said. "I was home reading at the time. Moby Dick. Herman Melville." Melville? I thought. Now why did I come up with "Melville?"

"And you're a liar, too."

"I swear."

She raised an eyebrow and shook her head. Why couldn't I be a good liar?

"Okay. I won't pry. For now. But sometime, I want to know the truth. I want to know what you saw." Her eyes cut villainously. "In detail. Blow by blow. Or should I say, stroke by stroke?"

"I can't very well describe something I didn't see, can I?" I said. "I'm innocent. And how come you know such vile words? Stroke by stroke! I don't believe you said that."

"I get around, babe."

"Talk. Talk is all. Everybody knows you're as naive as you look. Anybody who looks at you can tell you're pure as spring rain."

She nodded and looked away, her smile gone. "Sure I am. That's the way men want their women, don't they? Pure. Virgin. That's what I am, Jack." She stared out at the lake. "Wholesome Saxon Browne. Never been kissed. Not even on the forehead."

I had the urge to kneel and kiss her toes one by one. Instead I said, "How about on your..." I thought better of it. I was already sounding like something of a nut. "You sound like you're fed up with purity."

"Perry and I aren't seeing each other tonight." She eyed a nearby group who lounged on their beach towels as she leaned to scratch Willie's ears. She studied my buddy intently and continued, "We're going through one of our difficult spells. We may even stop seeing each other."

"Yeah?" I said happily. "That's terrible. Horrible. A real shame."

"It's not a pleasant time for me."

"I'll bet," I said. "But just think about Perry. I bet he can't keep his mind on football for worrying about losing you. Hell, he might even lose a game because of mental incapacitation!"

I watched her teeth as they smiled and she said, "You're sweet."

"You can bet I'd never give you up without a helluva fight!"

"I know you wouldn't. You're a real gentleman. When you're not sneaking around looking in parked cars."

"I told you..."

"Never mind. Where were we?"

"I was a gentleman. And I was about to predict that Perry will come whimpering back to you, begging forgiveness. You'll probably take him back, too. Doggone it."

I trembled as she smiled and leaned forward to cradle my chin in the palms of her hands. "Sweet little boy," she cooed. "Thank you for saying that. It makes me feel better."

Good god! I thought. Romeo, move over! Here comes Jack!

"Your hands are so soft," I said. "Little rose petals."

"It won't be long until you have to start shaving." She withdrew her fingers from my cheeks in a prolonged, faint caress.

"I shave all the time," I said. "Beard's so rough I wear out a razor blade every time, too."

"Such an innocent boy, too. Such a sweet baby. I don't mind your little beard."

No doubt, Saxon was a goddess. An archangel! She adored my frailties! I felt humble, for with little effort, really only a smile or two, I, Jack Smith, had brought this angel to earth. "God, Saxon," I breathed heavily, "I've always loved you!"

"Since fourth grade," she said. "I could tell. In study hall the other day."

"Every since I first saw you! It started back in 1944, when I first laid eyes on you. I remember it well. I'd just got back from the big fight on Guam. The Japs, the blood and all. You've read about it. I came home. And there you were. You were... You still are... the most beautiful girl in the world!"

Her mouth dropped open. "Huh? Liar! You never went to Guam!"

"I'd lie every word if it would impress you, Saxon."

She faked a gasp. "Such a flatterer! Why, I didn't know you were such a rogue, Jack! Where have you been all my life?"

"Listen," I said eagerly, "if you're not seeing Perry tonight, maybe you and I..."

"Yes!" she said, as though she had already thought of it. "We could, couldn't we? Maybe we could ride up to Ginny's and have a Coke."

"That would be fun. Where's old Perry tonight? Guam, I hope."

"Oh, don't worry about that wimp." Her hair swished as she tossed her head and took my breath away. "I can be ready, oh, six-ish. Will that be all right?"

"Perfect!" I said. A date with Saxon Browne? Fantastic! Impossible!

"You'll pick me up?" she said, her eyes sparkling. "Six o'clock?"

"I'll be there."

In an old Plymouth station wagon. Maybe she won't notice. Wonder if Jerry will loan me his Chevy? Maybe I'll just steal a car...

"Oh, we'll have such fun, Jack," she was saying as I mentally prepared myself. She squeezed my hands playfully. "Actually, I've wanted you to ask me for a date for a long, long time. Really."

"I've been a fool, Saxon," I said. "I thought since you and Perry..."

"Don't even mention that name, Jack." With a frown she pulled her hands from mine. "I get mad when I hear it."

"Great!" I said.

"There's my dad."

The sound of the outboard motor had been lost on me, so heated had been my attention to my idol and her words. She jumped to her feet, wiggled her fingers at me in parting, and pattered away toward where her father waited in his small cruiser. Mr. Browne was a dairy farmer, and had profited quite well by his trade.

"Bye, Saxon," I shouted after her. It was her father who turned to wave to me as he gunned the engine. Then Saxon's hand fluttered briefly above the windshield as the boat backed away. I watched until they reached the ramp on the opposite shore, and there began to pack their skis and vests and prepare their boat for winching onto its trailer. Six o'clock, I thought with a start. And it must be after three now. Gotta go!

With the passing of mid-afternoon, and on top of a mild sunburn, the October chill seeped into my body. By the time Willie and I reached Cherokee Rose, we were both shivering, despite closing all the windows and huddling side-by-side on the wagon's leather seat. "Southern dogs we are, Willie," I confided to him. "Not used to this damn Yankee cold."

As we pulled into the driveway of Cherokee Rose, there was a thoroughly intimidating loneliness in the dull windows and lifeless porticoes that belonged to the old house. Where in its past splendor there had been gaiety and frivolity, there now was peeling paint and mildew, wind-blown leaves, a stark desolateness that would sadden any compassionate observer. The forbidding spirit was further amplified when I pushed open the side door and fell back in the face of a humid breeze escaping the chilled rooms of the interior. There was a dank smell of bare earth, and I feared for a moment that a floor had disintegrated and fallen into the sodden basement. Paranoia, I thought then. Meatloaf Murray Malady. Football Fever. I kept a firm grip on the pistol and pointed inside. "Willie," I said, "you go first."

My trusted cripple accepted the offer and was soon sniffing about for crumbs under the kitchen table. Willie's nose detected no breach of security, and, his nonchalance having eased my fears,

I proceeded to check in every room and under every bed to be certain we were alone. I wanted no visitors while I soaked in my tub. "Keep a close lookout, Willie," I told the noble guard dog, "and there'll be extra dog biscuits tonight." I took time to straighten Jim's bed covers, which lay where Jerry and Archie had tossed them. My own bed was made.

Jerry refused me the loan of his Chevy. After I had completed my bath and dressed, I dialed his number, and when his mother got him to the phone, asked the favor. "I don't loan out my Chevy to nobody," he said. "Much a buddy as you are, Jack, I just can't do it."

"But I got a date with Saxon Browne, Jerry!" I shouted. "I can't take her out in a trash-can-on-wheels!"

"YOU got a date with Saxon Browne? You finally asked her?"

"She practically begged me. It's something she's wanted for a long time, and I finally consented. The woman adores me."

"I can't believe it!" There was a long pause. "Hell," he said then, "I know I ain't gonna loan you my car now. One thing I don't tolerate is bullet holes in my car." He snickered. "You're nuts, Jack. Saxon is Perry Norman's private stock. When he finds out about this, he'll tie you to a tree and use your body for blocking practice."

"Saxon told me she and Perry might be breaking up."

"Hell, she's using you! She's just trying to make Perry jealous. She'll run right back to him once he's pulverized your ass. Women are like that."

"Not Saxon."

"You'll see."

There was nothing to do but attempt to diminish the abhorrent state of our station wagon. The old rattletrap was reliable, and not really so old. But covered with dirt and grime, one headlight broken completely out, the antenna bent where Archie had once "adjusted" it so that the Nashville rock station could be received more clearly, a cracked windshield, and the rear cargo space littered with empty Early Times pints, the vehicle would have, in my opinion, been better suited for Morgan's Auto Salvage than squatted in the driveway of an antebellum home. It even had black-wall tires.

I filled a trashcan with liquor bottles, empty cigarette packages, half-filled oilcans, and an assortment of other debris, then swept the seats and floor with a whisk broom. A wet rag removed from the body and windows whatever portion of grime had not become a permanent part of the facade, but that left dry smears in wide circles that had to be cleansed with yet another damp cloth. The spots of body rust and mildew would not budge, but the antenna miraculously straightened without breaking. With the approaching grayness of nightfall, I was surprised at the improvement. There was actually paint under all the grime! No jewel, I thought, but it's all I've got.

I considered leaving my weapon at home, thought better of it as I recalled the comfort it had given me minutes before as I approached the lonely house, and took time to strap it above my privates. Then I grabbed a jacket, warned Willie once again to keep a lookout, and dashed out to my pumpkin carriage. Six o'clock was minutes away, and the Browne farmhouse at least five miles out. I had to move!

CHAPTER 15
THE DATE

A ND MOVE IT did! The station wagon's six-cylinder stick-shift was no pumpkin pulled by six mice; the vigorous little power train yanked us out of town and along Davis County's gravel roads toward the Browne estate with unbelievable swiftness, leaving behind billows of dust that settled thickly on the trees and houses along the way. I did not intend to be late on my first date with Saxon. And I wasn't. There were seconds to spare when the Plymouth skidded to a halt before the massive home of my darling. Relax! I told myself as I got out and stumbled toward the front door. She's only a girl! A goddess, sure, but still, only a girl.

Saxon's mother answered the door and stood for a moment staring at me along her lanky nose. Does she know me? I wondered as we eyed each other. Or does she think I'm a vacuum cleaner salesman? "Hi, Mrs. Browne," I said. "I'm Jack Smith. We've met before."

She was a thin, plain woman, once a noble, honest country girl, now, since her husband's ascension to wealth, a powerful city woman who cherished her prestigious position in the Smith Station Garden Club. Her opinion was regularly consulted in matters of religion and scuttlebutt by the Baptist Ladies. Apparently, however, she remained a country girl at heart, for her dress was without waist—one long, uninterrupted flow of wrinkled plaid gingham—the type of dress worn by the bony or the fat or the ignorant, women who would probably flaunt it if they had it, but since they didn't, wore dresses without waists.

A painful squint withered the skin about her eyes. "You're Jack Smith," she said accusingly.

"This is true," I answered, "and it's a pleasure to see you once again, Madam Browne. May I come in?"

"You're here for Saxon!"

"Yes, ma'am."

"Well!" Her eyes narrowed. "From what I hear about you, I'm not sure I want Saxon going out with you! What's wrong with you boys? Didn't you have any upbringing? I suppose not. With your background..."

"I heard about that nasty rumor, Mrs. Browne," I interrupted, "and I can assure you, it's all bull... it's all a lie. That Archie Jones! He's the culprit, and somehow my name got dragged into it. Darn gossipy people! Believe me, I'm innocent as a lamb."

"Well, that's not the way I heard it!"

"It's a shame, the way people talk, Mrs. Browne." I shook my head wearily. "So many righteous people get hurt that way."

Her sideways glare and wrinkly squint implied skepticism. "You're just telling me that, aren't you? If that had been me in that car, I'd have showed you a thing or two! You little deviates!"

If that had been you in "that car," I thought, I wouldn't have even wanted to watch, no matter what you showed me. But I tempered my reply. "Those boys should be horse whipped, Mrs. Browne. I'd help with it, too, because they've blackened the name of Smith."

"Well..."

"I hope they prosecute the bastards!"

Perhaps my language was a bit strong, for she appeared aghast for a moment. After blocking the door for another few seconds, she turned and stepped rapidly down a hallway toward the center of the mansion. "George," she barked as I followed, "George, the Smith boy is here for Saxon. You hear me? It's Jack Smith."

George relaxed in socked feet sprawled within a recliner placed near a huge brick fireplace that contained a huge fire. He dropped his newspaper in his lap as Mrs. Browne and I entered from the hallway and regarded me with eyes whose lids sagged in anticipation of an early bedtime. Mr. Browne was short and round with the rosy nose and face of either a cherub or a newborn dairy calf, and the body of Santa Claus. Except that he was bald. "Hello, Mr. Browne," I said. I took the limp hand he offered from his sitting position. "Good to see you, sir."

Mrs. Browne remained just long enough to give her husband a frown and a shake of one finger, then retreated without a word toward what must have been the kitchen. "Sit down, Jack," Mr. Browne said pleasantly, "I want to talk to you."

I sat in a stuffed chair near his and tried to anticipate his words. "Nice place, Mr. Browne," I said as I eyed the tiny wooden animals with lace bow ties that hung on every wall. "Decorated well, too." The room smelled of wood smoke.

"Thank you, Jack. Listen." He paused to leisurely spit into a can that he lifted from the floor beside his chair. He has, I noted, become one of his dairy cows. Years of association did it. Complacent. Slow. Chewing tobacco because he doesn't have cud. At least, I hope he doesn't have cud. Heedless of all but his own world.

His bare legs shined where his khaki pants had pulled above thin black nylon socks. "About Saxon," he drawled. "She'll be down in a minute. Have her home by nine o'clock. It's Sunday, and she has school tomorrow. I let her stay out only until nine o'clock on Sundays."

"Yes, sir."

"Drive the speed limit."

"Yes, sir."

With a finger pointed at my middle he eyed me and said, "Frankly, I don't give a damn about this escapade you were involved in. At your age, I probably would have done the same thing. Just didn't think of it." With a knowing look he continued, "Just hope you don't get in too much trouble over it."

"It's nothing, sir. A misunderstanding. I intend to file suit."

My denial passed without comment. "What are you planning for tonight?" he asked.

I suddenly felt guilty. He knew what I was planning. He'd had similar plans when he was my age. "Saxon wants to drive to Milldale and get a Coke at Ginny's," I said. "That's all. It's Sunday. We may even drop by church for a minute."

"Good." His face brightened and he relaxed as he relieved himself of fatherly duty with his warnings and my submission. "Think the team will win the rest of the games this year, Jack?"

"The team?"

"The football team. Think we'll be Little Dixie champs again this year? You should know. You don't play, do you, but you know the team."

"No, I don't play, Mr. Browne," I said. "I'm not much on softball."

"Softball? Football!"

"Oh. Well, Coach Murray will come through again," I said quickly. "We'll win the Dixie State Championship again for sure."

"It's the Little Dixie Championship," he said with a frown. "You know, Perry... Saxon's steady boyfriend... is Captain of the team. His father and mother... We're all members of the Country Club. Together. We all love Perry. Great kid. Great quarterback."

"Perry? Perry." I scratched my head and put on a puzzled frown. "I think I've heard of a Perry..."

Mr. Browne's body lifted in the recliner as his hands gripped the arms. I panicked for an instant, thinking he was about to beat hell out of me. "Damn, boy!"

I raised a discerning finger. "Yeah," I said frantically, "yeah, I do believe I've seen him somewhere. Perry, you say? Perry who?"

"Perry Norman!" he practically shouted. "Everybody's heard of Perry Norman, boy! Saxon's his girl!"

"Well." I leaned back into my chair. "I don't think we got the team we had last year, Mr. Browne. Weak in the backfield. I think we'll have a good basketball team, though."

"Hate basketball."

I decided to try a different tactic: "How's the dairy herd?"

His face brightened. "Banner year this year. You like farming, Jack? Dairy farming?"

Finally! I thought. "Sure do. I've thought about having my own herd one of these days."

"Damn fool," he said, shaking his head. "Anybody'd be a damn fool to go into the dairy business this day and age. Can't make it without the government. And a lot of luck. Too much competition."

"Maybe," I said weakly, "maybe I'll just go on to Mississippi State, be a Cow-College Engineer. Bulldog backer."

"I'm an Ole Miss Rebel myself," he grunted. He picked up his newspaper and resumed reading.

Having done nothing to alleviate the malice with which Mrs. Browne viewed me because of my date with Saxon and the possible consequences of same upon her relationship with the football star should the football star learn of it, I had now alienated Saxon's father as well. I didn't really give a damn. Saxon was what counted, and I guessed she liked me the way I was. I sat quietly and through a window studied the soaring fins of the Cadillacs parked outside. New Cadillacs. Flip side: Aged Plymouth station wagon. New, virile money. Flip again: Old, bygone money. Fine, new mansion. Antebellum hovel. New name. Old name.

Maybe Mrs. Browne would be the one. Maybe she would have Smith Station renamed "Brownesville" one day.

My eyes lifted to the sound of Saxon's light tripping on the stair treads. My heart stood still. As she skipped toward us, I thought that she was the most exquisitely lovely thing I'd ever seen. Her thick brown hair was fascinating, the way it always bounced about her cheeks and neck, framing an angelic smile that captivated any who saw it. Her white teeth gleamed from between lips parted in a deceptively timid smile that invited affection. She wore a pink sweater tonight, over blue jeans, brown penny loafers and pink socks, and a small silver barrette above her left ear. Her cheeks were pink to match. "Ready?" she called breathlessly at the foot of the stairs.

"Ready!" I said with a bound from my chair to stand beside her. "Bye, Mr. Browne," I said while steering his daughter toward the front door. "I enjoyed talking to you. I'll remember your advice, too. Tell Mrs. Browne adieu for me."

"Nine o'clock," he advised without lifting his eyes from his paper.

Would Saxon run screaming back inside when she caught sight of the Plymouth? I closed the front door of the mansion behind us. "Jim's old Plymouth was all I had," I apologized as we walked together toward the heap, "and it's not much of a car."

"I think it's cute." She stood back and examined it. I opened the door and helped her inside. "It kind of reminds me of a little lost puppy. It suits you, Jack. I love it!"

"Lost puppy?" I gulped. "It suits me?"

"I couldn't picture you in a new Lincoln or Cadillac. This car is perfect for you."

Pondering the implications of Saxon's words, and discouraged by my initial assessment, I got inside and got the Plymouth rolling toward Milldale. "I'm ready for a milk shake at Ginny's," I said. "Maybe a hamburger, too. How's that sound?"

"Oh, I don't care," she answered, twirling small curls of hair with her fingers as she studied the countryside. "Let's drive around town for a little while first. Drive by the cafe and see who's there."

"You sure?" I said. "I thought we planned on going to Milldale. Where did you say Perry was tonight?"

"Oh, Jack!" She wagged her finger at me and shook her head. In mock anger, she was more gorgeous than ever, and I was over-joyed again that she was here in the same car with me. "Don't worry about him! Don't even mention his name. We're through!"

"You are?"

"Yes. Do you think I'd be out with you if he and I were still going steady?"

"Who knows about women?"

"Of course not!"

"Well, then, we'll drive by the cafe. We'll drive every street in town if you want. We'll keep on until we run out of gas. Then I'll carry you on my back."

"You are SO sweet."

"Maybe we'll see Perry, and he'll start something. I'd like that. That way, I can lay down my life for you. You'll have beautiful memories of me lying there in a pool of blood."

She mewed contentedly and moved closer, a sudden bounce that pushed her knee against my leg. I froze for fear the contact was unintentional, but she seemed comfortable with that intimate maneuver. Her hand left my shoulder and squeezed my neck, then her fingers traced along my ear and up until finally her hand rested atop my head. As we neared Mary's Cafe, she began to absent-mindedly stroke my scalp with the tips of her fingers, while at the same time she slouched into the seat so that only that portion of her head above her eyes could be glimpsed by a casual observer. I wondered what people would think about me driving around in a ragged Plymouth station wagon with a strange hand perched on my head. We turned onto Main Street. I happily noted that there were few vehicles lining the street.

"You don't see Perry's Corvette, do you?"

"No."

"And Coach Murray's Fury? I don't see it. Do you?"

"No."

"Well, maybe we can sneak past without fear of injury."

"Of course we can," she said. "I'm not afraid of Perry. And I didn't slip up on Coach Murray while he was doing it in the gravel pit, either. It'll be you he'll kill, not me." She giggled as though it were funny.

"You're with me," I said. "They'll jump us both."

"They wouldn't hurt a girl."

"You know Perry. He gets mad and loses his head. And Coach Murray just likes to kill things. Anything that breathes. Male or female."

"Well, Perry's probably in Milldale tonight. With that blonde tramp. Coach Murray, I don't know about."

"You know about the girl Perry dated?"

"Dated? Dated?" she said a bit shrilly. "He's still dating her. And yes, I know."

"I saw her once. At the cafe."

"Thrill."

"I hope I see her again."

"Why?"

"I want to thank her."

"Jack. You're such a love." She bumped my shoulder with the palm of her hand. We were buddies. "And we're finally having a date, Jack! After all this time!"

"The first of thousands," I said.

We cruised silently past the cafe. "Just the same old people," Saxon said with a sigh as she ducked and bobbed and inspected the few vehicles parked along Main Street. "Nobody interesting. Smith Station is dullsville."

"We could go inside," I said in jest. "Maybe everybody's on foot tonight."

"I guess so."

"I was kidding!" I said. "I don't want to go in."

"Chicken."

"Let's go to Milldale."

"Circle the block one more time. Maybe we missed somebody."

"Who're we looking for? Anybody I know?"

The soothing massage ended for a moment as Saxon was lost in her thoughts. Does she massage Perry's head while they're driving? I wondered. She's so good at it. Nobody can stroke head like this without a lot of practice. Perry's hair is ruffled all the time. I bet she does! And I always assumed it was his football headgear that made him look like he'd just fallen out of bed and forgotten to shower.

Saxon straightened and nodded as though she had made a decision, and her fingers went to work again. I twisted my neck and head and groaned with pleasure. "Let's park and go inside," she said. "We'll have a Coke."

"You're kidding!"

"No." Her fingers softly patted the top of my head. She sighed, "If it comes to it, I'll protect you."

I turned the wagon into a parking space half a block from the cafe and killed the engine. Saxon sat with her hands clasped in her lap. Her eyelids fluttered expectantly.

"Me Tarzan. You Jane," I said after a few seconds. "Tarzan takes care of himself."

She patted my shoulder, a bit protectively, I thought. "You swing on vines and talk to elephants," she said. "You protect natives. I suppose I stay home in our tree house and cook."

"It's the American way."

"And at night, after you've had a hard day in the jungle, you expect me to cuddle you in bed."

"Yeah! We don't need to go inside. Let's go to my place and get started!"

"Chicken. Let's go to the cafe."

"You like to live dangerously?"

"I like to live."

I exited the wagon intent upon pleasing Saxon, patted my weapon to be sure it still hung in place, and opened her door. "You ever go out for track?" I asked when we were on the sidewalk. "What's your time in the hundred?"

"Sometimes I race Perry."

"I thought we weren't going to mention that name."

She grabbed my hand and pulled me after her. How many times had I imagined walking the streets of my town with Saxon Browne? I wouldn't have traded places with Elvis Presley tonight. I patted my hair in place and strutted.

The pool hall was nearly empty. Sunday night. I had forgotten. Sunday night was the slowest night of the week. We pushed inside, and at the door's eye-opening howl endured the prolonged glances of Mama Mary, the Boy, three or four of our classmates who were not close friends, and three drunks who sat at different tables. I winced as I recognized Josephine, seated in a low chair behind the counter where she was having a private conversation with Mama Mary. I avoided her eyes as I whispered a suggestion to Saxon, a table hidden from view of patrons or passersby "We can have some privacy," I whispered.

"Cluck, cluck, cluck," she whispered.

"But I always enjoy sitting at the counter, too."

"That will be fine. If you really want to."

There was no ducking Josephine now, and as Saxon and I sat, I greeted her with a hello, then saluted Mama Mary. Saxon likewise spoke to them, and, much to my relief, after Mama Mary had given us an eyebrow-raised but cheery welcome and had ambled away toward her cooler to fetch our soft drinks, Josephine smiled and returned our greeting. "You look so pretty tonight, Saxon," Josephine said from her chair. "You could be a movie star."

"Not me, Josephine," Saxon said. "You're the one. I've seen the way men look at you. You could have your pick."

"No," Josephine said with a sigh, "I'd have to do what my name-sake did to do that. My uncle loved Josephine Baker. He told me so. He said he saw her once in Paris. That's why he asked my grandfather to name me Josephine."

Saxon and I looked at each other. "Who's Josephine Baker?" I asked.

Saxon shrugged. We both turned back to Josephine. "A famous dancer," Josephine responded after a moment. "A famous NEGRO dancer." She stared at us for a few seconds, then pushed from her chair, said "Good night," and waved goodbye to Mama Mary. "Bye, Josephine," Saxon and I called to her as she left through the back door.

"I've never heard of Josephine Baker," I said after Josephine had disappeared.

"Maybe you're not the brain you think you are."

"And maybe Josephine has more brains than any of us."

"Let's finish these Cokes and get out of here."

"Ginny's?"

"How about the gravel pit?"

For a moment I feared that my just-swallowed sip of Coke was going to join the flyspecks and grease spots that embellished Mary's walls and ceiling. "The gravel pit?" I managed to choke out. "You want to go to the gravel pit?"

"Everybody goes to the gravel pit, dummy." She studied my face as if she were numbering every zit and freckle. "It's no big deal. You of all people..."

I felt my cheeks redden.

"You know the place, Jack?" she continued. "The big hole? In the mountain of rock? The place that's perfect for making out?"

The stories were true, then, I thought. Saxon knew all about the gravel pit. She had probably spent a lot of time out there. With Perry.

"But you..." I was caught off guard, and I floundered. "You don't... You're the nicest girl I know!"

"And nice girls don't go to the gravel pit?"

"Hell, I don't know," I said warily, though that was what I was thinking. "I'm not exactly Sigmund Freud. I just thought that nice girls went to the movies, and the rest went to the gravel pit."

"Damn, Jack, I wasn't born yesterday!"

"But..."

I had hit a nerve, I thought with regret. I listened, afraid to speak, as she raised her voice. "What's a 'nice girl' anyway? A virgin? Is that the definition of a nice girl?" Air whistled from her lips, a cool gust of anger. "Sometimes I get positively angry at what men think about women. They're so unfair. So immature. Hell, I AM a nice girl. But I know about things like the gravel pit and what goes on there. Girls talk, just like boys do. Boys just can't accept the fact that girls have the same rights they do."

"You're positively correct," I said. "I am a lost puppy."

"Just can't believe it, can you? So what if I go out to the gravel pit and mess around?"

"What?" I said, "You don't mess around, too!"

Her scowl meant my rating had taken another nosedive. She said softly, "Suppose I told you I was no virgin, Jack. What would you think? Would you want to take me home? Or would you want to go on to the gravel pit and try to get what someone else, maybe Perry, has had before you?"

Was my image of purity so distorted? I wondered. Had my opinions and values been misshapen by sixteen years of an uncle who spoke of honor and virtue and the merits of Southern manhood, yet cursed like a sailor, drank like a fish, and refused to admit that no one was fooled? Or was it the classics? Had that library of antiquated fantasy and treasured Southern rationalizations given me a warped perspective of what constituted propriety? Were virgins to be worshiped, non-virgins merely condoned? Were men above it all? Were men such fools? Was Saxon a tramp? How about Linda Murray? What exactly was a tramp anyway?

My spirits tumbled even further when Saxon whispered, "Take me home, Jack."

I whispered back, "Saxon, I'm sorry."

Her eyes trembled as she stared a hole through me. She continued, very softly, "I'm so sad. There was something special between us. I felt it. For a while."

I fought for the right words. "There still is, Saxon," I said finally. "Please, I – we—can't allow it to be lost now."

Her hand was resting on her knee, where I found it and squeezed it tightly. "You're just not like I expected, that's all. I don't know you!"

"That makes me madder! You expected a kitty and you found a tiger!" She squirmed away, pulling her hand from mine. "What's the matter, Jack? Do I frighten you? Or are you afraid of growing up?"

"No," I said, though I was far from being truthful. In a way, she scared me to death. However, more importantly, despite the delicacy of the moment, I recognized that all my years of yearning for her were guided not by mere lust, but by a kind of inner perception that there existed between Saxon Browne and myself an enduring fascination that was far too rare to allow it to be lost without a fight. I leaned as closely to her as the stools would allow. "When I look at you, Saxon," I breathed in her ear, "I know why Romeo couldn't live without Juliet. I know why Antony fought for Cleopatra. I love your name. Your face. Your body. So much you make my stomach hurt. I haven't figured out why just looking at you gives me a stomach ache, but I will, and when I do, I'll love that, too."

"I give you a stomach ache?" she said as she backed further away. "Jack, you're ending this thing before it gets started."

"It's more like a knife stuck in my belly. And I love it."

"Cleopatra?"

"Juliet, too," I reminded her. "Saxon Browne. A name that will join that of Aphrodite as a vision to mankind of all that is desirable."

"Do you use that line a lot?"

"Seldom," I said. "I'm jealous, too. Jealous of Perry, jealous of anyone who's touched you. I've had you on a pedestal all my life. You're a goddess to me. A queen. I should have tried to date you years ago. Then maybe..."

"Maybe you could have gotten there first?"

"Damn, Saxon" I said, looking away. "That hurts."

With a sigh she answered: "Now, I'm sorry."

We sat for several seconds without speaking while I bemoaned the fact that my angel had been robbed of her virginity by a meathead. Was there no fairness in this world? Just as importantly, how good was Perry Norman in the sack? Could my performance compare to that of the lean, mean, handsome, bastard? Probably not. Damn it all! The thought of my angel in bed with Perry was enough to cause important parts to shrivel.

"A goddess?" she asked.

"My idol," I answered as I turned back to her.

Long live depravity and wickedness. And wanton, wild, deliberate sex. Surely Saxon wouldn't tell anybody if Perry was a lot better where it really counted. "Let's go to the gravel pit," I said.

"No."

"I thought you said..."

"I don't do it with just anybody."

"Just for a few minutes. We can't stay long anyway. Your dad will kill me if you're not in by nine."

After hesitating for a second or two she said, "Don't count on anything. This is a first date."

What are the odds, I wondered, of a virgin making love to two different women in the same week? Slim, I'd guess. But I was on a roll.

Once back in the Plymouth, I pulled Saxon close for the drive to the pit. The radio was tuned to the Nashville station that played the latest rock-and-roll. The music faded in and out as, Jerry and I had speculated time and again, the mountains of clouds between Nashville and Smith Station rolled and churned and in the process disturbed the signal and hindered its long journey to our antennas. Saxon sat huddled next to me, one hand kneading the top of my head in the strange caress to which I was becoming addicted, the other loosely nestled in her lap. She did not speak as we drove, either lost in her own thoughts or else having decided that the lyrics sung by the Platters were preferable to conversation with me. "YOU'VE got the magic touch," I said once. She squeezed my scalp in silence.

As we approached the entrance to the gravel pit I began to ponder the possibility that Coach Murray might be there. That was doubtful, however, since Josephine had just been at the café. Later, perhaps. Perry? Perry, hopefully, was in Milldale with his slinky blonde friend. The possibility of a confrontation with either of the two, however, brought to mind a vision of tomorrow's headlines: ALLEGED PEEPING TOM MURDERED; TORN AND MANGLED BODY LEFT AT SCENE OF LOATHSOME CRIME. Followed by: MUTILATED REMAINS TENTATIVELY IDENTIFIED AS THOSE OF ONE JACK "CHEROKEE JACK JUNIOR" SMITH. SHERIFF SAYS JUSTICE SERVED; KILLING JUSTIFIABLE.

"Isn't there a better place to park?" I said. "The pit may be full."

My idol was stirred from her silent reflections to say absently, "Not on Sunday night. Anyway, the pit's safe. Nobody bothers you. Not even the police."

"I'm glad you're familiar with the routine," I said dryly.

She pushed away for a moment. "Don't be snide. You've made quite a study of the routine yourself. Just how many times have you been up here, Mr. Snoop?"

I pretended I was too busy looking for the turnoff to pay her any attention. Halfway up the gravel trail that led into the pit I turned off the Plymouth's headlights and continued with only the faint light of the moon to guide us. The crunch of the Plymouth's tires in the gravel was the only sound. I thought, the owls and crickets are scared, too. When we reached the crest, the darkness of the crater and the narrowness of the road forced me to turn the headlights on once again. "I don't see anybody," I whispered as we slowly descended toward an oasis brightened by the glare of our lights. "We'll park under that patch of trees ahead."

"Fine," Saxon whispered. "Why are you whispering?"

I doused the lights and circled the patch of scrub trees, then slowed to a halt beneath them. The Plymouth's nose was pointed toward the entrance road, the route to escape. "Is this the one you and Perry use?" I whispered.

"Perry and I have used them all at one time or another."

"Thanks. I needed that."

As far as I could see, there were no other cars in the pit. Only a million crickets. Now that silence reigned once more, the tiny revelers resumed their monotonous symphony. Late in the year for them, I thought. They'll all die soon. Too cool. Such is life. And death.

I cranked open my window to allow cool air inside, expecting Saxon would be forced to cling to me for warmth. She continued to silently fondle my scalp. Our knees touched as I turned to put an arm around her, and she shivered and moved nearer.

Linda Murray, I reflected as I held Saxon for the first time.

She and Saxon were so different. Or to put it better, the two of them affected ME differently. Linda was earthy desire, carnal fulfillment. The thought of her half-moon eyes and perfect breasts was enough to paralyze the muscles in my belly. I wanted her for sex. I couldn't live without her for sex. But I couldn't bear the thought of forsaking Saxon for her, despite the revelations of this evening. Before tonight, before the baring of her notoriety, Saxon had been a perception of my future. Purity. Fidelity. Quiet evenings at home with the children and the Baptist Ladies. Supper promptly at seven. PTA. In more apt term, WIFE material. So much for ignorance. But a burning love is hard to smother.

She jarred my private thoughts by asking, "Have you been dating anyone?"

"No one in particular. Actually, I've never taken anybody out in Jim's Plymouth. I avoid dating in this old trap."

"I like this old car," she answered. "Fancy cars don't mean anything. Perry's so proud of his Corvette. He's silly."

"He sure is," I agreed. "The childish bastard." Just because he was tall, handsome, rich, a gifted athlete, and drove the best-looking car in Mississippi, he thought he was special.

"You don't need a car to be a man, Jack."

"Good thing," I said. "How about tall, handsome, rich, and athletic?"

"Mandatory."

"Well, maybe they'll have me at some monastery."

"I was only kidding." Her hand curled around my shoulder and patted my scalp with a patronizing stroke. "You have a lot to offer any woman, Jack."

"I know I do." I raised a hand behind her and counted on my fingers. "Let's see. I don't have a car, but I can borrow a sure-enough prehistoric station wagon. I can afford to eat, but not much else. Egg sandwiches are my specialty. You gotta try one. My only relative is a drunk. Maybe I will be, too. Runs in the family. I have a dog, but he only has three legs. But, hell, he loves me, and I love him. We're very close. Next, I'm about to be the center of a major scandal involving a voyeuristic outing with two other dimwits. I'll be lucky if I don't have to move away forever. And don't forget the Smith name. A hundred years ago it really meant something. Nowadays, people point and laugh. Let's see, did I leave out anything?"

The sympathy ploy worked. Saxon pulled my head down by the hair she had been kneading and planted me with a juicy kiss. "I want to lick your teeth, Saxon," I said after a few juicy moments, "and I want to munch your tiny little ear lobes."

"Why the devil would you want to lick my teeth?"

"I've always wanted to lick your teeth. It's your smile. Your teeth are beautiful when you smile. And your ears. Small sweet grapes. Nibble size."

"Jack, you are weird."

"Only when I'm this close to you. Your body against mine provokes irrational thought."

In a while I decided we were the perfect pair because Saxon, I discovered, was every bit as weird as I. It was mainly her kisses. I only had one woman to compare her to, of course, but the contrast was astounding. When she wasn't vigorously pleasing herself, Linda Murray favored tender, dream-inspiring contact, a prolonged visit to a placid mountain stream in which we floated deliriously in a never-never land of bliss. Saxon chose instead to embrace furiously for a few seconds, a short, wild, white-water river jaunt that left me wild-eyed and aroused, gasping and grasping. We would collide, then she would pull away for a few gulps of air, peer into the darkness around us to be sure no one had witnessed her impetuosity, gather her strength, and make another charge. As she retreated across the seat following the first skirmish I wondered what was wrong. Then, as the scene was repeated and I realized this was the norm for her, I awaited her return each time in something of a daze. Every one or two minutes, I was ravished by a tornado. Before I could recover from one big blow, here came another. It was actually frustrating. A starving child might have felt the same if its dinner were snatched away after a bite here and there.

During one of these fierce encounters, she discovered the gun. If I had thought of it beforehand, I would have removed the pistol and stuck it under the front seat. But I didn't. And as jock strap and weapon had become quite at home on my pelvis, I hardly noticed the inconvenience anymore. Excitement got the better of me now, however. The state of my lower regions had reached a point of discomfort about the time Saxon bumped the gun with an elbow. "What in the..." she began.

"It's just a gun," I said. I pushed her away. "A pistol. Don't worry. I need to take it out. It's hurting me."

She bounded to the opposite corner of the seat with a suddenness that surprised me. "You men all think alike," she cried disdainfully. "So proud of your toys! Don't you DARE take it out!"

"But it's hurting me," I said.

"I don't care if it explodes! If you take that thing out, I'll never speak to you again!"

It struck me then that we had embarked on divergent conversations. "The barrel's so LONG," I said, "I have to get it out. It's really hurting."

"Braggart! Don't you dare!"

"But Saxon. You know all about these things. One more rod shouldn't shock you too much. You're a woman of the world, aren't you?"

"I'll get out of the car and run!" she cried. "Leave that thing in there!"

I pushed my door open and got out. In a moment I had the pistol out of my pants. I got back inside and tossed it onto the back seat. "There," I said. "I feel a lot better now."

"It really WAS a gun," she said wonderingly.

"Personal protection," I said. "Normally I depend on my Judo – what they taught us before we invaded Guam – to defend myself. My hands are registered weapons. But lately, I've taken to packing a firearm. Don't want to take a chance on damaging my weapons."

"My god!" she said, shaking her head. "I never know what to expect from you! I know you're the biggest liar I ever met. But Guam?" She sighed. "Heck, maybe you were on Guam."

"Third Marines. Nineteen forty-four."

The look on her face made me laugh. "Let's just get back to the necking," she said with a shake of her head.

In a little while I figured my lips were bleeding from the mauling. I imagined I tasted blood. Fractured my lips. Docile Saxon Browne. The woman with the instincts of a hungry shark. How did Perry hold up to her? Bloody lips and a battered scalp. Perry was sure to recognize the damage she had done to me. I would have to avoid him until I healed. And next time I saw him, I planned to examine his head for signs of similar treatment.

Another vehicle joined us in the pit. When its headlights flashed past us, I strained to make it out. "Ain't no Fury, is it?" I whispered to Saxon. "Or a Corvette?"

"No," she said, straining to see. "It's just Muledick's old car. He and Teeny."

I couldn't hide my surprise. "You know about Richard?"

Instead of answering she attacked. When she paused for air, I said, "You sure did get scared a little while ago. When I was talking about pulling out my gun."

"Not really, puppy."

"Yep. You acted like you'd never seen a gun before."

"Who would be afraid of one of those little things?" she said. "You just wish."

"Woman-of-the-world," I laughed

"That's me."

"You're as big a liar as I am."

"Not so. I'm no war hero, either."

"You're as virgin as Archie's Aunt Ethel," I said, "only you got a lot better chance of losing yours than she has. You're not a hunchback like she is."

"I'm not telling you anything. Except that Perry can kiss a lot better than you."

"I think I love you, Saxon. No, I know I do."

"Every since fourth grade."

It was getting late, and in a while I drove her home. "I've had a good time," she said at her door.

"Let's do it again."

"I thought that was settled." She pecked my forehead. "Puppy."

I licked her teeth. "See you at school tomorrow, Miss Chastity."

"Probably."

"That'll be me, floating down the hallway at break. Just reach up and pull me down."

"By your gun?"

I braved the dark doorway of Cherokee Rose without the protection of the courageous watchdog, who was probably out doing what I had been recently only contemplating. After I had the lights on, I went back out to the Plymouth and strained to lift the front bumper. That'll cure the ache every time. I was lucky to have such a knowledgeable uncle. He knew about things like this.

And I wondered about Saxon Browne. A man really never knows for sure whether his love has loved and been loved before, does he? Virginity. Would it really matter if Saxon were no virgin? Damn. Maybe I did need to grow up.

When I got back inside, the telephone was ringing. Nine-thirty. Late. Wrong number? Nope. Not a wrong number. Linda Murray was alone and lonely.

CHAPTER 16
MAMA MEATLOAF'S DILEMMA

RESH FROM THE slashing caresses of somewhat wholesome Saxon Browne, I acknowledged Mrs. Murray's friendly voice with the strain of one tolerating an intrusion into sacred meditation. She sensed the coolness, for after I answered her genial inquiries with a reserved "okay" and an impassive "fine", she asked what was wrong. "You sound as though you'd rather not talk to me," she said. "Would you prefer I just hung up?"

"You haven't called," I said, "and it's been two whole days."

There was silence at the other end for a moment before she replied, "I'm a married woman, Jack. I have other responsibilities. And there have been other complications as well."

"Complications?" I said warily, all sorts of alarming illusions coming to mind. "Like what? Nothing to do with us, I hope. Is everything okay?"

"Yes, everything's fine. It's just that... I'll tell you after you get over here. Come in the back door. And be careful walking over. Don't let anybody see you."

"What?" I croaked in astonishment. "Walk over there?"

"Melville is out of town," she said. "The kids are asleep."

"Melville is out of town," I repeated slowly, wheels turning. No wonder I hadn't seen Coach Murray this entire weekend. He probably hadn't even heard about Archie's big mouth!

"Tommy and Barbara Ann are asleep in their rooms. That leaves me here in this big bed all alone. I need you here in it with me."

"Holy cow!" I said. "What if somebody sees me? I can't just walk over there like I was taking a Sunday afternoon stroll!"

"You need to be careful. But you can do it. I walk a lot at night. There's hardly anyone out after dark."

"What if your husband comes home? Where is he? What if Gertrude is listening in?"

"Damn, Jack," she said impatiently, "do you think I'd take a chance like that? He left Saturday morning, right after he got in from his precious poker game. He's at some kind of football clinic, or so he claims, and believe me, he won't be back until just in time for his first class in the morning. He won't even stop here. He'll go straight to the schoolhouse. He's done it before. And Gertrude. Gertrude and I go back a long, long way. She'll never say a thing, believe me, even if she is listening."

Could I do this? I wondered. What if Coach DID come back early?

"Don't you want to come over, Jack?" she asked as I hesitated. "Or do you have other plans..."

The tantalizing memories overcame me then. Linda Murray's sensuous body crept into my brain and settled where moments before had dwelled the essence of Saxon Browne. Tender breasts. Soft lips... Love. Lust. Fulfillment. All in the seclusion of Linda Murray's bedroom. Only minutes away. "I'll be over in ten minutes," I said. "Wait for me at the back door."

I changed to a dark shirt, doused the lights, locked the doors, then stopped at the wagon to lace my weapon in place. Am I nuts? I wondered. Yeah. Pussy makes a man crazy. It won't be until AFTERWARDS that I'll admit nothing's worth this risk.

There were dark shadows beneath trees and near houses and parked cars along the way. I used them to advantage, skirting the well-lighted parts of the sidewalk, keeping close to the disordered lines of bushes and shrubs that graced the well-kept lawns. She was three blocks away, less than five minutes on a mundane sunny day, and tonight, no more than a ten-minute slither. I slithered past dark windows and silent homes, crept beside one house where a love song was beguiling some happy couple, then finally entered the side yard near her swimming pool, near to her back door, where I stopped to monitor the sounds and the scenery.

After a few seconds there was a noise at her door, and it opened. She had been waiting inside, and she spoke in a low voice when I hastily squeezed past her. "Be quiet," she warned. "The children." She was barefoot, but she clutched about her body a full-length gown that covered her from neck to feet. She must have read my mind. "It's so cool," she whispered in way of explanation as she closed the door behind me. "If it weren't so cool, I wouldn't have worn this."

"I would have liked that," I said.

The room was so dark I could hardly make out her face. There was a distinctly eerie, exciting feel to being here, in the den of the lion, so to speak. I shivered. I touched her shoulder. "Melville hasn't called, has he?" I asked.

"In the past ten minutes, you mean?"

"Yes."

"No."

I breathed a sigh of relief. "I'm glad you finally telephoned. I thought something was wrong."

Her hand touched my arm as she leaned and brushed her lips against my cheek. "Nothing's wrong," she murmured.

"You're sure your husband won't just pop in before morning?"

"He never has. Why would he start tonight?"

I let her pull me down the narrow hall past the two closed doors that led to Tommy and Barbara Ann. Her own bedroom door stood open. I hesitated once inside, my heart pounding as I thought of the hazard of being here. While I made note of which window I would jump through in case of emergency, she closed the door carefully behind us. I heard the click of a bolt as she secured it.

"My heart's pounding," I whispered.

"Stop worrying, Jack." In the darkness beside the bed the rustle of her robe being removed was deafening. "Pull those jeans off. Hurry!"

She discarded her underwear in urgent movements and was nude about the time I got that way. I thought, the sooner I do this, the sooner I can get out of here. I love Linda, but I sure don't want to die for her. As I jerked my shirt over my head and placed my gun atop a nearby chest, she lay down, naked, upon the bed, and even in the near total darkness of the room I could see that she was watching me with her arms outstretched, waiting. And then there was no time to think, no need to prepare, no opportunity for second thoughts. She clutched me with a wantonness that was astonishing. Though I needed no encouragement, her insistent struggling hastened our union, and when it occurred, she became savage. Her movements were convulsive, her hips and legs wonderfully strong and almost brutal in the fierceness of their thrusts. I was shocked at the same time by the series of incoherent groans that began to flood from her mouth in tempo with her movements. She seemed oblivious to anything but her own fulfillment. "The kids!" I whispered once. But she seemed not to hear, not, in fact, to even be aware of my presence, or of her own frenzy. I might have been hurt by her preoccupation if there had been time to reflect on it, but I was more than occupied with just hanging on.

Though only a junior in high school, and hardly cosmopolitan in education, I viewed myself, arrogantly, I admit, as somewhat more sophisticated than the average Joe. But as Linda Murray's mating instincts intensified to a virtual tantrum of sexual ferocity, whatever restraint I possessed vanished, and I soon became as reckless as she. To my eventual shame, her cries triggered my howls. Her movements brought my own, twofold. When she clawed, I clawed back. When her moans became shrieks, I shrieked with her. We were temporarily insane. We were wild animals. We were in another place where the worry that the commotion might bring our world tumbling down was insufficient to deter the hysterical rampage we had created. This was not love,

I thought later. This was the way it was with cavemen and cave-women. Or maybe what went on between grizzly bears.

In the moments before we became demented, I recognized in her groans my name, as it mingled with oaths and provocation. For what seemed a long time, then, we were delirious, and I neither paid attention to, nor, if I had been otherwise alert, could I have understood her cries of passion. Eventually, though, I tired, and with my consummation came the inevitable decline in my efforts and my interest. Her enthusiasm had likewise slackened. Yet, before she lay still, I was appalled to hear her mumble her husband's name. Her pronunciation of the word was almost unrecognizable, emphasis being placed on the "Mel" and, as though they were separate words, the "ville" grumbled in a deeper intonation that might have come from someone about to be sick to their stomach. She had, I realized with trepidation, been repeating his name, in between curses, for some time, and although I knew she was damning him, the fact that she could think of him while the two of us made love distressed me. What had been going through her mind as we worked?

The distraction affected me as scorn. Whereas after our initial experience at lovemaking I had clung to Linda Murray, dreading the separation of our bodies, now there was relief in rolling from her and allowing the cool air of the bedroom to chill my heated skin. We lay silently, and I listened for any sound that might warn us that Tommy or Barbara Ann had been disturbed, and, God forbid, had somehow witnessed any part of our indiscreet performance. "I sure hope the kids didn't hear," I said in a moment. "All the doors are closed. Maybe they didn't."

She rolled toward me, on her side. "They're heavy sleepers," she said lazily. "Don't worry."

"We should have stuffed pillow cases in our mouths."

I retreated as she tousled my hair with one hand, then felt badly about it and turned to stroke her blonde curls. We sprawled on our sides, facing each other. I was reminded for a moment of

Saxon's hand atop my head, and I felt ashamed. I wondered why. Deep down, I knew why.

"I guess I shocked you just now," she said after another moment. "I'm sorry. It was like so much had built up inside me, I would explode if I didn't get it out. I feel so much better now. I could sleep for a month I'm so relaxed."

"I never knew it could be like that," I said. "It was incredible. I'm glad you didn't have a knife."

No answer.

"You were so different," I went on. "You were wild. It was like you were drunk. Out of touch with reality. You could be hazardous when you're like that."

Now she said, "You didn't like it?"

"Hell, yes, I loved it! The sex part of it. I don't see how sex could be any better, though I certainly have a lot to learn. But it was so different from the first time. Almost scary. The first time we were so close we could have breathed for each other. This time was like combat."

"Well." She stretched and sighed. "I never enjoyed anything so much in my life. I'm absolutely exhausted."

"You kept saying 'Melville.'"

"I know, I know." She rolled and stared at the ceiling.

"Were you thinking about him while you and I made love?"

"Yes. For a little while."

"How could you!" I pushed myself upright with the intention of dressing and leaving. "You can't even forget him when you're making love to me? Why didn't you just wait until he got home?"

Her hand tugged at my arm, and I allowed myself to be pulled near to her. Her mouth brushed my ear. "It's not like that at all," she whispered. "I loved what we did. I enjoy being in bed with you. I love you. And I hate Melville."

"Then why... Can you imagine how that makes me feel?"

The bed shook as she rolled from it. "I think so," she said with a touch of anger in her voice, "So I'll explain. You want to know why I was thinking of that bastard while we were making love? Why I was cursing him? I'll show you."

The bedroom had a private bath. In only a couple of steps she stood at its open door no more than six feet from me. She flipped a light switch beyond. "This is why," she said. "This is why I hate him. This is why I didn't call you earlier in the weekend. I hoped I would heal. But I won't heal. I won't heal until he's dead!"

Her beautiful torso was marred by purple bruises. She turned slowly in the light from the bathroom bulb. Bruises on her hips. Along her rib cage. Her breasts. Her abdomen. Small bruises, pinch marks, around her pubis. Uncle Jim had been right. "I've stayed inside all weekend," she said as she pivoted. "I'm ashamed. I didn't want you to see me like this. I didn't want anyone to see."

"When?" I asked, shaken by the sight of her. "When did he do this? And why?"

"Saturday morning. Just before he left town. He thinks I wouldn't allow anyone to see me naked like this, not with all these bruises. It's insurance, Jack. He's always thought it would keep me from being unfaithful to him."

"The son of a bitch," I said fervently. "I hope someone does the same thing to him."

"I hate him."

"Do you need to see a doctor?"

"No. I told you, I don't want anyone to know. Anyway, a doctor couldn't fix what needs fixing."

"He's crazy, Linda," I said. "He's a cruel, crazy, lunatic, and you need to get away from him. He could kill you! Why do you stay?"

She shrugged. "I have two children. They need a father, despicable as he is. And I can't manage alone." She spread her fingers and covered her loins, then reached for the switch and turned off the bathroom light. "Something is bothering him now, too, something more than the story going around town, if he knows about it. Maybe his new girlfriend. Maybe he'll leave me for her."

I threw back the sheet and groped about for my clothes. Mrs. Murray's bruises were paltry in comparison to what would happen to me if her husband came back and found me, and the longer I was here, the more likelihood that would happen. Linda Murray rounded the bed and kneeled to embrace me, shivering in the coolness. "Please don't go," she said. "Am I that undesirable, bruised as I am?" She pushed, and I rolled back upon the bed. She rose and fell alongside me, curled her body against my chest, and held tightly to me. "Please don't go."

"But suppose he comes back early?"

"He won't. And I need you here." I felt her head turn to look up at me. "It's not just the sex, Jack," she said. "It's you. People like you. You're the opposite of Melville. You're proof to me that there are people who care, and love. Gentle people. People who wouldn't hurt another human being. I need to know that. You know what?"

"No," I said. "What?"

"I feel good about tonight. Damn good! I felt like I was beating Melville. I knew it was you, but I was punishing him. While we were making love, I... overcame him. I was the one dishing it out for a change. It was a wonderful feeling to know I was hurting him. I wish he would die!"

"My god!" I said. "Leave him! While he's gone, pack your things, take Tommy and Barbara Ann, and go somewhere where he'll never find you. I'll help you."

The lovely woman stiffened and sat up, hugged a pillow tightly to her breasts, and swayed with it as she might have rocked a baby. "I can't," she said. "I can't. He would kill me. And I have too much pride. My children... I'd rather hurt him, damn it. I'd rather kill him! Will you kill him for me, Jack?"

I knew she wasn't serious. "I couldn't kill anybody," I said. "Not even Coach Murray."

"I know. I know. I'll have to do it, if it gets done." She threw the pillow aside and snuggled against me once again. Despite my fear, the warm breath on my neck excited me. "You're sure he's not coming back?"

"I'm sure." Her husky voice, her lips, tickled my skin as she spoke. She used a fingertip to singe each place where it touched my back. "Let's do it again," she said, "only this time let's do it right. Just you and me."

"I'm so scared," I said, "I don't know if junior has the get-up-and-go for another bout."

"No bout, Jack," she said tenderly. "Heart and soul. Love. Just you and me."

Her lips were as soft and yielding as the first time she ever kissed me. I was reminded, by the tenderness of my mouth, of my date with Saxon, and again my conscience pricked me. But Linda Murray and I made love again, without thought of children or husband, or even of Saxon, and the experience was as extraordinary as it had been the first time. When I finally pulled away, at three in the morning by her clock, she was passive and quiet, and she allowed me to go without again begging me to stay. We shared a silent embrace beside her back door, then I hurried away into the darkness of the tree line. I was so relieved to have survived the experience without a confrontation with her husband that I felt like shouting for joy.

If my movements were witnessed along the way towards home, I was not aware, and when I fell into my bed at Cherokee Rose I slept the sleep of the dead. But I was awake long enough to wonder if that had been the final time for Linda Murray and myself. I could not explain why, but I felt sure it was.

Dredged from some hellish dementia, or torn from an engram rooted in childhood trauma, milady of the warm milk bath revisited me. I awoke from the nightmare as the sound of a freight train was fading in the south, and I lay awake for a while, unable to think of anything else. The dream was the same as always. But my perception of it had changed.

Warm, white, creamy, heavy-smelling milk. A naked lady in

the tub with me. Love-making. Shudders and ripples from the train. The mean drunk dragging her away. Her wild, crazy screams. That was what had changed. Her cries. They weren't screams of horror. The lady hadn't been afraid. She hadn't been crying. What the hell? I wondered as I lay half awake. Was she laughing? Was that wild, hysterical laughter?

It didn't make sense. But, then, nothing about the dream made much sense.

The faraway whistle from another freighter, this one approaching Smith Station, was unsettling enough after the nightmare to drive me to seek companionship. I jumped from bed, ran to the back door, and called for Willie. I hoped he wasn't on the prowl tonight, and I was delighted a moment later when he appeared and accepted my invitation to join me in bed. His tail wagged happily, and though he smelled of some grizzly carnage, I insisted that he huddle under the covers alongside me.

We'd had nearly three hours of sleep when the chime of the clock in the hallway struck the half-hour. Six-thirty, and a school day. Monday. I bathed myself, dressed, fed and thanked Willie for coming to my rescue, then decided to drop by Mama Mary's before going on to my first class. There were real people at the café. That's what I needed. A touch of reality to help offset the unearthly events of this morning and the past few days. I tied my gun across my belly before leaving.

They were all familiar faces seated around the tables, no one I specifically cared to engage in conversation, and especially one, Squeaky Bishop, whom I avoided by quickly taking a chair behind a pinball machine. Squeaky was busily protesting the presence of a cockroach on the floor beside his stool while Mama Mary leaned her chin on her elbows and consoled him by nodding her head and compressing her lips in serious agreement. Squeaky hated roaches. The cafe could be swarming with swooping house-flies and Squeaky paid no attention. But let a cockroach show its whiskers, and Squeaky would be threatening it with a slug from his thirty-eight. This particular bug must have been aware of

Squeaky's missing teeth and the favorable repercussions that held for him, for he refused to heed Squeaky's warnings to vamoose, and instead awaited the crumbs sure to drop from Squeaky's slapping gums.

I was encouraged by activities in the café. They confirmed that the world around me was as normal as I had left it last week. Mary served my breakfast. A recuperating drunk eyed the back door, probably wondering if he could locate the hidden stash out back. There was even a pool game and rock music. Smith Station, it seemed, was on routine. I was the one who had changed. Nothing seemed the same as it had been before I discovered the world of illicit pleasures. I had my breakfast and pondered my downfall, then wondered why I had ever lived otherwise. I'd had more fun and excitement and close calls the last few days than I'd had in all my life up to this point. I regretted none of it. Except, perhaps, the pain I had inflicted upon Josephine. Hell, I'd been SQUARE until this past week! I was changed forever now. Honor and virtue were fine in their place. But I could learn to forgive me my own transgressions.

Squeaky had disappeared, probably hastened along by the stalwart roach, and Mama Mary was answering the telephone when I stood waiting alongside her cash register to pay for breakfast. To my surprise, she took the bill I offered, then handed the receiver to me. "Jim," she said under her breath.

I took the receiver from her. "Uncle Jim?" I said. "Is that you?"

"You're alive!" he barked.

"Of course I am."

"We have to have our phone checked. Gertrude swears it's working, but that's not possible."

"Oh," I said. "Well, I've been out a lot lately. It's good to hear your voice."

"Out, huh? Have you gone and finally got yourself laid, boy?"

I was caught off guard. The way I stuttered my reply gave me away for good. "Well, I, you know...," I stammered. "I'm in a public place, you know. And Gertrude. No telling..."

"Well, I'll be damned!" he exclaimed. "You did it! Who was she? Anybody I know? White girl?"

"Now, I didn't say I did that, Uncle Jim." I glanced around anxiously to make sure nobody besides Gertrude could hear me. "And if I did, I wouldn't feel free to talk about it. Not on this public telephone system."

"Well, hell, you can tell me later. Congratulations! It's a memorable occasion! We'll have a drink to celebrate. Now. Can you be up here at one o'clock today?"

"Well, I've got school... Wait a minute! You haven't been locked up even a week! You always stay longer than that. You're not ready to come home already, are you?"

"Damn right I am. I'm sick of this damn food. And the nurses won't cooperate. I never want to see another checkerboard, either. And the worst thing is, I'm sober as a pig in a slaughterhouse. I've got to get out and get me a bottle!"

"No!" I cried. "You're there to dry out! To learn how to quit drinking. What does Doctor Blake say?"

"You ask him. You have an appointment with him at one o'clock."

"Oh, no!"

"Yep. We've been putting this off too long. Be up here at one o'clock."

"He'll lock me up!"

"Stick a pint in the Plymouth before you come."

"No!"

He hung up laughing. I glanced about the cafe to be sure no one had overheard that I was about to have to visit a shrink. No one was paying any attention to me. After I'd collected my change from Mama Mary, I headed for school.

The thought of seeing Saxon again quickened my steps, while the near-certainty of also running into Coach Murray slowed them, so that I was alternately loping and poking, depending upon the thought of the moment. There were no football jocks on the field, no doubt due to Coach Murray's delayed arrival this morning, and I rounded the long, curved sidewalk undaunted by their pompous antics. On the school grounds, after ascertaining there was nothing more interesting to do, I joined a group of my male classmates who had gathered below the second-floor window of the girls' bathroom in hopes of spotting or hearing something lewd. After a few minutes of fruitless observation, we turned as a group at the sound of first bell and reluctantly wandered toward our classrooms.

Archie was already seated in our English classroom, and although I wanted to brag about my date with Saxon, that would have to wait. He returned my wave as I sat across the room in a seat mandated by Mrs. Green a month earlier to separate the two of us. She was there already, too, and she waited until everyone was quiet, then began her lecture. I'd had about all of diagramming sentences I could handle for one lifetime—would you ever use such unproductive knowledge after graduation anyway? – so, I instead concentrated my thoughts on what I would tell Doctor Blake about the nightmare. Just how hard would he laugh? I wondered. A warm milk bath with a naked woman, after all. Hilarious!

Polynomials were about as useless as fragmented sentences, so during Algebra class I continued the mental legwork. The time was wasted.

Toward the end of Algebra class I was distracted from my preoccupation by Sandra Hull, a bright, freckle-faced, red-haired girl, who was trying to control her giggles. Richard, I decided before I turned. Sure enough, Sandra had her eyes cut to where the big man sat grinning, staring straight ahead as if he were concentrating on all the scribbles our teacher had created on the blackboard. Every so often, whether due natural phenomena or natural urge, Richard experienced an accidental rise in his famous appendage that established a distinct bulge in his jeans. Despite his avowed efforts to the contrary during such a predicament, Richard seemed unable to influence the constant twitching of his contraption. Sandra was only one of a number of girls who loved to watch its maneuvers. But Sandra had limited control of her snickers. I figured it was only a matter of time until Mrs. Green investigated and got the shock of her life.

The established routine of Archie and I meeting Jerry at the Chevy during recess was derailed in the hallway after Algebra class. Archie and I were on our way out when Saxon tapped my shoulder from behind. Archie's eyes bulged when he saw her. "Would you excuse us, Archie?" I said, the way I knew Gary Cooper would do it. Forceful. Grave. Suave. Shoo, Arch.

"Sure," Archie said. He backed away until his rear grazed one of the hot-water radiators. "But I need to talk to you, Jack," he said before he wheeled to leave. "Seriously."

"Ah, Miss Browne," I said as I turned full attention to her. "And you look a delightful wee filly today, ma'am. Surely your evening of last has agreed with your disposition."

"Well, that's for sure, Mr. Smith," she said. "And you are so silly."

"But your evening was entertaining, was it not?"

"Oh, yes. I think it was having my teeth licked that did it. I think I'll have it done again."

"Aha," I said, "and I hope you will consider your servant and slave, he who stands before you, when next you are in need of a good teeth-licking? Perhaps this very evening, if I may be so bold?"

"No, I have a date with Perry tonight."

My mouth dropped open. "Damn!"

"It's nothing. I told you, we're through..."

There was nothing in the classics I'd read that had language strong enough. So I said, "You're through with him, but you've got a date with the mother-fucker?"

"Now, Jack..."

"Damn!"

"He called and begged. Last night, after I got home. He was pitiful, Jack. Just this once. Okay? Just to end it once and for all."

My repertoire of the quaint languages was once again undone by natural and more modern and effective discourse: "Fuck!"

I might have continued to utilize contemporary instinctive colloquy to make my point regarding Perry Norman, except that the subject himself suddenly appeared. A noisy gnashing of his teeth must have attracted my attention. Or maybe I noticed him because conversation in the hallway had died down, with the effect that the exchange going on between Saxon Browne and myself was echoing around the hallway like two cats having a war in a metal trashcan. "I'll wipe the floor up with him," I growled as I returned the hero's frown from a safe distance of ten or twelve feet.

"Oh, no!" Saxon turned to look in his direction, then took a step toward him. "I'll talk to you later, Jack," she said hurriedly.

I watched and died a little inside as my girl took Perry's arm and pulled him in the opposite direction. He resisted meagerly, with only an evil glance over his shoulder at me, content, I suppose, that Saxon had made her choice. In public.

My chin and knuckles scraped along the concrete sidewalk as I walked toward home. Birds flew over and splattered the top of my head with digested birdseed. The shuffling of my feet wore holes through the soles of my shoes. I slobbered profusely without wiping. Finally, the impact of the City of New Orleans, southbound and flying low, hurled me from the rails and crushed my body against the north wall of the loading docks, where I slid to the ground and was thankful for an end to living. Anyway, that's what I think happened on the walk home.

No more school today. I couldn't bear the grins and "I-told-you-sos" from Jerry. The snickers from Arch. The pointing and giggling from my classmates. I was through. Washed up. End of the line. Public humiliation of the worst kind. Even being exposed as a Peeping Tom couldn't be this bad. Put down by a mere football super hero! In front of everyone! Mortifying. I'd ask Doctor Blake's advice during my psycho session. Maybe he had some good drugs to ease the pain. Maybe he had some good drugs to use for suicide.

I'd barely entered Cherokee Rose and had just thrown myself

face down on the sofa to try to stop breathing forever when I heard Archie calling my name. I raised my head long enough to yell, "Come on in, Arch."

"You're skipping the rest of school?" Archie called from somewhere in the direction of the front door.

I pushed to a sitting position and avoided looking at him. "You heard what happened, didn't you?" I said. "I may never go back."

No?" He came to the sofa and sat beside me. "Why not? All I heard was that you were talking to Perry's girl, and he walked up and saw you. So she left and you took off. What's the big deal?"

"The big deal is, I thought I..."

I wasn't willing to bear my soul, to share the depths of my feelings. Not with Archie. Not with anybody. "Nothing," I said. "No big deal."

"I didn't come over here to discuss your love life. Or lack thereof." He snickered, and I thought briefly of my weapon lying within unzipped grasp. "I told you I had something important to talk to you about. I ain't got but a minute. Mom'll kill me if I miss class."

I said, "I hope you haven't told Melba or another stoolie about Coach being out with Josephine."

Archie's fake smile displayed plenty of teeth. He bounced excitedly on the sofa. "No!" he exclaimed. "That would ruin everything! Cause we're gonna blackmail him, Jack! All that money he cheated Mr. Bass out of, we're gonna get back. Split three ways! You, me, and Jerry. We'll be practically rich!"

"What the hell are you talking about?"

Archie could hardly control his enthusiasm. "Meatloaf would be run out of town if anybody knew what he's been up to, Jack. You know that. He ain't got no choice. He either pays up, or we tell. So he'll pay up!"

The hair on the back of my neck rose, and for a few moments the loss of Saxon Browne seemed unimportant. "What have you and Jerry done?" I asked. "Tell me what you've done!"

"Well." Archie rubbed his hands together, pride showing in his red face. "Over the weekend—Sunday—I wrote a letter to Coach Melville Murray. I told him we knew all about Josephine, and that we thought it was a disgrace. We Certain Citizens of Smith Station, of course. I didn't give our real names. I told him either he left three thousand dollars in a certain locker in the gymnasium exactly three days from now—Thursday—or we'd inform all the other people of Smith Station about his repulsive behavior. Repulsive. I looked that word up. So, all we gotta do is sit back and wait for the loot."

"Arch, you didn't mail that letter yet, did you?" I said.

"Naw. I..."

"Great." I sighed, relaxing again. "Man, don't you think Coach Murray would know who sent it?"

"Naw, Jack, Meatloaf can't know for sure."

I felt my blood pressure rising again. "Hell, he'd have to be stupid, Archie! Which he ain't. A locker in our gymnasium? Good god! I'm glad you didn't mail the darn thing."

"I never intended to mail it. I put it on the front seat of his car between classes."

"Oh, hell, no!"

"Yep. You know Meatloaf. He ain't got classes third period. So he always goes somewhere. By now, he's read our letter. By now, the bastard's sweating."

I fell back limply on the sofa. "Oh, my god! As if we didn't have trouble enough already! We're doomed!"

"No, we're gonna score big, Jack." Archie got off the sofa and turned to go. "Just you wait. When you got a thousand big ones in your hands, you'll see. I gotta run."

"Archie," I said quietly, "if I survive another week, will you do me one favor?"

"Sure. What?"

I rose and bared my teeth. "Never darken my doorway again, you idiot!"

"You're kidding."

"Yeah." I said, nodding, "what the fuck difference does it make now? You can't get me killed but once."

Archie departed. I felt strangely safe with my cheeks crammed between the sofa cushions, a sort of ostrich-head-in-the-sand analogy that was protection from the world. It was not yet time to leave for Blake Sanatorium, so I gratefully secluded myself between cushions, images of Saxon and Linda and Josephine, Coach Murray and Jim, Archie and Jerry filling my thoughts. The potential withering of my relationships with close friends and with the females I had always admired and desired was not a comforting perception. But, then, maybe it was good. Maybe I SHOULD become a social wallflower. Other people were deranged. They were scary. All of them. Anyway, after my exposure as a Peeping Tom and adulterer, children would flee me. Mothers would mount a campaign to have me denutted. Fathers would regularly warn their sons and daughters of my peculiar habits. I would become a derelict. Maybe Jim would let me stay. I hoped.

Eventually I dragged my face out of cushions and washed it, then unloaded my jeans of jock strap and six-shooter. I didn't want Jim to know I'd been packing heat. I also removed chairs from under doorknobs and unlatched bolts on doors that hadn't been locked for years. I wanted no evidence left that Cherokee Rose had been fortified. Satisfied that I'd covered my tracks, I trudged out to the wagon for the trip north to retrieve my uncle.

CHAPTER 17

THE CLUE

A	FTER DOWNING A Mary's Special – ham, beans, pickle rel-
ish, white rice, cornbread, and pecan pie for desert—I had
time for a leisurely drive to the Sanatorium. The purple-haired
receptionist greeted me in her normally cheery fashion, and while
I held my breath and tried not to inhale the sick air around us she
examined her large appointment book, looked up after a minute,
and said, very sweetly, "Oh, you have an appointment with Doctor Blake at one, don't you?" as if she'd just discovered it.

"The appointment's not really for me," I insisted. "Doctor
Blake just wants my advice. It's that new patient of his, Tubby
Tyrone. Real lulu. I'm gonna help Doctor Blake with the psycho-
analysis. He knows I have a way with crazy people."

She didn't crack a smile. Probably, I thought, all the insane
people who come here try something like that. It's denial. Denial
that you're really sick, that you need help. Like me.

I was too nervous to be still, and walking around helped to dis-
perse the grimy atmosphere anyway. So I didn't sit. In a few minutes Doctor Blake came around a corner of the long hallway and
found me standing at a front window studying the bushes outside.

The doctor had been afflicted, I suppose, by a harelip from
birth, for his lips were badly scarred. The condition affected his
speech, which emerged with a distinct lisp from a corner of his
mouth. His appearance otherwise was unusual as well, but particularly his head, which seemed far too large for the rest of his
plump body. It had always reminded me of one of the bumpers
under the glass of Mama Mary's pinball machines. Bald as an

onion, much like a luminous pinball bumper, it glowed as if he'd just paid a shoeshine boy to work on it. A person could have shaved by the reflection cast by that head. Certainly, I noted today, with its stout neck and glossy patina, Doctor Blake's noggin WOULD make a perfect pinball bumper. And then I thought with a shudder: Damn! It's strange what peculiarities pop into my mind. Do other people think like this? Hell, maybe I AM nuts.

"Hello, Jack," Doctor Blake greeted me with his skewed lips. He took my hand in his limp, moist one, and shook it. "Come on back."

His office was clean and straight, not a piece of paper, or even a paper clip, out of place. Various credentials hung framed on the walls, near bookcases lined with huge gray books. His desk was large and dark, a pen holder and notebook the doctor's only visible tools. There were no photos of family anywhere. He probably had no time for family anyway. He smiled as we sat on opposite sides of the desk. "How's the world treating you?" he said pleasantly.

"Interesting," I answered. "Very interesting."

He rocked back in his chair and raised a brow. "That's an unusual answer. I don't think I've ever gotten that one before."

"Like Al Jolson said, Doctor Blake, you ain't heard nothing yet."

Blake took his pen and moved the pad into writing position. "Well, let's get started. Jim told me a little about your dream. You tell me about it, with as much detail as you can remember. Just relax, now. Would you like a Coke?"

I told him "no" to the Coke, and after a few seconds used for gathering courage and thoughts, began to relate the details of my nightmare. I wasn't surprised at how nervous I had become, but the way my uneasiness affected my speech was unexpected. I sounded like I was talking through a tin-can-and-string telephone. I felt myself trembling; I couldn't stop it. The doctor interrupted a couple of times for clarification of some detail or other, but for the most part he merely listened and nodded along the way, ignoring my anxiety. At a point near the conclusion he raised his hand and asked, "This man called you what? A 'little bastard?' A 'murderer?'"

"That's right."

"And you think the woman is laughing hysterically as she's being dragged away? Not screaming for help?"

"I think so."

"Go on."

"That's about all of it, Doctor Blake."

"Well," he said, dropping his pencil and leaning back, "that wasn't too bad. I can understand why it upsets you. But it's not so unusual to have strange dreams."

"Not 'dreams,'" I said. "'Dream.' And it's so real. I can't hear a freight train now without wanting to run for cover."

The doctor leaned back across his desk and took up pen and pad. "Now, Jack," he said, "we're going to do something different. I want you to start over. Tell me the whole thing again, only this time tell me why you think the people in your dream are doing what they're doing. Don't be afraid, or ashamed. I'm a doctor. This is just between you and me."

He interrupted several times during the second version. "What was the song she was humming?" he asked once.

"An old slave song, I think. A religious song."

"And why?"

"Who knows?"

"You think this woman is your mother?"

"Maybe."

"And you made love to her?"

"Maybe it wasn't my mother."

"And the milk had a strong smell to it?"

"Heavy. Warm. Musky."

"Did you think of your mother when you smelled it?"

"I don't know."

"A train?" he asked another time. "You heard a train?"

"Yes, sir?"

"The milk rippled when the train passed?"

"Like an ocean."

"And it stopped when?"

"When the caboose was down the tracks."

Later he asked, "This strange man said what? You were a murderer? And a bastard?"

"A 'murdering little bastard.' That's what he said."

"Why?"

"I don't know."

"And you blame yourself for letting the woman be taken?"

"I should've helped her."

"But you were a child. In your dream. How could you have helped?"

"I don't know. I should have done something."

"There was nothing you could do."

"Now, once more," he said when I was through. "Tell me every detail again. But this time, tell it as though you are an observer. You're sitting in a chair beside the bed, and you see the whole thing. Can you do that?"

"It won't make any sense."

"Try."

So I went through the thing again in somewhat chaotic fashion that developed bit by bit as I awkwardly visualized the scene from across the dream room. What emerged was a description of an incident of such absurdity that it was almost as comical as I had earlier feared. I even laughed at it.

"There's a kid in the bedroom swimming in a tub filled with warm milk. Why the hell's the tub in the bedroom?"

Blake smiled and added notes.

"So a naked woman, maybe his mother, jumps in the tub with him, and the kid hustles her. Pretty soon, they're doing it. They both love it. A family affair."

"Good. Good."

"But in a little while they hear the train coming, and they know that's trouble. So Mom jumps out to fix things, and lo and behold, the evil uncle comes through the door, and boy, is he pissed!"

"Who?" Blake asked.

"The evil..."

I stopped as though a bullet had struck my forehead. "The evil person," I said quickly.

"You said uncle."

I shook my head. "No. That's not what I meant."

Blake placed his notebook carefully on the desk. We sat and stared at one another for a while. Then he said, "The mind does strange things, Jack. It twists events, shades them, and amplifies them. Especially childhood events. We human beings are much more influenced by new and strange experiences when we're in infancy. We're like blackboards, waiting to be written upon by our environment. Others take a hand in what's written. But sometimes our blackboards record events in a very distorted manner. Sometimes things become so twisted we're haunted by deceptive memories. Or dreams."

I shook my head, "I don't know what made me say a stupid thing like that, Doctor Blake. I didn't get a look at the guy's face. It wasn't my uncle."

"Then who was he, Jack?"

"I don't know."

"Who was the man in your dream, Jack?"

"I don't know. I didn't get a good look at him."

"You said he picked you up and looked you right in the eyes. You must have seen him."

"I've never seen him before. Or since. I swear."

"You're sure."

"Yes, damn it!" I swore. "I'm sure!"

His writing pen tapped his fingertips as he stared. "We've been at this for over an hour," he said after a moment as he rose and came around the desk. "Jim's in his room waiting. Would you stay right here? I'll go get him."

"Do we need him? We don't need him."

"I'll only be a minute."

I grabbed his arm before he could get through the door. "Don't tell him what I said, Doctor Blake. You won't, will you?"

Blake smiled and said nothing.

My god! I thought after he was gone. What the hell was I thinking about? Uncle Jim? No! Never could I seriously believe that the kindest, best person I'd ever known was capable of such cruelty. Or murder? The very thought sickened me, and I prayed Doctor Blake would not divulge the slip to him.

There was nothing to do now but sit and wait. I settled into my chair and let my mind drift. An hour of psychoanalysis had been much more exhausting than I would have imagined. Blake's office was warm and quiet, and I began to nod. But it struck me soon that Blake had been gone quite a while. I became uneasy then. Jim's room couldn't be far, yet if I were any judge of time, Blake had been gone for twenty minutes or more. Maybe he had to see another patient. Maybe someone stopped him for a chat. Maybe I should investigate.

The muffled sounds of a heated conversation surprised me then. The room next door, I decided. Someone arguing. I quietly left my chair and tip-toed to the wall that Blake used to display his diplomas. There was room for an ear between them, and I carefully positioned one against the wood paneling. Two men arguing. Cursing. One of them cursing. Familiar cursing. The other shouting. His words distorted. By lisps. Jim and Blake!

The paneling proved too competent an insulator for me to distinguish words, other than an occasional four-letter burst from Jim. I tip-toed back to my chair. Had Jim been next door all the time? I wondered. Was it possible that he had been there, listening by some means, to my entire session with the doctor? I hoped not. Why would he want to eavesdrop anyway? Why would Blake allow it? And why were they having a knock-down-drag-out now?

The clamor subsided after another minute or two, and soon I heard the sound of a door being closed. Jim and Blake came in immediately afterwards. Jim looked fit and sound, sober as a rock. "Uncle Jim!" I said, rising to hug him. "Damn, it's good to see you!"

"I've missed you, too, boy." He hugged me back. We were always like this after one of his confinements, as if we had been separated for months.

We sat, Blake behind his desk, Uncle Jim and I opposite. Blake clucked and "hmmmed" a few times over his notebook, tapping a pencil against his Adam's apple. "Jack and I had a long talk, Jim," he said finally, still scanning the notes he had taken. "I've asked you to be present now because you are not only Jack's uncle and legal guardian, but because you are intimately aware of circumstances that may be contributing to Jack's problem. Jack has discussed this repetitive dream he's been having with you?"

Jim nodded.

"I know that the dream is a source of discomfort for you, Jack." He nodded to me, then turned back to study his notes. "Our talk today should have a positive impact. I think that you are much more aware now of its irrationality, and that in itself should help alleviate the symptoms. However, there is more we can do. With Jim's help, we can probably identify the events that during your infancy or childhood so affected you that they have manifested themselves in the form of a nightmare. Jim has been reluctant to discuss these matters with you before, for fear that such would be detrimental to you, and because the process is difficult for him. There are family members involved, and it's hard for some people to discuss events that, oh, depict them in less than shining armor. I am going to do just that, however, and ask that you, Jim..." He nodded to Jim. "You interrupt at anytime you want."

"I will," Jim said solidly.

"We believe that the source of your dream, Jack," Blake continued, "is a number of events that occurred about the time you were a year old. Plus or minus. You were barely one when your father died, so that conclusion is perhaps logical. Now." Blake squirmed in his chair and glanced for a moment at Jim. "Whether you've been told or not, your father and mother had a difficult marriage. These things happen sometimes. Unfortunately, your father was possessed of a rather fiery temper, and, especially after, uh, imbibing, he sometimes took out his frustrations on your mother. There were disagreements between the two. On more than one occasion, incidents occurred in the bedroom, perhaps even when your mother was nursing you. That could explain your association of an unpleasant act with milk, though hardly a tub filled with milk."

He smiled at me as if it were a joke, and after I dutifully smiled back, he went on. "Certainly these must have been disturbing events for you to witness, young as you were. Your subconscious mind has, however, perverted this memory. It has, and again, this is somewhat speculative at this point, mistakenly equated an argument with the kidnapping of your mother. Imagine the effect, Jack. It's no wonder you are tormented by a dream."

Jim's hand patted my arm, and I nodded.

"You loved your mother," he went on. "You depended on her. Your subconscious has distorted this fact to the equivalent of physical love. Making love. You were too small to do anything to help her when these disagreements occurred, even though you may have wanted to. So your subconscious has given you a guilt complex. And the man in the dream?" He looked to Jim, then back to me. "You never really knew your father. I did. And I can assure you, the resemblance between your father and his brother, your uncle, is remarkable. Your subconscious mind may remember that face, but, again, it has deceived you."

"You told him?" I said, glancing at Jim.

"I had to. It was important that I do so."

"It's all right, Jack," Jim said, patting my arm again. "It doesn't mean a thing. It's just a dream, after all."

"I'm sorry, Uncle Jim." I stared into my lap in misery.

"Forget it," he scoffed, "It's nothing. It's just a dream."

"One other thing, Jack," Blake said. "The woman who's the victim of the assault. Your mother, presumably. You've indicated you think she was kidnapped. However, we know that this cannot be so. There would have been an investigation. Jim would have seen to that. After your father's untimely death, your mother left Smith Station and has not been heard from since. The inference from your dream is, again, only an improper consequence of cognitive processes."

"How do we know that?" I asked.

He glanced at Jim. "Well, we may never know all the details. But people just don't kidnap other people and go about their lives as though nothing happened, Jack. There would have been evidence, an arrest." He sighed and rose from his chair as though he were weary. "We will need to get together again, Jack. Next time, I want you to tell me the effect all this has had on the dream. Call me if you need to."

"Thank you, Doctor Blake," I said.

"And I'm sorry we've had to reveal such unpleasantness. But it is necessary if we're to help you. We may have to do more of the same."

"Yes, sir."

Jim and I rose to go. "One other thing, Doctor Blake," I said before walking out the door. "Why does the man call me a 'murdering little bastard?'"

"That's easy," he smiled. "Your guilt complex. You feel to blame. The man in your dream just confirms it for you."

I accepted his explanation with a nod, then Jim and I thanked him and the three of us headed back toward the reception area. The tile floor and walls of the clinic were spotless and sunshine-bright due to the strong unnatural lighting, though the dry sparkle of wax on the floors made the place feel dusty. The absence of windows and furnishings created a sensation of unreality. A cool, stark, sterile home for misfits, I thought, filled with hollow echoes and an adhesive atmosphere of lost hope. How easy it was to hate.

Blake apologized for having other duties. "I really must see another patient," he said as he turned into another corridor. "We'll talk soon, Jack. Stay sober, Jim! Good- bye."

We thanked him again and walked on. Jim said, "I have to pick up my things from my room, Jack. Why don't you wait for me up front?"

"I'll go with you," I said. "You may need some help."

"No, no. I can handle it."

"I've never seen your room," I insisted. "I'd like to."

He hesitated, then nodded. "Down here." I followed him along another corridor. "Place hasn't been cleaned today, so don't expect much."

"I'm familiar with your foul habits. I don't expect the bed to be made."

"Insolence," he grinned. "What have I told you about insolence?"

His room was nothing as I had expected it. Perhaps ten by twelve feet in size, excepting the presence of furnishings and a pile of soiled clothing, it had the same barren brick and tile appearance as the hallway. An iron bed and single mattress, rumpled white sheets, wool blanket, and a crumpled pillow attesting to its recent occupation were positioned against one wall between a small corner bathroom and the window. Along the opposite wall a small, shaded lamp glowed atop an oak-veneer desk scarred and chipped from years of wear. A worn checkerboard occupied a prominent position, the two nearby chairs obviously meant for the players. And as I might have guessed, an old print depicting Jesus Christ with rays of light spraying from His face, a halo over His head, hung over the desk in a warped wooden frame.

But as, too, I might have guessed, the stench of the room was its most conspicuous quality. There was the inevitable residue left by a thousand burned cigarettes, and, surprisingly, in addition to the presence of other ingredients in the soup of odors, there was alcohol. No drinking was allowed on the premises, so there was only one way alcohol could have been present. Perspiration! I thought. What I smell is the warm, stale, remnant of a hundred binges and a thousand cigarettes that has made its way to my nostrils through damp pores and clammy skin. And phlegm, too!

The caustic odor of phlegm! Phlegm coughed from the depths of unhealthy lungs, its pervasion and disposition a torture to both patient and physician, and even to visitors.

Good God! I thought. The same smell as Jim's room at home!

It was, I thought with a shudder, the familiar, though concentrated, smell of death.

"Nice room," I said. "Not as messy as I expected, either."

"Don't patronize me, boy," he replied, rummaging through a desk drawer for whatever he had in mind to take with him. "This place is almost unfit for the roaches that live here. Blake raises hell all the time, wants me to take a suite up front. But I don't want it. I'd rather stay here." He paused and looked up at me, swung his hands around to encompass the entire room, and said, "And the reason is simple, my boy. I know what's in store for me when I take that first drink. It's kind of a deterrent. Of course, it doesn't work real well."

"You are not coming back here, Uncle Jim," I said. "This place stinks. You are going to stop drinking."

"Hope you're right," he laughed. "But I wouldn't place any bets on it."

"Well, take a room up front next time. Like Doctor Blake wants."

"I'll think about it."

"You are not coming back..."

"HAL...LE-LU...IAH!"

"My god!" I cried in astonishment as a glorified shriek echoed in the hallway outside. Chill bumps formed on my neck and arms. "What the hell was THAT?"

Jim walked quickly to the doorway and peered down the hall. "Shut up, you old bat!" he shouted. "Shut up! Shut up!"

"Old bat gives me the red-ass," he said as he came back through the door.

"HAL...LE-LU...IAH!"

"Shut up!"

But the "old bat" refused to heed Jim's warning. After a couple

more "halleluiahs" she began to wail, a development that had Jim
gnashing his teeth. "I'll go in there and strangle the bitch," he said
through gritted teeth as he continued to pack.

"She's in the room next to yours, isn't she?" I said with an ear
tuned to that direction. "You really do need to move up front. For
your sanity."

"She'll pipe down in a minute. She just has to purge her soul of
sin occasionally."

"Who is she?" I asked.

"Damned nut. Like all the rest of us in here."

"A Colored lady? She sounds like a Negro."

"White woman." Jim looked at me. "Let's get out of here."

"She does this often?" I asked, following him out the door with
the bag. The Rattler hung from Jim's arm.

"Fifteen or twenty times a day, on average. Varies. Sometimes
only five or ten times. Really fucks up a good game of checkers
when she howls like that. But I guess it does her good, and it's for
damn sure the Lord can hear her, if she don't just piss Him off
with all that yap. Hell, let the bitch bark, I always say. I only get
real mad when we have visitors, and that's not often."

"You ain't coming back here," I said forcefully.

As Jim closed the door behind us, the shrill words of the insane
woman caused us to glance at each other once again. "LITTLE
DAVID!" she cried, her voice clear and melodic and filled with
African dialect. "HAL...LE- LU...IAH! LITTLE DAVID HE
WAS A SHEPARD BOY. HE KILLED GOLIATH AND HE
SHOUTED FOR JOY. HAL...LE- LU...IAH!"

"Something about her voice gives me the creeps," I said. "She
and Barbara Jones could carry on a good duet."

Jim kept walking. "That beautiful young Jones girl sings?" he
asked.

"When she's in the tub. Probably."

"I'd like to see that," he said.

My eyes widened. It's in the blood! I realized with a shudder.
It's not MY fault I'm a Peeping Tom. It's in the blood!

Jim whistled when he saw the Plymouth. "Damn!" he said as we neared it. "No wonder you finally got a little. New car?"

"When I washed it, I found paint," I said. "And it gets twenty-six miles-per-gallon now. The weight of all those whiskey bottles had the sucker stalled out."

"Get it in the front seat or the back?" he said evilly. "Back's a lot more comfortable." He raised an eyebrow and grinned even more evilly.

"I had a mattress. Pillows," I said. "Sheets. You said I'd always remember the first time. I wanted a beautiful memory."

He tapped the Plymouth with his cane and said, "You're a true Smith, Cherokee Jack Junior. Your dad would be proud. Your grandmother would raise hell, though."

"Why?" I asked.

"Cherokee Rose. I always had to sneak around, myself. Your grandmother didn't think much of copulation between unmarried couples, not under her roof."

"Good thing it's just you and me, Uncle Jim."

We had turned onto the highway and started south toward town when Jim's body was wracked by a fit of noisy coughing. He lowered his window and heaved spittle, then pulled out the ever-present pack of Camels, lit up, and tried a few puffs. "Damn things don't taste right without a drink," he complained, tossing the cigarette after the spittle. "Better stop at Mary's."

He pretended interest in Davis County's rolling pastureland and the heavy cattle that roamed near the gray cypress barns. He was trying to avoid a fight. I knew that. But I was prepared to do battle. "You're going to go on a binge already?" I said accusingly. "You just got out!"

"A twenty-team mule train couldn't stop me," he said. "I've gotta have a drink. For days, now, I've been thinking about how great a man-sized slug of Mr. Times would be. Now that it's ten minutes away, I'm about to have an accident of the most indecent nature merely from the suspense."

"You'll ruin your health. Doctor Blake said so."

"Blake is full of shit."

"All your brain cells will wilt and die. Your dick won't work."

"No way."

"You'll make an ass of yourself. I'll endure all manner of shame. They'll take me away from you and put me in a foster home."

"Jack," he said patiently with eyes cut in my direction, "even after a fifth of Early Times I can outfox and out think any man living, sober or not. Within reason. Einstein, maybe, had a slight edge." He grinned. "When he was sober."

"You'll have to go back to that flophouse and put up with that crazy, cackling old witch."

"Home sweet home."

Desperate times demand desperate action. "Well, by God!" I said, "I didn't want to have to do it. I didn't want to scare hell out of you. But I'm going to have to do it anyway."

"What the fuck are you talking about?" he said, craning his neck at me.

I hated to lie. But these were desperate times. "Doctor Blake," I said. "Remember how long it took for him to finally tell you I was there today?"

"No. I didn't notice."

"Well, it was because he and I had a talk. A private talk. About you."

"No, you didn't...," he began.

"Yep. Before we went to his office. He told me you were sick, Uncle Jim. Real sick."

By the way he sat up in the seat and rubbernecked, I knew I had his attention. "Your heart. Blake said you could keel over anytime. Time bomb. Walking, talking, ticking time bomb. A few more drinks, and.... BOOM! That's all, she wrote."

"Goddamn!" Jim said. He'd sat straighter on the seat with every word from my lips, hanging on every syllable. "I don't believe it!"

"You think I'd lie?"

"No..." He eyed me suspiciously. "You never lie."

"Time bomb," I said, shaking my head sadly. "Tick, tick."

"Why the hell didn't Blake tell me?" he said angrily. "That cock sucker!"

"Cussing, too," I said. "Get upset, cuss a few times, get the old heart overloaded, and... Bingo! Blake said Mr. Campbell would be happy then, cause he'd have another customer for one of those fancy mahogany caskets." I peered across the seat at him. "You don't look good in mahogany, Uncle Jim."

"Blake said that?"

"I probably haven't quoted him exactly."

"Fuck!" Jim said softly as he reclined into his seat. He glanced in my direction. "I mean, darn."

"It'd be better if we went straight home, so you could get the rest you need."

"Yeah."

"I'll go on to the five-and-ten."

"Sure."

"Maybe we can have supper at Mary's tonight. Just the two of us. I don't have plans."

He shook his head and rubbed his chest and frowned. "I'm not feeling too well, Jack. I'll probably skip supper. I got some thinking to do."

"Come on. It'd be fun."

He shook his head. "No, you go on. I'll come by later if I get hungry. Remember, I'm a sick man. I've got to think about this." He seemed to shrivel with each word.

"Uncle Jim?"

I hesitated, ashamed of what I'd done. It's not worth it, I thought, just to keep him from drinking. Hell, he loved to drink! "Uncle Jim," I said, "I didn't exactly tell you the truth about what Doctor Blake said. He didn't say anything about a time bomb."

"No?" He perked up.

"He has warned you about drinking, though."

"What exactly did Blake say?"

"Well, I didn't exactly talk to him."

Jim stared at me for a long while, during which time I refused to turn and face him, snorted and coughed a few times, hung his head from the window and spat, lit a Camel and puffed fiercely on it, then addressed me. "You know how I feel about lying, Jack Junior," he said. "It's dishonorable. It's beneath a Smith. A Smith's word is as good as a written contract."

He waited for me to agree. "Yes, sir," I said finally. "A contract."

"Your father never lied. Your grandfather, either."

"Never."

"You want me to stop drinking so bad you'd lie to me?"

"You're killing yourself, Uncle Jim," I said earnestly. "Drinking doesn't make any sense if it's killing you."

"I'm not killing myself," he said with an air of impatience. His hands fluttered in front of him. "And if I am, it's MY business. Let's not talk about it again."

"Yes, sir."

"Go on to Cherokee Rose."

"Yes, sir."

"Now," he continued with a note of joy, "you haven't even bragged to me about your conquest, my boy. Tell me all the juicy details."

I stalled him until we had reached the driveway of Cherokee Rose, which gave me an excuse to give the Plymouth my full attention.

"Who is the girl? Is it the Browne girl? Why aren't you going out with her tonight?"

"She's got other plans," I said as we got out of the Plymouth.

He got out on the other side. "Ah, competition," he called. "Just makes the game interesting, boy."

The sudden thought of Saxon squashing Perry Norman's mouth with her powerful lips made me ill. "The hell with women anyway, Uncle Jim," I said. "I'm going to work."

CHAPTER 18
MAMA MARY'S REVENGE

M R. BARNES WAS a welcome sight. With his wheelbarrow walk and blazing stub of cigar, he was bedrock Smith Station, and further confirmation that there was a sane world out there. I hungered for the sound of his Perry Como tunes. The chatter of his adding machine. His gruff orders. The world would be a better place if there were more Benny Barneses. He and I exchanged greetings and inquiries about our weekend, and after we had each overstated the accomplishments of our off-day, I was placed in charge of a broom. "Whole store needs a good sweeping and cleaning," he told me, "and you handle a broom almost as good as Rastus Williams, who is out sick this afternoon. I know I can depend on you to do a good job."

"Yes, sir, Mr. Barnes," I said, leaning on my handle. "And sweeping is one of my favorite chores. Why, I'd almost sweep floors for free."

"Uh-huh," he said, his stained teeth showing in a grin as he left me.

The truth was, I did enjoy sweeping floors. There's not a lot of brain work required in pushing a mop or broom once the mechanics of the operation are learned, and that doesn't take a great while. That leaves plenty of brain left over to think and muse and plot and plan. So I never avoided floor duty, but merely accepted it as an opportunity to think about women. I did so this afternoon, meditating over two women in particular, my thoughts straying occasionally to Jim and Doctor Blake and the events at the Sanatorium. I had a lot of thinking to do about what Dr. Blake had told me. I thought about Coach Murray, and almost casually wondered what his reaction to Archie's note had been. I had developed a mental callus, I guess, for I was not overly concerned whatever the consequences of the letter or the scandal. Coach Murray and the rest of Smith Station could kill me, beat me, ignore me, whatever. I didn't care. Just so they got it over with. Meanwhile, my strategy would be: Ponder women.

The floors were in spit-shine condition by five o'clock, by which hour most of the eligible females in town had been thoughtfully stripped and examined by my mind's eye. One by one, each had fallen short of the standard set by Linda Murray. Even Saxon's snow-white teeth, the spell she had on me, her possible virginity, couldn't match the blood-boiling excitement I felt when I thought of Linda and her loving ways.

The naked girls steaming round inside my head reminded me of one of Jim's classics, a conversation between an old bull and a young bull standing on a hillside overlooking a herd of cows. "Let's run down there and make love to one of them cows," says the young bull. The wise old bull shakes his head and replies, "We'll WALK down there and make love to ALL them cows." "Them cows" were swirling in my mind like the clouds of dust around my broom.

I waited until Mr. Barnes had locked up, wished him a good evening, then crossed the street to Murphy's Dry Goods Store to see if Archie were still alive. The store's front door was locked, but a light glowed beyond the back partition, near the shoe storage rack, suggesting that someone was still inside. Maybe Arch, I thought.

Mr. Murphy's store, like Mr. Barnes', had a back door used almost exclusively by the employees. I made my way through the alley leading in that direction, and in a moment verified that the back door, too, was locked. However, as I attempted to turn the doorknob, the door cracked. Locked, but not latched, I saw. Light spilled through the crack as I shoved the door open. "Archie?" I whispered.

A sound much like that of a loose floorboard groaning when it's stepped on caught my attention. I thought, that's no one walking, unless they're stepping on the same board over and over. So what? The frantic squeaking continued as I stole past a small men's bathroom, noting at my feet that the straight edge of light cast on the floor from around the corner of the shoe rack was moving in cadence with the squeaks. The entire shoe rack was pulsating. Then I heard the grunts. I'll be damned! I thought. I'll be damned! Archie ain't been lying all this time after all!

There was no resisting the urge to take a peek, but as I stuck my head around the corner of the creaking shoe rack, I thought, here I am, a Peeping Tom, peeping on my buddy, who's also a Peeping Tom. Is there no end?

And there they were, intently engaged in an activity as ancient as man. They had not removed their clothes, which was of some relief since I had no desire to scrutinize the privates of either of them, but had loosened or removed only those articles necessary to allow contact of essential portions. Skirt hiked, Melba sat upon a wooden box shoved against the shoe rack at a height a bit too elevated to allow Archie total comfort as he toiled. His hands gripped her knees tenaciously; he teetered precariously on tiptoes as though he were lodged on the seat of a bicycle that had gone out of control. She likewise clutched his shoulders, apparently to prevent her rear from being thrown off the box and onto the floor as a result of Archie's lunges.

The two were oblivious to the rest of the world. Archie's acne scars were blood red, the welts on his cheeks quivering with every puff from his open mouth. His eyes were closed, as were Melba's, hers so tightly locked in something near a grimace that long wrinkles extended to her ears. With every stroke she grunted. Sounds like a pig, I thought. Like one of those ninety-year-old women who come in the store sometimes. With every step, a grunt. The faces of the two of them and the sounds they made were such that, viewed out of the context of the act in which they were engaged, one might have exclaimed "funny farm!" on the one hand, and "torture!" on the other.

The urge to scare hell out of them was intense. Could I sound like Mr. Murphy, come back unexpectedly? Would Archie or Melba faint? Suffer heart failure? Would either of them ever speak to me again?

I thought better of it, carefully retraced my steps, and closed the door behind me. Let them be, I thought. They're happy with what they've got, and probably nobody else in the whole world would have either of them. They're lucky they have each other. The rest of us should be so lucky.

Jerry was parking the Chevy in front of Mary's Cafe as I walked past. I stopped and waited for him. "Jerry Bass decides to venture forth once more into the world about him," I said as he approached, "ascared no more of the terrible wrath of vengeful pit patrons."

"Fuck. Can't stay cooped up forever," he said, dragging deeply on his Lucky. "If he ain't done nothing by now, he ain't going to."

"He was out of town all weekend," I said. "He wasn't around to hear the rumors."

Jerry's eyes darted nervously. "He was?"

"Yep."

"You wouldn't lie, would you?"

"Not until lately. I'm reformed now."

He grinned and gestured toward the café's door. "Let's have a beer."

"I need to go home for a minute," I said. "I'll be back."

Jerry leaned close and whispered, "We need to talk. We need to decide how we're gonna spend our loot. Two more days, and we'll be rolling in cash, Jack."

"Down payment on a tombstone," I said. "That's what I'll use my thousand for."

Jerry, with a flip of his head and hair let out a shocked, "Holy Toledo! You worry too much! This plan is foolproof!"

"You've been listening to Archie again. Don't you ever learn?"

"Yeah," he snorted. "Like you do."

"This is true. I am certainly as much a dumb ass as you are."

Jerry shook his head, wrinkled his nose, and tried to convince himself. "Naw. The runt's got a winner this time. We'll get my dad's money back. The runt's coming by the cafe in a little while. Said he would be a little late, had to give Melba a good screwing." He chuckled and picked a small piece of tobacco from his lip. "He don't give up, does he?"

"Maybe he's telling us the truth."

"You know better."

Jerry disappeared into the cafe, and I turned the block toward Cherokee Rose. Jim had been home all of three hours now, and I was anxious to learn if he'd already fallen off the wagon. Fifty-fifty, I figured, based on past experience. As I walked in, he looked up from the sofa where he was reading the Davis County Observer. He slipped his reading glasses from his nose. "The goddamn Yankees are going to force us to integrate yet," he said crossly. "Have you seen a newspaper lately?"

"No, sir," I said.

"Well, it's coming. It'll be the ruination of the South. They weren't satisfied with killing our patriots, burning our houses, and stealing our land and everything else that wasn't buried. Now we're the slaves! Goddamn the cock-sucking Yankees anyway!"

"Yeah," I said, taking a seat beside him, "I can't imagine being in class with Josephine Rossetti all day. It's bad enough with Saxon Browne and Teeny Wright. Add Josephine, and any chance to educate the male population will end. Future graduating classes will be strictly feminine."

"If they were all like Josephine, it'd be fine," he said irritably. "You know what I mean."

"I guess."

"And nothing we can do about it. It'll be forced on us by a bunch of morons from Massachusetts who have no idea what we'll be faced with. And furthermore, they won't give a great goddamn, either. The uncivilized, pompous, tyrannical, despotic, gluttonous mother-fuckers."

"Obviously, you're sober, Uncle Jim," I said, patting his shoulder. "The quality of your slang is excellent. More than that, even. It's monumental."

"Be serious," he retorted as he pulled away. "This is enough to drive a person to drink."

"I'll have them stop delivery of the newspaper."

"On another note," he said, dropping the newspaper and raising an eyebrow, "I'm still dying to hear the details of your triumph over virginity. Tell me. I love a good lust story."

"Now, Uncle Jim," I said, squirming, "I don't feel comfortable talking about that."

He said evilly, "You had to hold a gun on her, didn't you?"

"What?"

"I noticed the thirty-eight in your bedroom. Poor girl wouldn't cooperate, so you pulled a gun on her."

Had I forgotten to put the pistol back in Jim's room? "It was a noise I heard the other night," I said dryly. "I thought we had a burglar."

"There hasn't been a robbery in Smith Station in years."

"Yeah. It was only Willie."

"So," he said eagerly, "back to the blessed occasion. Was it good? Did she enjoy it? Did she say she did? Did you enjoy it? Did you hang in there? Did you remember what I told you?"

"Yes, yes, yes, yes and yes. She said it was terrific. And I remembered what you said. I kept on going until I had blisters. Hours on end. She owes her total fulfillment to you and your advice."

"Even after she popped her cork, you kept on?"

"Yep. Even after she popped. I guess."

He smiled and relaxed into the cushions of the sofa as though satisfied with my performance. "The real joy in sex," he said with a contented sigh, "comes from pleasing your partner, Jack. From pleasing a woman who wants just as much to please you. That's what makes it all worthwhile."

"None of the guys at school talk about it like that," I said. "It's more wham-bam-thank-you-ma'am with them."

"Their words are drivel, my boy." He nodded wisely. "Their intimate relationships will always be inferior. You should ignore what they say. The physical union of two people who love each other, intensely love each other, is the most satisfying experience life has to offer. If you remember only one thing I've told you, remember that. And never settle for less."

"Okay," I said, "I swear I will never allow any woman who fails to swear intense love for me to use my body for any sexual purpose whatsoever."

Jim sighed in disgust and went back to his newspaper. I grinned at him and asked him, "I'm going to go up to the cafe. Jerry and Archie are there. Want to come up and have supper with us?"

"I might," he answered offhandedly without looking up. "Might just go to bed early, though."

"Want me to stay home? We could get a good game of checkers going."

He growled under his breath and kept reading. I took that to be a "no," and I left him to try to find Willie. The guard dog was nowhere to be seen, having probably found more interesting business than waiting around for me, so I filled his bowl, told Jim so-long, and headed back uptown. By the time I arrived back at Mary's and had taken my seat at our table, Archie had finished his "chore" and was waiting. "Archie Jones, too," I said before he had a chance to speak, "abandons his humble abode and the maternal protection afforded therein, for an opportunity to prove his mettle against the forces of evil. Meaning, of course, the Mighty Meathead, Melville."

"We got the Evil One by the balls," Archie grinned. "I ain't scared now. He ain't gonna start nothing."

I eyed him, then turned to Jerry. "Did either of you two bump into him at school today? And did he threaten to rip off your privates then and there?"

"No," Jerry answered, "I don't think he came back to school after third period this morning. After..."

"Reading my note made him ill," Archie snickered. "He probably went home and got sick."

"Or to get a shotgun," I said.

"I been screwing Melba!" Archie said proudly. "I was great! Girl had to crawl home. Couldn't walk!"

Jerry sneered and said, "I've heard all that shit I want to hear, runt. Even though Melba ain't much to brag about."

"Melba's BUILT."

"Built?" Jerry said incredulously. "If one of Mr. Browne's bulls caught sight of her, he'd break a land speed record running down the hill for some!"

I joined in. "She probably grunts, too, like a well-fed cow."

"Melba don't grunt!" Archie said angrily. "And she ain't that fat!"

Jerry rocked his chair back onto its back legs. "Only about a hundred and fifty pounds," he chuckled. "If she was a hog, they'd have butchered her when they found out she couldn't squeeze through the barn doors no more."

"Think I'll have a special," I said, turning to eye Mary's blackboard. "Let's see. Corn-beef hash, collard greens, black-eyed peas, chitlin bread, and bread pudding for dessert. All that, and a cold beer to slosh it down. Yummy!"

Archie said to Jerry, savagely, "I found out some more about Teeny and Muledick. I heard they was laughing at you, Jerry. They was..."

"Let me tell you two about my date with Saxon, guys," I interrupted loudly, as the two glared at each other. "You've heard I dated her, haven't you? Did I tell you? Saxon is the most divine human being on the face of the earth. I don't mind that I've had thoughts of suicide since she rejected me at school like that. That's just life. Guys, for a few minutes that night, I thought she liked me! It was fantastic! Now, of course, I've suffered the total destruction of my ego. But that doesn't change the fact that

Saxon's a goddess. She can't help being perfect. She just is. She's my loss and the football freak's gain. Hail the conquering hero! But I promise you, in the fine tradition of Scarlet O'hara, that I will hide in a dark alley and run that football fucker through with a dull hoe handle first chance I get. I'll be a lot better then. I won't have to talk about it so much after Perry's lying there kicking."

Archie relaxed. "I'm gonna use my thousand dollars to buy a motor scooter," he said wistfully. "I'm gonna ride all the way to Louisiana on it."

"Archie," I said, "I was just pouring out my soul to you. You're my buddy. You're supposed..."

"I'm gonna have my heads shaved," Jerry sighed from across the table. "I can get maybe forty more horsepower out of that baby when I shave the heads."

"Saxon can really use her lips," I bragged. "Why, I bet she could suck the chrome off a trailer ball!"

"What?" Archie said, suddenly interested. "She sucked your... No!"

"Hell, no! Archie," I said angrily "Saxon ain't like that!"

"You ain't gonna live long enough to find out, either," Jerry snickered.

I couldn't help the grimace. "I'm sure Saxon's total rejection of me earlier today will satisfy her hero's desire for vengeance. I don't think he knows we had a date anyway."

Jerry yawned as if the argument had sapped his energy. "But he'll find out," he moaned. "And imagine what it'll be like when he does. "

"I'll pack iron."

"You'll need it." He looked around. "Let's eat," he said, "and play pool and drink beer and relax for a change. Seems like a year since we did that."

The collard greens were terrific with half a bottle of pepper sauce poured on top, and the bread pudding was excellently flavored with bourbon. But the corned-beef hash could as well have been bacon and eggs, so drowned in grill residue as it was. The mid-meal round of beer, however, purchased by myself as a gesture to the 'durable friendship' enjoyed by the three of us, discouraged any complaints we might have had. I suggested a toast—"to the navel environs of the female anatomy"—to which my two buddies drank heartily. Afterwards Archie unwisely yelled, "Nother round of Schlitz, Mama Mary!" The look he got from her reminded him that he had better watch his manners.

"You know better than that, Archie Jones," she cried, standing over him and shaking her fly swatter in his face. "You want a beer, you see my Boy. We don't serve beer to the tables. It's illegal!"

Archie whispered when she was out of earshot, "Hell, having beer anywhere in Davis County is illegal. What's the big deal about serving at the tables? Old bat is crazy as a swamp rat."

"Maybe you should straighten her out," I said.

Archie's eyes rolled. "Uh-uh," he said. "I'm too young to die."

More beer and several games of eight ball later, the three of us had become once again masters of our fate, qualified to take on all comers, sure of our superiority. I recognized that fact when Archie developed a swagger and began to miss the easy shots. If I were sober, I thought, I might actually beat him! I pulled him aside once and asked if he thought the time might be right for additional research from astride the old kitchen roof. "No way," he answered. "Gotta let things cool off."

The rewards of drinking any good beer, inspiration and confusion, were being so well appreciated by the three of us that we failed to notice the swelling ranks of the patrons of Mary's Cafe. But at some point, the twang of the cafe's front door spring was coming so often that even a dim-wit would have noticed. When my deadened senses finally reacted, I shaded my beer-tender eyes to ease the glare from the bulbs over the pool tables and scanned the tables and chairs in the restaurant. Nearly all the chairs were taken, and the door spring was still twanging like a country band. Sure is a bunch of folks for a Monday night, I thought, surveying them. Several of the school crowd. Few drunks. Bookie or two.

The poor guys all seemed so straight-faced I thought about buying them a round of beer.

"Can you buy a round in this joint?" I asked Jerry. "We're the only ones having fun. Look out there. The rest of this crew needs a picker-upper."

Jerry staggered to my side, squinted, and shaded his eyes with his cue stick. "Damn!" he said. "Looks like a funeral parlor. Somebody die?"

"Maybe they heard we was having a party!" Archie giggled from his chair against the wall, where he'd perched after allowing Jerry and me to play each other for a change.

"All these people probably heard about our game," Jerry said. "They came to watch! We are that good! Olympic class! Bring on Minnesota Fats!"

The clatter of pool sticks being dropped on the adjacent table delighted us. "Other guys are quitting," I said proudly as the two players left their table. "Guess we showed them up so bad with all those bank shots they felt outclassed. Won't even play in the same pool hall with us."

I leveled my stick to demonstrate my new-found pool-prowess by lobbing a double-bank end-pocket missile across the felt. I heard Jerry say, "Uh-oh," at another squawk from the screen door. Archie agreed with a soft "Oh, shit!" from his chair.

"The Team," Jerry whispered as he leaned near my ear while averting his eyes. He maneuvered carefully around the table to Archie's side. I decided more study was necessary of the various angles required for my double-bank missile.

"The Team?" I whispered while studying the green felt. "You don't mean The Football Team, do you? The Little Dixie Champs?"

Jerry and Archie decided to help with my shot. Heads together, we studied position, bearing, heading, angle, and windage. Jerry whispered, "Perry Norman just walked in."

"Over half the football team is here," Archie said nervously. "Fifteen or twenty sets of hungry eyeballs are watching us."

"Maybe they decided to drop by for a beer after practice," I said.

"At nine o'clock at night?"

"Food, then. They heard about the collard greens with pepper sauce."

"Ain't nobody eating."

"Meatheads everywhere," Archie whispered, peeping around his cue. "And they look awful restless. Kinda fascinated by us."

"I feel a strong sense of doom," I said under my breath. "An odor of death in the air. Do you suppose they're here for what I'm afraid they're here for? Tell me I'm wrong."

"They even brought their girlfriends to watch," Archie said.

"Saxon?" I asked, refusing to look. "Perry's supposed to have a date with her tonight."

"Naw, Saxon ain't with Perry."

"Well, I wouldn't want her to see this," I said. "It'd probably embarrass her. The blood and all."

"It's only pain and injury," Archie said. "You'll probably survive it. The broken bones will heal. In time. I just hope they don't think me and Jerry are with you."

"What?"

"Jerry, what say let's haul ass?'

"Reckon that's really why they're here?" I said nervously. "I was only kidding. That's not it, do you think?"

"It don't look good."

Jerry smiled at the pack and said loudly, "Well, I gotta be getting home, Jack Think I'll go out the back door, get the Boy to get me one last beer. One for the road."

"Sounds good to me," Archie said even more loudly.

"Now, wait, you bastards," I whispered. "You're always leaving me when I need you most. I'll go with you this time."

Together we hung our cue sticks and pretended ignorance of The Team by laughing at each other's wisecracks while we paid Mama Mary. "Archie Fats!" I joked, "Southern pool legend."

"I can beat him," Jerry quipped. "Did you see that shot on the fifteen I made?"

"I actually felt sorry for you two pussies," Archie cracked. "Maybe I'll lose a game on purpose next time."

Mama Mary had taken note of all the additional customers present tonight, and although the gleam in her eye was probably caused by anticipation of an earnings bonanza, she must have sensed the tenseness felt by the three of us as well as by others in the cafe. "Something queer about the crowd," she said from over her cash register. "They're not talking to each other like normal. Too many, too. What's going on, Jack?"

"Full moon," I answered. "We're in a hurry to go watch it, too." I turned and strolled toward the back door alongside Archie and Jerry, feeling the eyeballs following us out. The Boy sat perched on his stool, his uneasiness obvious in the way his eyes darted from Mary to the crowd to us. He stood as we approached, unsure of our motives, his eyes focused on the crowd behind us. Then, with a sudden leap to one side, he avoided the two forms that hurried around Jerry to block our exit. Two tackles, I observed. Two tackles and three blockheads. We ain't got a chance. And no piece in my panties....

"Hello, Pig," Jerry said cheerily to the bigger of the tackles in his front. Then, turning slightly to face the other, "Pigmy, how's it hanging?"

Pig and Pigmy, aliases, of course, were brothers who played tackle position. The two fondly accepted their nicknames as emblems of their size and power, unaware that the source of their monikers was actually their pig-like snouts. Pig, the bigger of the two, glanced over to the table where Perry Norman had taken a seat. "Wanna let these two go, Captain?" he said loudly. "Or you wanna include them in our party?"

Perry must have signaled his lack of interest in Jerry and Archie, for Pig and Pigmy stepped aside to allow them passage, then took their blocking position again. Archie hesitated for a moment at the door, and in a quaking voice called across the room, "Perry, why don't you let Jack go with us? He ain't done nothing."

The taut ring in the words of Perry's reply was chilling. "You wanna die with him, Stub? Huh? You wanna die, come on back in here."

"Naw," Archie said quickly, "naw, I don't want to die." He gave me one long last look, shrugged, and disappeared behind Jerry.

The Boy watched from near a pool table, his long arms hanging motionless at his sides. Mama Mary backed away from her cash register and stood with one hand on the counter, the other covering her mouth. "Now don't you...," she began as she frowned and shook her head at the rows of spectators who were leaning forward on the edges of their chairs. Some had sadistic smiles on their faces. All I could think was, All this over one lousy date?

Perry Norman had always reminded me of what a "Greek God" must have been. Adonis, or Eros, I had grudgingly conceded. Dark, curly hair. A rugged face with heavy black stubble of growth. Clear, dark skin. Muscles. Perfect teeth. It was damned unfair, I had decided, that one person could be so handsome. The perfection ended with his looks, however, and was seriously impugned whenever he opened his mouth and divulged his ego. He was known for his volcanic fits of rage, and his arms were scarred here and there, the consequence of that blazing temper. He came from a wealthy family and would have been a "spoiled brat" if not for his physical attributes and abilities. These, however, were enough to accord him "hero" status in the eyes of most of the population.

A quick look around during the few seconds it took for him to cross the room in my direction convinced me there was no escape. There were athletes at both doors, athletes leaning on the pool tables, more athletes pitched forward in their chairs, all apparently eager to get on with the blood-letting. No law officer was around to save me, either. I thought of Jim's thirty-eight, lying uselessly somewhere at home. Never again, I thought. I'll always pack a rod after today. If I survive.

Perry's face was red with anger, the vertical blood vein that centered his forehead bulging so conspicuously that I would not have been surprised had it exploded and splattered everyone around with drops of blood. "Know what?" he whispered when he was near enough that our noses were in danger of contact.

"No," I said, backing away.

His finger tapped against my chest. "You'll be lucky to be out of the hospital for Christmas."

"Now, look," I gulped, noting with disgust the shrill, surging quality in my voice, "what are you so mad about?"

"You don't know?"

"If it's about Saxon," I squealed, "I don't understand. She pretty much proved she was your girl this morning. She doesn't care about me."

I could feel his breath. Deep, gushing streams of warm air. Like an angry bull. "You took her out last night!"

Hastily, I answered: "If you want to call it that. But what the heck? She practically fell all over you this morning at school. And she had a date with you tonight, didn't she?"

Hands balled into fists at his sides, the vein in his forehead bulged to breaking point, Perry pushed me along with his nose. "No," he hissed. "No, you little son of a bitch."

I had backed as far as the two tackles at the back door, and when I felt them jab my rear I moved to one side, back toward Mama Mary's lunch counter. Perry matched every move, so that our faces remained inches apart. We could have been slow dancing. "Know what Saxon said when I went by to pick her up at seven?" he said. "She wasn't feeling well. That's what she said. So I told her I'd heard she had gone out with you, and I asked her if she was going to do it again. Know what she said?"

I shook my head and continued to wiggle away.

"She said, 'Yes. I like him.' And when I told her she better not ever even speak to you again, know what she said?"

I shook my head.

"She said we were through. Finished. Forever. So you know what I said? I said I was going to find you and cut your dick off and feed it to you one slice at a time."

"Look," I stammered. "I know Saxon means a lot to you, Perry. She's a woman. She might cool off and change her mind."

"No!" he thundered. "This is all your fault! But there's one thing I want you to remember, Jackie boy, before I tear your heart out!"

My back struck a corner of Mary's big brass cash register. Perry turned to make sure the spectators were paying attention. He said loudly and boisterously, "Every time you screw Saxon, IF you ever do, just remember you ain't giving her half the fucking I've given her a thousand times before you! And don't be surprised afterwards if she dumps you and runs back to me. You're minor league, boy!"

I knew I should keep my mouth shut. But I couldn't help it. "You never have, Perry!" I said madly. "Never!"

His mouth fell open. "What? Fuck Saxon?"

"No," I said. "Saxon's as virgin as a fresh red rose. Hell, Saxon's a goddess! An angel! She'd never let you touch her. That way."

My feet almost left the floor as he grabbed the neck of my shirt, twisted and pulled it until our faces were nearly touching. "A goddess?" he said loudly. He turned to the crowd. "God!" he cried, laughing raucously, "I can't believe this little shit! He says Saxon is a goddess!"

There were a few giggles and sniggers, but no groundswell of amusement like Perry probably expected. My feet almost left the ground again as he jerked violently on my collar. His angry red eyes were petrifying as he pushed me away so he could use his fist. I brought both hands up to protect my face, but not soon enough: my chin suffered a glancing blow from a big right hook.

Backed against the counter, I used its leverage to push Perry away. His stout body hardly moved, and the maneuver only succeeded in nearly knocking Mary's cash register to the floor. With a forearm in my throat, Perry had tilted my chin and head backwards over the counter even as I strained to fend off with both hands the fist that had again landed in my face, and that was now being cocked for another punch.

The back of my head slammed against the counter. It was, I knew, about to be removed by the sheer force of Perry's big forearm. Curiously, now, Mama Mary's outraged features came into view, above us, behind me, near the cash register, her hand no longer covering her mouth. As the upside-down image of her face appeared before mine, and before I could ask to borrow a knife, I recognized that there had been an upside-down change in her mood. Her cash register! I realized at once. Her cash register was teetering near the brink of destruction! And while Mary might not have interfered with Perry's clobbering of me for any other reason, the threat to her cash register was a threat to her very existence.

"Get away from my goddamn cash register!" she screamed. "You hooligans! You'll break my cash register!"

There was no indication from Perry that he intended to heed Mary's warning, nor was there any sign that any of the spectators intended to interrupt his pounding of my chin. Another deflected punch grazed my cheekbone. I tried desperately to keep a grip on his forearm, but he was as slippery as he was strong. Gary Cooper wouldn't put up with this, I thought. He'd knock this guy's block off. But Gary was big. What would a little guy do? Cagney! He's the one! Cagney would break a gin bottle across the counter and slice the guy up with it!

There were no gin bottles within reach, and, regardless, Perry had sealed his doom by meddling with Mary's cash machine. His cry of anger as Mary's fly swatter slapped against the top of his head changed the complexion of the brawl for good. "My cash register!" she screamed as she beat him.

"You old bitch!" he shouted while he pinned my head to the counter with one arm and fended off the swatter with the other. "Don't you hit me with that fly swatter!"

The cash register teetered and tottered. Mary eyed it in horror, placed a hard hand against it to balance it, and continued to work on Perry's head. "Get out of my cafe!" she shrieked. "Get away from my cash register!"

"You better leave me be!" Perry shouted, and, turning to the crowd, barked, "Boys, hold this old bitch until I'm through with this bastard. Grab her!"

Now, even meatheads were smart enough to know that there was quite a bit of difference between the beating of a high school kid and the physical restraint of the owner/operator of a restaurant, especially an owner/operator with the contrary nature of Mama Mary. There was no telling what she would do if one of them laid a hand on her. Since their response to Perry's order was of paramount interest to me, I squirmed and twisted enough to see from my counter-level view that the various tackles and guards were eyeing each other, each trying to decide if the consequences of their actions might be more adverse than the outrage of their leader. The question quickly became irrelevant. As Perry indignantly awaited the intervention of his comrades, Mama Mary quietly dropped her swatter and seized upon another weapon. Perry's sudden stiffening, the look of terror on his face, his abrupt shriek of pain, and the welcome relief that came with the withdrawal of his arm from my throat, followed Mary's unexpected pounce upon his rear.

"Goddamn!" Perry screamed, bolting upright and groping at his posterior. "Goddamn, she's killed me!"

Mama Mary moved to one side after her assault, but as Perry's startled leap from atop the counter, and from atop my body, gave her cash register a final, fatal nudge, she leaped forward in a vain attempt to save it. Too late. The heavily-coppered old machine crashed to the concrete floor with a sickening metallic clang of little bells. "My cash register," Mary groaned, dropping to her knees to caress it, "my cash register."

No one paid her cash register any mind. All eyes were glued to the wildly gyrating attempts by Perry to remove the knife from his posterior. "She's stuck him in the ass hole with a butcher knife!" I heard one guard yell frantically. A tackle roared back, "It ain't in his ass hole! It's in a cheek of his ass!" Another screamed, "Let's pull it out!" And another, "Let's get him to the hospital!"

The crowd seemed to gather direction from the last assertion, and they milled about their stricken hero expressing their sympathy to a man who cared not an iota for it, but rather raved for someone to pull the butcher knife "outa my butt." With all attention temporarily diverted, I eased carefully from the counter and toward the back door, where the Boy stood, probably wondering if he should detain me so that Mary or Perry or a few of the tackles could retaliate for all the trouble I'd caused. "See ya, Boy," I said as I slipped past. "Have a good evening."

Jerry and Archie were waiting in the shadows. "You okay?" Archie asked as the two of them fell in step beside me on the sidewalk. "You're bleeding," Jerry added.

By the light of the street lamps I saw the blood on the front of my shirt. "Your nose," Archie said, pointing. "And maybe your chin. Your lip's cut."

My shirt was ruined anyway, so I used the tail to wipe my face as my buddies and I walked hurriedly down the sidewalk toward the safety of Cherokee Rose. I'll never leave you again, Rose, I said to myself. I'll be a hermit. It's a tough world out here.

"Sorry we had to leave," Jerry alleged, shrugging as he walked. "We wouldn't have been much help anyway."

"I know," I said. "Anyway, it was my fight. Poor Perry. He'll be out of action for a while."

"What?" they chirped in unison, their eyes suddenly interested in my face.

"They're carrying him to the hospital, fellows," I said. "I hope he's not hurt too bad."

"I ain't believing this," Archie said sarcastically. "But," he said admiringly, "you sure ain't beat up bad as I expected."

"Of course not," I said, "And I'll bet you five dollars Perry don't show up for the next football game. He'll be limping around for days. Maybe weeks."

Jerry was incredulous. "You whipped Perry Norman?" he nearly shrieked. "You couldn't whip him in a fair fight! You musta hit him from bchind!"

"Something like that."

"And all those meatheads. His buddies. They just let you walk out of there?"

"I think it was a matter of respect," I answered. "A kind of fighters' code. You see, once your best man has been whipped..."

"Hey, the City's stopped!" Archie interrupted, pointing down the railroad tracks. "It's stopped where it ain't never stopped before. Wonder what's wrong?"

Jerry and I followed Archie's gaze and saw that, indeed, the City of New Orleans sat idly on the railroad tracks that paralleled our path, her throttling engine abreast of Cherokee Rose and the nearby street intersection. Her orbiting headlamp spun a cone-shaped ray of light, alternately illuminating automobiles and the figures of people who peered at the tracks in front of her. A considerable departure from the normal obscurity and serenity of the docks at night, the spectacle was eerie, alien. "Chief Hancock!" Archie exclaimed in awe as we drew nearer the scene. "The City must have hit somebody!"

There were five vehicles at the scene, and, as we approached, a sixth arrived, apparently another passerby who was as curious as we. Two cars, sedans with the SSPD emblem on their doors, had been parked so that their headlights helped to brighten the rails before the City. A number of people stood to one side, twenty feet or so from the victim, watching Chief Hancock and his deputy as they examined the tracks and the railroad ties and the body that lay sprawled before the City's cow-catcher. We joined them and silently strained to make out the identity of the casualty.

"It's a girl," a voice from behind us said. "A colored girl. I was the first one here."

I turned and recognized, standing behind us in the swelling crowd, Ben Dowdy, a farmer who lived about two miles outside of town. He was an eighty-year-old whose sun-shriveled skin was as orange and mushy as a December pumpkin. He liked to talk; I normally avoided him. "Mr. Dowdy," I said, moving closer, "when did it happen?"

"'Bout ten, fifteen minutes ago."

"Did the City hit her? Is she alive?"

"Couldn't tell. I heard the train lock wheels after it pulled out of the depot. Engineer musta seen her. The City was honking her horn and sliding on the rails when I pulled up. I don't think it hit her, though. She'd be up under the cow-catcher if the City had hit her. Good thing for her he'd just pulled out of the depot and wasn't going too fast. So I drove up to the station and told Hancock. Hancock was real surprised. City ain't hit nobody for two or three years now. But he came right on. They been up there, he and that smart-ass deputy, huddled over her for ten minutes now. Wonder if they called the ambulance? Hell, the girl could lay there and die. Serve her right anyway. Stupid. Plain stupid to walk too close to the railroad tracks. Now, if I was Hancock..."

"Thanks, Mr. Dowdy," I said as I eased away. "I think we'll try to get a closer look."

"Now, don't get too close, boys..." Dowdy warned as the three of us moved on. I wondered how his wife took it. Maybe he didn't have a wife. More likely, an ex-wife.

Nothing would do but that we had to have a closer look. We crept nearer, almost into the orbiting beam of the City's powerful headlight. We stopped within ten feet of the prone figure, near enough that we could hear the words of Chief Hancock and his deputy, the "smart-ass," who was addressed by everyone but the Chief by his last name, Willis. Chief Hancock always called Willis "Fice." The two of them had apparently tried to make the victim more comfortable, for she lay between the rails on her back, her hands folded on her chest. She wore a dark skirt that had been pulled neatly below her knees, shiny red shoes, a white blouse, large gold earrings... "Josephine!" Jerry and I exclaimed at once.

Josephine was alive, for we heard her mumble as the police officers attempted to talk with her. Her words were unclear, but we deduced from Hancock's actions that the girl was dazed and making no sense.

"Still can't remember what happened, Josephine?" Hancock asked her.

A slight movement of her head indicated that she could not.

"Ambulance will be here in a minute. Just rest easy. Fice?"

Willis answered his boss with a "yes, sir."

"You told the Boy?"

"Couldn't find him, Chief."

"Damn it, Fice."

"I'll go look for him again. He must have been out back at the stash the first time."

"You told Mary."

"No, Chief, I didn't know..."

"Damn it, Fice."

"I'll go now, Chief."

Why Willis lied I have no idea, but lie he did; after all, we had just left Mary's Café, and if Willis had been there... He spun away now leaving a vapor trail and a bit of rubber on the street behind his vehicle. The small crowd sneaked nearer to Josephine. Chief Hancock, in his normally languid manner, warned us away. "You folks stay back," he said quietly. "Ten feet away, at least."

So we backed away and awaited the ambulance and the arrival of the Boy. "The Boy will be shattered," I whispered. "Josephine is his life. I hope she doesn't die."

"She's moving around," Jerry said hopefully. "She'll be okay."

"Man, oh, man," Archie whispered, his eyes rolling. "Are you two thinking what I'm thinking?"

Jerry and I stared.

Archie continued, "Reckon it was an accident? Or you reckon..."

Good God! I thought at once. Would Coach Murray do it? Would he try to murder Josephine? The words flooded from me: "Coach could have been trying to destroy the evidence! Beat her up, and put her on the tracks! Let the City run over her! No evidence, no crime! Is that right?"

"He wouldn't!" Jerry said, aghast and shaking his head in disbelief. "He wouldn't really try to kill Josephine!"

"Helluva coincidence," I said, "right after you two tried to blackmail him with that note. I told you not to..."

"We've got to tell the Chief, then. Meatloaf can't get away with trying to murder somebody!"

"Coach and Chief Hancock are big buddies. Maybe Coach figured he could get away with it. After all, Josephine is colored."

"The Chief's not like that," Jerry insisted. "He'll do what's right, whether it's a white person or not."

I nodded agreement. "I think you're right. The Chief's honest. And fair."

"Let's tell him tonight. Right now," Jerry said, tugging at my arm. "I'll sleep better knowing that bastard is in jail. After all, he might come after US now."

"Wait. Aren't you forgetting something?" I said. "Like The Plan? Like attempted blackmail? We'll have to tell it all. What about our reputations? You want a permanent visit to somewhere north of northern Canada?"

"We gotta do something!"

"Let Josephine tell him," I said with a shudder. "She'll fix Coach Murray's ass, as soon as she comes to and remembers what happened. IF she does. IF it happened the way we think."

"Yeah!" Archie agreed.

"It could have been an accident, after all."

The "ambulance," a dark old Cadillac hearse owned by a local colored funeral home, arrived. The driver and his assistant, another colored man in a dark suit, exited their vehicle and, as we watched, bent alongside Chief Hancock to examine Josephine. Josephine was evidently coming around, for we got an occasional glimpse of her hands above her head. Just then the Boy arrived on the run, apparently jogging the block-and-a-half distance from the café. Mama Mary was right behind, a passenger in Willis' squad car. In a moment Josephine was surrounded by so many people that we could not see an inch of her body.

"She'll be all right, I think," Hancock told the Boy as we watched and listened. "Just bruised up from where the train hit her. She's lucky to be alive."

"Did you hear that?" Archie said. "He said the train hit her!"

Josephine was on her feet, and we moved aside as she was led tottering toward the hearse. The Boy held her tightly from one side, Mama Mary from the other. Police and ambulance attendants strolled alongside, giving Josephine no more assistance than the concerned frowns on their faces. As we followed, and as we approached the ambulance, Chief Hancock waved us away. We waited and watched as the hearse was driven away, Josephine and her grandfather on board. Willis opened a door of his patrol car for Mama Mary, and in a moment they, too, were gone. Jerry, Archie, and I then wandered away to the front steps of Cherokee Rose, where we held a powwow.

CHAPTER 19
PAST IS PRESENT

ONCE THE VEHICLES of the remaining spectators had left the scene of Josephine Rossetti's brush with death, the City of New Orleans gave a few quick blasts of its powerful horn, its diesel engines rumbled, and the big train pulled slowly away. My two pals and I remained seated on the front steps of Cherokee Rose and watched warily – I fought the urge to go inside – until it was gone from sight. Jerry spoke first: "Something like this can't happen in Smith Station. Attempted murder? I can't believe Meatloaf would do that!"

"We caused it," I said. "Us and our dumb trip to the pit that, incidentally, was entirely the brain child of Archie Jones."

"Naw," Archie protested. "It woulda been her own fault. She did it to herself. She shouldn't have been messing around with a married man."

Jerry groaned, "Where does this leave us now? Do we go on trying to collect from Meatloaf, or do we forget the whole thing? I sure could use that dough."

"Are you kidding?" I said. "Drop it."

"Three thousand bucks," Archie said slowly.

"My life's worth more than that," I said. "If Coach Murray tried to do away with Josephine, why not us? It just might be over now, though, if we keep our mouths shut. I bet Josephine does! She'll be too scared to talk! I'll also predict that if the City runs over Archie Jones tomorrow night on its way back through here, Jerry Bass and Jack Smith, too, will develop a bad case of amnesia that lasts the rest of their lives."

Jerry nodded. "Got a point. Hope it's the runt, and not me."

"I just hope we don't get run out of town. When this thing blows over, maybe things will get back to normal."

"Unless Coach did do it. And Josephine talks," Archie said.

"She won't. I'll wager your life on it."

"He's probably waiting out there." Jerry peered into the darkness about the dock. "Watching. Planning his next victim."

Archie used a finger to emphasize each point as he said, "What we're saying here, to sum up, is, one, Coach has made a meaningful point, and, two, we have to forget we ever heard of the gravel pit. That way, three, Coach continues to live happily ever after, and, four, allows Josephine, and, five, us, to do the same. Right?"

"Eloquently spoken."

"Right, runt."

It was late, and in a while I sat on the front steps and watched the two of them walk away. Willie limped up to me in a few minutes and with his whipping tongue reminded me of my injuries. He insisted on giving my face a good scrubbing, and though it was a sloppy piece of work, he cleaned the dried blood from my chin and nose. I remembered how awful he had smelled the night before, and so I refused his offer to wash my lips. When he was satisfied he'd done a thorough job, I asked him, "Want to sleep with me tonight, old buddy? You ain't been wallowing in cow shit, have you?"

As Willie and I stepped inside the house, the familiar odor of alcohol and cigarettes jolted me to sensibility, to anger. Jim was back on the bottle.

He slept clothed, snoring, passed out upon his bed. His last Camel had scorched a ragged black spot on the edge of one of the sheets, adding the acrid smell of charred cotton to the other repulsive odors. Anger overcame me. I crossed the room and shook him. "Uncle Jim!" I said roughly. "Uncle Jim!"

He twitched at my prod. "Squeaky," he said drunkenly, his eyes half open while he clawed the air over his head, "Leave me lone, Squeaky!"

Squeaky Bishop! I silently cursed his name and vowed revenge. "I'll get you, Squeaky," I said aloud. Then I took my dog to bed.

Whether due to Doctor Blake's counseling, or to the exhaustion that comes with days and nights of exceptional stress, I slept deeply, dreamlessly for most of the night. Even the worry that Perry or some of his devotees might drop by for a little vengeance wasn't enough to keep me awake. Willie remained on the foot of the bed until morning, and when I awoke with a start and found it was after seven o'clock, he was pawing the back door. Still groggy, I put him out, fed him, and fell back into bed for an extra wink. I dreamed for what must have been mere seconds. Strangely, it was not of Josephine and her misfortune that I dreamed, or of Linda and her majestic breasts. It was upon Barbara Jones, bouncing provocatively among the sponges and bubbles in her warm bath, that my fantasy concentrated. As Barbara scrubbed her back with a washrag she sang to me, and though her curves would normally have fixed my attention, it was the song she hummed in a lulling monotone that commanded it now. I felt her song in my throat, a deep rasp that aroused me, made me cling to her, even to fight to be near her elastic breasts. I knew the song. Somehow, the rhymes were thrilling. They were the lines from a Negro spiritual... "The Lord loved David, and he loved him well..." and "...Halleluiah..." I couldn't remember all the words.

The stupor could have lasted no longer than a few seconds, but when I awoke it was with the feeling that I had found something long lost. A final piece of the puzzle. A bit of the past extinct, somehow scooped from below the level of conscious perception. The insight led me to silently swear: DOCTOR BLAKE! DOCTOR BLAKE! DAMN!

How could I know that reassuring lullaby, the Negro spiritual that Barbara Jones mimicked in her bath? For a long moment before I forced the idea from my mind, I thought I recognized the real songstress... For a moment I even knew where she was....

I could not face the truth. Not now. Not yet. My life, my perceptions of my life and of my Uncle Jim, all would change too radically if I allowed that door to open. There was time. Plenty of time. And time for explanations, too.

And there were happier thoughts.

Saxon had dumped Perry! That exhilarating fact was obvious from Perry's words last night. She'd dumped him for me. Hadn't she? And with Perry fettered with a butchered posterior for at least a few days before he healed, wasn't now the perfect time to pursue her? Yes! I would see her at school today. I would be irresistible. I would do my Cary Grant impersonation. She would swoon and hunger for me.

First, though, I planned on playing hooky, at least for a little while. I was dying to know firsthand what Chief Hancock had learned from Josephine.

And my excuse for missing school? A simple cold would do for today, but colds were lackluster, trite. Dysentery? Too messy. Malaria? Rather protracted. Gonorrhea? That would shake them up. Gunshot wound? No, I'd save that one in case it came to pass. What then? When I glanced in the mirror and was shocked by the sight of my cracked red lip and bruised cheekbone, I found I didn't need a better excuse. The idea of having my friends at school see me like this was utterly disgusting, though it would have been satisfying to rebut their taunts with a few wisecracks about Perry's derriere. Malaria, I decided. With Malaria I could skip classes the rest of the day. Or even a week!

Jim was completely sober, or he appeared to be so when I woke him after I had dressed. He noticed the damage done by Perry immediately, and examined me with his bloodshot eyes in obvious amazement. "You ought to see the other guy," I said before he could ask about it.

"You got into a fight?" he said with a lingering note of astonishment. "Are you okay?"

It wouldn't do to have Uncle Jim upset with the truth about my altercation at the cafe. With his temper, he might grab his thirty-eight and storm Perry's parents' house, ready to "shoot first and ask questions later." "It was nothing," I said. "A minor incident and just a small bruise. Believe me, the other guy is in worse shape than me."

"You've never been in a fight before," he said pointedly. "You're not one of the riffraff. You're better than that."

"I have mingled with the peasants," I said. "But I have learned my lesson. The peasants are meaner than me."

"Who was it?" he demanded. "I'll kill the ruffian!"

"I told you. He's a lot worse off than I am. He had to be taken to the hospital."

"You, of all people! Fighting! Don't you realize how petty and vulgar it is to brawl?"

"I fight. You drink. We all have our failings. I'm going to kill Squeaky Bishop." I heaped pillows behind his head and lit his first Camel of the day. "I know Squeaky brought you a bottle. You took that first drink because that bastard brought a bottle into this house."

"He didn't twist my arm," Jim said. "I know where to buy the stuff." He shook his head at me, unwilling to let me off the hook. "I can't believe you allowed yourself to be drawn into a fight!"

"And once you've had one drink," I retorted, "there's no stopping you. You try to drink up the world's entire supply of booze. Someday you may actually succeed."

"What a bittersweet thought."

"On another subject, Josephine Rossetti almost got killed last night, Uncle Jim. The City of New Orleans almost ran over her."

"What?"

"Right in front of Cherokee Rose."

"Christ!" he exclaimed incredulously. "The girl just walked out in front of the train?"

"Who knows? All I know is, she was hurt, lying between the tracks in front of the City."

"Well, I'm sorry. There ought to be more like her. Was she hurt bad?"

"Don't know. Chief Hancock had her taken to the hospital."

"Hancock, eh." Jim snickered. "Bet Hancock was real glad it wasn't fatal."

I didn't understand. "Why would you say that?"

"You know."

"No, I don't."

"Hancock. And Josephine. Sure, you know." He cocked his head at me. "Hancock's been tuning that piano for a long time."

"No!"

"Yes. Hancock doesn't like it to be known, of course. Not him and a little colored girl. He might not get elected next time around if it became public knowledge."

"Well, I'll be damned!" I said.

"I need a drink."

"No!"

"Emphatically 'yes!'"

I stormed, "I will find your hidden stash and break every bottle!"

"There is no stash." He grinned. "Only a standing order with a certain bootlegger. Delivery should occur within the hour."

"Now look, you're almost sober now," I pleaded. "Why not stay that way? Why do you have to have a drink?"

"Because of your grandparents. My iniquitous parents. My father died before I was born; we buried him when I was twenty. My mother never lived. So I drink to thwart the absence of joyful memories."

"That does not make sense."

"Oh, yes it does. Perhaps when you're older and wiser you may discover meaning in these words, and thereby comprehend the miserable legacy that is yours."

"You ain't sober. And you're drunker than I would have thought."

"And I love it. And don't say 'ain't.'"

As I walked the sidewalk toward the police station, the morning sun vanished behind a mass of churning gray clouds that had earlier appeared on the western horizon, and now stretched across the heavens, leaving only a long curved slice of blue in the east. A rumble of distant thunder made me shiver. Rain, and cold, I thought. Summer may finally be over. Good!

Though the circuitous hike via Forrest Street to the police station was a block out of the way, the route avoided Mary's Cafe and the possible consequences of being seen by Mama Mary. I feared she might still be mourning the fate of her cash register, and might even explode out of the cafe to use her butcher knife on me. It could happen. Last night wasn't the first time I'd seen her in action with her knife. Once, when Teeny Wright's dad had had a bit too much to drink, and had slapped his wife while they sat together at one of Mary's tables, Mary had chased Mr. Wright out and down the street, threatening as she ran after him to cut off one of his fingers tonight, and another one for every time he ever slapped her again. Mr. Wright was always on his best behavior after that. Mary hated men who roughed up their women.

A sprinkle of rain had begun when I reached the station. Chief Hancock's car was parked in front of the red brick building, which looked more like a post office than headquarters for Davis County's two crime fighters. Nearby was the car of Hancock's deputy, "Fice," the red-faced, red-haired, quick-tempered, skinny mouse of a "smart-ass" who used belligerence instead of brawn to intimidate lawbreakers. I wasn't particularly happy at his presence. But I climbed the steps in front and pushed inside, pausing for a moment to take a look at the combination police station and jail. As long as I had been in Smith Station, I had never visited here, and after a quick survey I decided I wasn't particularly anxious to come back, for dark wood paneling and dark carpeting lent a dungeon-like feel to the interior. Quite apt, I decided. A sign on a steel door far in the back was marked "JAIL" in large white letters. The remainder of the place appeared to be office space more suitable to the needs of Dracula than the Law. Like Blake Sanatorium, the station had its own peculiar odor. It smelled of stale obsolescence.

Voices in one of the gloomy offices attracted my attention. I walked to it. Chief Hancock and his deputy ceased their conversation when I stuck my head inside and tapped on the open door marked "Hail The Chief."

"Hello, Chief Hancock, Deputy Willis," I said from outside the door opening. "Can I speak to you for a minute, Chief?"

Hancock slouched in the chair behind his desk, twirling a pencil between his fingers. At my words Willis rotated his rear where he sat on the edge of the Chief's desk and gazed suspiciously at me. "Why ain't you in school, boy?" he said, without acknowledging my greeting. "You think it's Saturday or something?"

The Chief's expressionless face reflected his indifference to his deputy's remark. He nodded in my direction. "Yeah," he said. "Come on in, Jack."

"I only need a minute," I said. "But I'd rather it was just you and me, Chief. Private."

Willis' mouth opened, first for what I suspect was to have been an angry blaspheme, and then, as he got a look at me, a grin. He glanced at Hancock, then back to me. His grin widened. "Looks like Perry got in a few licks before Mary got to him with that bayonet of hers, Chief," he chuckled. "The boy's lucky Mary saved his ass. We might of been parking cars for his funeral today."

"Leave him alone, Fice," Hancock said. "Come on in, Jack." The Chief straightened in his chair. "Fice," he continued, looking at the deputy, "you see what you can get out of that prisoner."

"But, Chief..."

The Chief waved him away. "Damn it, Fice."

The corner of Fice's mouth that Hancock couldn't see twitched in frustration as the deputy rose and left without another word. The Chief pointed me to a chair, and I sat before a desk strewn with the business of its owner. Hancock wearily shuffled a pile of paper and said without looking at me, "Now, what is it, Jack?"

He was not a tall man, and he must have been fifty, but the Chief had such a wide and powerfully-built body that there could be little doubt of his strength. He had never, to my knowledge, had anyone challenge his authority. He spoke with the command of one accustomed to being obeyed, and he always was. Though there were sometimes rumors of impropriety in his conduct, such was viewed as inevitable for anyone holding the office. In the eyes of many of the county's residents, he maintained a stature approaching that of God Almighty.

"Mama Mary's not in any trouble because of me, is she?" I asked.

He shook his head without letting his eyes stray from the paper before him. "I doubt it. Not unless Perry's folks press charges. But they won't. The Norman's are smart enough to be cautious about bucking that old gal."

"It was partly my fault anyway."

"Partly, huh?" He placed reading glasses on his nose. He peered over them at me. "Is that what you came about?"

"No, sir," I said. "It's about Josephine Rossetti. How is she?"

He frowned. Then sighed. "She's all right. Spent the night in the hospital. They'll let her go this morning. Just bruises."

"Good," I said. "I'm glad. Has she said anything about how it happened? Did the train really hit her?"

Hancock studied me for a moment. "Is there any particular reason why you're so interested?" he asked pointedly. "You need to tell me anything?"

"No, sir," I said. "Josephine's just a friend. You know. She's a friend to everybody. I just wanted to see how she was, and find out how it happened."

"She wasn't watching what she was doing," he said bluntly. "Besides that, she'd been drinking. She was drunk. People get hurt when they get drunk and careless, Jack. You know that, don't you?"

"But Josephine doesn't drink," I said.

Hancock's eyes narrowed. "I said she was drunk, boy. I know

a drunk when I see one. She smelled like a brewery. She had so much whiskey in her she couldn't stand up." He threw up his hands and rolled his eyes. "And I don't have to explain this to you. I've got enough on my mind without having to put up with you, boy. You get about your business."

He'd been watching too many Edward G. Robinson movies. All he needed was a Tommy gun. "Did you ask her if she'd been drinking?" I asked. "Did she tell you how it happened?"

The Chief's thunderous response nearly bowled me over. "I don't have to...," he roared, then stopped, gritted his teeth, took a deep breath, and continued, "You can read about it in the newspaper. Get out. I got work to do."

I couldn't help myself. I said, "I guess you wouldn't want Josephine to say too much, would you?"

He stiffened and glared at me. "Why the hell would you say that?" The Chief's bushy eyebrows quivered. "I'll tell you something, Jack," he continued hoarsely, "I've overlooked what I've heard about you and those other two boys lately. But you come in here acting holier-than-thou, acting smart and making threats, and I just might not look the other way. You understand?"

"Yes, sir," I said.

"Coach Murray is a married man. Those tall tales of yours, that you've seen him with another woman, a colored girl at that, could cause problems for him. Don't you care that you might ruin a man's life?"

"A colored girl?" I said. "I haven't heard anything about Coach and a colored girl."

"Why, you know..."

The Chief appeared to think about what he'd said. I could picture the wheels spinning inside his head. Had he made a mistake? Had he just admitted he knew about Coach Murray and a colored girl, Josephine? Neither Jerry, Archie, nor myself had mentioned that little fact to anyone else. At least, I didn't think we had. And, I thought, Coach Murray probably knows about Josephine and

Chief Hancock, too. So maybe Hancock knew about Josephine's "accident." He could even be in on it!

"I guess I better go," I said. "I'm late for school."

I got out of my chair. His eyes followed me. He insisted on a last word:, "I want you to remember, Jack, you can be sued for libel. Coach Murray might just do that. You boys better keep your mouths shut."

I nodded. "Yes, sir," I said. "I know. I've already spoken with my lawyer about that. He's advised me not to say anything."

"Your lawyer?" Hancock choked. "You talked to a lawyer? Now, why the hell did you go and do that?"

I waved good-bye without answering. Let him worry. He'd tell Coach, and Coach would be furious. But as mad as either of them got, I figured neither Hancock nor Coach Murray would dare try anything now that I'd "talked with my lawyer." They just couldn't be sure how much "my lawyer" knew.

I headed home by the same sly route as before. Despite the continuing cold sprinkles, I made one small detour past Kosser's Grocery in order to pick up a treat for the dog. "Willie's gonna love this," I observed aloud as Mr. Kosser wrapped a giant bone in white waxed paper. "The dog will probably wash my face again."

The sprinkles had become a steady downpour by the time I reached Cherokee Rose. I was shivering with cold and wet by the time I walked through the front door. Willie, likewise cold and wet, and smelling of gore to boot, met me at the back door, and, after sniffing at my package, with a mighty flourish lunged inside. I gave him the bone to enjoy there on the kitchen floor. Nothing was too good for a great guard dog, even if he did wallow in manure and things departed.

I had to have a change of clothes, a hot bath to warm myself from the bite that had crept inside my wet jeans and shirt; a steaming tub is a noble prescription for a chill. Jim, I assumed, though I had not checked to see, was getting quietly bombed in his bedroom. In a way, this was good. Maybe he wouldn't notice

I'd skipped classes today. I reclined in the hot, soapy water for a long while before drying and dressing.

When I walked into his bedroom to check on him, Jim, propped on his pillows reading yesterday's Observer by the lamp beside his bed, dropped the newspaper and looked up. A half-empty pint of Early Times peeked from beneath yet another pillow. He cocked his head. "Pardon my curiosity, nephew, but if my calculations are correct, this is Tuesday. And normally, on Tuesdays, you go to school. Is there something wrong with this logic?"

"Malaria," I said, easing onto the opposite side of the bed. "The Malaria I contracted in the jungles of Guam. It's flared up again."

"How sad," he said. "A little quinine and a few days for those bruises to heal, and you'll be good as new, I bet."

"Quinine. Yes."

"I still want to know who the bastard was that did that to you. I plan to have him anchored to the bottom of Davis Lake."

"No need. He's been humiliated enough already," I answered while mentally thanking Providence that Perry was either at school or at home recuperating. "He may even have to turn in his cape."

Jim sighed and uncapped his bottle for another drink. "Like some?" he asked after a nip, extending the bottle toward me.

"Sure," I said, reaching for it. "Family tradition, after all. Gimme a big slug. I won't need the quinine after a pint of this stuff."

"No you don't!" he screeched, jerking the bottle away with a look of horror on his face. "You've got school!"

"My malaria, Uncle Jim," I argued. "Can't make it to school today. Anyway, it's a fine day for a drunk. Rainy. Cold. Let's you and me just hang around together all day and get good and plastered. You know what they say. The family that boozes together suffers DT's together."

"I'll send you to Chamberlain Hunt if you ever take a drink!"

I grinned. "I was kidding. Anyway, I wouldn't fit in with those toughs over there."

"Good." He settled himself more comfortably into the bed covers and sighed contentedly. "I knew you were kidding. Well, what are your plans for your day off? While I get pleasantly intoxicated, will you return to your paramour for another round of canoodling? Or is la belle in school today?"

"La belle is indeed in school. But don't get the wrong idea, Uncle Jim. La belle aka Saxon Browne is a virgin. Never even been fondled. Within reason, of course. No matter what the rumors."

"Then who did you..." he began.

"You're a prime candidate for membership in the Baptist Ladies," I said uneasily. "You're a natural gossip."

"Damn!" he screeched, "I'd rather you accused me of being a New England Yankee! Gossip, my ass! I'm merely expressing semi-parental concern for my only nephew. I want to make sure you have been properly laid. I'm merely doing my duty."

I guffawed. "You're just nosy," I said. "And I'll never tell. My duty is to honor. Remember?"

A rap at the front door interrupted our conversation, ending Uncle Jim's sarcastic inquisition. I was glad. I couldn't tell him about Linda Murray. I jumped up, grateful for the excuse to go and see who was on our veranda.

Compared to what was waiting at the other end of the hallway, the torment I was enduring at the hands of my uncle was peanuts. Before I reached the front door, through the varnished glass of the huge windows along the front of Cherokee Rose, I recognized Coach Murray's Fury parked behind our wagon. The sight of it was so instantly disheartening that I immediately turned back and ducked into my bedroom, where, for a few panic-stricken moments, I searched for the pistol. It was not there. Jim had either returned it to his closet or hidden it under his mattress.

There was no way to retrieve the weapon from his room; to do so would alert Jim. And there was no telling what would happen if Jim heard Coach bawling me out! Why, Jim would try to whip Joe Louis if Joe slandered the family name!

Christian words, I decided as I left the bedroom and sneaked up the hallway. I'll calm Coach Murray with a few Christian words and hope Jim stays in bed, out of hearing range. Then I'll tell Jim it was the paperboy at the door. Unless Coach Murray's found out I screwed his wife. I sure as hell won't be worried about Christian words or a paperboy if that's the case.

"I know you're in there, you prick! I can see you in the mirror. Come out here and act like a man. Or do I have to come in after you?"

It wasn't a mirror, but the silvered face of old grandfather clock that had given me away. I turned at Coach Murray's derision and saw the warped outline of his towering figure, wet clothes, frown and all, squatting between twelve noon and a cheery moon. Damn clock, I thought. And how would a good Christian respond to such harassment?

"Whaddya want?" I said in my James Cagney voice while I swaggered toward the front door. "My malaria's acting up. I ain't well. Be brief."

His face glowed red. His cheeks bulged as though his mouth held a pair of eggs. He kicked at Willie, who was nearby growling like a good guard dog, and missed. Then he jerked the screen door open and charged inside, dripping water onto the floor as he came. "Don't you kick William Wing!" I practically bellowed as I backed away. "The last guy to do that is now sprouting algae in Bayou Pierre."

"Don't you get smart with me, boy!" He shook a fist at me. "You went to see a lawyer? Tell me the truth."

"Didn't take you long to find out," I said. "Chief Hancock call you at school?'

He growled, "Do you remember what I said I'd do if you boys ran your mouths?"

"Now, look," I said, rather anxiously, for he was obviously intent on closing the distance that separated us, and I sure didn't like the look on his big red face. I backpedaled as he advanced. "My lawyer has a big mouth, too!"

"Nobody would blame me whatever I did to you," he said, raising a fist again. "You boys are all liars. Troublemakers. It's your word against mine."

I circled and wondered if I could beat him to the bedroom and the pistol if it came to a matter of survival. "Yeah," I said, "Josephine learned her lesson. She sure won't say anything now, I bet."

"By god, I'll finish what Perry started!"

"Ha! Perry learned his lesson. You don't fuck around with a Smith."

Coach Murray snorted and lowered his fist. He snickered, and his voice boomed. "That's funny as hell boy!" he howled. "Cause you ain't even a Smith!"

"What do you mean?" I demanded. "You crazy?"

I don't know how long Jim had been standing in the hallway watching and listening. Coach Murray hadn't noticed him either, until we both jumped at his hoarse, "What DID you mean by that, Murray? That Jack is no Smith?" Jim had gripped the Rattler tightly in one hand, wielding it like a long, knurly club as he entered the room.

"Jim!" Coach barked in surprise. His hands dropped to his sides. "I didn't know... I thought you were in Blake's looney bin."

Jim's face dropped. "Looney bin? LOONEY BIN!" He raised a fist and shook it. "My HEART, goddamnit. My heart was acting up again!" He stopped and glanced at me. "I'm better now." Then he shook the Rattler in Coach Murray's face. "Now, tell me what you meant by what you said?"

"By what? Which part?" The coach had begun to back away, toward the front door. His eyes shifted side-to-side as he felt his way. "It was a slip, I guess. He just don't act like no Smith. You know..."

"Jack's a Smith through and through," Jim said as he advanced toward the coach, waving the Rattler before him. "And you know it. I'm gonna make you a new poop hole with the tip of this cane, meathead..."

As Jim's words trailed he ended his charge at Coach Murray.

A look of bewilderment covered his face. The energy seemed to leave him. His mouth dropped open and he groped his way toward the sofa, where he dropped onto it and sat motionlessly, eyes on the floor before him, for several seconds. The Rattler fell from his hands. For a moment I thought he was terribly ill. But he wasn't ill. He was just weird. "You were the one!" he whispered softly after a moment. He raised his face to stare at the coach. "You were the ONE..."

Coach Murray backed another step toward the door. "I gotta be going," he said. His voice shook as he shook a finger at me. "You remember what I said..."

Jim's face glowed. His voice shook as he interrupted Coach Murray's admonition with, "I should have known! I should have figured it out. God, am I dumb! All that time..." He looked as if he were miles away. "All that time you were acting like his good friend, and you were..." He glanced in my direction and smiled. He chuckled. He howled with glee!

Coach and I were astounded by the sudden transformation. We stared at one another with our mouths open. We jumped away when Jim leaped from the sofa and began to shriek. "Meat-head, you miserable bastard!" he screamed, pointing with a finger. "You have made this the most wonderful day of my entire life! If you weren't such worthless scum, I'd shake your hand, you poor dumb fucker!" He raised his eyes to the ceiling and lifted his arms and the Rattler over his head. His shirttail flew. "There really is a God!" he shouted. "After all these years of cursing the simpleton, there really is a kind and loving God! Forgive me, God! Thank you, God!"

Coach Murray and I again regarded each other in awe of the scene. Jim practically danced the jitterbug around us, whooping and praising the Lord, as the coach and I stared in amazement. We were too dumbfounded to speak. As Jim pranced non-stop about us, I heard the coach mumble, "Old bastard's finally lost his goddamned mind. You better call somebody. The nut house. Send him back."

"I believe for once I agree with you, Coach," I said as I revolved in order to keep track of Jim's maneuvers. "They'll need a strait-jacket this time."

"Maybe it's that cheap booze."

The coach dashed out into the rain, and I watched as he cranked the Fury and roared away, then I turned back to Uncle Jim, who had by now sprawled upon the sofa on his back, breathing heavily. I walked to the sofa and looked down at him. "You have made a complete fool of yourself," I said. "Was it some asinine act to save our lives? If so, I forgive you. But I'm not proud."

"No act. Couldn't help it," he gasped. "It was too good."

"I believe I am missing something here," I said. "Perhaps you should explain."

"Private joke." He sat up on the sofa to catch his breath. His face was red from the exertion of the past few minutes. "Private joke," he repeated, "between Coach Meathead and myself."

Then it hit me. It hit me harder than anything I had ever experienced before. I was dazed beyond comprehension.

After a long, endless moment I dropped to the sofa beside him. I said then, "It's not a private joke anymore."

I had never seen fear in my uncle before, but now he was terrified.

"It doesn't take an Einstein to figure this out, Uncle Jim," I went on. "Even I can do that. God, am I humiliated now! What else can happen to me? Will there be no woman around to save me the next time my life is in danger? Will I find out my mother was a streetwalker? My father was her pimp? Will Willie lose another leg? Will I find out that Saxon likes girls?"

Only under stress could Jim lie. "Now, Jack..." he began.

I shouted, at close range, "Coach Murray was having an affair with my MOTHER! He thinks I'm his SON! My God! I can't believe this! I am in a total state of shock! And I am leaving Smith Station forever!"

"Now, you don't know that..."

"Hell! It's obvious! I'm not THAT stupid!

"Well..." Jim hung his head. His voice shook. "There's no reason to be concerned. There are worse..."

"Damn!" I shouted. "What could be worse? No wonder the guy has always acted so nice to me while he was treating the rest of civilization like it was a leper colony!" I paused for a second, then repeated with a croak, "He thinks I'm his SON! Oh, God. Could it be..."

"Well, you ain't."

I rose and began to pace the floor. "How do you know? How the hell would even my mother? I may be the offspring of that goon!"

"Nope. You are not."

"How can you be sure?"

"Cause."

"CAUSE WHY?"

"Because, Jack," he answered with a wicked smile as I stopped before him. His fear had vanished. "Melville Murray is as sterile as a dog turd. Football accident, maybe. The only thing he ever fathered was a handful of dead wiggle-tails."

It took a few seconds for me to comprehend his statement, so agitated was my state of mind. "Are you sure? How can you know that?"

"Infertile. I know. I know for sure."

"Well, don't tell his two kids he's sterile. They might disagree with you. Or..." I got off the sofa, as shell-shocked as any veteran of Omaha Beach, and crept away from him. "...or are you telling me that Linda Murray snuck around and..."

I caught a glimpse of the mysterious, self-satisfied George Washington of one-dollar-bill fame in his placid face and slightly raised brows. Archie couldn't have done a Mona Lisa any better. My breath caught in my throat.

"Oh, my god," I said softly. "Oh, no..."

CHAPTER 20
A LADY LONG GONE

"I'M GOING TO school," I told him. "I'm going to school where there may be a few sane people I can talk to. After that, I'm going to ride off into the sunset with Saxon Browne screaming across my shoulder. When I reach Hollywood, I'll tell everybody I was born in Florida and I never heard of Jim Smith and Smith Station, Mississippi."

Jim's fingers played along the smooth knurls of the Rattler. "What's the matter?" he said from his seat on the sofa, his voice muffled as if he had a rag in his mouth. "Did I say something?"

"Did you... My god!" My face must have reflected the incredulity I felt. "You said a humongous mouthful! My god!"

"I think you've just got the wrong impression, Jack..."

"Wrong impression?" I said. "Wrong impression? The impression I'm getting is that I have new first cousins. Or are they any relation to me at all? Who are the real Smiths around here? And Mrs. Murray! I can't bear to think about her! I'm going to commit suicide!"

"Shhh," he said, glancing around the parlor. "If Murray found out about all this..."

"Aunt Linda! That's who she is!"

He squirmed noticeably. "She's not your aunt. At least, I don't think so. Legally. Anyway, you don't need to mention it out loud. Just keep it to us."

"You don't have to worry a damn about that!"

He cocked his head as though all this were behind us, and deftly changed the subject. "What the hell was Murray doing over here anyway? The sorry bastard! If I weren't so happy it was him, I'd kill the bastard. I heard something about a lawyer, too, and Hancock. You're not in any trouble over this altercation, are you?"

"No. I wish all my problems were as simple as a fight."

"Well, tell me about it. Maybe I can help."

I shook my head and thought, Uncle Jim, if you find out about my little caper, it'll be through the grape vine.

I had him on the defensive now, and I didn't intend to allow him to gain the advantage. So I said, "I'd rather hear you explain to me exactly what happened the night my father died. I want the truth. Including Melville Murray."

"There's not any more," he said weakly. His eyes shifted, the way they did when he had to lie. "You've already figured it out anyway. What else can I say?"

He eased from the sofa and walked to a window and looked out onto the lawns of Cherokee Rose. There he stroked his cane nervously with the fingers of one hand, his eyes darting from oak to oak as he rolled over in his mind whatever lie he planned. In a moment he began, "I guess since you've found out what you have, I might as well tell you the rest. What little I know." He turned. "We thought your mother was seeing somebody. Your father and me, I mean. We never found out who."

Jim's eyes went back to the oaks, as if for solace, but more likely so he didn't have to face me. It's easier to lie that way. "It didn't last very long, I don't think. But long enough that your father suspected her. He made life hell for Maggie. She didn't have a minute's peace. He would crash in here from one of his all-night drunks, and he'd jerk her out of bed and beat hell out of her. Even when she was pregnant with you. Your grandmother and I tried to talk to him, even though Maggie's behavior roused no sympathy from either of us, but it was no use. Jack was sure she was pregnant with another man's child. It made him crazy. It made him crazier that she denied there was someone else."

I leaned forward from my seat on the cushion, anxious, sure, but dreading, too, whatever I was about to hear. "What did Maggie say about it?"

"She said you were Jack's child. She was an arrogant woman, though, and even though she was telling the truth, that made things worse. She practically taunted him at times. She raved and fought him until the end. Until that last night, when Jack died. And when he was dead, she disappeared. She left for good."

"Then what?"

With a shrug he continued his deposition, along with his inspection of our oaks. "People naturally suspected she killed him, that she poisoned him, then took off for parts unknown. With whoever she had the affair with. But Doctor Blake, of course, put an end to all those rumors. Jack died from ptomaine poisoning."

"Doctor Blake again."

After receiving a quizzical glance, I continued, "Maggie didn't leave with Coach Murray, though. We know that much. Do you think he knows what happened to her?"

"Don't know," Jim said thoughtfully. "Don't know."

"Aren't you curious to find out?"

"Wouldn't change things."

"Or maybe you already know."

"Already..." Jim's face screwed into a frown, and he raised his voice. "Now, Jack, why the hell would you think that? You know I would have told you."

"Ptomaine?" I said. "Ptomaine poisoning?"

He walked back to sit on the sofa near me. With a weak laugh he said, "Something he ate. Probably at Mary's place."

"An honorable way to die," I mused aloud.

"What?"

"Not original. Not unusual. And, other than questions about Maggie's disappearance, certainly not dishonorable."

"What do you mean by that?"

"The family name was about as secure as you could want, under the circumstances. No murder: Doctor Blake saw to that.

No one to blame for infidelity: Maggie was nowhere to be found. And no witnesses. None that would talk, anyway."

The Rattler did a rat-a-tat on the floor.

I said, "I'll bet Coach Murray has no idea what happened that night, or even what happened to Maggie."

Jim said testily, "Murder? Witnesses? Hell, I don't know what you're driving at, Jack. You're trying to make it sound sinister. It was unfortunate, for sure. But not sinister. Not criminal."

"There's something else that doesn't make sense to me," I said. "I'm no judge of mothers, obviously, but from what I've seen of Archie's mom, and Jerry's mom, those gals would sooner get run over by a school bus than risk losing their children. And here we have Maggie Smith, who has just seen her husband die, and who is maybe still hot for old Meathead, suddenly deciding to abandon her lover and her one-year-old baby for a lonely bus ride to Hollywood, where she plans to become a movie star. Does that make any sense?" Jim shrugged. I continued, "Hell, no! Maybe she was arrogant, and mean, and unfaithful. But mothers don't just up and desert their babies. Something happened to change everything, and I think you know what that something is. I want you to tell me, damn it! Be truthful with me. I can take it."

"Jack."

Betrayal. I hated that the word popped into my mind. But I loved him. And his was an honorable betrayal. Wasn't it?

In those light blue eyes inches from mine, I recognized the immutable determination that I had learned to appreciate. There was strength. There was the notorious Smith pride. And there was more. Before he spoke, both my uncle and I knew what would be said. And we both knew the words would be false. My uncle was no better liar than me.

"Jack," he said in his most gentle voice, "I'm sorry you had to find out about all that mess. I never would have told you. It doesn't change anything, though, except that now you have to live with it. Believe me, if I could change things, I would. But what's done is done. Your father died in a very inglorious manner. Your mother disappeared and caused a lot of talk. And you had to be reared by an uncle who still believes that the South will win the War, and that our line of Smith's will lead the final charge to victory. But you seem to have adapted to all that, and you've even grown into a fine young man. I'm proud of you. I'm proud you're a Smith."

"What did you think, Uncle Jim?" I said then. "What did you think of me when you found out about Maggie's lover?"

"I never doubted for a moment!" he said furiously, pounding the floor with the silver rattlesnake. "You're Jack Smith, son of Cherokee Jack of Smith Station! Never could that buffoon have fathered you!"

"You sure were dancing with joy a little while ago."

"Nonsense," he said with a smile that seemed genuine. "But you can imagine how such a revelation would substantiate my faith in my own good judgment."

"Well," I said, "I sure hope Coach Murray doesn't find out his reproductive works are inoperative. He might have a few questions for YOU, then."

"Not me," Jim said. "Linda. He'd kill Linda..."

He stopped and eyed me, his blue eyes cold with the hatred he must have felt for Melville Murray.

"Aunt Linda," I said aloud. "Aunt Linda told you Coach was sterile? How did she find out for sure without him knowing?"

"Don't ever mention my relationship with Mrs. Murray to anyone, Jack," he said firmly. "I'm sorry you found out about it. I'm not proud of it."

"Dishonorable," I said. "Unworthy of a Smith."

"True." He paused for a moment, and then told me, "She had his, uh, sperm checked, from a... sample after one of their, uh... You know."

"You can do that?"

"Sure. It's not a hundred percent accurate, of course, but in this case, well, it's pretty obvious that the diagnosis was correct."

"Cousin Tommy. Cousin Barbara Ann."

"Stop it!"

"We'll have to have a lawyer check the relationship for us."

His horrified expression was quite gratifying. "No, we won't! We won't mention this to anybody!"

We leaned back into the pillows of the sofa and were silent for a minute or two as each of us attempted to envision the changes to our lives decreed by this day. It was, I thought, a kind of editing of our attitudes and our opinions and suspicions of each other that had been initiated and directed by events of fifteen years before.

As for my own soul, the events of the past week had already lent an air of unreality to everything that went on around me. But the confrontation with Coach Murray, the revelations of our clash, had left me feeling as if I were no longer on the same planet. How does one accept a mother's infidelity, the possibility that she was a murderess? That father may not have been really father? That instead of one known relative, one suddenly has three or four? And that maybe, just maybe, your only uncle did something terrible to your mother...

Five, I thought with a quickening heartbeat. I have five relatives. My mother. Five.

"Think I'll go out to Lake Davis and drown myself," I said to Jim. "Mind if I use the wagon for a little while? I'll leave the keys where the sheriff can find them."

"No," Jim said absently, staring off into space from his hollow between cushions. "You know I don't. But it's raining. You should wait until the rain slacks up to drown yourself."

"Bury me somewhere on the other side of the cemetery," I said as I got up. "And please. No marker."

He sighed and refused to acknowledge me, preferring instead to stare vacantly at the painting of Great-grandfather that hung above the mantle. I joined him for a moment. "Wonder what the old man would think of us?" I said as we confronted the whiskered gentleman together. "Bet he had a few skeletons in his closet, too."

Jim smiled and nodded. "You're right," he said. "He probably did. Makes me feel a little better. Old bastard wasn't perfect." He looked up at me from the sofa and said, "I hope you won't blame me too much, Jack."

I shook my head "no," left the room, and slipped quietly into my favorite space in Cherokee Rose, the library. I made sure Jim hadn't followed me, or had even heard in which direction I headed, for I wanted a few minutes alone with the books. I had already decided where I had last seen the small black volume that contained the verse that would confirm my suspicions, and when I spotted it, high on a dusty top shelf, I swung the small vertical ladder into place and retrieved it. The tiny book was in poor condition from age and wear, and several pages fell to the floor when I opened it. I stooped to gather them, and as I was reinserting them, the frontispiece caught my eye. There I saw the inscription that I remembered and for which I was searching: *To Margaret Meribaum, From your loving mother Aimee, Christmas, New Orleans, 1928.* And there was a note: *I love you, Margaret! Sing for me!*

I found the hymn for which I searched on page 64, and as I read the words it seemed as though they were meant for me alone. I knew the clumsy poetry, but I could not have recited it. I knew the melody, but only as a throaty hum. In an instant, even as I read, I recognized the tranquility of a prescription that had calmed me many times before. The hymn was a Negro spiritual from "befo de War." "Little David" was its title, and it went like this:

Little David he was
A shepherd boy.
He killed Goliath
And he shouted for joy.
Little David play on your harp
Hal-le-lu-iah!
Little David play on your golden harp
Hal-le-lu!

The Lord loved David
And He loved him well.
He sent Goliath
Right down to hell.
Little David play on your harp
Hal-le-lu-iah!
Little David play on your golden harp
Hal-le-lu!

It must have been a song of my mother's favor, for its page was dirty and ragged from wear and tear. I gently replaced the small tome, grown from its African roots, into its hallowed lair, and wondered why a white woman from south Louisiana would display such preferences. One never knew about south Louisiana, though. That was Creole country. If my skin weren't so red-haired white, I would have wondered about Maggie's past as much as my own.

I resisted the impulse to drive past SSHS and maybe snag a glimpse of Saxon, or perhaps giggle at Perry Norman limping along holding his rear. It was too early, anyhow, not yet noon, and all the good kids were busy with their classes. Too bad for them, I thought. Hooky was always more fun.

Not today. Fun was not what I had on my mind. I wasn't sure how I was going to manage to get inside Blake Sanatorium without being collared, but I had the idea that if I could hide the Plymouth in the woods, there would be a door somewhere at the end of one of Doctor Blake's long hallways that somebody had forgotten to lock. I regretted that I hadn't paid more attention to the setting during my frequent trips with Jim in tow, but always during those times I was more concerned with his welfare and with dodging the awful smell of the place. So I would have to wing it and hope I could get inside and out, fast, without being seen.

Ten minutes later I was there. The parking lot was full, which, of course, improved my chances for anonymity. Nobody pays attention to old Plymouth station wagons anyhow. And, naturally, the spaces at the far end of the lot were the empty ones, which again enhanced the possibility that I could accomplish my mission without being noticed. A thick line of pine trees bordered the paved area. Immediately adjacent was a front wing of the hospital. Aha! I thought as I selected a space and killed the engine. If an orderly shirked his responsibility, just this once, and left the door cracked...

I waited for a moment while a visitor noisily slammed the door of his car and jogged across the wet lot to the Sanatorium's front door, then eased from the wagon, looked around to be sure no one was watching, and slid into the pine trees and around the corner of the wing. A second later, I tried the door. Locked. Locked, and emblazoned with a large red and white sign that warned of the penalty for unauthorized entry. Oh, well. There were other wings, other doors.

The certainty that there were gloomy eyeballs staring from many of the unadorned windows lining the brick walls, and the further guarantee that nothing could brighten a mental patient's day more than reporting a prowler in the woods, convinced me that I should stay out of sight. Pine trees can hardly be considered good cover, since they're built more like toothpicks than bushes, so I had to trek far back into the wooded hillside until there was enough tree bark between the hospital and myself to hide my movements. Then I made a wide arc and approached the next wing from its extremity. Another locked door. With the steady drizzle of rain, I was being soaked for the second time today, but that was no real concern. I repeated the dodge once again and approached a third wing. Again, the door was locked. And here, I noticed, the windows were barred. Probably where they keep the real sickos, I guessed. This was not the wing for unauthorized entry. All the ax-murderers were back here.

But an intriguing thing about this wing was that one window, about halfway along its length, was unbarred. Not only that, it was open. This might be my only chance. I crouched and duck-waddled along the brick wall, making sure my head stayed below the sills, hopping from pine tree to pine tree in an effort to avoid being seen by the patients in the opposite wing. I paused long enough below the open window to listen for any sound that would mean that the room was occupied, then, hearing nothing, leaped up and over the sill. I fell into an open laundry hamper, the bottom third of which was filled with dirty towels and linens. Immediately I recognized that the rags smelled like Squeaky Bishop's breath, the totally loathsome thought of which had me bounding from the hamper and onto my feet, dusting myself to remove all manner of imagined contaminants. From the hallway outside came the sudden click-click of footsteps on the hard tiled floor. I ceased slapping my jeans and glued my body to the wall behind shelving lined with stacks of linen. I was in a small storeroom.

The sound of footsteps faded, and after waiting a minute to be sure there weren't more, I cracked the door leading out of the room and peered up and down the long passageway. The doors on either side were closed; no one was in sight. Now I had to get my bearings, since I wasn't sure where I was relative to Jim's room. That would take some exploration. I stepped into the hallway, closing the door behind me, and resisted until there was no other choice than to suck the foul smell of the place into my lungs.

I remembered Archie's advice and walked on my toes "like an Indian," but still the leather soles of my loafers were unbearably noisy in the echo chamber created by the concrete walls and floors. I wondered if the patients could hear me. I wondered if all those murderous inmates that were resident in this wing had been locked in their cells, or if one might suddenly open his door and split my head open with a lamp, or a bedpost, or even a fat fist. I was imagining how the headlines of the Observer would describe my mysterious death when voices from around a corner ahead warned of the approach of hospital staff. I had no choice. I tried the nearest door, and when it opened, stepped inside and closed it behind me.

It took only a moment's adjustment to the somber light in the room to establish that the patient in this room was no ax-murderer. The only thing resembling an ax here was the skinny old man's Adam's apple. And his skinny nose. He sat on his rumpled bed with his hands in his lap. He seemed not to notice me as I entered his cubicle, and only continued what he had been doing before: staring blankly at a spot on the wall. He hadn't been shaved in several days, and the gray stubble made his face rugged and primitive. His thin hair was uncombed. I stopped at the door and wondered if I should apologize for my rudeness. But the old man continued to ignore me, and I remained silent.

The sound of footsteps disappeared after a few seconds. During that time, the old man's gaze never wavered from his chosen spot. He never made a sound or seemed cognizant of my presence. As I eased from his room and closed his door, I decided that this was one of the most disturbing scenes I had ever witnessed, and I was ashamed that I'd assumed that nothing more than ax-murderers were incarcerated here.

At the intersection of my hall with the next, I knew where I was. To the right: Doctor Blake's office. To the left and around one additional corner: Jim's room. I padded as silently as an Irish Indian could be toward my destination, and rounded the last turn without hearing or seeing anyone else. I slowed. There was no one in sight, and the hallway was quiet.

I now stood before Her door, the room next to Jim's. My heart pounded. The moment seemed artificial, as if I were outside myself, watching someone else acting for me. Did I know what I was doing? I wondered. Could it really be true? Could I actually be about to meet someone who for my entire life had been only a hopeful illusion? I cracked the door and peeped inside.

The room was a duplicate of Jim's: Small corner bathroom, bed, window, desk with lamp and Jesus. Bureau. A chair. A framed print of frolicking green cherubs. And a missing occupant. The room was unoccupied. I slipped inside and closed myself in. If I were not going to be able to see her, then I could at least examine her belongings. Maybe there would be evidence to confirm or disprove my supposition. A photo. An heirloom. Maybe some newspaper clippings, or a birth certificate.

There were four drawers in the bureau, and as I pulled each open, I found them amazingly bare. There was underwear, and an article of clothing here and there. A Bible. Even some small tubes of makeup. But things like nail files, or small mirrors, or even hairpins, were missing. Suicide! I decided. There's nothing here that could be used to kill.

The bathroom contained towels, a plastic hairbrush, toilet paper and the like, and was quite clean. The single desk drawer contained not even a pencil or writing paper. Life here must consist of simple meditation, I thought, for there was little else to entertain oneself. Not even a checkerboard. I wondered if Blake ever let his deranged patients outside for a little sunshine.

I had been so intent in my search that I failed to notice the approaching footsteps. When they became apparent I also heard voices just outside the door. With no time to open the window and leap, there was only one place for cover. I dashed into the small bathroom and pulled the door nearly closed, leaving only a slight crack through which I could see a portion of the room. I heard the hallway door open, noisily, the sound echoing hollowly about the room, and then followed the sound of clicking heels as someone entered. A slight form in hospital gown passed my view for a moment, and the lady sat on her bed, out of sight from my hideaway. But the doctor, one of Doctor Blake's assistants, I supposed, stood in plain view. He was a short, chubby gentleman, dressed in suit and tie and wearing a white hospital gown. He pulled at a white-bowled pipe clamped between his teeth. He faced the lady and spoke around his pipe as she sat.

"How do you feel now, Margaret?" he asked.

No reply.

"Better? You feel better after our chat?"

The lady must have nodded, for the doctor said, "Good."

Then he smiled and said, "We'll have our walk later this afternoon. If the rain stops. Would you like that, Margaret? A walk?"

"Yes. A walk!" the lady answered. There was excitement in her
simple voice. "A walk!"

"Maybe the birds will be out. Maybe the squirrels, too."

"Birds!"

"Perhaps the sun will come out of hiding. Maybe we'll have
sunshine."

"The sun!"

"I'll come for you in a little while."

"Yes! Yes!"

He reached out with one hand and patted her, then wheeled
and left the room. After he closed the door, the lady remained
seated on her bed, out of my sight. I waited and wondered what
to do next. I could just walk out and act normal, except that she
would probably wonder who I was and why I walked out of her
bathroom. Or I could wait until she occupied herself with something else, and then leap out and pretend I'd entered in a more
customary fashion. In the meantime, I hoped she didn't have to
use the john.

As the minutes passed and the lady remained seated on her
bed, I began to wonder if she were occupied with a spot on the
wall, much like the ax-nosed old man. Maybe that's what insane
people did to pass the time. She might sit there for hours. At
any rate, there was no telling when the doctor would return for
their "walk," and when he did, he just might notice the intruder
in the bathroom. I took a deep breath, slowly pushed the bathroom door open, and proceeded to face her much as the doctor
had a few minutes before. I prayed that she wouldn't pick just now
to break into a noisy rendition of "Little David" just to prove she
could do it and no one could stop her.

She did not. The lady was clothed only in a plain gown, her
hands clasped loosely in her lap. Head bowed, her long dark hair
spilled over its front like thin black thread blown in the wind.
I made no sound, only studied her, and it was several seconds

before, with a slight movement of her eyebrows, she appeared to notice me. She took her eyes from her lap to peer up at me, and to my surprise she smiled when our eyes met.

"Jack!" she whispered.

My word! I thought. She recognizes me! I said, "Yes. It is I."

"You've come to see me again!"

"Again?"

"Have you been here long?"

Her complexion was as clear and pale as a newborn babe's, though the hollowness of my mother's cheeks and the prominence of the bones in her face gave her a gaunt look of mere hanging-on. Even so, she was beautiful, and I thrilled for a moment at the recognition that I had been born of this lovely creature. Her wasted form, I suspected, was the result of physical or mental insufficiency rather than starvation. Eyes bright with excitement, she lifted her hands to take mine. I clutched them both eagerly, and drew nearer at her tug. "I've been here a little while," I said. "How long have you been here?"

Her puzzled expression was answer enough. But she said, "I don't know." She squeezed my fingers. "Don't you know?"

"Are they treating you all right?"

She grinned mischievously. "Doctor Thorn," she said. "If it weren't for you, Jack..."

If it weren't for me... Why? I wondered. Then, it hit me. She was talking to my late father! "What?" I said. "What would you do if not for me?"

With a whirl of her head that sent her hair flying, yet with her eyes pinned upon my face, she said, "I can always make you so jealous, Jack. I can just look at another man, and you go crazy."

"Why would you want to do that?"

"Tamales," she said. "You love hot tamales. The hotter the better."

"Yeah," I answered, "Hot tamales seem to be real popular around Smith Station."

"The secret's in the sauce. Terrell's hot-hot sauce." She shook her head. "I'm sorry, Jack. I told you. Tamales are not my idea of fun."

She would not have had to say a word to give the impression of insanity. The condition was obvious in her eyes, in the way she stared vacantly for a moment, then perked up, eyes lighted as though a great idea had popped into her head. She squeezed my hands and looked expectantly up at me, like a child, as if she were about to let me in on a secret. "Maggie," I said. "It's been so long."

"Maggie," she repeated with a frown. "I'm not Maggie. Nobody calls me Maggie anymore. Not even you, Jack. Why did you call me Maggie?"

"Well...," I began.

"Jim. Jim is the only one who calls me Maggie."

This was sapping my strength. I pulled the chair from her desk and dropped clumsily into it, then sat and stared into her sallow, empty face, dazed from the reality of actually being there before her. I said, "Jack Junior, Margaret. Your son. Does he ever come to see you?"

"Junior?" Very carefully, as an affected child might have, she shifted her expressionless gaze to a spot somewhere above my head. "I don't want to talk about Junior," she said.

"Why is that?"

"Don't. Just don't."

Her breathing had quickened. Her chest expanded and contracted with each quick breath, and she began to softly hum a panted version of "Little David" under her breath. Eyes fixed on an unseen mark, she pulled her hands from mine and rubbed her arms as if she were cold. Her humming ceased, and she said anxiously, "The angels don't like me. They don't want us, Jack."

"Why is that?"

"The angels loved Jack Junior." Her dull stare remained as her eyes dropped back to mine, and with a sudden lunge she knelt on the floor beside me and laid her head in my lap. "They don't like what happened, Jack," she said, her lips against my leg. "They tell me all the time. I never think of him. The angels come when I think of him."

And suddenly I was back in that warm milk bath, making love to my mother, gasping for air, clawing for my life, wanting to hold to her forever, aware that she was being torn from me by an act that would forever separate us, but thankful for my breath just the same as she was dragged away. Her scent was the same now as then, a familiar fragrance that made me by instinct feel protective of her. With both arms about her shoulders I drew her upright and held her close. Unwelcome but undeniable tears began to stream from my eyes. I held tightly to her so that she would not be aware of my humiliation; she struggled and groaned as if I were hurting her.

I squeezed her thin body and thought that I'd known the truth forever, a vagabond truth purposely obscured by love and hate, and perhaps by a desperate longing to deny what now was so obvious. The realization saddened me, and the uncertainty of my own sentiments gave me pause to wonder. Should I love her, or hate her, or was there some emotion somewhere between the two that would be the eventual consequence of the unveiling past? Was past really PAST? Was a truth of fifteen years ago to be allowed to color the present?

I felt now as if a load had been lifted from my shoulders. I felt a strange calmness. I felt what I supposed was love for her.

"The angels have forgiven you, Margaret," I whispered in her ear. "Jack Junior is in heaven. He's happy. I know. I've talked to the angels. And they promised me they won't bother you anymore."

"They can't hear you, Jack."

"Sure they can. I'm in with the angels."

"No, they know you're from the bad place. They won't listen."

I held her at arms length so that I could memorize her face. She touched my lip with a finger. "You've been fighting with the boys again," she said simply. The wry twist to her face made apparent her pleasure at the sight. "Fighting over me again? Jack!"

"You're worth the fight, Margaret," I said.

She struggled for freedom from my grasp. "I have to go now. Doctor Thorn. We're going to see the birds."

There was nothing wrong with her ears. Only after she mentioned Thorn did I hear the distant click of heels on tile. He was coming.

I released her and pushed her away. "Goodbye, Margaret," I said. "I'll leave the way I usually do. Through the window."

She was surprised by that. "But you always fly away when the doctor comes. Through the transom, and into the hall."

"Not today," I answered.

The window screen was held in place by two small clips, which popped loose with little effort. There were no bars, a circumstance for which I gave fleeting thanks. In a moment I stood on the ground outside, and as I pushed the screen back in place, my eyes probed the room for one last look at her. She faced the door, her back to me, probably unaware now that I had even visited. She was more interested in Doctor Thorn and her walk in the sunshine than in the ghost of her late husband. After all, the ghost was a frequent guest.

The rain had stopped, though drops falling from the pine trees overhead added to the miserable state of my clothing. Once I had retraced my route and made the roundabout trip to the Plymouth, I jumped inside and got the wagon headed for Smith Station.

I wasn't sure what to do now. I wanted to go home, to see Uncle Jim. To thank him. To question him. To condemn him? He was a part of what happened that night fifteen years ago. But I knew him well enough to know he would never admit the truth. And what was the truth anyway? Would I ever know?

I thought of my visit with Dr. Blake. Much of what he had told me must be true. But would I ever know the total, absolute truth? Did I really want to?

For some strange reason, then, I had a vision of Mama Mary running along Main Street as she chased Teeny Wright's father with her butcher's knife.

I needed time to think. So much had changed in such a short period. I needed an interval to assimilate it all. I was discovering that there are times in one's life when the normally ordered cranial processes can become so encumbered by chaos and turmoil that the moving parts of the brain misfire. "Right" goes up in smoke. "Wrong" unravels and becomes a bickering contest. Solid earth is a despairing memory. Confusion is supreme. One needs the counsel of trusted friends at moments such as these. I didn't need snickers from Jerry or Archie. "Aunt" Linda was out. To whom could I entrust the details of my incredible story without fear of ridicule?

Saxon Browne! The baring of my story would be with her as natural and as casual as my conversations with Willie. Her counsel would be discerning and meaningful. Our souls shared the same covenants. I was lively when she was near. Her spirit nurtured my own. She was exactly what I needed!

It was already past two o'clock. Saxon would walk down the front steps of the schoolhouse at three, and if her big former boyfriend were nowhere in sight, I would slyly snatch her away. I would tell her everything, and in the course of our therapeutic session, we would discover what made Jim tick. We would decide on a course for the future.

To kill time, and to straighten my hair and allow my damp clothes a chance to dry, I drove to Lake Davis and parked near the waterline in one of the gravel turnouts provided for people who, like myself, were desperate for serenity. There were egrets stalking the small fish in the shallows, ignorant fish that were too intent upon leaping out of the water to snap at flying insects to notice that their ranks were being steadily thinned. They reminded me of certain of my friends, and I watched with a kind of malicious glee for nearly an hour as the witless fingerlings were eaten alive.

Exiting vehicles lined Main Street by the time I reached the vicinity of the high school, and I feared for a moment that I had enjoyed the bream slaughter a bit too long. I parked the Plymouth a half-block from the school's front entrance and used the shrubbery planted near the walls of the building for cover as I skulked through the slackening mist of rain to a corner with a view of the front steps. A number of students, walking home instead of riding, observed my cowardly performance, and I even heard two of them giggling. I turned my broken lip to one side, safe from their view, and kept going.

With mixed feelings I saw from the corner that Mrs. Browne was seated in one of her Cadillacs across the street, waiting for her daughter. She certainly wouldn't be glad to see me. Too bad, I thought. But thank goodness Saxon is still inside. There's no other way. I sat cross-legged behind a shrub and waited.

The schoolyard was deserted when I finally heard her voice. Saxon's words always held a kind of breathless quality about them that resonated the affection she felt for everything and everybody. I would recognize her happy lilt from a chorus of a thousand others. She was coming down the steps, talking with Tish Baker, when I stepped from my haven and strode across the school ground toward her. She saw me immediately and stopped, a curious expression on her face that bared her surprise. Tish Baker stared at me as if she could hardly control her laughter. I turned my bad lip away. "Hi, Saxon," I said when I was close enough to speak.

"Tarzan," she said good-naturedly, her features cordial with the same smile that I always wanted to lick off her lips. "Tarzan has a boo-boo. And he got caught in a shower while he was out in the jungle playing with his lions."

"Do you have to go straight home?" I asked.

"Mom's waiting. I guess so."

"Would she let me take you home in a little while? I need to talk to you. The wagon is right over there."

Saxon turned to her friend. "See you tomorrow, Tish." Tish took the hint and said goodbye. In something of a sanction of Saxon's association with me, she even said goodbye in my direction.

"It's important," I said.

"She'll probably pitch a fit." Saxon glanced toward the Cadillac. "She doesn't want me seeing you again. She blames you for what happened between Perry and me. She even wants Chief Hancock to arrest you." She grinned. "For what you did to the poor sweet dear."

"Me? I didn't do anything. Mama Mary..."

She interrupted with a snicker, "Oh, it's all around town that you stabbed Perry in the booty. You sneaked up on him. Backstabbed him. Perry has promised everybody that he will break every bone in your body as soon as he's able. As soon as you get up guts enough to come back to school."

"I don't wish him a speedy recovery."

"I bet. But I'd protect you anyway. You puppy." She grinned.

"Me, Tarzan. Remember?" Desperation in my voice, I continued, "Please, go ask your mom for her blessing."

Mrs. Browne had my number. Her snarl was obvious to anyone within a hundred yards even before Saxon reached the Cadillac, and when she growled and glanced in my direction, I looked the other way. Nobody could hold up to that withering glare. Saxon persuaded her, however, and after she opened a back door of the car and tossed her books inside, my darling joined me back on the schoolyard lawn. "Mom said okay, kind of," she said. "But you've got to have me home in less than an hour."

We hurried together toward the Plymouth. When we were out of sight of her mother, I grabbed her hand. I said, "I'll bet Perry gets more than an hour at a time."

"Not anymore."

The sorrow in her voice had the effect of immediately dampening my spirits. I opened the wagon's door for her. "You want him back, don't you?" I said. "You sound down. Maybe you should give him another chance."

She shook her head. "No." A moment later, when we were in the Plymouth and headed out of town, she went on, "I'll never go back to that kind of relationship with Perry. I don't want it. But it makes me sad just the same. Anytime you lose a friend, you should be sad."

I felt better. "I know you're right," I said. Then I joked, "He's sad. I'm happy. Kind of a good balance there."

She gravely shook her head and said nothing, and I loved her all the more for her concern for the football jerk. When she wasn't picking on me, Saxon Browne was the most compassionate person I'd ever known. It was a quality that melted me. She deserved the pedestal.

I parked the wagon in a small roadside park a mile from town, and sat quietly for a moment trying to decide how to begin. As I deliberated, courage slowly drained from me. How does one quietly admit that he is of a family of honorable liars and insane murderers? That he has his choice of fathers? A brand new aunt and new cousins? Worst of all, at least to my perverted thinking of the moment, was that Uncle Jim was no doubt more intimately acquainted with the body and soul of Linda Murray than I. God! We were not only Uncle and Nephew, but... what would you call us? Lovers-in-Law? Lovers-by-proxy? Adulterers à trios?

Saxon sensed my uneasiness and reposed silently a foot away. She studied the leaves on the trees around us, patted my knee once, then finally turned to me and said, "Did you bring me out here to talk, or do you want to play around for a while?"

"I want to marry you," I said.

She blinked lavishly, several times in succession. Her lips parted in a smile, and she said, "Gosh, I really don't know you that well, Jack. And besides, when I'm eighty, you'll only be seventy-nine. I'm not sure I could handle that."

"I'll lie. I'll tell everybody I flunked a grade and graduated a year late."

"And suppose I meet someone in college that I just can't resist? You'll still be in high school. You're still a puppy."

"Let's do it now, then. Let's go to Hollywood for the wedding. I'll call Coop. Gary will put us up while we're looking for a castle to live in."

"Jack." I breathed a deep sigh of satisfaction as Saxon fell against me and snuggled into my chest. Heaven. This was heaven. She said, softly, into my throat, "I'm flattered. I think we have something special. But you're sixteen, and I'm only seventeen. We have lots of time. Let's get to know each other first. Okay?" She raised her head to look at me when I made no reply. "Okay?"

"How many children will we have?"

She leaned back and pursed her lips for a minute. "Lots," she said then. "Lots of kids. I love children. But later."

I held her close to me and groaned. And groaned. They were groans of complete satisfaction. I said, "I wonder what your mom and dad would think of a Browne stooping to marry a Smith."

"Don't be silly. Smith is the oldest name in town. It doesn't mean a thing anyway."

"Suppose I had murderers and mad-dog lunatics in my family. What would they think then?"

She eyed me suspiciously. "You don't, do you?"

"Yep. My mother resides in an asylum where she spends her days staring at a spot on the wall. Except when she's entertaining my dead father. And my dad... Who knows what happened to him? Maybe he was murdered by a psychopathic lunatic. You know about my uncle."

Saxon giggled. It's funny how people don't accept the truth when it's so macabre that it's preposterous. "I've heard all those old stories about your mother and father," she said. "I know they're just mumbo-jumbo." She nuzzled my ear and straightened every hair on my body. "You're not going to get out of marrying me by fabricating some tall tale."

I sighed, "Let's go to my place and make love the rest of the afternoon. Uncle Jim's drunk. He won't even know we're there. And if he did, he wouldn't bother us. He'd only watch and suggest improvements."

"Uh-uh. If you don't get me home in the next few minutes, we may never get a chance for that. Let's boogie."

She stayed very close to me on the way to her house, kneading my scalp and nibbling my ear. She didn't move away until we passed through the white fencing that surrounded Browne Farm. From there in, Saxon said, her mother could see, and there was no sense in giving the woman another excuse to try to end our inevitable union. As if she needed another. I vowed, as Saxon waved goodbye to me from her front door, that someday Mrs. Browne would thank me for marrying her daughter.

CHAPTER 21
REMEDY FOR
INNOCENCE

R ELUCTANTLY, I TURNED the Plymouth from Browne Farm toward Cherokee Rose, driving a speed which I hoped would get me there no sooner than midnight. The thought of facing Jim was not a pleasant one, the more so because what I had learned at Blake Sanatorium had created that many more questions for him. Sure, I knew a lot more than before. But I wanted to hear it all from his lips, damning truth or not. He and Doctor Blake had the answers. And what of Doctor Blake? No doubt, Jim's relationship with the good doctor had taken a decided twist that night fifteen years ago. I would have bet it involved the very land that Blake Sanatorium was built upon, too.

In a much shorter time than I had hoped, the Plymouth crept onto the downtown streets of Smith Station. When the Merchants and Farmers Bank clock came into view, I realized with a curse that it was nearly five o'clock, and I had forgotten my work. I had not even called Mr. Barnes to tell him how badly my malaria had flared up, though with him I would probably not now have used that sarcastic excuse. I slipped the Plymouth into a nearby parking slot and hurried inside to apologize. He was, of course, understanding, and he accepted my apology with a laugh. I promised to report on time tomorrow. As he smiled and puffed on his cigar and joked with me, I was aware again of just how much I needed his respect. I guess people are much more cognizant of their own immorality, and ashamed of it, when they've misbehaved as I had, and are then threatened with exposure. My face felt as if it were burning in a hot summer sun as Mr. Barnes made light of my delinquency. Here he stood, righteous, conscientious, genuine, sincere, steady, and honest; I hoped he would never learn of my indiscretions and think less of me for them.

Five o'clock. I backed the Plymouth out of the parking space at just the right time to catch a glimpse of Archie's rear end wagging along the sidewalk toward Mary's Café. Beer and pool, I thought. The essence of life. What an astute observation on the part of my friend Archie! I made a U-turn opposite the police station and in a few seconds parked the wagon beside Jerry's hot-rod Chevy. My two friends were in a heated discussion when I arrived at our table, something about Melba's big boobs and Jerry's little pecker. They stopped long enough to say hello, that my face looked like hell, and that they didn't blame me for playing hooky today. They added that I was dead anyway, just a matter of time, then went back to their argument.

Mama Mary was punching, with exasperated concentration, the keys of her rather canted register as I sat. The old lady ignored me, calming my fear that she might head my way with a butcher's knife. My friends' debate raged as I sat. They had even ignored my bedraggled appearance. Some things never change, I thought. "I think I'll move to Alaska anyway," I said between their barbs. "A change of scenery would be nice."

They had the courtesy to glance at me when I spoke, then went back at each other. I listened a while longer, refused to order anything when the Boy came over, and was glad he was waiting tables instead of Mama Mary. "You two want a beer?" I said after a while. "I'll pay."

They grinned broadly and nodded and affirmed my suspicion that in this brotherhood of man, respect and friendship are there for the buying. I went with a sigh and whispered my order at the knotty ears of the Boy. He seemed preoccupied with his own thoughts, and hardly smiled when I inquired of Josephine. She was home, he said, and aside from a few bruises, the only remaining manifestation of her ordeal was her refusal to discuss the incident at all. Though I didn't say so, of course, I thought that such was entirely predictable, given the size of the muscles in Coach Murray's arms together with his inclination towards the use of them to intimidate women.

The Boy brought three beers and presented them to me with the same lack of enthusiasm with which he had greeted me, then headed off in the direction of the kitchen. I sighed again and returned to my table, where my two comrades were nearing physical hostility. "Why don't you two bastards just shut up and act like adults," I said as I sat and handed them their beers. That got their attention. I said, "Archie screws a fat girl every day, and Jerry needs a dick job just to be able to use the thing anyplace but the toilet. Sure, it ain't the way either one of you would have it if you were running things from some cloud-on-high. But you ain't. Life ain't fair. It won't ever be, and that's the way Jesus Christ planned it. So you might just as well relax and get used to being barfed upon by the angels."

"Damn!" Jerry said. My buddies stared down at me as if I were six inches tall.

"Melba ain't THAT fat," Archie said vehemently.

I said, "I ain't in a good mood. What's it like to drown in beer? Will I feel it when the lights go out?"

Jerry whistled and wagged his hand as if it were injured. "Talk about down and out," he said, speaking to Archie. "Archie, this boy needs to be watched. He's suicidal."

Archie sneered. "We should murder him before he kills himself. We couldn't enjoy it if he just killed himself. I want to help him die."

"You'd be doing me a favor," I said.

"What's wrong with you?" Jerry asked. "You're not still worried about Meatloaf, are you? Or about everybody finding out about the pit operation?"

"Now it's the 'pit operation,'" I said. "Sounds almost noble. And no, I'm not worried about Coach Murray anymore. The big man practically castrated all three of us when he draped

Josephine's body across those railroad tracks. He knows we don't have the balls to say anything now. Anyway, he has the law on his side."

"I'm not scared of him!" Archie said.

I said, "Me neither, of course."

"Wow," Archie said abruptly as he craned to see out the café's front windows. "Mrs. Murray! Good God! Lookit them long legs!"

Jerry and I craned with him, as did several other males seated nearby. Linda Murray was waiting for a car to pass to cross the street, and when she did so, groans of desire charged the air around us. This was not the usual prim and proper Linda Murray, dressed just so, made up just right. This one wore short-shorts and a short T-shirt, and tiny sandals, and that was all. She was dressed the way she normally was when she was doing housework, or lounging around her pool on those days when she wasn't trying to hide her bruises. Which she hadn't managed to do today. Below her shirt and above the waist of her shorts, several small purple spots were visible, insulting blemishes on otherwise flawless skin. Something, I thought with a shudder, is wrong! Linda would never be seen in public like this, half-clothed and with signs of her husband's abuse obvious. Unless something bad had happened. What could it be? A sense of apprehension filled me then.

Her rapid steps slowed as she reached the café's front door, where she paused for a moment to peer into a window and roughly brush her hair. The screen door slapped shut behind her. She surveyed for an instant the occupants of the café with a cool stare of indifference, as though she dared anyone to question her presence. She gave me no particular note, and I stared along with the rest of salivating hornydom. With a stride that was too careless to be proper she moved around the counter to where Mama Mary stood watching. After a moment of whispered conversation, during which Linda patted her belly a time or two, the two of them left through the back door and disappeared. "Did you see them tits?" Jerry whispered in awe. "You could see the imprint of them big nipples!"

"And those legs!" Archie crooned. "Wrap-arounds! She's got the longest legs for a little woman I ever saw."

Half rising, I said, "Something ain't right here, boys. That ain't like Mrs. Murray. We better get the hell out of here before World War Three starts. The gunfire is due to erupt any minute now."

Jerry looked at me as if I were crazy. "Are you nuts?" he said. "There ain't gonna be no gunfire. I'm staying right here to see her when she comes back through that door. Maybe she'll stay a while. And if SHE stays, I stay."

"Maybe she'll sit on a stool," Archie said, licking his lips. "Maybe we can shoot her squirrel!"

A glimpse of Aunt Linda's "squirrel," though tempting in a nowadays odd sort of way, was not appealing enough to ease my fear that the world might be about to end. But the thought of going home to Jim was equally uninviting. After fidgeting over it for a minute, I decided I might be overreacting, and I sat nervously and listened as my buddies described how completely they could satisfy Mrs. Murray's sexual needs if they got half a chance. Jerry had begun to characterize himself as a virtual "Muledick," and Archie was categorizing his personal cache of erotic talents, when Mary and Linda returned. Mama Mary's face was red and mean as she resumed her work, but Linda looked businesslike, although a bit square-jawed and wild-eyed as she bustled around watching the old lady and whispering to her now and then.

"Strange," I said, "I never saw Mrs. Murray help out up here before. She acts like one of the crew. Reckon what's going on?"

"Lookit them thighs," Archie whispered, his hands clasped before his mouth to hide his lips. "Lookit how they curve up around her..."

"My tongue's so hard I'm gonna choke on it," Jerry murmured.

The screen door growled and slammed, and Coach Murray walked inside. We, and every other man or boy in the place, had been so intent on removing what little clothing covered Mrs.

Murray's body that her husband surprised us all with his sudden appearance. Immediately fifteen or twenty throats cleared, chair legs scraped the concrete floor, and all eyes were diverted from tanned legs and taut T-shirt to the more important concerns of menus and hang nails. "Dum-de-dum-de-dum," Archie said softly as he squinted at the backs of his hands. "And twiddle-dee."

As it became obvious that the coach either hadn't seen us or would ignore us, I said, "You fooled him, Arch. He never suspected you were wondering about his wife's undies."

"Hope he don't start nothing," Jerry said, his voice a pitch higher than normal. "Surely he knows we won't say nothing about nothing for the rest of our lives. And that three thousand... forget it."

Coach Murray had apparently not expected his wife to be in the café. As he strode past on his way to a stool, he glanced ahead to see her leaning across the counter, watching him, her bountiful parts bulging from the well-filled shirt and shorts. He stopped immediately, and both hands doubled into fists as he stared, first in surprise, then in anger. He was about to speak when she smiled at him and said, "Hello, dear," in an amiable voice that would have disarmed the most irate cutthroat. "I guess you're wondering what I'm doing here, Melville, dear."

The coach recoiled in surprise and hesitated. Then he remembered his anger and growled, "You might just say that." He looked around at the rest of us. To a man, or woman, we were all of us intent upon being anything but interested in what we were seeing and hearing. "And why the hell are you out in public half naked? Aren't you cold without any clothes on?" He took a stool and put his elbows on the counter opposite her, stared directly at the tiny bruises above her waistline, and said, very quietly, "You ain't got good sense, broad. Get the hell out of here." Then he looked around once again to be sure no one heard. No one had, of course.

Mrs. Murray said, "Mary was kind enough to share a recipe with me, Melville. I know how much you like those hot-hot hot tamales. She and the Boy are giving me a kind of firsthand look at how to cook them. Dear." She backed away from the counter. "I don't wait tables, though," she said coldly. "Mama Mary will take your order in a minute."

Linda Murray wheeled and walked away toward the kitchen before her husband could complain. His upper lip had lifted to snarl at her, but he controlled his temper and sat half-cocked on his stool, stretching occasionally to scrutinize his wife and her activities while impatiently awaiting Mama Mary and her pad. When the old lady stood before him, pencil in hand, Linda Murray could be seen through the small window of the kitchen's swinging door conversing with the Boy. Coach Murray hissed his order for a plate of hot-hot hot tamales, and I thought of my conversation with my mother. Hot-hot hot tamales were truly big here at Mama Mary's Café.

"He ain't even paying us any attention," Archie said cautiously. "I think we're home free."

At the moment Archie's words were uttered, the coach glanced in our direction and frowned. For a second or two I thought he was going to get off his stool and pay us a visit, but after glaring at each of us, he instead returned to his previous diversion, that of watching his wife as she watched the Boy prepare hot tamales.

"The Boy's in the kitchen playing cook today," I observed. "How many times have you guys seen that?"

"He's helped cook before," Jerry said. "I've seen him. He's a good cook."

"Odd though, ain't it?"

"The main cook must be sick," Archie said. "What's the big deal?"

"Just seems strange. Mrs. Murray and the Boy cooking. You don't see that everyday. That don't seem strange to you two?"

"If she cooked here everyday," Jerry sighed, "I'd weigh two tons."

Archie ginned evilly. "Maybe certain portions of your anatomy would benefit from all that fat." Jerry tapped the butt of his cigarette against his cheek and regarded Archie with subdued hatred.

In a while Mama Mary banged the plate of hot tamales on the counter before Coach Murray as his wife watched from the kitchen. Linda Murray's face glowed with a kind of distasteful fascination, the type of expression you might have while you watched a snake eat a frog. Before I could pull my eyes from her face she caught me watching her, and for a long slow moment our past and our future were bartered in a telepathic exchange. To my horror, and with obvious indifference to anyone else who might notice, she then lowered one eyelid and winked at me!

My reaction was to immediately turn to see if her husband had noticed. Thank God! I thought as I watched him stuff hot tamales into his mouth. I may survive yet another day. But this is too much! "Boys, I'm scramming," I said as I pushed my chair back and rose. "Coronary thrombosis is no better way than gunshot wound for a sixteen-year-old to die. If I stay in here another minute, you may have to give me artificial resuscitation."

Archie looked up and said, "Ugh. I'd let you lay there."

"My pal."

"Where you headed?" Jerry said.

"Costa Rico. Argentina. Haven't really decided."

"Later, maybe we could..."

Jerry stopped and stared. By the drool from his lips and the lust in his eyes, I gathered that Linda Murray was on the move. I turned for a cursory glance, and panicked when I saw her walking quickly toward our table. "So long," I blurted. I turned and strode toward the door, but slowed my flight when Linda Murray grabbed my arm and turned me. "Jack," she crooned, tugging at my elbow and smiling, "you're not leaving, are you?"

"Yeah," I said, wheeling to face her after a sidelong glance at her husband. He had paused with a mouthful of tamales ballooning his cheeks and was watching us with what I took to be disbelief. I couldn't believe it myself. "I've gotta go check on Jim," I said to her. "He's not feeling well."

"Oh? Nothing serious, I hope."

"No, no. But it could get serious if I don't get out of here and go on home."

"But I want to play a game of pool, Jack," she said loudly. "Play a game with me."

Archie and Jerry were eyeing each other, probably thinking, like I was, that the situation was a lot like standing over a toilet after you've flushed a cherry bomb down it. Coach Murray was getting off his stool, and Archie and Jerry were lifting their rears from their chairs, and every other person in the café was on the edge of his or her seat, waiting for the concussion that was certain to come. I was eyeing the door, wondering if the coach really could run the hundred in eight seconds, when Mama Mary shouted from the kitchen door with a mouth so wadded with soggy brown leaves that we could hardly understand, "I done had one goddamn fight in here that nearly ruined my café, and I goddamn sure ain't gonna stand for another! Murray... " She shot him a fire-and-brimstone scowl that would have worked well at Sodom, and continued, "sit your ass on that stool and finish them tamales. I ain't gonna have good tamales thrown out. Jack... " I gave her a big grin, hoping she would have mercy and let me the hell out of there. "Jack," she ordered, "you play pool with the lady if that's what she wants. You act like a gentleman. You ain't hurting nothing, just playing pool." She shot another frown at Coach Murray, and ended, "And Jim Smith don't need nobody to baby him."

"Yes, ma'am."

"The rest of you folks." She immobilized them all by swinging the rolling pin she had brought with her from the kitchen in a wide, bobbing arc around her. White powder flew from it. "You just sit back and enjoy your meals and keep your goddamn mouths shut." She turned her back to us all and headed for the kitchen, confident that no one would have the guts to argue with her.

And for sure, few people disputed Mary when she was mad, and nobody would for a while, at least until the memories of what had happened to poor old Perry Norman faded. So all of us did as we were told. I kept a wary eye on Coach Murray while I racked the balls on the far table, and he watched and waited his turn at the revenge he no doubt planned, violently chewing his tamales as he sat and blooded his wife and me with his eyes. Nonchalance, I thought as I watched him. My only hope is nonchalance. With maybe a little begging thrown in occasionally. I said in a loud and respectful voice, "I didn't know you played pool, Mrs. Murray," emphasizing the "Mrs. Murray" ending. "I bet your husband taught you. He's a hell of a fine shot."

"No," she said loudly as she launched the cue ball. "An old boyfriend of mine taught me. He was from Birmingham, before I got mixed up with Melville. Now, he was a fine shot. Hell of a lot better than Melville."

"Hmm," I said. The café was so hushed that "hmm" echoed off the walls and about the room. Mary's little fan buzzed softly. There was an occasional clatter from the kitchen, where the Boy was loading the sink with dishes while keeping an eye on the proceedings. And, of course, there was the sound of Coach Murray's teeth grinding tamales.

I sank the thirteen in a side pocket, then missed the fifteen. "I still gotta give your lawn that last cutting, Mrs. Murray," I said loudly. "Coach Murray's lawn, I mean. I got the stripes. You got the solids."

"The end of the week," she answered, walking around the table to take aim at the cue ball. "Come Friday afternoon. Melville probably won't be around." She lifted an eyebrow at her husband, snickered, and said loudly, "But that's okay."

I leaned and pretended to help her line up a shot at the six. There was the smell of liquor on her breath. I whispered, "Have you lost your mind? Have you been drinking? You act like you're trying to make him mad! Have you got a gun on you? Are you suicidal?"

She giggled, and my ears tingled. "The kids will be spending the night with my neighbors Friday," she whispered. "You know what that means?"

I spoke from the side of my mouth so no one else could hear. "No. And I don't want to know. Never, ever again."

She raised her face in surprise. "You're kidding. Why?"

I thought of Uncle Jim. But I said, softly, "I'm in love with another woman."

She shrugged. "So what?" She pulled at the hem of her T-shirt, deliberately stretching it across her breasts. She leaned to take her shot. At the flash of firm breasts outlined under the thin material, and despite my eminent demise, the dagger struck under my navel.

"You're right," I said weakly. "So what?"

The six disappeared into a corner pocket after a solid thump against the leather. She said, "I'm in love with another man, too, Jack. But love and lust are two different things. I plan to have more time for both in the future." She grinned broadly.

My skin was crawling. Costa Rica? Argentina? I said, "Great. Great." Louder, I said, "You play a mean game, Mrs. Murray. You're better than me."

"Who is this 'other woman' anyway?" she giggled. "Anybody I know?"

"Saxon Browne," I answered softly. "You're definitely drunk, Mrs. Murray."

"Saxon Browne." I thought she looked impressed as she repeated the name. "Very pretty girl. And smart. But Perry..."

Despite her inexplicable contempt for the wrath of her husband, Mrs. Murray, between proficient pool shots and witty words, glanced time and again to where he sat on his stool finishing his meal. More than once he gave her a look that could only mean disaster for her when they were once again alone. There would be more bruises this evening, perhaps more than ever before. I shuddered at the thought. Yet Mrs. Murray seemed unconcerned, carefree, as if she had been playing pool here every evening. A restrained flow of conversation resumed among the café's patrons, masking, I hoped, most of her conversation with me, and which in itself contributed to some semblance of normality. But the situation was anything but normal, and I managed a quick look myself every now and then to verify that the coach hadn't left his stool. None of Mary's customers left, either, and the old lady herself stood motionlessly beside her grill, deliberately pulverizing the plug in her mouth and casually driveling into her Crisco can while contemplating the coach as he noisily chomped Mexican cuisine. "Good tamales, eh, boy?" I heard her say once. "Hot enough for you?" Coach Murray grumbled a reply under his breath that I couldn't make out.

Soon the coach had completed his meal. He sat brooding before the lunch counter as Mrs. Murray and I began a second game. Mama's Boy, I noticed, was no longer in the kitchen, but instead had perched himself on his familiar "runner's" stool. He, too, seemed interested in just how much Coach Murray had enjoyed the tamales, for he watched the coach with hardly a glance at anything else. In fact, I noticed, there were even several of the customers who had dropped their knives and forks and were no longer absorbed in the pleasant routine of downing mashed potatoes and gravy. Jerry and Archie remained seated at our table, but unlike many around them, their blank stares and nervous gestures merely exposed the confusion and concern the two of them felt.

I had squatted beside the pool table and was squinting between balls in order to add at least some appearance of authority to my next shot, when I heard a groan from behind. Mrs. Murray was standing opposite me, and at the sound I saw her eyes immediately flick toward the lunch counter. If you've seen the eager look on the face of a squirrel dog when there's mention of a hunt, you've seen what I saw in her face. I jumped up and wheeled around in time to see Coach Murray, clutching his belly, slide from his stool and roll onto the concrete floor. He groaned once again, more loudly, his face distorted, then bellowed, "My stomach! I'm on fire! Get me a doctor!"

Mama Mary had ceased, at least temporarily, chewing and spitting, and she watched with detached acceptance the scene before her. The Boy now sat on the edge of his stool. I was shocked when I caught his fleeting grin, a passing snicker, as if he were enjoying the sight of a man rolling on the floor in pain. Jerry and Archie had each grabbed the other's shoulders and appeared to be on the verge of breaking for the door. The remaining customers sat glued to their chairs, watching Coach Murray roll and groan, taking it in as if they were at the drive-in theater. I turned to Mrs. Murray, not knowing what to say. She looked at me without blinking an eye and said, "Your shot, Jack. You got the stripes."

Mama Mary was the first to act. She walked too casually to the telephone near her tilted cash register. In a moment I heard her say, "Gertrude? Hey, Gertrude?" A pause. "Yeah, yeah. Later, Gertrude. We got a man ill up here at the café." Another pause. "Maybe we ought to get hold of Doctor Blake." Still another pause. "Yeah, just make sure it's Blake, now, we want a real doctor, you know, not one of them interns of his. Make sure Doctor Blake gets the message."

While Mary chatted with Gertrude, Linda Murray strolled, with me right behind her, around our table and across the room to where an assortment of Mary's customers had now surrounded her stricken husband. Their ranks parted as she approached. After propping on her cue stick to stare for a moment, she dropped to a squatting position and began an inspection of her ailing mate. "What's the matter, pumpkin?" she said soothingly. "Tummy ache?" She gingerly patted his tummy between the massive arms holding it. By this time Coach Murray was twitching and gasping for air. His head was bent backward at a terrible angle that had half the spectators rubbing the backs of their necks with sympathy pain. "Told you those green beans you had yesterday didn't smell just right," Linda said, still patting. "Told you you'd get a tummy ache. Now you have to go to the doctor."

"You... bitch... ," the coach managed to gurgle, "I didn't..."

"Give the man air!" Mama Mary bellowed loudly. "Can't you see the man's sick? Get back!"

The Boy jumped from his stool and began to enforce Mary's order by herding people with his two outstretched arms. "Ya'll get on back, now," he said as he urged us away. "Ya'll heard Miss Mary."

In a moment only Linda Murray and Mama Mary were near enough to the coach to hear him if he spoke. Linda remained kneeling at his side as we all watched, occasionally whispering into his ear and patting his stomach. The coach's seizure continued, his body arched. We could all of us hear the awful sound of his gasps and his moans of agony. Someone pinched my arm, and I turned to find that Jerry and Archie were right behind. "Don't tell me there ain't no God," Archie whispered.

Jerry nodded agreement, but said, "Bad as I hate the bastard, I still wouldn't want him to die like this."

"That's not what you were saying the other day," I said. "You were ready to do it yourself."

"I wasn't serious."

"Anyway, what makes you think he'll die? It's probably just gas. And Doctor Blake's on his way."

"Don't look now, but I think he's already dead!"

The coach's body had relaxed, and his arms had slipped from around his belly. One hand lay open-palmed on the floor. But he was still breathing. His wife pinched his cheek and shook it, the way you would a child's, and continued to talk softly to him. We couldn't hear the words, nor could we see that Coach Murray spoke again.

My thoughts were interrupted, and I shuddered at the sound, by the steaming wail of a passing freighter as it imposed its presence upon the show. With the intrusion of its intimidating howl came sudden deja vu. Had I been here before? In this café? Fifteen years before, and nothing changed? Had I seen a man die, just as Coach Murray was dying? Had I felt his pain and wept at his death? Had I run from the scene in panic, frightened then and ever more by the agonizing rattle of steel wheels on steel rails?

The ethereal and the corporeal; they had become the same.

Within minutes Doctor Blake burst through the café's front door and pushed his way past the spectators to kneel at the side of the victim. His black bag he set beside him, and he opened it and withdrew a stethoscope. After a moment of sober listening to the sounds of Coach Murray's innards, he jerked them from his ears and demanded an explanation: "How long has he been like this?" he said, directing the question to Linda Murray. "What did he have to eat today?"

Linda Murray briefly described the circumstances leading up to the illness, including the fact that her husband had just enjoyed a serving of hot-hot hot tamales that she herself had helped Mary and the Boy prepare. "Maybe the peppers didn't agree with him?" Linda ventured. "He loves peppers, though."

Meanwhile, Coach Murray's breaths were coming at longer and longer intervals, and his tongue had fallen quivering onto the dirty concrete. Doctor Blake and Linda Murray didn't notice. "Maybe it was something he ate this morning," Blake continued. "Or yesterday? I ought to get him to the hospital. Mary?"

Mama Mary, standing nearby, answered, "Reckon I ought to call the ambulance, Doctor Blake?"

Blake replied in the affirmative, and as Mary made her way to the telephone, he returned his attention to the patient's wife. "Looks like ptomaine poisoning to me," he told her, loud enough that we all could hear. "Has he eaten any home-canned food today? Or yesterday?"

Linda Murray nodded, and with her eyes cast to the floor in front of her, said, "Green beans, Doctor Blake. Some I canned last summer. He had them for supper last night. I told him they didn't smell right, but you know Melville..." She turned sorrowful eyes upward to the doctor's face. "You don't think..."

"There, there, Mrs. Murray," Blake said tenderly to her. He patted her shoulder. "You couldn't have known. It wasn't your fault. And that might not have been it at all."

"But I shouldn't have let him..."

"Well," Blake insisted, "we all know how..." Blake paused, searching for the right word. "...how intractable your husband is. There was probably nothing you could do to stop him."

He turned his attention once again to his patient, who was now motionless and quiet. Even the coach's tongue had ceased its quivering. Blake listened intently once again with his stethoscope, felt for a pulse, and said, "Mary, I don't think we'll need that ambulance. I'll send one of ours. I'll have to perform an autopsy." He rose and took Linda Murray's arm in his hand. "I'm awfully sorry, Mrs. Murray," he said, patting the back of her hand. "But I'm afraid your husband has passed away."

"Oh, no!" the widow said, her hands over her mouth. "I can't believe it!" For the first time she exhibited what I took to be real concern, even sorrow. A tear trickled down her cheek. "Oh, no," she repeated.

The Boy turned to me when I approached him from his blind side and said, "Terrell?" He didn't answer, merely stared as if he were seeing me for the first time. "You make a mean tamale sauce, Terrell," I said. "I'd like to get the recipe sometime."

His expression never changed. If there was remorse behind those dark eyes, I couldn't tell. Some eyes can keep secrets.

I pushed past Archie and Jerry and through the rest of the crowd and onto the sidewalk and then the bricks of Main Street. The freighter had left the usual fallout of sulfur fumes and soot, the latter of which was still raining upon the town in tiny bits of soggy black ash. For a moment I was lost, unsure of which direction I should turn, uncertain even of who I was. This seemed a strange place, far removed from the security of my hometown. The clang of the Merchants and Farmers clock striking the hour galvanized my soul, and with a sense of nostalgia I climbed into the old Plymouth wagon and headed it toward home.

Willie was crossing the street when I arrived, probably bound for an all-night social with his buddies. I whistled for him, and when I opened the passenger door, he jumped into the front seat and sat beside me. Mutt and man. Can one conceive of a more perfect union when the chips are down?

The gravel pit was shadowy and silent when I arrived. The lovers in Smith Station were not as energetic on Tuesday evenings, I observed, and I pulled my Plymouth beneath the premier scrub tree. No longer did the crickets chirp; no owls spooked the night with their hoots of greeting. November was nearly upon us, and the cool breeze brought chill through the open windows. "Old pal," I said, turning to my friend, "you and I are probably the only two sane people in Smith Station." Then I thought of what I had said. "Correction. You're the only sane person in the county."

Willie appreciated the recognition, and he pawed his way to my lap, where he struggled once again to cleanse the healing wounds on my cheeks. I let him. "Willie," I said between laps, "if anybody drives in here and sees me out here at the gravel pit making out with you, then there will be no question. I will move to Alaska."

It was a long while that I sat there reflecting on the events of the past week. Had it only been a week? It seemed more a lifetime. I thought of Uncle Jim, of his pride and of his deceptions, and I knew I couldn't leave him to face the music. I naturally then thought of Linda and the lure of her softness, and even of her ferocity, and wondered if I could resist the temptation of her bed. But Jim... My god! How could I even think of Linda and her bed? Uncle Jim. Aunt Linda. And me! Damn! I couldn't do that again. Could I? Lord, I hoped Uncle Jim would never find out.

I thought of Saxon, her beauty, her hopeful virginity, and wondered if my one true love, virgin or not, would eventually marry me. I thought of Archie and Jerry, and marveled that the three of us had survived. Bullets and bedlam, I thought, and we brought it all on ourselves. I thought of Josephine, and I cringed. I thought of Mama Mary and her Boy, and of Dr. Blake, and... I could hardly make myself think the word, but there it was... murder. Murder across a lunch counter. Murder callous, and even routine.

My father. My mother. No, I couldn't. I put them and events of fifteen years ago out of my mind. That was for another day, a day when I was more prepared. Despite it all, I was glad my mother was well hidden.

Most of all, though, I thought of Uncle Jim. I loved him dearly, despite whatever had happened fifteen years back. I was sure now... he was just caught in the middle. Cleanup man. Desperate to protect the family name, he had cleaned up the best way he knew how.

When Willie was satisfied I was scrubbed clean, I cranked the Plymouth and steered it down the small gravel road toward the pavement. I hesitated for a long time where the gravel met the paved road, wondering if immorality and impropriety lay to the right, honor and virginity to the left, or whether it really made a difference which direction I turned. I put my arm around my dog and pulled him close. I looked him in the eyes. "Which way, Willie?" I asked.

Willie cocked his head and peered at me with his deep, dark eyes. Eyes can talk, you know.

So I took his advice and steered the Plymouth onto the blacktop. I nosed it toward Cherokee Rose. Willie barked his approval.

END

Made in the USA
Monee, IL
29 December 2023

50780732R00208